The Hermit of Humbug Mountain

Mike Nettleton & Carolyn Rose

Nettleton, Mike & Rose, Carolyn
ISBN: 0-7443-0732-5
The Hermit of Humbug Mountain – 1st ed.

SynergEbooks
1235 Flat Shoals Rd.
King, NC 27021
http://www.SynergEbooks.com

Cover art by Robert Nettleton
Visit the authors' website at www.deadlyduomysteries.com

Printed in the USA

The Hermit of Humbug Mountain

Also by Michael Nettleton and Carolyn Rose:
The Hard Karma Shuffle

Also by Carolyn Rose:
Consulted to Death
Driven to Death

Dedication

This book is dedicated to all of our honorary children and their children, with thanks to the many friends who keep us writing and to the sharp eyes and red pen of Eunice Abrahamsen.

Prologue

Spid, the demon troll, leaned against the polished black marble of the imperial throne set atop a stalagmite in a massive chamber, miles below the surface of the earth. With great satisfaction, he looked down at his minions marching on the pockmarked lava flows of the Plain of Misery. He, the Exalted Garboon, had recruited a vast army of demons, ogres, trolls, skrees, grammits, and gronnks.

Turning to the squat, muscle-bound ogre beside him, he chortled. "It won't be long now, Yurk. All of Earth will be ours."

"Yeah, boss. All of it. Ours." A glob of green drool slid from the protruding lower lip of Spid's second in command. Small, beady eyes, out of place on his massive chopped-meat face, darted from side to side as if yanked on strings.

Acrid smoke from smoldering coal torches rose along with a hellish mantra from the assembled multitude below. The guttural cry echoed among the stalactites that hung far above. "Heek, Hak, Hophul, Heek, Hak, Hophul." Spid bowed his head in reverence, translating the ancient words into English, the language he'd mastered in order to communicate with those he would soon dominate. "If we take it, it is ours."

Raising his head, he squinted into the gray, reeking air and saw a thousand skrees circling in formation, hungry to rip the flesh from their opponents, razor sharp talons flexing in rhythm with the beating of their featherless wings. Their limited vocal chords could not form the words of the chant, so they were content to scream their own names at deafening volume. "Skree, Skree, Skree!"

It's taken me hundreds of years to achieve this, Spid thought as he watched another wave of troops pass his reviewing stand. *It's taken every waking moment since the last convergence of the full moon, the planets, the summer solstice and the mating dance of the Darksuckers, the inhalers of perpetual night.*

"But I've brought them all together," he muttered.

"Through bargaining, bullying and bloodshed, I've bent them all to my will, honed them for the battle to come."

He scowled and twirled the thick ring encircling his stubby forefinger. The stone glittered like a snake's eye.

Yes, his troops were ready for the battle. But before that battle, he must meet the challenge that would open the portal to the outer world. If he missed his opportunity, it would be hundreds of years before he could attempt to breach that portal again. It might be a millennium before he, Spid the Devious, son of the Troll King Glaub the Wrathful and his captive consort Dismalia, queen of the gammits, could bring enlightenment and discipline to the creatures of Above Skin. Perhaps a millennium before the power of the Darksuckers could be harnessed for the good of . . . well . . . of him, Spid.

He scowled again. Only two people stood between him and his dream—a mere boy and his younger sister.

Chapter One

Noah Keene knew better than to look directly into the setting sun—his mother had warned him many times—but he couldn't stop himself. The distant corona of fire somehow helped to lock her image in his mind, to keep it from fading any more then it already had. And doing something she'd cautioned against almost let him hear her voice.

"Ow." He felt the red laser of sunlight stab his brain.

"You're right, Mom." Squeezing his eyes closed, he dug his fingers into the rough rock of the ledge, struggling to keep his balance as dancing stars lit up inside his eyelids.

When they twinkled out, he shaded his eyes with his right hand and moved his gaze back to a spot on the blue-green water just short of the sunset. The whitecaps lapping at the horizon had doused a quarter of the orb's fire, but the rest of it raged crimson against the cloudless Oregon sky.

He wondered, as he watched the fireball slowly slide into the ocean, if someone, maybe someone his age and feeling as lonely as he did, was watching the sun come up in an eastern sky. Where would that sky be? He tried to remember his geography and time zones. Three to the east coast, three more to England? Then a few more.

Maybe some kid in the Middle East. Perhaps an Israeli girl on one of those communal farms. What did they call them? Kibitzers? Kibbutz? Yes, that was the word. Or perhaps a Russian boy, staring out an apartment window at first light, wondering what was ahead for him and his family. Just as Noah wondered what was ahead for his.

Not that he thought of them as a family anymore, not since his mother died. More like three people living in separate dimensions within the same house—him, his father Sean, and Abby, his younger sister. Dad, silent, unsmiling, on edge, and working too hard; Abby lost in her world of books and chess; and him hammering the drums hour after hour, trying to drown out the silence that filled the house.

A passing gull canted its wings and for a second hovered eye-to-eye with Noah, the June breeze puffing its feathers slightly. "I don't have anything for you." Noah held up his empty hands and the bird swooped away, gliding toward a nearby outcropping where dozens of other gulls hunkered over their nests. Noah smelled their gamy aroma mixed with the sharp scent of the low evergreens at his back and the rank and salty smell of what the tide had deposited on the beach below.

A thin rind of orange sun remained. Noah let his eyes slide past it, looking north up the coast. He spotted two fishing boats, stragglers from the small fleet at Port Anvil, heading toward twin jetties bent like beckoning fingers into the Pacific. *They're running wide open,* he thought, watching their bows slap the waves. Racing the night.

His eyes followed the jetties to the shore, to the broad curving sweep of sand that began at Massacre Rock and dead-ended into Humbug Mountain. A few beachcombers meandered along the tide line, searching for agates, sand dollars or other treasures overlooked by others.

He thought about the stone Abby had plucked from the surf two days ago. The size of a softball, it seemed to glow with an almost lunar light. Not quite opaque and not quite translucent, and polished smoother than any piece of quartz he'd ever found on the beach. It almost seemed to quiver and pulse in Abby's hands, and when he'd touched it, it had felt warm, too warm for a rock just pulled from the ocean's chilly grasp. But perhaps that had been his imagination. Maybe tonight, now that school was out, he'd get out the rock and mineral book and try to identify it.

Noah glanced at the vinyl-banded Timex on his wrist. Almost nine. Almost curfew. He knew he needed to head home. Dad would be hacked off. As usual. But he wouldn't say anything, just point to the kitchen clock and motion for Noah to go to his room. Noah vowed that tonight he wouldn't bite his tongue and slouch off in silence. Tonight he'd answer back, force his father to talk.

"Rules are rules, Noah," he spun the scene out in his mind, hearing his father's words. "When I make them, I expect you to follow them."

"But dad, tomorrow's Saturday," he'd argue. "And school got out today."

"Makes no difference. Nine o'clock is late enough."

"Dad, it's summertime. It's still light outside. And I'm sixteen years old."

"Horsehockey, Noah. Nine o'clock."

"But, Mom would have—"

And that would be the end of it. "I said, enough!"

After the final words, his father's face would compress into the grim mask he'd worn ever since he and Noah's mother came back from the doctor's office the day before Noah turned fourteen. Cancer. She'd been gone more than a year.

Maybe tonight, he could make Dad see that time had passed. He wasn't fourteen anymore. Noah considered different strategies. What if he said, "Abby and I are growing up, we should be allowed to help make the rules."

No, that wouldn't work. His father wouldn't listen. There was no point in even trying to talk to him anymore. He kicked at a clump of ferns sprouting from a crevice beside the ledge. "It wasn't fair!" A frond broke off and twirled toward the rocks below. "It isn't fair."

It didn't seem like Abby missed Mom as much as he did. But then, Abby, after an initial tantrum, had always been more willing to accept what she couldn't change.

11

Thirteen years old going on thirty, Dad called her. At school they had her doing college math. Calculus, no less. Noah had heard one of his teachers call her a child prodigy. He knew that meant she was way ahead of everyone else, including him. Not that he thought he was dumb or anything. But sometimes his little sister made him feel almost backward. She could already smoke him at chess, spotting him two pawns and still making short work of him. Of course, she did that to most everybody; she was one of the best players in the state.

Even though his nickname for her was Ab-normal, most times he was proud of Abby for her brains. He wouldn't let her help him with his math homework, though. No way. They'd fought about that more than once. Abby could be a little pushy. But Noah wouldn't back down. Stubborn as a starfish clinging to the pier, Dad had once said. That's where Abby got her nickname for him. No-way, she called him.

Noah got his feet under him and stood, glancing south along the coast to the mountain. Strange to be able to see the grassy strip and the rocky knob at the top. Most of the time a layer of fog covered that. He'd always thought of Humbug Mountain as mysterious, even spooky, but today, silhouetted against the darkening sky, it seemed almost ordinary. There were lots of stories about the mountain, about sightings of the hermit, and Sasquatch and even the ghost of Noah's musical idol, Felix Delacroix. A young, gifted jazz drummer, Delacroix had blazed through the music world twenty years ago, playing to sell-out crowds and making half a dozen inspired recordings. He'd married a talented young actress, learned to fly, and was on a honeymoon tour of America when their small plane, tossed by a near-hurricane-intensity storm, had crashed into the side of the mountain a month before Noah was born. Neither had been found.

When Noah had been younger, he'd believed every tale about Humbug Mountain—rumors of people hearing Delacroix's moans on the wind as he called his wife's name over and over, stories of hikers sighting a woman melting in and out of the coastal mist in the dense woods of the lower slopes. Now, at sixteen, Noah was inclined to think the stories were just things people had imagined when they were tired or had had too much to drink.

A cool breeze made him shiver and he became profoundly aware of how alone he was, high above the beach, above the foaming surf and the sharp rocks far below. He felt queasy, and for one scary moment, as if forces beyond his control might push him over the edge.

A small voice, harsh and taunting, rose from a dark and hopeless place deep within him. "You won't even feel it.

Do it. Why not? Dad won't miss you. Do it."

"No!" He backed away from the edge. He'd promised Mom he'd be strong, believe in himself. She never gave up, right to the very end. Noah couldn't let her down.

Hurriedly, he shrugged into his backpack and scrabbled up the brushy trail hacked into the cliff face.

The ledge where he'd watched the sun's descent was fifty feet below the edge of the bluff and the Cape Misfortune lighthouse. Standing up there, you couldn't see anyone on the ledge because of the gorse and Scotch broom plants and a natural brow of rock that jutted out. Noah thought of the ledge as his secret spot, but he knew he wasn't the only person who used the rocky hideaway.

Often he found cigarette butts, beer cans and fast-food wrappers. He would pick the litter up and cart it away, furious at those who left it behind. How could you trash a place that was so beautiful?

Noah climbed the last fifteen feet hand over hand, automatically finding grips and footholds he'd used hundreds of times before. At the top, he levered himself up and around to a sitting position to take a final look at the purple light that smudged the horizon. "Goodnight, Mom," he whispered, wiping a solitary tear from his eye with the back of his wrist.

Clambering to his feet, he strode to the porch of the old lighthouse keeper's cabin where he'd chained his bicycle. He covered large chunks of the rocky ground with his long-legged gait, but several times he snagged his toes and once he fell to his knees. God, he was awkward these days. He hoped he'd outgrow it, but feared he'd go directly from being a spaz teenager to being a spaz grown-up.

He unchained the bike, wrapping the chain around the seat stem and securing it with the combination lock. Running the bike a couple of steps to build momentum, he threw his leg over and started the fifteen-minute ride home. Sometimes he felt like a baby, still riding a bike.

All of his friends were learning to drive. Their parents and older brothers and sisters gave them lessons. But Dad wouldn't let him behind the wheel. Dad said he was too young, too careless, too oblivious to what went on around him. He'd argued about that, but Dad ignored his protests.

The last thirty yards he had to stand on the pedals to make it up the steeply sloping street. Panting, he hopped off and walked the bike up the driveway, catching sight of Abby lounging in the porch swing, reading by the light of the yellow bulb beside the front door. As he came around a gnarled rhododendron bush, he noticed that his father's pick-up wasn't in front of the garage. Good. Maybe he'd escape the curfew lecture. He laid the bike over on the barren, untended lawn and let himself down onto the concrete steps, calf muscles twitching from the ride.

"Hey, Ab-normal. Where's Dad?"

Abby didn't look up from her book, Stephen Hawking's *A Brief History of Time*. Theoretical physics, she'd explained when Noah asked. He wondered if she really enjoyed it, or felt like she had to read egghead stuff like that to meet everyone's expectations. Personally, he liked science fiction and mom's favorites, murder mysteries.

"He's out," she said without looking up.

"Well duh, Abby. I know that. His truck's not here."

"Oooohhh. Amazing powers of deduction, Dr. Watson." She raised her right hand and twirled a strand of ebony hair around her forefinger, eyes still focused on the book.

He sighed. "Okay, Sherlock, where's out?"

"The movies."

Noah felt his eyes widen. His father worked, cooked their meals, labored in his vegetable garden and read books about history. Serious business. "But, he hasn't been to a movie—"

"—since way before Mom died." Abby finished the sentence and set the book aside. "And he has a date. Cool, huh?"

Noah felt the words tear into his heart. A date? But what about mom? "Who? Who did he go out with?"

"Mrs. Ramsden from down the block."

Noah felt a surge of relief. "That's not a date. She's married."

"Nuh uh. She's divorced, No-way. Don't you ever pay attention to what's going on around you? Mr. Ramsden left six months ago. Moved to California with that lady who used to work at the souvenir shop."

No. No. No. The word pounded through Noah's brain.

"Anyway, they drove up to Coos Bay to see the new Julia Roberts' flick. It's supposed to be funny. I hope it makes Dad laugh." Abby, who usually chose her words wisely and used few of them, had gone into her other conversational extreme, motor-mouthing. "He left you some meatloaf in the refrigerator. And Mrs. Ramsden brought us chocolate chip cookies. With nuts. I divided them up, fifty-fifty. Yours are in the sack on the counter. She wants us to call her Jennifer."

"Never. No way!" Noah leaped to his feet and tore open the screen door.

"Noah, where are you going?" Abby called after him.

"Inside," he shouted. Passing through the kitchen, he seized the sack of cookies and slammed it into the wastebasket. "No!"

Abby sighed, set the book aside, retrieved the sack of cookies and returned to the porch. Munching, she lay back in the swing, tapping one foot to the wild beat of Noah's drumming. Even though he'd put up makeshift soundproofing, lining the walls and windows of the garage with leftover egg cartons, it barely dampened the thumps, thuds and crashes he created. Tonight the noises were louder than usual, discordant and arhythmic. *He's angry,* she thought, *angry that Mom's gone, angry that Dad doesn't seem to hear us, angry that it can't be like it used to be.* Sometimes Abby wished she could let it all out like Noah did, scream at the top of her lungs, hit something, anything, run down the beach until she collapsed with exhaustion. But she couldn't.

Abby remembered one of the last conversations she'd had with her mother. She could almost hear Mom's voice, feel her soft hand against her forehead. "You're the one with all the common sense in the family, Abby.

You're the logical one. It's up to you to help your Dad and Noah keep it together when I'm gone."

She ate another cookie, closed her eyes and imagined her mother again, telling her the story about Noah's first drum. A Christmas present from Aunt Susan, it had been nearly as big as the two-year-old boy who'd unwrapped it.

An hour later, he was keeping time to Christmas carols and leading their old dog, Ranger, in a parade around the house. By the time Abby was old enough to have memories of her own, Noah had a complete drum kit.

Through the years, he'd saved money to buy congas, timbales, and other percussion paraphernalia at yard sales and secondhand stores up and down the coast. He'd even fashioned a Caribbean style steel drum out of an empty oil container they'd found on the beach. Mom had helped him clean it and found little mallets to strike it with.

I should go talk to him, Abby thought. *Tell him that I understand. Let him know that I hurt too, but we'll get through it together. His drumming and my math serve the same purpose. They're different sides of the same coin.*

She knew he'd locked himself in and wouldn't hear her pounding on the door and she felt anger flare at the back of her head. Keeping the world away was easier for Noah than facing his problems and admitting that he might be part of them. He'd have a turntable spinning an old jazz or rock LP. With the heavy black Koss headphones plugged into the amplifier and the volume maxed out, Noah could ignore an H-bomb exploding next door.

She'd made the mistake of slipping on the headphones one time when he'd set them down. "Aoooooh," she'd howled, snatching them from her ears. She'd thought her head would explode. Noah had just grinned that silly grin – Mom's grin – and said, "I know, it rocks, doesn't it?"

Maybe girls had more sensitive ears than boys. She smiled. Girls had other skills, too. She darted to her room and got the nail file from the manicure kit Mom had given her. The simple knob lock on the side door to the garage was old and worn. In less than two minutes, she had it open. She slid inside and shut the door as quickly as possible. The neighbors had complained repeatedly about the volume of Noah's drumming.

The lingering aroma of old motor oil and rusty tools filled her head as she watched him play. He snapped out syncopated rolls and riffs, going from snare, to tom-tom, to cymbal, all the while keeping a steady thump, thump with the foot pedal on the bass drum. Although she didn't understand most of the music he played, she still knew that he was special, talented. Someday he'd make a name for himself; his picture would be on a poster like those stapled onto the egg carton walls. Keith Moon, long-haired and shirtless, sweating and attacking his drums.

He'd played with a group called The Who. He was dead now. So was Buddy Rich, a lounge-lizard looking jazz drummer on the next poster. Next to that was Noah's favorite. Dela . . . Delaroy? She looked at the banner across the bottom of the poster. Delacroix, that was it. Lix Delacroix. Anyway, he was dead too. Crashed his plane into Humbug Mountain, Noah had told her somberly.

She'd once asked him why he didn't like any live drummers. He'd just groaned, put his headphones back on and turned up the volume.

Noah hadn't seen her yet. No surprise. He liked to play with his eyes squeezed tightly shut. Told her it helped him feel the music. She moved closer to him, waving her arms, hoping, if nothing else, that the fanning air would distract him. No luck.

Finally, she walked around him, to where the snake-like black headphone cord plugged into an ancient Marantz lamp. With her index finger, she punched the power button in. The tone arm skidded to a stop on the turntable.

"Hey, what the—Abby!" Noah bellowed. He opened his eyes, but kept his headphones in place. "What's the big idea?"

Abby leaded over and pulled one side of the headphones away from his ear. "We've gotta talk, dude. Take those things off."

He peered over the snare at his sister. "Nothin' to talk about, Abby."

"Horsehockey, Noah."

Glaring, he thumped one more short and angry riff on the snare and cymbal, then set the sticks down. He nodded sullenly and slid the headphones off, setting them carefully beside the drumsticks.

Abby jumped right in. "C'mon Noah, why can't you cut Dad any slack?"

"Me cut *him* slack? Like he does for me with all his stupid rules? Hah."

"You know what I mean. With him going out tonight with Jennifer. Mrs. Ramsden."

She saw the veins in his neck stand out as he fought for control. "None of my business. He can do whatever he wants. It's not like he cares about what I think."

"Noah, maybe it will be good for all of us if Dad finds a lady he likes. Mom's been gone more than a year now."

"You don't have to tell me how long she's been gone! She made us a family, made everything all right. Your precious Jennifer can never replace her. Never."

"I never said she could replace Mom. I just think—"

But by then, her brother had punched the amp's on button, sheathed his ears with the headphones and begun thumping an insistent beat with the kick pedal of the bass drum. It vibrated so intensely she thought the face of the drum would burst. As he began a machine gun sequence on the other drums, he opened his mouth and howled at the top of his lungs. Abby started to reach for the off button again, but stopped herself. Maybe tomorrow they could talk. She covered her ears and backed out of the garage, closing the door carefully behind her.

* * * *

Noah glanced at his digital alarm clock. Two a.m. He needed to leave soon. Tying his shoes, he considered what he should stuff into his green canvas backpack. Not a pack really, just a glorified book bag. Still he could cram in all the junk he'd need for the trip: three extra pairs of underwear, two T-shirts, socks, cut-offs, and fourteen dollars and seventeen cents left from mowing lawns. He suddenly regretted the eight dollars he'd spent on a movie and video games last weekend. No way of knowing he'd need it later, he thought glumly. No way of predicting something like this. The only thing left from last week's splurge was some salt-water taffy in a plastic bag. He tossed it into the pack along with a toothbrush and a mangled tube of toothpaste, a comb and a small block of spicy fragrance deodorant.

He glided silently to the kitchen, wrapped a slice of cold meatloaf in aluminum foil, snagged an orange from the bowl on the dining room table and filled his small canteen with water. Tiptoeing to the closet to retrieve his sleeping bag, he stepped on a squeaky board. He halted, holding his breath, hoping he hadn't awakened anyone.

The door to his father's room was closed. Around midnight, Noah had heard the pickup truck skid to a stop in the gravel driveway. Hunkering in his bed, he'd listened to his father whistle that "Jeremiah was a bullfrog" song as he walked up the steps. He and Mom used to embarrass Noah by singing that song at the top of their lungs when they were happy. Now it sounded like betrayal.

When Dad looked in on him, he'd pretended to be asleep. Dad had chosen silence, Noah reminded himself. He'd use the same weapon. The dead air had seemed to press in on him, making it hard to breathe.

It didn't matter now, he told himself. Nothing more to talk about. By the time Mrs. Ramsden moved in and took over, Noah would be long gone. He didn't need Dad anyway. He didn't need anyone. He could make it all on his own.

Abby's door was also closed, which was unusual. She was skittish about the dark and generally slept with it open. He wished he could take one more look at her, but decided against messing with her doorknob. What if she heard him and woke up? She'd want to know where he was going. She'd argue with him. Wake Dad. He'd be grounded for the summer.

After a moment, he crept back to his room and paused to look longingly at his boom box and small collection of compact discs. No. No space. His drumsticks, strapped safely to his belt, would provide the only music he could carry with him.

Back in the living room, he stopped at the piano to look at a picture of his mother, slim and smiling, holding three-year-old Abby up to pluck an apple from the ancient tree in the backyard. Noah pulled a T-shirt from his backpack, wrapped the picture, and wedged it in the center of the pack where it wouldn't break. The photo of Mom and Dad in the porch swing he left on the piano.

Time to go, he told himself. *But where?* He slipped the pack over his shoulder. *Somewhere. Anywhere.* For tonight it was enough just to be going away.

The bicycle lay where he'd left it. Carefully, he set it upright and walked it halfway down the driveway before hopping on and starting to pedal. The night was still clear; stars twinkled by the thousands and the moon shone brightly over his shoulder. *Not full,* he thought. In a few days, though. He wondered where he would be in a few days. California, maybe. Mom's sister, Noah's Aunt Susan, lived somewhere near Los Angeles. Maybe he'd go there.

He gripped the handlebars and pumped his legs harder. Could he ride all the way? How far was it? Five hundred miles? Eight hundred? What if he got a flat or the chain broke? Well, then he'd have to hitchhike. Or walk. It didn't matter. As long as he kept moving.

At the stop sign at the bottom of the hill, he looked both ways and turned onto Old Coast Road. Off to his right, the black ocean rumbled, somehow louder in the stillness of the night. He heard the distant clang of a harbor buoy, sounding as lonely as he felt. The slender beam from the lighthouse swept above glistening whitecaps and shot over his head. He pedaled faster, faster.

His eyes on the revolving light, Noah didn't see the pothole until his front wheel rammed into it. He flew over the handlebars, his head thumped the pavement and blazing pain ballooned behind his eyes. Colors flashed through his head – reds and yellows and whites. A sharp throbbing drowned out all other sound.

"Owwwww!" Rolling from side to side, he clamped his hands to his forehead.

Eventually, the pain receded. He sat up slowly, rocking back and forth. On wobbly legs, he clambered to his feet Taking several deep breaths, he tried to clear his head.

He was about to retrieve his bike when he heard quick footsteps behind him. Before he could turn, a hand clamped down on his shoulder.

Chapter Two

"Noaaaah. Noaaaah Keeeeene." Menace dripped from the gravelly voice.

An icy fork of fear scraped Noah's backbone. Wrapping his arms tightly across his chest, he tried desperately to get a message from his brain to the rest of his body. Run! Fight! Scream! But it was like someone had chopped the phone lines. He couldn't move. Gory scenes from every horror movie he'd ever seen thrashed through his imagination. A wave crashed against the rocks far below, the retreating water hissing in the darkness. And then he heard the ragged breath of whoever had caught him. Paralyzed, he wondered if he'd be thrown from the cliff, or if his captor had something worse planned, something horribly painful.

The grip on his shoulder released slowly. The hand withdrew. Noah's feet still refused to move. A puff of warm breath tickled his ear. "Tee hee."

Noah felt the fear that had held him captive seep away, leaving him weak and rubber-legged. A flush of anger and embarrassment replaced the fear. "Abby! Dang it anyway. You scared the living peemore out of me." He whirled to see her leaning against the guardrail, convulsed in laughter. The nearly full moon cast an eerie orange-yellow light on her tousled dark hair.

"Sorry—" she choked off another giggle. "I couldn't help it. I wasn't gonna, but I couldn't stop myself."

Noah clenched his fists, scowled at his sister, then eased himself onto the guardrail beside her and took several slow, deep breaths. He turned his face from hers. Sometimes she reminded him so much of Mom that it hurt to look at her. She had the same hair and olive skin, the same flashing eyes, the same way of waving good-bye using just her fingertips. Even the "tee hee" she'd used as a punch line for her prank came right from Mom's catalogue of gentle teasing tricks. Noah knew he took after his father—fair haired and freckled with lanky limbs. Just a pound this side of skinny. The tendency to brood came from Dad, also. And, he admitted to himself, the tendency toward silence.

For a moment, Noah considered revenge. Abby was starting to slim down, but she still carried some baby fat at thirteen. Sometimes he teased her about it, calling her "chubby cheeks," even though he knew that would make her cry and argue that he ate lots more than she did. Three times as much. It seemed like he was always hungry.

He remembered the cookies he'd dumped into the trash and wished he'd brought them along. Then he recalled where they'd come from, and his earlier anger returned.

He remembered his father and the song, recalled the faint fragrance of cinnamon and something flowery that lingered in the air later that night when he'd crept into the kitchen for his getaway supplies. Her scent. Dad had already forgotten Mom, it looked like. How long before he replaced Noah and Abby with another family?

"Yo, big brother. Earth to No-way, earth to No-way, come in Noah."

Abby's voice snapped him back to reality. "How the heck did you find me, Ab-normal?"

"Hey, I'm a brain, remember? I made use of zee leetle gray cells, mon ami."

Noah groaned. The other night, they'd been watching a mystery show with a short, weird detective who pronounced his name Hair-kewl Pwah-roe. He was what, French? No, Belgian. He'd made a big deal about that.

Ever since, Abby had been mimicking him and spouting off about her "Leetle gray cells," and how everything was "quite simple, mon ami." She was right about being smart, though. Her I.Q. was one eighty-five. He remembered Mom and Dad's amazement when the test results had come back. Mom had— No. He chased the memory out of his mind and asked, "How so, braniac?"

"It means, goofwad, that when I hear someone rummaging in the refrigerator in the middle of the night, it is of no consequence." Abby began larding her words with the Belgian accent. "But when zat same person begins rummaging in zee dresser drawers, then, mon ami, I say zere is zee fox in zee hen house." She dropped the accent. "Or, as Sherlock Holmes would say, 'the game is afoot.'"

"So, you followed me?"

"Right in one, Noah."

"Well, you need to go home. Now. If Dad finds out you're gone he'll—"

"He'll what? How about you, dude? Way I figure it, you're out," she glanced at her watch, "almost seven hours past curfew. You'll be grounded until you're old enough for Golden Hills." She named a retirement center up the highway from their house.

"I probably would be," Noah sighed. "But I'm not going back."

Abby squinted at him; she raised her chin. "You have to go back, Dad will miss you."

"No he won't. He'll be too busy with Jennifer. He probably won't even notice I'm gone."

"Oh boo hoo. Poor No-way. Nobody loves him," Abby taunted.

Noah's fists clenched. "Shut up, Ab-normal."

"I won't shut up, Noah. Dad loves you. He just has trouble showing it. He's not like—" She didn't say "Mom," she didn't have to. They both fell silent. The lighthouse beam swept by them again and again, marking off the minutes.

"Where are you going, Noah?"

"California. At least at first. To Aunt Susan's. Maybe she'll let me sleep in her garage or something. Maybe I'll get a job mowing lawns, save my money, buy some drums, get into a band."

Abby threw back her head and laughed.

"What's so funny?"

"Aunt Susan moved. To Ohio. Last fall."

Noah felt his jaw drop. "How'd you know that?"

"From the return address on her Christmas card, dummy." She flashed him an impish grin. "I guess I'm going to have go with you whether you want me or not. Somebody's got to be the brains of this outfit."

"No way, Abby. I don't need anybody else. You'll just be in the way."

She grinned. "Well, I sure wouldn't want to be in your way when you get to California and start looking for Aunt Susan."

Noah fought the grin, then let it spread across his face. Smart aleck little sister. He'd really miss her. He made a fist and laid it gently against her temple. "Twirp. I oughta..."

Abby laughed again. "Yeah, but you won't, because I'm your little sister and you love me even if I am a pain in the rear. And besides, I brought a blanket and more food and some money, cuz I broke open my piggy bank, and I even snagged us a bag of frosted animal cookies, see?" The words came out so fast they sounded like they were chasing one another. She fished around in her backpack, found an iced cookie and popped it into Noah's mouth.

"Mgfff. Pfanks," he mumbled, trying to chew and think. He should take her home. But how would he make her stay? Wake up Dad? Tell him to watch Abby while he ran away?

"Poor Noah," Abby said, "he's having a bad brain day."

She stood, stretching her arms above her head, then rubbed her shoulders. "I'm getting cold. It will feel good when the sun comes up."

The sun? Noah bolted to his feet and seized his backpack. The one valid part of his plan had been to be off the road by sunrise in case his father called the police and they organized a search. He ran to his bike. "I've got to get going."

"Not without me, you aren't." She raced after him, shrugging her backpack onto her shoulders.

"No, Abby. Go home."

"Not without you."

"Go home!" Noah swung a leg over his bike, found the pedal with his right foot and stood on it. The front tire went sideways. The bike bucked and screamed. Metal grated on stone.

"You blew out a tire," Abby informed him. "Bent the wheel, too."

"Yaaaargh!" Noah screamed in rage and frustration. He leaped from the bike and slung it against the guardrail, hot tears blistering his eyes. Why couldn't something go right? Anything?

"Take my bike," Abby offered in a business-like tone.

"I'll ride on the handlebars."

"How many times do I have to tell you, Abby? You're not coming."

Abby raised her chin defiantly. "Might as well take me. I'll follow you anyway." She sighed melo-dramatically. "There I'll be, walking along the highway. All by myself. At the mercy of every weirdo on the west coast. Gangsters. Thugs. Ax murderers."

Brother and sister stood, hands on hips, eyes locked in a classic standoff. Finally, Noah gave up. Kicking the wreckage of his bike, he growled, "All right, let's go. We can make it to the cave before sunrise. I don't want to be on the road in the daytime."

"What cave? Where?"

"It's over on the ocean side of Humbug Mountain."

"Right in the mountain?" She turned to look down the coastline at the dark craggy mass.

"Yeah. It's a big cave, but you can only get to it during low tide. Which oughta be," he glanced at his watch, "in about two hours." He straddled her bike, helped her balance on the handlebars, and began to pedal.

"Noah?" Abby's voice was a quavering whisper on a quickening wind. "If the cave's in the mountain, aren't you scared of . . . of . . . you know?"

"Of the hermit?" He formed an O with his mouth and made a spooky moaning, whistling sound. It was payback time. He did his best creepy monster impression in a cracking adolescent voice. "You mean, the Homicidal Hermit of Humbug Mountain." He capped this with a cascade of diabolical laughter that echoed from the rock wall that hemmed in the road on their left.

"Quit it, you creep," she moaned. "Just knock it off."

"Oh I see," he snapped back. "It's okay for you to sneak up on me and get my shorts in a bunch, but when it's you who's scared, the shoe's on the other foot."

"The hermit is different, Noah," Abby said in her I-make-the-rules voice. "You don't joke about the Hermit."

"Whatever," Noah puffed. He didn't have the breath to argue anyway; pedaling took all his energy. In fact, he didn't say another word until after they turned off the road, hid Abby's bike in a patch of gorse and struggled across rocks and logs to the beach. There, they fought a stiff breeze blowing out of the south that lifted Abby's long hair and rippled it out like a dark contrail. Noah dug his stocking cap from his pack and offered it to her. She shook her head in refusal and continued to trudge three steps to each of Noah's two.

They stayed close to the water where the sand was hardest and made steady progress toward the looming, barren face of Humbug Mountain. The earthy perfume of low tide blew into their faces—a pungent stew of sea brine and decaying shellfish. Two sea gulls, silhouetted against the barely gray sky, circled down to the sand and an early breakfast buffet spread by the retreating tide. The surf was a steady roar; white noise as Noah struggled to put together a list. Build a fire, he thought. Get warm. Figure out how to get little sister to go home.

"Darn." He'd forgotten matches. He hoped that Abby, the organize-ma-tron, hadn't.

"Abby?" He paused and tilted his head a little, expecting to find her just off his left shoulder.

No answer. A sour taste rose in his throat. His heart fluttered in his chest like a captive moth. He swiveled and screamed full out. "Aaaaabby!"

"Gahh, you wanta deafen me? I can hear you fine."

As suddenly as she had disappeared, she was beside him again. And she was holding something round and wet—the smooth stone she'd found two days ago.

"Where'd you go?"

"Down to the surf." She held out the stone. "See how pretty it is when it's wet? You can almost see down inside of it."

"Why'd you bring that, Abby? You're like, hauling an extra five pounds around. I mean, it's pretty and all, but—"

"Three pounds exactly," Abby interrupted smugly. "Weighed it on the fish scales. And I couldn't leave it behind. I've never had anything like it before."

Noah understood. Being beach kids, this was not the first glass ball either of them had found. But it certainly qualified as the coolest. During certain times of the year, the round floats broke free of Japanese fishing nets and drifted across the Pacific. He'd heard his Dad tell of times they'd been plentiful, but now they were fairly rare. The Japanese didn't use as many of them, and crack-of dawn professional beachcombers, who sold to the local gift shops, scooped up most of them.

Abby stretched her arm out, offering the stone to the moon drifting toward the ocean. "Look at how it glows.

Like it's alive, almost."

Noah watched the orb, fascinated. The stone seemed to cast a light of its own, a greenish luminescence that shifted to violet and then to an icy white. "Yeah. Cool. Maybe we can sell it to a gift shop for some more traveling money."

"Not a chance." Abby rubbed it on her jacket and placed it carefully in her backpack. "We can't sell it. It's important."

"Important? Important for what? How can a rock be important?"

"I don't know how." She was emphatic. "I just know it is."

"Okay, brainy one, if you say so. Let's boogie. We've got forty-five minutes to make the cave before the tide turns." He strode ahead toward the mountain.

Abby ran to catch up. "Noah, what are we going to do about Dad? He'll be worried sick."

Noah didn't answer; didn't remind Abby that Dad didn't care about him. Yeah, he'd be worried about Abby. But Abby should have gone home when he told her.

"I don't want him to worry," Abby moaned. "He's been through enough." She stumbled over a piece of driftwood and Noah stretched out an arm to help her. "And what if he starts to look for us and finds your wrecked bike? He'll think you got hit by a car. It's not fair, Noah."

Fair? Didn't Abby know that life wasn't fair? Noah sighed. "Okay, I know what we can do."

"What?"

"You can call him later on, and tell him we're okay and we're in California. Tell him we caught a couple of rides last night and got as far as San Francisco. Then the cops will look for us there. Meanwhile, we'll find a road that'll take us east, to Ohio."

"Highway 199, south of Brookings." She patted her backpack. "I brought a map. You can't find the right way without a map."

He shook his head and smiled at her. She was so efficient. "I knew that." He turned back to the south.

"Hey, look up there." Several hundred yards ahead, in a small natural cove carved into the face of an enormous rock, a campfire flickered.

Abby clutched his arm. "Stop. Maybe we oughta walk around." She jerked her head away from the beach toward a jumble of logs littering the high tide line. "We can get through there as soon as there's enough light to see by."

"No. That will take too long. It's probably just a couple of bums by the fire. They won't hurt anyone. And we have to get to the cave before the tide."

Abby relaxed her grip. "Let's walk by them fast though, okay?"

"Right," he agreed. "We'll just keep going."

They kept close to the retreating surf, sneaking looks toward the campsite. As they drew alongside the small bonfire, they heard it crackle and spit. Noah picked up something else, too. Music. A strange kind of rhythm. One of his Dave Brubeck jazz LP's had a cut where the drummer Joe Morello kept a syncopated beat like that. A tango. He ventured a look toward the fire and saw two people, illuminated by the flickering flames, advancing and retreating with the rhythm. Whirling and dipping.

He couldn't remember seeing any stranger sight in his life.

He halted. "Abby, look."

"Shhh." She put a finger to her mouth. "You said we'd keep going."

But Noah couldn't seem to move, and he couldn't take his eyes from the dancers. They were very graceful, moving almost as one person as the music built to a climax and, with a chattering of castanets and a crash of cymbals, ended. The two separated and honored one another, he bowing stiffly from the waist, she answering with a prim curtsy. The man reached toward what appeared to be a boom box and punched a button.

"We need to go talk to them." Noah heard the words leave his mouth as he started toward the fire.

Abby grabbed his sleeve. "You're crazy, Noah. We don't know who—"

"We have to talk to them." Noah pulled away and walked steadily to where the two dervishes had collapsed on the sand. He heard Abby's feet shuffling behind him.

"Welcome, children." The voice of the woman was husky but had a smile in its tone. "Sit down. Enjoy the fire."

Noah obeyed immediately, but Abby hesitated at the edge of the firelight, glancing around. After a moment, she sidled up beside him and squatted, tensed and ready to run.

"You kids runaways?" This voice came from the grizzled man who put something in a brown paper bag to his mouth after he spoke.

"Of course they are, George," the woman answered. "What else would they be, out here at this time of night?"

As she spoke, Noah recognized her. Old Hannah. Almost every day, she hobbled up and down Highway 101 picking up bottles and cans and putting them into a supermarket shopping cart. He'd never seen her up close before, and he was surprised to note that she didn't look all that old. She was small, probably not much taller than Abby. Her hair was brown and tangled. Her face was smudged with soot from the fire. She smiled warmly at him.

"We're hitchhiking," he found himself muttering. "Heading south."

"Better head for the road then. Ain't many cars pass by here on the beach," the old man cackled, took another pull at whatever was in the bag and punched a button on the boom box.

Old Hannah smiled at Noah again, and nodded slowly. She stood and swayed gracefully as the opening chords of another song roared from the speakers and held her hand out to Noah. Without a conscious thought, he took it and led her toward the surf. Abby gaped open-mouthed from her spot near the fire. The old man belched, swigged from the bottle and slapped out time with his hand against his knee.

The song wasn't a tango. Its rhythm was slow and dreamlike. Hannah guided Noah in a flowing whirl around the perimeter of the rocky cove, shedding her usual rocking, limping walk as she moved with the beat of the music.

Noah had never before danced, although Mom had been promising to teach him when she—

He put the thought aside as he danced across the sand, his eyes locked onto Hannah's. The steps seemed to come to him automatically. They were complex, taking the two of them over wide stretches of the beach, forward right to the edge of the water, sideways down the beach, then a series of spins and stutter steps that brought them back to the fire. As they danced, an extensive silent conversation took place. Images passed from her piercing green eyes to Noah's mind, as if projected from a lantern onto a screen in his. Images, words, pictures, even sounds and smells— so jumbled and fractured, he could make no sense of them.

Suddenly he heard the snap and pop of the fire and a hiss of white noise from the tape player. Hannah curtsied toward him, smiling slyly. Without thinking, he bowed from the waist. "Don't ever be afraid to dance, Noah." Hannah counseled. "Remember the steps. Can you do that?"

Noah, nodded, wondering if he could. "I . . . uh . . . think so."

"Good," Hannah said. "You may need to dance some time. Some time soon." Her eyes flashed into his again, sealing something into his brain.

Noah nodded again. "We can go now, Abby." He walked quickly away from the fire down the beach.

She caught up to him. "Mundo bizzaro, big brother."

Her voice quavered a little. "What was that all about? How did she know your name?"

"It was—" He tried to find words to explain but couldn't. He looked back at the fire and saw Old Hannah and the man huddled together, the bottle in the bag passing between them. The homeless woman turned her head and caught his glance. She flicked her fingers at him, shooing him on his way, then picked up a walking stick and limped to a rock at the edge of the darkness.

Noah raised his hand tentatively, then turned his back on the fire and shrugged, letting his silence replace the answer he didn't have for Abby's question.

Even though the tide was nearly out, they had to take off their shoes and wade through ankle-deep water to reach the pathway to the indentation in the base of Humbug Mountain. As they slogged through the cold brine, Noah tilted his head to look up the sheer ocean-side face. It seemed dark, ominous, cold, and impossibly high.

But, in a few moments, they found the trail and hauled themselves up to the cave.

Too tired to talk, they ate a few cookies, unrolled their sleeping bags and crawled into them. Abby fell asleep almost immediately, but Noah lay awake for a time, looking out at the brightening sky and listening to the tide. Finally, he closed his eyes and let sleep take him.

He dreamt vividly, of his mother and father, Abby and the hoary old couple at the campfire. And then his dreams became strange and horrible, filled with dark passages and strange creatures, dwarfish baboon-like animals with wild, dreadlocked hair and round, black blotches for eyes.

The stench of the creatures, their warm and foul breath, seemed to fill his nostrils.

It was only when Abby screamed that he realized the horrible truth. He was not asleep. They were not alone in the cave. And the nightmare face of one of the creatures was just inches from his own.

Chapter Three

Frozen with fear, Noah tried to scream. No sound came from his throat. He squeezed his eyes closed as tightly as possible, employing the defense he'd used against monsters under the bed when he was little.

Perhaps, if he didn't look, he'd drift into a warm peaceful sleep and wake up to find the leering beast hovering over him had been only a fragment of a bad dream.

His ears and nose betrayed his hopes.

Vividly, he heard the rhythm of the beast's chest rising and falling. A snuffling, snorting intake of air. A lip-quivering fooof. Then again. And again. He smelled sickly-sweet, rotten breath. The stench hung over his face like a damp and dirty washrag. He stifled the impulse to throw up, forced himself to remain utterly still.

Then Abby screamed. "Get your hands off me, you scuzzy little dirtbags. Noah! Noah, help me! They're—"

Her words were cut off with a strangled "mmffk."

"Aaaabbbbbyyyyy!" Noah bellowed, kicking his sleeping bag-covered legs as hard as he could. He felt his knees make contact with something, heard a whoomp and a squeal.

He forced himself to open his eyes. Gray light surrounded him. Dawn? Or twilight? He tried to stand and got tripped up by the tangled sleeping bag.

Wriggling frantically, he finally managed to kick it off and get to his feet.

"Abby! Abby!" His shout bounced off the rock walls of the cave. "Abby, where are you." God, please don't let them hurt her, he thought. And where's the— What the heck had it been? He swung around toward the entrance and saw the creature he'd kicked rubbing its midsection and backing away furtively.

It's scared of me, Noah thought. Good. He took two steps toward it and the creature cowered. Noah figured it to be about a foot shorter than he was, but much brawnier. Its skin was a sickly gray and it was bald except for a cascade of braided hair falling from the top of its head, clumps of feathery black hair around each foot and a fringe hanging from its waist to its knees. The feet themselves were more like hands and reminded Noah of monkeys' feet.

Noah took another few steps toward the mouth of the cave and was about to lunge for the creature and throw it down the cliffside when he saw the other two. They were perched on a narrow ledge thirty feet above him. One carried Abby, slung over its shoulder like a sack of potatoes. The other held a huge gray hand clamped over her mouth.

As he watched, Abby's eyes darted back and forth, pleading silently with him to do something, anything.

"Where are you taking my sister? You let go of her right this minute," he bellowed.

Abby's eyes widened even farther and she looked down. Noah clapped his hands over his mouth. If the kidnappers let go, she'd fall and crack her head open.

Why was he so stupid? Why did he always seem to make things worse instead of better?

The creatures laughed, a sound like bacon grease spitting from a hot frying pan. The one covering Abby's mouth pointed at Noah and shook its finger. It was then he noticed they all wore sunglasses—specifically Ray-Bans. He recognized them; he had a pair in his backpack. He'd saved his allowance for two months and bought them because he thought they'd make him look cool while he was whaling away on the drums, make him look just like his idol, the immortal Lix Delacroix. Abby had laughed and said that other than being too white, too young, too short, too skinny and too alive, he was a dead ringer for Delacroix.

"Tuh-cht-cht-cht-cht-cht," the creature Noah had kicked made a clicking sound with his tongue. The one holding Abby answered with another clucking rhythm, adding a click or two, and began scaling the cliff. Its companion followed, carrying Abby's backpack slung over its shoulder.

"Noaaahhhh!" Abby screamed as the creature took its hand from her mouth. "Help me!"

"Where are you taking my sister?" Noah's voice cracked. The two creatures above him didn't stop. He whirled on the one he'd kicked. He was no longer frightened. A calm had come over him. "You tell them to bring her back this minute."

The nightmarish beast now looked somehow pathetic and perplexed. It bared its teeth, showing red-tinged gums and raised its arms in a karate stance.

Noah kept coming. "You make them bring Abby back or I'm going to kick your butt." He'd never fought anyone in his short life, but a red rage engulfed him. He was certain he would win.

The creature backed away and shook its head, snarled braids flopping like worms. Suddenly, with a final chtcht-cht-cht, it turned and scampered up the rock face outside the cavern.

Without thinking, Noah set out in pursuit. The rock was slick, with only small crevices and knobs he could use for handgrips and toeholds. Glancing up, he saw that the creature he'd kicked was only a few yards ahead, but Abby and her captors were merely distant blobs of color on the wall above him. "Oh God, Abby," he moaned, "I'm so sorry. I should have taken you back home. I should have gone with you. I dumbed out and got us in trouble."

Reserves of strength and agility he didn't know that he had kicked in. He clawed his way upward like a mountain goat. He didn't dare to look down, but knew that he'd climbed a long way. As he scrambled for another foothold, and wedged his fingers into cracks in the rock, he found himself wondering what it would feel like to fall. Would he have time to be afraid?

He lifted his head and saw his quarry just a few feet away, its head cocked as if it were listening to something.

Noah pulled himself onto an inch-wide ledge and pressed his chest against the rock. Then he heard it. Or perhaps felt it. It was a low thoomp, thoomp, thoomp, as if Humbug Mountain had become a massive kettledrum.

Thoomp, thoomp, thudda, thoomp, it went. Thudda thoomp, thoomp, thudda thoomp.

The creature above him was transfixed, listening, hugging the rock face with all four of its hand-like feet, rocking gently to the beat. It seemed oblivious to Noah, oblivious to anything except the rhythm.

Noah found another foothold and pulled himself a few feet closer. He, too, found himself temporarily mesmerized by the rhythm of the mountain—*thudda thoomp thoomp*. And then he realized something very strange. The rhythm he was hearing, the sound that the creature moved to, was identical to the beat of his own heart. His ears were filled with it now. He couldn't tell where his pulse ended and the vibration from the mountain picked up. *Thudda thoomp thoomp thudda thoomp.*

But he had to save Abby!

"Arrgggghh." He howled. He lunged upward and grabbed a hairy ankle.

"Cht!" The creature stiffened, then kicked, trying to shake Noah loose. Noah held on. The creature frantically shook its leg.

"You tell them to bring back Abby!" Noah shrieked. Lodging his toes against another small outcropping, he thrust himself upward and clutched the creature's other ankle with his left hand.

The mountain continued to thump, faster now as Noah clung desperately to the creature's legs, exhausted from the effort; hyper with fear and anger. *Thudda thoomp thudda thoomp thudda thoomp.* Noah's heart remained in lock step with the rhythm.

Above him, his adversary growled low in its throat and directed a warning cht-cht-cht toward him. It reached a pudgy paw down to swat at Noah's hands. The movement threw its center of balance backward, toward the open air and the water below.

Noah felt his left foot swing away from the cliff face.

"No." He tried to swing his foot back. Too late. He felt the creature's weight start to peel him from the rock and toward the long fall to the water. Time slowed to a near standstill. Two words repeated over and over again in his mind, providing a strangely calming mantra as his last handhold gave way.

Uh oh, he thought. Uh oh, uh oh, uh oh, uh, oh.

Wind rushed around him. He somersaulted through the air, hands clamping tighter around the creature's ankles.

Their eyes locked for a moment just before they hit the water. Noah saw the animal's lips move and form the words. "Uh oh."

Chapter Four

Abby looked around at the rock walls of her chamber and munched on a mouthful of the dried fish she'd been given to eat. Salty, but okay. At first, she'd been too frightened and confused to take anything from the seemingly contrite little grungoid who'd brought her a tray of strange-looking food, but eventually hunger and common sense took over. She needed strength so she could think. Think and plan. Her watch had been broken as she struggled with the grungoids, so she didn't know the time. She tried to calculate how many hours had passed since 5:59 AM when it had stopped, but found she couldn't even guess. Four hours? Eight? Time seemed to twist around itself in her mind. At least, she consoled herself, she'd gotten beyond being terrorized and into analyzing the situation.

As Abby chewed, she noticed her jaws keeping time to the deep, throbbing rhythm of the inner mountain. The thumping she'd heard as she was carried up the cliffside had subsided for a time, but now the mountain seemed to pick up the beat. It seemed to serve as a tympanic reminder of her plight with its low-pitched rumbling thudda thoomp-thudda thoomp. Was the sound random?

Was it caused by the shifting of different strata of rock, expanding and contracting with changing temperatures?

Or did it mean something? If so, what?

Noah could probably figure it out, she thought. After all, he knew everything about drumming. He'd once told her that all the rhythms he heard in his head, and conveyed through his drums, were born in the earth.

She'd scoffed. The whole concept was a little too mystic for her. She put her faith in science. Numbers, probabilities, and nature's finite laws.

"Noah," she whispered, as tears rolled down her cheeks. He'd tried to follow the creatures that took her.

She'd wiggled around in their grasp, trying to keep her eyes on him. But her captors climbed quickly and the distance between them had widened. Finally, Noah appeared only as a speck clinging to the side of Humbug Mountain. And then the speck disappeared. Had he fallen from the cliff? Was he hurt? Dead?

She sobbed for a few moments, then knuckled the tears from her eyes. Crying wouldn't do any good. She had to think, had to recall and memorize everything about how she got here—in case she found a way to get loose.

She remembered the second rhythm. After her kidnappers had carried her almost to the top of the mountain, they'd stopped on a small rocky ledge. One of them had picked up a large stone and thumped it against a chipped and gouged spot on the wall in front of him. The pattern of thumps had been very intricate and precise.

When the creature had finished, Abby had heard a loud click and a section of what had appeared to be seamless rock wall swung open. Four tunnels converged onto a narrow landing inside the door. When they'd passed through, the door slid shut behind them and the squat, muscular creature that had been carrying her set her down. Immediately, it had pulled her by the hand into the opening on the right. It scuttled through, barely clearing its head; she'd had to duck. As the first creature yanked her along the tunnel, the second one prodded her from behind if she stumbled or slowed down.

Something occurred to her and made her smile at her own preconceptions. Why did she call the creatures "its"?

She'd assumed they were male. But assumption without evidence wasn't scientific. She needed more facts. She visualized the creatures. Without parting the fringe that hung from their waists, you couldn't tell if they were male or female. And she wasn't about to try that. But the 'grungoids,' as she decided to call them, could well be 'grungettes." The word caused her to giggle a little, despite her fears. She decided to think of them as male.

Sometimes you had to make an assumption in order to test it.

She returned to her review of the rest of the journey to this place—a perplexing hodgepodge of twists and turns. Still, terrified as she'd been, Abby knew she could find her way back to the stone door if she had to. The same ability that allowed her to think six or ten moves ahead and overwhelm her older brother when they played chess would allow her to retrace the route.

In the meantime, she was a prisoner, there was no question about that. One of the grungoids paced regularly between her and the door. This particular one disgusted her. Truly. From time to time, it would plop down on the dirt floor, use a gray thumb and forefinger, and extract some kind of little bug or something from its own hair.

After examining it for a moment, the grungoid would pop it gleefully into its mouth. Ooh ickkk! Abby shuddered at the thought of what that morsel might be.

She'd given up trying to communicate with them. After she'd calmed down, she'd attempted several questions about what they meant to do with her. She'd tried asking where she was in English, Spanish and French. In frustration, she'd even tried Igpay Atinlay. Pig Latin only brought a blank stare and another probe for food. Even acting it out didn't work. Her pantomime only drew another "cht-cht-cht-cht." Variations on that sound seemed to be the long and short of their language.

But there had been pleasant surprises. She'd spent the night on a waterbed—or, to be more accurate, a gel bed.

She knew because one of her friends at school let her lie down on her parents' bed one time. It had felt just like this, sort of squishy but still fairly firm. A crude wooden frame had been built around the mattress. How the grungoids had gotten it and brought it into the mountain was a curiosity.

Something else about her quarters baffled her—the lighting. At first glance, she thought a solid panel illuminated the entire high ceiling of the chamber. But soon she saw individual little pinpricks of light, clustered so tightly together they melded into one galaxy of light.

Like the Milky Way, only more so. They cast a different kind of luminescence—fuzzy, but at the same time somehow warm and clear. Intrigued, she'd climbed on her bed for a better look, but couldn't get close enough to see if there were wires or sockets. Strangely, when she'd laid her head down and tried to nap a little, the lights had dimmed immediately. She'd thought at first the grungoid had done it, but she when she opened her eyes and sat up, the light increased. The grungoid hadn't touched anything other than the buffet he knew as his body.

After eating some of the dried fish stuff and a cooked root that reminded her of squash, which she hated, she pushed the tray away. One of the other grungoids, not her guard, had come to take it and offered her something that totally blew her mind. Sealed in its original plastic wrapper, there was no mistaking it for anything else.

Deep within the mountain, held prisoner by nightmare-spawned creatures that spit instead of talking, and feasted on their personal parasites, she found herself eating a Twinkie.

She thought again of Noah and blinked back fresh tears. This was all her fault. She should have forced him to go back. Or gone home and finked him out to Dad. Her father would worry himself sick. She visualized him trudging up and down the highway where they'd left Noah's bike, saw him plunging into the surf after a log he'd imagined looked like a body. No matter what Noah thought, she knew Dad loved him, worried about him, and would mourn him if he died.

Once again, she fought tears and sat up straight.

Maybe Noah wasn't dead. Maybe he'd survived. If he had, she'd find him. She didn't worry much about her own safety. Something told her she was in no immediate danger. That same sense also nagged her about making rash assumptions. But she'd always had the knack of keeping herself calm in a crisis. She was sure she could come up with a way out, if only she could concentrate. When the chance to escape came, she'd make the most of it.

"Cht-Cht-Cht-Cht."

Abby snapped from her trance to see two more grungoids enter the chamber. She thought one might have been the one who'd carried her up the mountain, but she couldn't be certain. They were different sizes, but their faces all looked the same to her. And they all wore Ray-Ban sunglasses. She found that surprising, given the soft light in the cavern. Still, the eyewear didn't seem to be much of an impediment to getting around. They moved swiftly to her side and gently but firmly pulled her to her feet.

"So where are we going?" Even though she didn't think they understood her, talking helped her stay calm.

"Big plans for you, baby. It gonna be too cool."

"You know I could have you all arrested for—"

Suddenly what she'd heard registered in her brain and she thought she would wet her pants. The creature at her right elbow had just talked. Well, mumbled might be more accurate. She struggled to regain her equilibrium as they moved her toward the opening. "Y..Y..you talk?"

"Of course, little chickie, don't everybody?"

She hadn't been hearing things. Not only did he talk, but he sounded like . . . like that beatnik character she'd seen on an old black and white TV show. The one with the silly little goatee and the ripped-up sweatshirt.

"But why didn't you say anything before?"

"You and me only, like just now met, baby. And the others can't fling people lingo, dig?"

She didn't, but nodded anyway. "But I thought . . . Sunglasses?"

"We all wear shades, chickee. All of Lix's posse, anyway."

"Posse? Where are we? Who are you? What are the big plans? And what happened to my brother?"

"Whoa, little princess. Cool your jets. All in good time."

"But—"

The grungoid turned and drew a finger across his mouth. "My lips is zipped, chickie baby. Don't waste your wind."

Abby ducked as they entered the passageway and debated whether to ask another question. The grungoid seemed to read her mind.

"The Grand Exalted Pettifog has the answers, dudette. But he don't deal 'em out often or easy." His grip tightened on her wrist.

Suddenly, Abby was afraid again.

Chapter Five

Turbulent dreams ravaged Noah's sleep. In them, he saw himself on a towering precipice, unearthly twinkling light above him, a crowd of—

What were they? Not people. Beings. Creatures with humans mixed sparsely among them. An ebony giant pointed toward him. He peered down, saw Abby in the giant's shadow. Abby! He'd found her! But he couldn't get down. Couldn't get to her.

Suddenly, all light was extinguished. He heard the howl of the wind. Or was it the keening of some voracious beast, closing in on his prey? The rankness of the animal flooded his senses and he felt his nostrils flare.

He flailed his arms, tried to lift his feet to run. He couldn't.

Something metallic clicked against his teeth and another pungent aroma replaced the first. A taste— organic, tangy and foreign—made him splutter involuntarily. He jerked his head. Hot liquid ran down his chin onto his bare chest.

"Careful boy. You'll be burnin' us both." The voice, guttural and gruff, filled his ears, echoing around him as he attempted to focus his just-opened eyes.

An old disheveled man, long tangled gray hair afly, eyes like stone, spooned more liquid from a clay pot and extended the spoon toward Noah's mouth. "Eat some.

But go slow. You coughed up the last."

"Whuh . . . what is it?"

"Scrubbage stew. Good for what ails you. Don't worry, boy. I'm not trying to kill you. You came close enough to doing that yourself."

Before Noah could protest, the spoon found his mouth. This time he swallowed the liquid without problem. On second tasting, it wasn't bad; kind of a cross between broccoli and carrots, with maybe a dash of celery tossed in. He accepted several more spoonfuls while he studied the rocky chamber in which he lay. "Where am I?"

"Not under the Pacific Ocean, that's where ye be.

Lucky for you, I happened along when I did," the grizzled codger cackled. "Saw you peel that little worm-headed thing off the cliff."

In a rush of images, Noah recalled the frantic climb up the rock wall after Abby. He remembered grabbing the squat little creature's ankle and then . . . uh oh. The rough mattress below him made crunkly noises as he sank back for a moment, his head swimming. He breathed slowly, concentrating, then sat up again and took in several more spoonfuls of stew offered by the thin, hunch-shouldered man. Feeling its warmth coursing through him, he swallowed hard, then blurted out. "Abby. My sister.

Where is she?"

"Can't rightly say. Never saw her. Just you."

"Who—"

"Am I? Good question. I am who I am. Except when I'm somebody else. I live here. In and around the mountain."

"Humbug Mountain, you mean?" What he'd teased Abby about came back to him. The hermit. Along with Bigfoot and the midnight-hook-wielding teenager slasher, the hermit was the bogeyman of local campfire stories.

Noah had never thought he really existed. But this man did. He sure looked like a hermit was supposed to. And, like the legend said, he apparently lived inside Humbug Mountain.

The old man ladled more stew into Noah's mouth.

Noah doubted he'd ever relish the taste. No question though, it made him feel better. He sucked it from the spoon, his energy level inching up. As soon as he could, he needed to get up. He needed to find Abby. But his eyes still felt heavy. Time jumbled. He felt himself slipping back into sleep.

It was pitch dark when he opened his eyes again, but immediately, as if it sensed his sudden consciousness, something seemed to throw a switch. A soft warm light began to glow from somewhere above him, illuminating an oval-shaped chamber defined by four rocky, damp walls with an opening on the side opposite the bed. As he sat up, the mattress-stuffing made a scrunchy sound beneath him.

His ears also picked up the distant hum of someone mumbling. The hermit? He stood, walking wobbly-legged across the uneven rock floor, realizing he was quite naked. He blushed at the picture of the hermit peeling his wet clothes from him and drying him off, but the flush subsided quickly. After all, the scruffy old codger was a guy. No big deal.

Noah looked around the area, and saw his clothes, dry and folded neatly on a sort of natural table formed by the rock. Still shaky, it took him a few minutes to put them on. Bending down to tie his tennis shoes, he felt the room spin around him and the floor tip. He sat with a thump.

The dizziness passed.

It was then he noticed his backpack and sleeping bag on the floor beside him. But how? He'd left them behind when he'd chased Abby's kidnappers up the rock face.

Hadn't he? He checked through the zippered pockets quickly, his hands pausing for a moment over the drumsticks he'd put in the pack before he went to sleep in the cave. Everything seemed to be there. He tied the sleeping bag to the pack, shrugged himself into it, and staggered to his feet.

"Got to go. Got to go get help for Abby." He thought aloud. His words echoed from the walls and he realized how impossible his mission sounded. Go where? How would he get out? And if he did get out and get home, what would he tell his father? What would he tell the cops? Little monsters from hell kidnapped his sister and he'd fallen into the ocean trying to catch them? The hermit of Humbug Mountain had rescued him and fed him scrubbage stew?

No one would believe him. Never in a million years. They'd think he'd been drinking or doing drugs. A sudden spasm of fear and revulsion tugged at his nervous stomach. They might even think he'd hurt Abby. Killed her.

"Oh, God, got to think." He crossed back to the bed and sat for a moment, trying to slow the images zooming through his brain. After several moments, he became aware again of the one-sided conversation coming from the next room. The hermit. Talking to someone. But who? Who else was in this cave?

If they got in, he told himself, I can get out.

Making his way to the door, he ducked to pass under it and found himself in a larger chamber. Twenty yards away, the hermit sat in the lotus position, his eyes lifted toward the high roof of the cavern. Noah followed the old man's gaze, but saw only the same soft glow that illuminated the smaller room. As he walked toward the hermit, moving his gaze from the ceiling to the floor so he wouldn't trip and fall, he noticed something strange. As the hermit spoke, rocking back and forth on his haunches, his hands forming a tent in front of him, the lights changed color. Not only that, but pinpoints of light rearranged themselves on the surface of the rock, forming images and patterns. Noah also heard a faint, but unique humming sound, like a whispered chant filtered through a thick quilt.

Approaching the hermit, he cleared his throat. "What are you—"

"Shhh." The old man put a hand up to halt Noah's question, then used it to point at the ground. An order to sit. Noah obeyed, sprawling with his face turned upward.

"And if he can overcome that obstacle, what will come next?" The hermit intoned toward the ceiling.

Noah heard the distant hum change pitch, the rhythm and the light shifted hue again, forming a pattern unlike anything he could identify.

"Of course, the mountain's pulse will quicken before it begins to fail. That will make old Spid sit up and take notice."

Test? Mountain's pulse? Old Spid? Noah squirmed on the cold hard rock and looked up again to watch the shapes shift again and the light become violet, then almost lemon yellow.

"What will he need to do to find the Orb?" The whispered growl floated another question toward the lights. "What is his destiny?" The hermit turned slightly and studied Noah before looking to the lights for the answer.

Is he talking about me? Noah squirmed again. Crazy.

This was crazy. He wondered, for just a moment, if he might still be asleep and dreaming. He pinched the flesh on the back of his hand and felt the sharp pain, a reminder that the visage of the hermit talking to his ceiling hadn't sprung from his imagination.

"I see." The hermit rocked slowly, nodding his head in affirmation. "The girl will be critical then, to his quest."

The girl. Could he mean Abby? "Abby? Are you talking about Abby? Where is she?"

The hermit turned his gaze on Noah for a moment, and Noah recoiled from the pinwheeling power he felt emanating from the man's eyes. Images flooded through his brain. He felt himself falling, then flying, felt a throbbing beat reverberating in his chest. Then the hermit returned to his communication with the pulsating ceiling lights. As he spoke, the pattern changed once more. The colors become shades of red, from crimson to soft cherry.

"His sister. He wishes to know if he will find her."

Noah sat transfixed as the lights moved, dancing on the surface above him and the hermit rocked back and forth, back and forth. "If Spid doesn't lure her to his side first," the hermit acknowledged the message from the lights.

"He must rescue the Methuselah Stone from the Temple of Cheltnor and return to help the Pettifog finish the ritual and seal the Skin? And how will he—"

Noah felt as though his head would burst. Leaping to his feet he yelled "Noooo!" at the top of his lungs.

What were they talking about? A quest? And who was Spid, and why would he want Abby? What temple? What stone? Why him? Maybe he'd gone crazy and this was what it felt like. He had to get away. Get out into the air. He staggered away from the hermit and broke into a dizzy-footed run.

"Wait," the hermit called. "Come back."

"No!" Noah screamed as he stumbled across the rough floor. On the opposite side of the chamber he found another opening and ducked into it, running with his head down. He'd gone only a few yards before the glow from the big room faded behind him. Fearful of the dark, Noah stopped, panting, feeling sweat, cold and clammy, on his back. He looked back, expecting to see the hermit loom in the entranceway, but there was no sound, no movement.

Think, he told himself. Think like Abby would.

Up, he decided after a moment. He needed to go up. Eventually he'd reach the top of the mountain and find a way out. There had to be a hole or there would be no air.

Encouraged by this logic, he continued onward, keeping one hand in front of him and one on the tunnel wall.

His mind reeled; his nerve-endings tingled at the very surface of his skin. He felt a light spray of water splash onto his forehead and dribble down his nose, onto his upper lip. He arced his tongue upward to taste it. It had a strong mineral flavor. Water was a good sign, he told himself. Water flowed downhill. Maybe he'd find an underground stream he could follow.

Noah soon lost track of how long he'd been walking.

His wristwatch was gone—lost in the ocean or acquired by the hermit. He tried counting seconds and adding minutes, but soon lost his place. At first, he'd turn every few minutes and look back into the darkness or stop and listen for footsteps to see if the hermit had followed him.

But he couldn't hear a thing except the pounding of his own heart. The head-high tunnel wound around and around, tightening in some locations, opening up in others.

After a time, he saw a dim dimple of light. Outside! He'd made it! He moved more quickly, then slowed, wondering if perhaps he'd walked in a huge circle and would find himself back in the hermit's cavern. No, he was sure he'd been going up all the time. He stopped for a minute, then staggered on. He had no other choice.

He emerged into a lighted room about twice the size of the one he'd slept in. With a final burst of strength, he ran to its center, hoping to glimpse the sky, the sun. But the only light came from a blanket of the glowing pinpoints on the ceiling.

He slumped to the floor, feeling tears of frustration burn his eyes. "Where am I?" The whisper sifted into the air around him. The lights on the ceiling seemed to dim.

Noah felt the weight of exhaustion and despair on his shoulders, the hopelessness of his situation flooding through him. Abby gone, probably dead, him trapped inside Humbug Mountain, with no clue as to how to get out, to find help for Abby if she was alive. Some maniac, probably an escaped mental patient who talked to tiny fluorescent lights and thought Noah was supposed to save the world, or some incredibly insane stuff like that, hot on his heels.

"Keep going," he told himself. "There's got to be a way out." Looking around, he saw three openings cut into the rock wall. Three! Which one would take him out? What if he chose the wrong one? He might die inside this mountain. He imagined, years from now, spelunkers finding his skeleton, wondering who he'd been and what he had been doing here.

Noah covered his eyes with the palms of his hands. If only he'd listened to Abby. If only he'd given Dad a chance. God, no way things could be more screwed up than they were right now.

It was at that instant he felt a small hand on his shoulder.

He froze. Abby! She had been playing an elaborate joke on him. He smiled and relaxed, waiting for her "tee hee" giggle. It would all be okay.

Then a musty aroma reached his nostrils. He heard a small, strange, warble of a voice say the words that had been on the nightmare creature's lips as they fell together into the ocean. "Uh-oh," the voice chirruped. "Uh oh."

Chapter Six

The biggest, brownest, baldest man Abby had ever seen hung upside down from the top of a low natural arch in the middle of the rocky cavern. As she approached, she saw his eyes flutter open and a sly smile curve downward. The immense man wore nothing but a pair of cream-colored canvas painters' pants. A small gold tambourine earring dangled from his left earlobe.

"Little princess," the soft, low voice rumbled musically from the inverted giant. "*Comment allez vous?* Just five more crunches. I'll be wid you in a shake." At that he drew his muscular upper body toward his gravity-booted feet and paused with his body in an L position.

She heard him exhale smoothly and watched him lower himself until his head hung at the level of her knees. In a moment, with another slow intake of air, he pulled himself back to the L.

His pleasant voice and deferential manner made her relax. Then she stiffened again, thinking he might be acting, trying to trick her into dropping her defenses.

Warily, she peered around. She stood in a large chamber, with a great distance to the rock ceiling above and dozens of entrances, including the one through which she and her captors had come. The room was bathed in mellow amber light, emitted by the same kind of wispy, luminescent pin-points she'd noticed in her room. A pleasant, sweet, almost fruit-like fragrance drifted through the room, cutting the faintly moldy smell that permeated all of the chambers she'd been in. Incense? Air freshener? Down here?

"Five-Fwoo." The man exhaled slowly, lowering himself for the final time. The mellifluous voice rumbled at her again, making a request. "Time to descend to earth orbit. If I was you, I'd be motoring backways a little, ma petite."

Abby checked over her shoulder to avoid bumping into the strange, jive-talking grungoid and his two sunglassed sidekicks, then scuttled back a few yards. They shuffled along with her, never more than a yard away.

"*Merci.*" The strange man again rewarded her with his upside down grin and flexed his shoulders and neck. His accent reminded her of a travel show about Haiti she'd watched a few days ago. It had that mix of French and English, but it had something else, too, some of the same jive the gross little grungoid spoke. And, even though it was upside down, she knew she recognized his face. She just couldn't pin down where she'd seen it.

As she watched, the man jack-knifed himself up so his head was at his ankles. In one almost-too-fast-to-follow motion, he used his teeth to yank open the Velcro fasteners on the gravity boots, bent his legs and did a backward tucked somersault and a half. He landed with a soft slapping of bare feet on the rock floor in front of her.

It was only then that she noticed he had no hands and no forearms. Both his arms ended in rounded stumps approximately halfway between shoulder and elbow. She stood gaping at him, too stunned to speak.

"The Grand Imperial Pettifog of Humbug Mountain at your service, Mademoiselle Keene. I hope we shall be friends." He displayed an ear-to-ear grin and bowed deeply from the waist.

Any fear Abby felt dissolved in an explosion of anger.

"Friends? You order these demented little Rasta baboons or whatever they are to snatch me out of my sleeping bag and kidnap me. You hold me against my will in some dark, smelly cave and feed me dried fish and some kind of gakky squash and you want to be friends? Get a life."

The man's grin stayed firmly in place, but his eyes narrowed.

The grungoid who'd spoken to her laughed. "She got a definite point there, Lix. I feel her pain, man. Can you dig it?"

Lix? Abby felt another faraway twinge of recognition, but she couldn't enlarge it, couldn't bring it into focus.

"A point she does have, Chillout. Deny I can't, no. Gunnysack the best laid plans go again." The huge man motioned at the grungoids and bowed to Abby again.

"They mean you no harm. But when you scream, they freak out, you know? They went up to that ledge for a little confabulation and got doinked by the fuzzy, frapulations of fate. Couldn't be helped."

Before Abby could decipher his words, the man motioned for her to follow him with a jerk of his head and strode to a small cove in the large chamber. Smoothly, he lowered himself into a lotus position on one of three large, fringed pillows and waved Abby toward another.

She approached it hesitantly. "How do you know my name? I've never met you."

"Ah, but we've had the pleasure, little chickie," chortled the creature, the Pettifog—is that what he'd called himself?—had referred to as Chillout. "We've grokked you the most." "Grokked me?" Abby sputtered and backed away, clenching her hands into tight fists. "If you touch me, I'll scream. I'll—"

"Calm yourself, little princess. No one will hurt you," the brown behemoth insisted. He made a disapproving face in the direction of the grungoid. "Big goof, no? I read *Stranger in a Strange Land* to him. He spit out whole everyting he hear. What he mean is, he like you. Please, sit you down."

Abby thought about it for a moment. The man's calm, matter-of-fact tone calmed her. Plus, she reasoned, if they'd mean to do anything to her, it would have happened a long time ago, right after they took her away from Noah. She felt tears scorch the corners of her eyes.

"Noah." She squeezed her eyes shut against the pain, saw him tumbling toward the ocean.

"Your brother survives his plunge into the sea, Abby. The Darksuckers, they have the message sent."

Abby didn't realize she'd spoken her brother's name aloud. And who were the Darksuckers? "Noah's okay?"

"He grooves on, chickie," the grungoid spoke. "He's digging the hermit the most."

The hermit? Abby felt dizzy. Images and thoughts swerved and dove around her head like bees. Noah and the hermit? Darksuckers? Grand Imperial what? This must be what Alice felt like when she fell down the rabbit hole. Abby felt like screaming at the top of her lungs: "Where am I? What's happening to me?"

"I know, I know, Abby. It seem like one big borgle right now. But it all gonna be revealed in due time. Trust, ma cherie." The musical bass voice reassured her again.

She lifted her eyes to see the armless man gesturing again for her to sit on the soft cushion beside him. She sank to her knees, then tried an awkward imitation of his lotus posture.

"Most excellent." He favored her with a warm smile.

Sitting so close to him, she noticed that his head was not entirely bald. A short fringe of curly dark hair created a sort of horseshoe effect, with the open end toward his broad, handsome face. He also sported a frazzly clump of hair just under his lower lip and another under his chin.

"Can I offer you some refreshment? Dr. Pepper, Evian water, cranapple juice? Ocean Spray, I believe. Oh yes, and we have espresso, of course. But a little young you probably are for that habit. Non?"

"Uh . . ." Abby tried to think of a good reason not to accept his offer and couldn't come up with one.

Espresso? He had an espresso machine down here? For a moment, suspicion crept into her thoughts. Maybe she shouldn't touch anything he offered. But he hadn't poisoned the food or anything. And she was thirsty. Very thirsty. Besides, why risk making him angry? "Uh, yeah, I guess juice would be nice."

"Chillout, could you could?" The man turned his head a few inches toward the grungoid. Without a word, the beast shuffled off, touched a spot on the wall and ducked through the opening that appeared.

Abby sat wordlessly, sizing up the gigantic armless acrobat across from her, trying to analyze her situation.

That was the first rule of chess; think about what you're seeing. Try to understand the goals of the opponent. Try to figure out what he might do, and how you'd respond—the "what ifs." The more "what ifs" you could visualize, the better player you became. Her coach, Mr. Prentiss, told her that Bobby Fischer, at his prime, saw the board sixty or seventy moves ahead. At this moment, Abby didn't understand the game or the board. Her opponent was still a shadow; a shadow with a familiar face and friendly manner, but a shadow nonetheless. She decided she'd attempt a move and see what happened.

"My brother's not with any old hermit. He's probably gone to get the police. If you don't let me go, you're going to be very sorry."

The Grand Imperial whatever pursed his lips as if considering the possibility. She wished she could remember where she'd seen him before. Slowly but effortlessly, he bent one flexible leg upward and scratched his chin with his big toe. How did he do that? It hurt her just thinking about it. "Well? Are you going to let me go, or what?"

This provoked a deep-throated chuckle. The man scratched his chin again. "Or what is the correct answer,

Abby. Or what? Your jail is not the room you slept in. And your jailer, I am not." His voice changed, became deep and mournful. "Fate is your jailer. As it is mine. The choice is not ours. We dance to the music of the spheres until the solstice. We listen to the heartbeat of the mountain. And then, at that moment," he paused and gazed up at the ceiling, "poon shazam, all will be decided."

The gravity of his voice and words sent a creeping chill through her chest. The feeling of apprehension she'd felt watching Noah dance with Old Hannah, and the premonition that accompanied her discovery of the mysterious orb on the beach, returned.

He seemed to read her mind. "You hold the Chameleon Stone, Abby. Its magic, it is a tool to help you play your part. Noah must also follow his path, play his part. His journey begins with the hermit, little princess. He must meet his fears head-on, conquer them, and join us at the Skin. When he arrives with the Methuselah, we will kickstart the mountain's heart, ne c'est pas? He and I and you, if we are ready, if we are worthy, we will send the evil back for a long sleep. If not, nothing more will matter."

Nothing more will matter? What did that mean? What was the evil and how would they send it back to sleep? What fears did Noah have to conquer? If the Chameleon Stone was the one she found in the surf, where would Noah find the Methuselah? As the questions flew around in her mind, her frustration and fear grew. And most importantly, why her, why Noah? They were just average kids.

Before she could ask, Chillout returned with a tray containing two glasses filled with a ruby red liquid. Both drinks contained straws with accordion joints and brightly colored miniature paper umbrellas. Leaning down, he set a small paper napkin on a level spot beside Abby and carefully placed her juice on it. Moving to the right side of the Pettifog, he duplicated his actions. Then, bowing at the waist, he spoke in an affected, almost effeminate voice. "I'm Anton and I'm like, your waiter for the evening. The fresh fish special is braised bass and the soup is cream of rock worm. I'll be back in a moment with your breadsticks." At that, he slammed his heels together and pranced out of the chamber.

Forgetting her anxious questions, Abby rolled her eyes back in her head and tried to stifle a giggle.

The big brown man smiled and sipped his drink. "A smartass, yes? I'm almost sorry I taught him people talk. But I am desperate for conversation down here after so many years, you know. So . . ." He shrugged and bent his neck to sip his drink.

"Is he the only one?"

"Who can talk? Yes. The others understand some of what they hear, but are not interested. Except for Chillout, they are all a little, how-you-say . . . dense? Not the sharpest pencils in the packet?"

"What are they? What are they called?"

The Pettifog raised his eyebrows an inch and pronounced a word that sounded to Abby like someone gargling a razor blade.

"I call them grungoids," she blurted.

"Grungoids? Hmmm. Like it, I do, princess. Easier to say." He repeated the gargle. "Grungoids we call dem."

Abby noticed that as he spoke, the toes on both his feet wiggled. It reminded her of her brother. He had the same habit, only with him, it was his fingers. Her fears returned in a rush, like a sneaker wave. "Where is my brother?"

His eyes wandered to a spot above her head.

"Somewhere. Not far, but a zillion miles away."

"But that doesn't make—"

"I got no more answer right now, cher. It all have to play out, you know?"

That gambit hadn't worked. She took a sip of her juice. It smelled pungent and fruity and tasted sweet and tangy. She decided to shift tactics. "Is your name really Pettifog? How did you get into the mountain?"

"Ahhhh." The man took a deep draw on his own drink and regarded her. "Pettifog is only a title. It sounds a little silly, I know, but necessary it is, yes?" He shrugged his shoulders. Here, they are very fond of their titles, and the roles people are expected to play, non? Pettifog is the role I play, the cog I have become in the machinery of the mountain. Irony was always my bag, you know? But my mama and papa given name is Delacroix. Felix Delacroix. Lix for short."

The name jangled within her tangled mind, but she couldn't draw out what it meant. She felt slow and stupid, not a worthy opponent. She decided to try a memory trick she'd used successfully before—rapidly change the subject, shift her brain into another gear. "Why do you wiggle your toes all the time?"

"Aha!" Delacroix was gleeful. "She cuts to the chase."

"I do?" Abby was mystified.

"Oui. Don't you recognize me, Abby?"

"No. Uh, well, maybe. Yes, definitely yes. But I can't figure out from where."

"Chillout," Delacroix summoned the grungoid, who appeared as suddenly as he'd disappeared. Delacroix made a quick gesture with his head to draw the little creature closer to him. They huddled in a rapid and whispered conversation.

"I'm hip, Lix," chortled the grungoid as it scampered out of the chamber. "I'm picking up what you're layin' down, daddy-o."

Delacroix clucked his tongue in mock disapproval at the departing Chillout. It was clear they had great affection for each other, Abby recognized. But who were they, and how did they get inside the mountain? Where did the fruit juice come from and—

Suddenly she heard the sound of a needle dropping onto a phonograph record. A hissing sound seemed to come from all around her. She swiveled her head. Where were the speakers? She saw nothing but solid rock. Not too solid, she reminded herself. After all, the grungoid had passed through a door in it.

Delacroix smiled. "The needle searches for its groove, yes?"

Abby nodded, noticing that his toes had stopped moving for the first time since he sat down. The hissing sound ended with a pop and suddenly the chamber was filled with jazz. Piano notes wandered wildly up and down the keyboard. A soulful sax sang and sputtered and soared. A bass guitar explored the bottom of the improvisation.

"Cool, huh? Delacoix smiled. "The music it is all on compact disc, too, but I am a devotee of the black wax. Believe the notes sound purer, more alive on the vinyl."

He cocked his head. "Here come my big moment, *cher*.

The others, they provide the rain, I bring in the thunder and lightning."

Abby heard the thud, thud, thud of a bass drum and then the click and tat-a-tat-tat of a snare. She recognized the style instantly, amazingly delicate and intricate, yet impossible to ignore with its penetrating clarity. The drumming provided a framework for the rest of the piece and stood on its own. Point and counterpoint, the drummer created rhythmic stories, journeys with beginnings, middles and heroic endings. A shock of recognition forced Abby to acknowledge exactly who sat beside her on the tufted pillow in the bowels of this mysterious cavern. She'd heard his music just days before in the garage where Noah had played along to a record.

Lix Delacroix was Noah's hero. Noah called him the greatest drummer who ever lived. But this man couldn't be Felix Delacroix. He and his fiancée, a promising young actress, had died during a violent storm when their small plane crashed into the top of Humbug Mountain, years before Abby was born.

Searchers never found any trace of them. They speculated the two had been thrown from the cockpit and their remains had been eaten and scattered by scavengers.

The man on the cushion smiled serenely. Was he lying to her? Was he someone else? Or had Felix Delacroix survived the crash? If he had, why hadn't he let anyone know? Why was he living here, inside the mountain?

And what had become of his fiancée?

Chapter Seven

Noah couldn't force himself to turn around. He couldn't breathe, couldn't think. The gray thing he'd pulled off the cliff, the thing that went "uh oh," had followed him to wreak vengeance. Strangely, that realization made Noah somehow calm and ready. A strong but controllable energy coursed through his veins and he conjured up a mental picture of the animal he was about to engage in mortal combat—short, muscular with dangerous-looking teeth.

Swiveling around quickly, he grasped at the creature, but found himself holding only air. Where was it? Noah snapped his head back around, expecting an attack. Instead, he heard an alarmed cht-cht-cht sound and spotted the dreadlock-haired gray monkey thing clinging to a ledge over the middle doorway. Noah got the impression the animal was every bit as frightened of him as he was of it.

His mind raced as he tried to think of what to do. He could run through one of the three openings and try to get away from the thing. Monkey? Baboon? His mind seemed to lock up, spin around that question. What was this creature? What should he call it? The only thing he could think of was the sound that had signaled the creature's return. "Uh-oh."

He scolded himself. That didn't make any sense. It was like calling the creature "oops." But, unable to come up with another label, he went with it. He was trapped by an Uh-oh. Noah shook his head, trying to clear his brain, trying to think what to do. He recognized that if he bolted for a tunnel, the Uh-oh could easily pounce on him. The gray tangle-haired thing quivered on the narrow ledge over the middle opening, but kept its eyes glued to Noah.

Going back the way he came was out of the question, Noah decided, glancing behind him. That tunnel led back to that crazy old codger's lair and his wild talk about quests and stones and skins and—

The creature sprang from the overhang and landed with a plop on the rocky surface a foot or two in front of Noah.

"Yikes!" Involuntarily, Noah took a step back. Then adrenaline pumped through him again. He crouched, preparing to tackle the creature, wrestle it to the ground. He bent his knees, ready to spring.

The gray thing shook its curls, fluffed them out around its head and struck a familiar pose. It grinned at Noah, walked away from him and began to sashay back. Noah stood open-mouthed. The thing had captured the essence of his sister—her posture, the way she walked, even the crinkly smile was dead-on. As Uh-oh drew near, it stopped, wrinkled its nose a la Abby and emitted her distinctive giggle. "Tee hee."

"That's Abby's laugh." Noah sprang toward the creature. "Where is she?"

The creature dodged away and scurried back to the ledge. Hunkering there, it put one hand, palm down over its eyes and swung its head back and forth, all the while pointing to the cavern floor below.

"I don't have time for charades! Where's Abby?"

Before Noah cold react, the creature sprang to the floor, and once again mimed a perfect recreation of Abby. Except this time, the Uh-oh acted out Abby in the mode she'd been in just before they'd gone to sleep on the ledge.

The creature mimicked her responding to an imaginary Noah, combative, argumentative, and ultimately frustrated. "That's Abby in the cave, before we went to sl— You were spying on us!!!" The animal recoiled a step, put a hand over the O of surprise it had made with its lips, then shrugged its shoulders in resignation. "Of course," it seemed to be saying.

"Why? Where did you take Abby?" Noah clenched his hands into fists. "Tell me or I'll . . . I'll . . . stomp you."

The creature closed one eye and trained the other on Noah. Clasping its very human-like hands behind its back, it stalked back and forth in the small chamber, stopping every now and then to extend a forefinger and scratch a spot in the middle of the dreadlocks. It seemed to be thinking. Finally, it stopped mid-stride and turned to do the single-eyeball gaze at Noah. A beaming smile appeared on its face and it held a finger in the air in front of it as if to signal, "I've got it."

"Well? Tell me! Where's Abby? Why did those other creatures take her?"

Both of the animal's eyes opened wide, and then, very slowly, very deliberately, it shrugged. It stood in front of Noah with an apologetic frown on its face.

"You don't know why you were taking her? Or you don't know where she is?"

Another shrug, followed by a wrinkle of the creature's brow as Uh-oh signaled upward with an extended finger.

"Up? They took her up. Up, where?"

Uh-oh pantomimed walking up stairs, feigning exhaustion as it reached the top step. When it got there, it used its hands to create the sense of a large chamber, an expansive room.

"So she's somewhere else in the mountain? Further up?"

Uh-oh smiled sadly and nodded.

Noah cast an eye at the openings in the rock wall. Going up would also get him closer to the outside. "Do you know how to get there? To where Abby is?"

The creature shrugged and became thoughtful again, pacing the floor of the rocky chamber for several minutes, hands clasped behind its back, a determined look on its baboonish face.

Noah couldn't take it any longer. He pointed at the tunnels opening off the chamber. "Well? Which way do we go?"

Uh-oh shrugged again and shook a clump of hairy ringlets out of its eyes, then cast a glommy expression toward Noah and shook its head back and forth. "No dice," it warbled.

"What do you mean, No? Hey, I thought all you knew how to say was Uh-oh."

"Uh-oh," the creature echoed back. "Can you talk, or do you just mimic?"

Uh-oh shrugged.

"Do you understand everything I say?"

Uh-oh shrugged again.

Noah considered for a moment. "Do you understand this: I'm going to get a rock and beat your head in if you don't run for your life."

Uh-oh shrugged a third time and then went to sit on an outcropping of rock a few feet away.

Either it didn't understand me, or it doesn't think I would hurt it, Noah decided. He studied the creature as it huddled on the rock, picking at its knees with a long finger. It? Was it an it? Or was it male? Or a female?

Male, Noah decided. The idea of being down here in the dark with a female thing that wasn't his sister made him a little nervous. Stupid, he told himself. But still, that's how he felt.

Thinking about Abby made him miss her even more. Missing Abby made him miss home, and that made him realize his stomach was growling. When had he eaten last? He'd lost all sense of time. He peeled his pack from his back and dug through his extra clothes and other supplies. His hand closed over the foil-wrapped leftover meatloaf he'd stowed. Pulling it out, he dove in again and found the orange. All of his food. After that, starvation city. Unless he found his way out. Abby, of course, had brought the equivalent of a week's food. She was always thinking, always a step ahead of him. He fought back a sob. How could he ever find her? He was lost in this maze of a mountain with a strange little creature and a demented old hermit who wanted him to go on some crazy quest or something.

The creature cast longing eyes at the hunk of hamburger wrapped in tinfoil, but made no move toward it. Instead, he stood and walked to the three openings in the wall, poking his head into each one in turn and shrugging. After a while, he seemed to give up and returned to sit on the rock.

Noah held the meatloaf to his nose, trying to decide if the cold meat and onion aroma was tainted, a sign the stuff had turned south. He didn't know how long he'd been unconscious in the hermit's cave. It could have been days. It was cool down here, but food would still turn bad and the meatloaf could make him sick. He couldn't afford that. He had to find Abby. He started to set the meatloaf aside, but hunger overruled caution and he took a little bite. If seemed to taste okay. Noah wolfed down half of it, then picked up the orange.

Uh-oh sat morosely, watching him intently, like a dog hovering under a dinner table, but making no move toward him or the food. A tear appeared in each of the creature's eyes.

"I must be nuts," Noah mumbled. Grasping the corners of the foil, he extended it toward the creature.

"Take it."

Cautiously, the creature scuttled across the floor and seized the offering. Carrying it back across the chamber, he squatted and began pulling morsels from the foil with two fingers and dropping them into his mouth.

Meanwhile, Noah peeled the orange. The pungent aroma filled his senses, and for a moment he forgot the wet, metallic smell of the interior of the mountain. He sectioned the fruit off and ate a segment, chewing slowly and licking his fingers afterward. When half the orange remained, he offered it to Uh-oh. The creature took it and ate it in a perfect imitation of Noah, carefully chewing each segment, then stopping to lick its fingers. Noah smiled and the creature smiled back.

Noah pointed at him. "From now on, your name is Uh-oh."

"Uh-oh," the creature echoed, pointing at itself.

"That's right. You're Uh-oh." Noah pointed at himself. "And I'm Noah."

"Noo-ahh," the creature murmured. "Noo-ahh. Nooahhhhhh."

"Good. Now we have to figure out how to find Abby."

He stood and walked to the first of the tunnels. "Should we go this way?"

Uh-oh shook his head.

Noah strode to the next tunnel. "This way?"

Uh-oh shrugged.

Noah marched to the final tunnel. "Then it's this way, right?"

Uh-oh flipped out his hands, palms up in a "search me" expression.

Noah felt tears of frustration burn his eyes. He'd have to try each tunnel in turn to see which one led upward. But what if he ran into cross-tunnels along the way? He returned to his pack and threw himself down beside it. He should have brought a compass. Maybe he had some string. That would help. He dug through his pack again. No string. Nothing but his clothes, money, the picture of his mother and his drumsticks. He pulled them out and threw them against the wall. What good were they?

Uh-oh scuttled to retrieve the sticks and return them.

Noah tossed them away again. Once again, Uh-oh ran after them.

"This isn't a game!" Noah shouted at the creature. "I don't want them. We can't eat them. They won't even make a decent fire to keep us warm. They're worthless. See." He gripped one in each hand.

Uh-oh cowered and backed a step away.

"It's okay," Noah lowered his voice. "I'm not going to hit you. I'm just going to show you. These are drumsticks. All you can do with them is this." He began to click the sticks against the surrounding rock, pounding out a rhythm of fear and frustration.

"This is bad, Noah. This is really bad." He heard himself say. "No way out. No way out," he mumbled, keeping time with the sticks.

Uh-oh bobbed his head up and down in agreement, moving his lips as if trying to mimic the sounds Noah made.

Exhausted, discouraged and tired of searching for answers where there were none, Noah let his mind go blank. As he did, he began to hear rhythms that weren't his own. The thudda thoomp, thudda thoomp originating deep at the core of the mountain began to reverberate through him as it had when he clung to the cliff. He drummed along with it, and slowly, even over the sound of his sticks, he became aware of other sounds: water dripping onto rock, Uh-oh's soft breathing, his own heartbeat. The sounds became counter-rhythms and punctuations flowing through him. Automatically, he reached out with the sticks and began tapping on the wall, his pack, his own body, trying to recreate the sounds he could hear in his head.

Disconnected from the world, eyes tightly clenched, hands flying, his spirit soared with the thunder of the tympanic creation rolling around him. As his fervor grew, and the speed and frenzy of his playing accelerated, he heard Uh-oh gasp. Noah opened his eyes to see that the light in the chamber had become liquid, rolling and flashing with his tempo changes, glowing in changing shades of red, blue and green as he drummed toward his crescendo. "Cool," he mumbled. He drummed harder, faster, leaping to his feet and clicking the sticks off the ceiling, darting back and forth between the walls.

The beat of the mountain speeded up. Noah kept pace. The sounds ratcheted up to a crescendo and he struck the sticks a final time against the floor, then sank back beside his pack. When the echo from his final blow finally died away, Uh-oh leaped to his feet and stood before him, a look of undisguised admiration in his eyes. He drew his hands apart and brought them together again with a soft pat. He repeated the gesture twice, a one-creature audience for Noah's spontaneous performance.

Grinning in spite of himself, Noah stood and bowed, then raised his arms, waving the sticks triumphantly in the glowing air. He blinked. The light on the ceiling was brighter than he'd ever seen it. It was also lime green.

And, unless he was hallucinating, the pattern of the lights formed an arrow pointing toward the left-hand opening.

Noah seized his pack and started for the tunnel, then stopped, wondering if this was a trick. Did somebody, someplace, somehow, want him to go down the wrong tunnel? He tried to think, tried to clear his head. What would Abby do? Would she go? Would she wait for more information? Or would she see something here that he didn't? She'd been right, he admitted to himself; she *was* the brains of this operation.

Finally, he made a decision. This was a trick. He wasn't going to let anybody manipulate him. "I'm going," he told Uh-oh. The creature looked at the lights and then at Noah, but didn't move.

"All right, I'll go alone." Throwing his pack over his shoulders, he took a deep breath and, with much more confidence than he felt, entered the center tunnel without looking behind him. As he advanced, the light from the small cavern faded. He fought the urge to go back and take the left hand tunnel. Stubbornly, he stumbled forward in the near-darkness.

He counted steps as his mind raced, going over the details of everything that had happened. A hundred steps, he left his house, two hundred, he met Old Hannah, three hundred, the creatures captured Abby, four hundred, the crazy hermit and his wild talk, the scrubbage stew, his long flight into the winding tunnel.

"Darn." He'd lost count, lost track of how far he'd gone. What if he had to find his way back? He looked behind him down the dim and empty tunnel, feeling exhaustion bowing his shoulders. "Five hundred and fifty," he guessed and made himself go on, step after slowing step, counting carefully.

He'd reached a thousand and forty seven when he saw a glimmer of light. He increased his pace, desperate to emerge from the heavy gloom of the tunnel, to have gotten somewhere. "Eleven hundred," he muttered. Then he stopped, gagging. A stench like rotting eggs, decaying meat and old slime filled his nose.

He bent over, holding his stomach, and heard the low, bloodthirsty, back-of-the throat growl of an animal ready to pounce on its prey. Noah froze, remembering the cougar he'd seen at the zoo in Portland. This sounded bigger, nastier, scarier, hungrier.

Slowly, he slid one foot behind him, preparing to pivot and run. His heel came down, not on rock, but on something soft.

"Uh-oh."

The creature had followed him unseen. They were both prey for whatever lurked in the tunnel ahead.

The hungry growl filled the air around them. Closer now.

Uh-oh gasped and Noah heard an uncanny reproduction of his own cracking teenage voice. "Bad, this is really bad, Noah. No way out. No way out."

Chapter Eight

"Ooobaladoo, scoobaladoobaladoo fa-foom!"

Chillout, Delacroix's grungoid sidekick, flailed away at imaginary drums, while contributing his own vocal punctuation to the frenzied percussion climax thundering through the hidden speakers. Abby listened to the last notes ping-pong off the stone walls of the massive cavern, a crazy quilt of sound that seemed to take forever to dissipate. She glanced at Delacroix, who sat Buddha-like, staring into space through hooded eyes, his lips sagging in a melancholy frown.

Peering over her shoulder, she wondered if she should take the opportunity to run for it. The grungoid didn't seem to be paying any attention to her. She drank the last of her juice and searched her mind for the sequence of twists and turns they'd taken when she'd been carried into the mountains. She could probably backtrack successfully. But which of the many openings in the rock wall of this cavern had they emerged from when they'd left her room? Could she find her way there for her backpack with her food and extra clothing? And what were the chances she could outrun Chillout or any of his other little grody friends? They were stronger than they looked, and they knew the cavern and tunnels well.

Besides, she thought, what was it Delacroix had said, just a few moments ago? About fate being her jailer, not him? What did he mean by that? The analytical part of her brain overrode her fear. She'd stay, for now, she decided. She'd gather information, stockpile food and try to find out where Noah might be.

"Time for answers to some of your questions, ma cherie."

Delacroix's basso rumble startled her and she made an involuntary hiccup. She felt like he was inside her mind, reading her thoughts like a newspaper. Okay, well, maybe he was. Maybe he had that power. She'd make some headlines for him to peruse. She concentrated on putting aside her questions about Delacroix and thought instead on more important ones, forming them into distinct words and displaying them on her brain:

"Where's my brother? How can I find him? How do the mysterious lights sense when I'm awake or asleep and how do they read my moods?

Another hiccup escaped from her diaphragm, loudly echoing in the airy chamber. Ohmigod, she thought, embarrassed by her physical failing. What a terrible time for this to happen.

"You've swallowed some air, non?" Delacroix's voice took on a tone of sympathy. "Try holding your breath for a count of ten," he instructed.

"I know what to do," Abby sniped. But she obeyed, gulping and taking in a deep breath. She felt like a two-year old.

She'd counted to three in her mind when the next spasm caused her to exhale loudly and hiccup at the same time. "Urkkip." The sound left her lips. "Gleep," it bounced back to her ears on the return trip. She felt herself blushing. A person who was cool and in control did not hiccup like a baby. She covered her mouth with both hands, muffling the next spasm.

"Do not be embarrassed, Abby. We will fix it for you. Chillout, some moss-water, s'il vous plait."

Abby didn't know if she wanted to drink anything called moss-water, but decided she'd wait until she saw and smelled it to turn it down. Besides if it, (urkkipgleep) could end these (urkkip-gleep) hiccups, she'd try (urkkip-gleep) anything.

Delacroix studied her, a small smile tugging at the corners of his mouth. Finally, just when she was about to scream at him to stop staring, he spoke. "Another cure is to take your mind off the muscles and think of other things. Perhaps you'd like to hear how you came to be here? And why Noah, your brother, is destined for mortal combat with the forces of Spid, the evil one?"

"Spid? Urkkip-gleep! Mortal combat?" Noah wasn't a fighter. He'd always run from bullies when they were little. He didn't know anything about guns or spears or other weapons and he certainly didn't have any with him.

All he had was his drumsticks and maybe a little jackknife. She felt another spasm and tried to stifle it, but a loud gasp escaped from her throat and reverberated even more loudly from the recesses of the room. "Oh, ex-(urkkip-gleep)-cuse me," she apologized.

"Not to worry, ma petite. It happens to all of us. I once heard of a man who got the hiccups at about the age you are now and had them for forty-seven years."

"Thanks a (urkkip-gleep) lot." Abby snapped. "Uh, (urkkip-gleep) sorry." She didn't want to hear about the hiccup guy, but was afraid to be rude, afraid that Delacroix wouldn't tell her about Noah. "Did he ever get rid of them?"

"Yes, eventually he did. Do you know how?"

She cringed inwardly at the prospect of Chillout's return with the requested beverage. She grimaced. "Moss (urkkip-gleep) water?"

"No," Delacroix smiled, "although I do think that will be of help to you. This man, after years of standing on his head, holding his breath, eating sugar, putting paper bags over his head and so on, had finally given up. He determined to die, to pass on to another life where he would not have the hiccups."

She felt herself drawn into the story despite her preoccupation with her own dilemma. "So what (urkkipgleep) happened?"

"This man, though, he did not want to die, he decided to embrace his malady. He coveted every 'hic and every

77

'up because it meant he was still breathing, he still had life. No longer did he try to cover the sound in company.

He refused to be embarrassed by the air bubbles and muscle spasms that lived within him, and instead allowed himself to be as one with them. Instead of being a social outcast, he forced himself to seek out people, to carry on conversations, hiccups and all. He stopped thinking of the gulps and hics as invaders into his body and instead considered them part of what made him a unique creature, as punctuation for his thoughts, for his life."

"And then (urkkip-gleep) what? Did he wake up one morning and they were gone?"

"*Non*. He had become quite content with his lot, no longer worried about his hiccups and totally at peace. And then one day, when he was looking the other way, his wife of thirty-five years snuck up behind him, stuck her fingers in his ribs and yelled 'Boooo' at the top of her lungs. Voila, no more hiccups." Delacroix chuckled.

Abby sighed. "That's probably the (urkkip-gleep) stupidest story I've ever heard. Is there a (urkkip-gleep) moral or something?"

"Beverage boy here with your elixir, little chickie. Scarf this down and those hiccups are gonesky." The growl-rasp of Chillout's voice announced the arrival of the promised glass of moss-water. He held a small glass out to her on an oval tray inlaid with what looked like abalone shell and ivory. The concoction was an ugly brackish green with bits of slimy, moss-like stuff floating on the top. It smelled like a wet cow pasture. Abby felt her stomach lurch in apprehension. She looked desperately back and forth between the little grungoid and an expectant Delacroix.

"Surely, you don't expect me to drink that glop?" She protested. "No way. I wouldn't drink that stuff if you paid me all the—" She noticed Delacroix's lips twist into a grin and heard Chillout chuckle. Her hiccups had vanished.

"The moral of the story, ma petite, is that sometimes a little fear is good for what ails you. And also, sometimes you can shrink your problems when you quit worrying about having them."

"I'll drink to that, Lix." Abby watched open-mouthed as Chillout put the glass to his lips and poured the mosswater down his throat. "Ahhh." He smacked his lips.

"Smooth, real smooth." With that, he turned on his heel and disappeared through another spot on what had appeared to be solid rock. Abby squinted into the small tunnel before the rock sealed itself again. How many of these places were there; places where the rock would open? Were they shortcuts?

Was there a map anywhere? She remembered her vow to stockpile food for her escape. She wouldn't have to do that if she could find the source of the food. A kitchen, or storage room. She could stock up in a few minutes.

"Where does all this stuff come from?" She gestured at the glasses they'd been drinking from and toward the hidden stereo speakers. "Does somebody go outside the mountain and bring it back?"

"Yes. And no, not exactly." Delacroix's toes twitched. "We do have a—how shall I say—intermediary to the outside world. Someone who can come and go at will. But . . ." Delacroix stopped and seemed to search for his next words. "This person only provides occasional treasures. Such as the Twinkie. You enjoyed it, non?

"Uh, yeah. Sure. But where does the rest of it come from?"

He pondered that, scratching his chin with a big toe.

"This, it would be better to show you. We will take a short journey, you and I and the—" He began to pronounce the gargle-name of Chillout, then coughed and corrected himself. "—the grungoid. Chillout. We will take you to the place where lost dreams live."

"Lost dreams?" It reminded her of Peter Pan and the lost boys, of the movies about Shangri-la and Brigadoon she'd watched with her mother. She felt suddenly very small and alone, her confidence ebbing away.

"Oui. And many other lost things, too."

"Noah's lost. Will he be there?" She heard the quiver in her voice and blinked back a fresh set of tears. "I'm lost, too. When can we go home?"

"In a few short days, as you call them. Although, in the mountain, time is told in rhythms instead of hours and days." Delacroix powered himself to his feet. "Come, ma petite. Do not waste your time on tears. We will go to the place of lost dreams. And on the way, perhaps you will learn a lesson. Knowledge that will help you aid your brother with his final challenge. With your help . . ." Delacroix paused, "with our help, Noah will be armed with all he needs to defeat Spid."

"What kind of a lesson?" Abby didn't move.

Questions swarmed from her lips. "What kind of a challenge? Who's Spid? What can Noah and I do? If you can go outside the mountain, why don't you get some real help? Get the sheriff. Get the army. We're just kids.

What can we do?"

"Tut. We are all as children, little one. But you have been chosen. Noah, too. He must do what I cannot. What no one else can. Now come."

"No." Abby clutched the cushion. This all had to be some kind of twisted joke. A nightmare. It couldn't be real. No way. "I won't go. I won't do it. I want to go home!"

The gigantic, brown, stub-armed man regarded her sadly. "Abby, if we do not defeat Spid, there will be no home. Not for you. Not for any of us. Never again."

Chapter Nine

The cheer was supposed to go, "two, four, six, eight, who do we appreciate? Spid! Spid! Spid!" But since most of the officers in Spid's demon army couldn't make any sounds outside of grunts, whistles and growls, the echoing cacophony sounded more like feeding time at the zoo than an organized cheer. They hadn't even mastered the choreography, Spid noted, simple as it was.

Still, he contemplated, it's the thought that counts. He raised long and twisted arms, prying the green-nailed fingers into a victory salute. They like me, he thought. They really like me. On the other hand, he considered, perhaps they only fear me. Close enough, he decided. When he took over the world of Above Skin, everyone would like him. They'd have to. If they didn't, they'd die.

The important thing, Spid concluded, was that when the time came, his forces would obey his orders. He twitched his thick lips into a predatory smile. No matter how bloodthirsty and unmerciful those orders were.

Spid leaned back in the sculpted granite chair and looked out over the banquet tables. Trolls, ogres, demons, and other denizens of the land of Beneath partook of a traditional pre-apocalypse feast of roasted rock borer and fossilized fackus soup. A shiver of joy ran down his spine. A shiver of fear ran up it. As the Grand Exalted Garboon, he was the guest of honor at this particular banquet. However, if his troops failed in their effort, he could just as easily become the entrée at the next meal.

Rubbing the large wart growing from his cheek, he calmed himself. He had nothing to worry about. They couldn't lose. Not this time. His plan was perfect.

He took another bite of the braised stone-lizard on the table before him. Grimacing, he chewed the rubbery meat and reached for his flagon of deadly nightshade wine to wash the acrid taste out of his mouth. The red liquid wasn't much of an improvement, but it packed an alcoholic punch and cleared the palate. He set the wine goblet down, looked at the stone-lizard steak again, then pushed his platter aside. One of the first things I'll do when I take power, Spid thought, will be to get my own chef. Maybe Wolfgang Puck or one of those other white-hatted guys on the cooking channel. Spid wondered how Puck would make the gross, leathery lizard more palatable. Maybe infuse it with tangerine juice and slowroast it. Next to planning the grisly death of Delacroix and the residents of Above Skin, Spid's favorite pastime was watching cooking programs on the Shadow Stone.

Spid glanced at the smooth, black elongated crystal beside his place at the table. The Shadow Stone stood about two and half feet high, cast a cold glow, and never left Spid's side, as it had never left his father's before that. When Spid slept, which was seldom and uneasily, he lashed the stone to his chest and clutched a sword in his hand. All power Below Skin lay with the possessor of the stone.

He knew some of his predecessors, those who had held the stone and focused its power to marshal the forces of evil Below Skin, would frown upon him using it as a kind of satellite dish to tune in television shows. But he, Spid, was the Garboon now. The others who had held the stone were dead. Besides, even a leader of his importance, his magnitude, his girth, needed relaxation now and then.

Plus, he didn't need practice, he knew full well how to wield the Shadow Stone's dark power.

Spid tapped the stone with his ring. "Shadow!

Abraltos. Commenvarque. Find Noah Keene for me," he commanded.

The black pillar began to emit a high, whistling tone. Its frequency increased, soaring out of Spid's hearing range. He saw the gammits try to cover their multiple ears and was glad once again that auditory excess was a recessive trait. Although gammits were able to pick up sounds originating miles away, they couldn't screen out near-by noises. Gammit females often pleaded headaches and gammit males usually wore dazed looks and thick hats made of gravel badger skin. Spid's mother had had seven ears, his father two. His father's genes had prevailed and Spid himself had only two ears, each in what he thought of as the correct place, on either side of his face. They had long and dangling lobes that he'd pierced and studded with dark and gleaming gems and metals from the mines of Below Skin.

A young gammit shrieked in pain and Spid turned his eyes toward the Shadow Stone. Shards of light flashed within its ebony depths and a spinning irregular mass of murky jelly began a frenetic random journey within the boundaries of the stone. Spid bent closer, watching an image of the boy take shape.

Noah crouched in a dimly-lit tunnel, rigid with fear, anticipation, even dread. Behind him, cowering near the boy's leg, a gray, dreadlocked creature trembled and made cht-cht-cht noises in his throat. As Spid watched, they advanced slowly, in tandem toward the tunnel's mouth. The young gammit stopped howling and fell from its rock, gasping with relief. Good, Spid thought, the whine has ceased, the stone is locked in. Leaning close to it, he heard the growl of a creature—carnivorous sounding, if he wasn't mistaken—rumbling from somewhere ahead of the boy and his companion.

Beside him, the ogre who acted as his second-in-command hovered, as fascinated as Spid with the images within the black pillar. "Looks like he's got big trouble, Boss."

"Good. Maybe they'll both be eaten. What kind of predatory creatures live in that part of the mountain, Yurk?"

"Dunno for sure, boss." Yurk shifted from foot to foot, his curved nails scratching the stone floor. "Could be a burrowing throat weasel. Or maybe a razor-beaked Phlemus. We gotta watch out for those when we head topside, boss. They can make confetti outa yuh in nothin' flat."

"If the boy becomes a heap of shredded flesh, it certainly would eliminate any shred of doubt that we will prevail, Yurk." Spid smiled at his own versatility with the language and his dexterity with adjectives. "Shredded, shred, get it?"

Yurk scratched his snout. "Uh, yeah. That's a real knee-slapper, boss. I get it."

Spid doubted he had, but didn't pursue it. He'd promoted Yurk for his loyalty, not for his brainpower.

"Let us then root for the appearance of the Phlemus, shall we? And for its triumph."

"You got it, boss. A cheer for the Phlemus." Yurk, the ogre, snorted mightily through his large snout-like nose and turned to the assembled forces of darkness.

"Give me a P!" He roared.

"F'noorg." The beasts tried their best, but couldn't manage a P.

Paying no mind, Yurk continued. "Give me an, uh, an H!"

"Fnooorg." The H sounded just as the P had. Spid sighed and turned back to the Shadow Stone. With the boy about to become subterranean supper for some roaming beast, all that stood between him and victory was the girl, Abby. She was smaller and weaker than her brother, but handling her promised to be more difficult.

"Give me uh L!"

"Fnooorg."

Yes, Spid thought, he'd have to be much more careful with the young one. She was very smart, extremely logical, not apt to plunge into danger like her brother. He'd have to use that to his own advantage. As he watched Noah and the small, gray animal advance toward the growling creature before them, Spid smiled to himself.

Perhaps, if he played his cards right, the girl could be convinced to help him realize his dream. If not, she would have to die with the others.

"Give me uh E!"

"Fnoooorg."

Chapter Ten

As he crept fearfully down the tunnel, the gray creature trailing just behind, images and ideas careened inside Noah's mind. Flashes of Abby being carried off by Uh-oh's companions, his father shaking a finger, Old Hannah dancing, his mother making dinner, all collided and overlapped. "Don't give up, Noah." He could almost hear Mom's voice. Going back would be giving up on the choice he'd made, the tunnel he'd picked. It had continued upward. It had to be the right choice. His mind grew still and empty of all thoughts except two: Keep going, Find Abby.

"Do you know what's making that noise?" He whispered to Uh-oh.

The creature shrugged, and Noah saw his eyes dart back and forth between the widening tunnel ahead and the distant opening marking their starting point.

Maybe we *should* retreat, Noah thought. But the other tunnels could be even worse. And we'd lose time backtracking, hours, even days. And this might be the only way out. Maybe this thing sounds worse than it is, the echo could magnify its growl. Maybe, like a skunk, it's relatively small and depends on smell to force predators to give it a wide berth.

Urging himself to move forward, a step at a time, was the hardest thing he ever did. The stench of the beast grew, and its low sputtering growl escalated as he and Uh-oh inched toward the glow of the opening. Maybe, he thought, as he visualized something huge with flesh-ripping claws and fangs, this thing wouldn't be right where the tunnel emptied into the chamber. Maybe they could skirt around it, perhaps scale the rock wall and stay above it. Of course, he thought, that's assuming this thing can't climb. Too many unknowns, he thought. We're walking into a nightmare.

Cowering beside his left leg, Uh-oh moved with Noah, making faint, frightened sounding cht-cht-cht noises.

Several times, Noah caught him peering back down the tunnel longingly, as if deciding whether to retreat. Funny, Noah thought. He's going through the same thing I am. Fear. Indecision. I guess stuff like that is universal.

After what felt like hours, they emerged onto a ledge overlooking a deep depression inside an enormous, high-ceilinged chamber. The chamber was so vast that the opposite wall was lost in the gloom, but it appeared to Noah that the cavern, like the tunnel they'd just traveled, sloped upward. With Uh-oh all but glued to his leg, he stood unsteadily on the narrow outcropping, searching for the best way through the cavern. The growling had ceased. The smell was worse than ever.

To their left, the rocky ledge ended. Noah edged over and saw a sheer drop of several hundred feet onto the boulder-strewn chamber floor. And to the right? A narrow trail led down to a larger, flatter area. Halfway along that trail, some kind of stumpy animal slid silently back and forth.

"What's that?" Noah pointed down at the creature.

Uh-oh peered down the trail, scratched his head and then adopted his palms-up shrugging "beats me" posture.

Some help you are, Noah thought, scanning the cave for the creature responsible for the putrid smell and frightening growls. He saw nothing. Maybe the noise came from some kind of huge lizard. Maybe it had moved on. It couldn't possibly be the creature on the trail. It looked fairly small, slow and stupid. He could probably jump over it with a running start. Then he'd race to the other side of the cavern. Good plan. He took a dozen quick steps down the trail.

"Roawwwwwrrrr!"

Noah froze and stared at the lumpy creature ahead of him. Had the throaty snarl come from it? He couldn't spot anything resembling a mouth.

The creature growled again. Noah retreated a few steps and studied it. Vaguely round, with short fur or something covering it, it bumped along the surface clumsily. It wasn't much larger than a beanbag chair.

Definitely the source of the stink though, Noah decided, wrinkling his nose. Glancing over at Uh-oh, he noticed his companion using a finger and thumb to pinch off his own nose. Apparently, he agreed. Although, to be honest, Noah thought, Uh-oh didn't smell like a bouquet of flowers, either. More like really grody gym socks.

Maybe, he concluded, he thinks I reek too. It's been a while since my last shower.

Concentrate, Noah, concentrate, he scolded himself. You can survive the smell. Just figure out how to get past this thing. Noah watched the animal watching them, and tried to formulate a second plan. The trail widened out down where the creature skittered back and forth. They could probably circle around it. It didn't appear to be very agile. And when it had roared, he hadn't seen any fangs or claws. "Okay," he said, with much more confidence than he felt, "let's start down."

"Okay. Start down," croaked Uh-oh. Then, almost under his breath, "Uh-oh."

Noah wondered again if his companion knew what he was saying or just mimicked what he heard. No time to think about it. He moved forward in a slow jog.

As they drew closer, Noah decided the creature most resembled a big bag of goo—pudding, maybe, or melted ice cream. Instead of moving from place to place, it kind of oozed. What had looked like fur, now more closely resembled the mold that formed on left-too-long-overs at the back of the refrigerator.

The mold thing began to change shape, its fuzzy surface swirling and rippling as it morphed into a new but still random glump. Prune-sized dots that Noah guessed were the creature's eyes danced along the surface of the thing, stopping to stare through the fuzz at the approaching intruders, then sliding off to somewhere else.

Okay, Noah thought, so it's weird and moldy and its eyes move around. For all he knew, that was normal for this part of the mountain. He edged ahead, looking for an opening. Should he hurdle the creature, or make a dash around it?

"Roooaaahhhrrr."

The mold-thing convulsed from top to bottom, shuddering as it rearranged its skin. An opening formed in the center of the lumpy body, an opening that expanded rapidly into a huge and gaping mouth. Noah skidded to a stop, staring straight into the writhing purple belly of the beast. Slimy red stuff dripped from the upper rim of the mouth. "Tssst." The red stuff spattered onto the ledge, sizzling, eating into the rock. Noah crept backward. He couldn't turn. He couldn't tear his eyes from that horrible mouth. And then, with a sort of squishing sound, the mouth closed on itself and disappeared. Would it, like the eyes, appear again, somewhere else on the thing's body? What was this thing, this mold monster?

"Mold monster," came the echo from Uh-oh. "Not good."

Noah didn't even remember speaking the words aloud. But he must have, he thought, otherwise how would Uh-oh pick them up?

"You got any ideas on how to get around him?"

Uh-oh scrunched his face into a caricature of thoughtfulness, holding a forefinger in the air in front of him as if an idea was imminent. But then, as usual, he shrugged and shook his head no.

"Well, it's not coming after us. I bet it's really slow." Noah forced himself to sound confident. "I bet if we get going, we can run around it. We'll back up a few more steps and then sprint as fast as we can." Uh-oh frowned, but then nodded and they began edging up the trail.

"Okay." Noah crouched. "Get ready."

The mold monster's oval eyes stopped darting around the surface of its body and locked in on Noah and Uh-oh.

An eerie hissing sound started to intermingle with the low, burbly growl. The hiss grew in volume and the wavering growl became a short, sharp snarl. It sounded to Noah like a warning.

He was right.

The mold-monster's flesh vibrated and another mouth formed. As it did, the monster sprang, flying through the air in a blur, landing with a loud splat in front of them.

Noah's reflexes took over. He darted around the monster to the left. As he passed, something stung his leg. He tried to ignore it and ran on. The pain grew worse. His leg felt hot. The trail narrowed and ascended onto another rocky ledge. Pausing in his flight, he looked at his leg. A glob of some kind of red yucky stuff stuck to his jeans. He felt it burning. He smelled his own scorched flesh.

"Ooowww," he moaned, hopping up and down. He wanted to get the red slime off of him, but knew if he grabbed it with his fingers, it would burn them too.

Reaching into his backpack, he groped for something to protect his hands. He found a pair of spare underpants. Using the cloth as protection, he grabbed at the glob of gunk, trapped it between layers of cloth and pulled it away from his skin. "Sssstt." The stuff made an angry sound as it came away. Noah flung it from the ledge and peered through the hole in his jeans. An angry-looking spot the size of a half dollar glowed on his skin. Small wisps of smoke curled from it, but there was no goo that he could see. He touched the spot gingerly and shrank back from the pain.

"Big trouble. We got big trouble." Uh-oh's panicked impression of Noah's voice came somewhere farther back on the rocky shelf on which he'd stopped. In his pain and desperation to peel the fiery glob from his leg, he'd totally forgotten about the mold-monster. He looked around frantically. Where was it?

He spotted Uh-oh, fifty feet away, perched on a very narrow outcropping a few feet above the main ledge.

Yes, get higher, Noah thought. Get off the trail. Maybe it won't be able to follow. He tried to scrabble further up the wall, but there were no hand or toeholds and his efforts only led to a shower of small stones falling around him.

"Rooahhr." Noah looked down. The mold monster waited below Uh-oh, its fuzzy flesh rippling wildly in expectation. Although Noah couldn't see its mouth from where he stood, he could have sworn he heard the thing smack its lips. If Uh-oh falls, he thought, he'll plummet right into its stomach.

His mind raced frantically. What could he do? A part of him said, just run, jump to the next ledge, get away and let Uh-oh fend for himself. After all, it was his creepy little friends who started this whole thing when they kidnapped Abby. He didn't owe Uh-oh anything.

As if he could read Noah's mind, Uh-oh moaned. "Uh-oh. Bad trouble."

Impulsively, Noah picked up a baseball-sized stone and hurled it at the mold-monster. It struck with a resounding thrump. The hissing and growling stopped. A rusty squeal replaced it.

"No!" Noah commanded, his voice quavering with fear and doubt. "Leave my friend alone. Get away from here. Shoo."

Shoo? Noah grimaced at his own stupidity. Brilliant, No-way, he could almost hear Abby's taunt. Shoo?

Exactly the right word to terrify a mold monster. It will probably shiver the whole time it eats me.

The fuzz on the creature began to vibrate again, and the hissing returned, low and threatening. The acrid smell of the beast flooded Noah's senses. He bent over, gagging.

The mold-monster spun and leaped, whirling upward and forward. It landed with another loud splat in front of Noah, gaping mouth dripping red ooze, black eyes glued on its prey.

The stench alone nearly slammed Noah against the wall, but surprisingly, he felt a calm settle over him. He couldn't leap to the next ledge now, so this was the way it would end. Maybe Uh-oh could get away, maybe he'd find Abby, act out what had happened. Abby's smart, maybe she'd figure it out. But then what?

Well, it didn't matter. It wouldn't be his problem.

Resigned, he braced for the mouth to engulf him, for red slime to cover his body and burn him to death. He hoped it would be over quick.

A rock flew from behind the monster and embedded itself in its soft back. The mold monster squealed and its eyes migrated toward Uh-oh, who'd descended from his perch and now prepared to throw another rock. The monster opened its massive mouth again and roared at the coil-haired gray figure. One eye traveled back toward Noah. It seemed to be deciding which of them to attack first.

That's when Noah got the brainstorm. There was something else he'd forgotten he'd brought. It probably wouldn't work, but he had to try something. Reaching back into his pack, he groped through the jumble of clothes and other junk. A hissing sound drew his attention back to the mold-monster. It seemed to have made up its mind to eat Noah first, then take care of the annoying little gray thing. Uh-oh tossed another rock, but it drew only a warning hiss. The mold-monster's eyes trained themselves on Noah. The mouth gaped open further and Noah felt the heat of the putrid breath on his face. He saw orange wormy things, wiggling grossly in the monster's stomach, waiting for their feast.

With one smooth motion, Noah's hand closed around the plastic bag of salt-water taffy, pulled it from his pack and threw it into the cavernous mouth. The lips closed behind the bag. The flesh constricted.

Noah tensed, ready to run, but the mold monster emitted a loud, warning hiss that froze him in place. I'm still the main course, he thought. That was just an appetizer. Life's too short, eat dessert first. He remembered the sign from a restaurant where the family used to eat. He marveled that he could still make jokes to himself when he might die at any second. With grim fascination, he watched the creature digest the bag of taffy. Flesh bunched and released, twisted and relaxed.

Noah heard a cross between munching and squishing and saw the monster's flesh quiver. Uh-oh hefted another rock, a bigger one. Once again, Noah wondered whether he could gather himself for a desperate leap.

The monster seemed to rear up. It snarled. But the sound came out muffled. "Grymmph." Uh-oh raised the rock over his head with both hands. Noah backed away as far as he could. When the rock hit, the monster would react.

But Uh-oh paused, up on tiptoe, peering at his adversary. As Noah stared, the monster's gyrations increased, its mouth opened, closed and twisted, then spread into a weird grimace. Its fuzzy flesh began to vibrate rapidly, and Noah heard a faint humming. The mouth appeared, but opened only an inch, just enough for Noah to see a gummy mess of taffy.

The monster tried to roar again. It spun around, banging itself against a nearby boulder, trying to dislodge the sticky candy.

Noah raised one hand slowly and motioned Uh-oh to put down the rock. Then, as the mold monster's mouth closed, he swung his pack at it. Reflexively, the monster rolled away from the blow, skittering to the very edge. It teetered there for a moment, convulsing as it tried to swing the balance back. Failing, it tumbled down the face of the cliff.

"Run," Noah shouted. He raced to the far edge of the outcropping and leaped to the next ledge. Uh-oh followed at his heels. In a few minutes, they paused and looked down.

The mold monster lay far below in a tangled heap on the floor of the cavern, moaning loudly. Noah almost felt sorry for it. He blinked and had to remind himself that the thing had nearly eaten him. And now it appeared to be digesting itself. As they watched, its body became a puddle of steaming red ooze.

"Whew," said Uh-oh. "Close call."

Noah grinned over at his sidekick. He didn't remember ever saying "close call," out loud. Where had Uh-oh picked it up? Maybe he could always talk Noah's language, but simply hadn't. But no, that didn't explain why he echoed Noah's unspoken words so accurately.

Uh-oh scratched his head with a thin, gray finger and pointed along the steadily rising trail toward the far side of the cavern. Noah nodded and followed the creature who'd tried to save his life. He hoped they'd find something to eat or drink soon. He had a little water left in his canteen. They could share that the next time they rested. He realized that he needed to do that soon. He felt lightheaded and vaguely sick to his stomach. It must be a delayed reaction to the fight with the mold monster, he thought. And I'm so hungry.

It will pass in a few minutes, he told himself. But it didn't. He began to sweat and his leg throbbed and stung. He looked down and saw the spot where the red goo had burned him had changed color and begun to swell.

"I . . . I . . . need to rest for a minute." Noah stumbled to a halt and leaned against a rock.

Uh-oh glanced back. "Uh-oh." He trained his gaze on the swollen leg. Noah could tell by his expression that the leg looked as bad to Uh-oh as it did to him.

"It's nothing," Noah said. "Just a little burn. The swelling will go down in a little bit." Ice, he thought, I need some ice. And aspirin. He felt his forehead with the back of his wrist the way his mother used to do. It felt warm. Did he have a fever? Was his leg infected? No.

It couldn't be. It had only been a few minutes since the fight.

Noah slid to the ground and closed his eyes for a few seconds. The dizziness passed and he opened his eyes, sat up and looked along the rocky path toward what appeared to be a lush, green valley. Stranger yet, even though they were inside a mountain, he was certain he saw a forest of tall, brown limbless trees. If there was a forest, they might find water. He pulled himself to his feet. "I think I'm okay. Let's get going again."

Hot green nausea clawed at his stomach and his eyes swam out of focus. He dropped to his knees. Maybe if he rested just a little longer, he'd feel better. Just a little nap and he'd be fine.

Uh-oh's face hovered just inches away from his own, a look of undisguised concern written all over it.

Noah's head seemed to balloon with heat. Sharp pains ripped at his gut. A dark wave washed over his mind and shut it down.

Chapter Eleven

They took a steep path, so steep that Abby found herself gasping by the time they reached the top.

Delacroix, the Grand Exalted Pettifog of the Upper World, led her into a small, rounded chamber about the size of a bathroom and stood waiting for her to catch her breath. Chillout lingered nearby and Abby caught a whiff of his gamy body odor. Strange, though, it didn't seem to bother her as much as it had at first. *I guess you can get used to almost anything,* she marveled.

Delacroix bent at the waist and looked into her eyes. "Faith, you know, is a very important thing to have," he said quietly.

This puzzled her. What was he talking about? Faith like in church, with miracles and prayers? "I don't—"

"—understand." He finished her sentence and continued in his lilting patois. "Ahh, but that is the crux of the matter, yes, that is what faith is all about—believing without understanding. Sometimes, suspend our disbelief, we must."

Abby wrestled with the idea for a moment. The concept didn't appeal to her. Understanding, knowing, that was everything. Reasoning, gathering evidence, then using her mind to generate logical conclusions. Faith, on the other hand, felt like leaping off a cliff without knowing what was below.

Delacroix's voice took on an almost trance-like quality. "Having faith begins in very small ways. C'est vrai. To begin, you must have faith in me, little one. Faith in the ways of the mountain. You must believe I would not do anything to cause you pain; that I would put my life down to protect yours. Can you do that?"

Fear made her nerves jangle and she felt her heart begin to pump faster. What did he mean? What was he going to do? She wanted to scream, for Noah, for Dad, for anyone who could help her. But she didn't. It would be a waste of breath.

She forced herself to take a deep breath and think logically. If Delacroix intended to hurt her, he could have done it a long time ago. "I'm . . . not sure what you mean." Her voice was a strangled squeak.

"You will know when you know," Delacroix told her.

"Let's boogie on down, Lix, she's copasetic."

Chillout's hipster growl wheedled. The grungoid moved closer to Abby and she was suddenly glad to have him near, even glad about his scent. He was warm and funny.

He was safe, even though he'd held her captive. "Time to play between the notes, baby," Chillout told Delacroix.

"Shhh, Chillout. Not yet. The vibrations need to be exactly right. Listen."

The grungoid took a deep breath and held it, cocking his head. In the sudden calm, Abby heard the faint heartbeat of the mountain again, this time a distant and reassuring thrum-thrum, thrum-thrum, thrum-thrum. As she listened, she felt herself disconnect from the reality of the moment and drift. "Thrum-thrum, thrum-thrum, thrum-thrum." She looked up at Delacroix and saw a beatific smile on his large, brown face. Chillout, too, seemed to be blissed out. She put a hand up to her own face and realized she must be smiling too. "Thrumthrum, thrum-thrum, thrum-thrum.

In her dream-like state, she heard Delacroix's words almost as if they were spoken through water. His head turned up toward the ceiling of the chamber and he began to chant something over and over.

"Alameezos gravititos," she thought she heard.

Thrum-thrum, thrum-thrum, thrum-thrum, answered the mountain.

Delacroix chanted again. Maybe he was saying "Gravuhmeezos Alamitos."

Abby felt her heart answer the mountain. *Thrum-thrum, thrum-thrum, thrum-thrum.* She looked at the ceiling and saw the light begin to swirl and blink with the increasing intensity of Delacroix's chant, which now sounded to her like an indistinct mumble, mumble, mumble.

Beneath her feet, the surface of the rock shifted and began to sway and jiggle, as if it was melting. She looked down to see the floor dissolving at the edges of the chamber. She seized Chillout's hand, the skin and hair rough beneath her fingers. The grungoid smiled at her, then gazed at Delacroix, who continued to chant.

Abby glanced at the floor again. The solid rock on which they stood was now a small island in a lake of liquid. Her stomach churned and a scream rose in her throat.

"Faith, little chickie," Chillout whispered.

Faith? Faith won't let me walk on molten rock! She tried to tear her hand from Chillout's. Maybe she could leap over the lava or magma or— wait a minute. Rock had to be very hot to melt. And yet, it was cool in this cavern, almost chilly. So perhaps the melting floor was an illusion. An illusion couldn't hurt her.

She relaxed, concentrating on the *"thrum-thrum, thrum-thrum, thrum-thrum* and Delacroix's repetitive chant. Then she had a horrible thought. Everything was different down here; maybe rock could melt without getting hot. She felt a wave of panic and tried to pull away from Chillout once more.

"Faith," he whispered again. "Let go and believe."

Let go? But how? How do you just decide to believe?

Blind panic swept through her brain like a tsunami wave and she gripped Chillout's hand tighter. They'd fall together. Down, down, deep into the mountain. She closed her eyes. She couldn't look. The chanting and thrumming became an ocean-like roar in her mind, the rock beneath her feet oscillated in time with the mountain's beat. She felt herself swaying and suddenly realized there was nothing beneath her feet.

But she wasn't falling! She was merely twisting gently, like a windsock in a gentle breeze.

She opened her eyes slowly and saw Delacroix and Chillout smiling at her. The Pettifog looked up at the ceiling once more and simply nodded. The grungoid seemed to giggle and extended a long gray finger downward. Abby could have sworn she heard him say something like "Cowabunga." Or maybe it was "Wobucanga."

Then the bottom fell out.

She heard a sharp sucking sound, as if a giant were drawing on the other end of an enormous drinking straw.

"Voorrrvvvv." She felt herself plummeting downward, going faster than she'd ever moved, even in Dad's car on the freeway.

Her heart dropped into her stomach. Cold air rushed by. Rock walls flashed past. Everything around her was a blur, including two other figures that may or may not have been Delacroix and the grungoid. The shriek she'd held onto before escaped her throat. The sound was torn from her lips and faded away.

She closed her eyes. Faith. It was all she had. But how do you get faith? Do you just have it? Or do you have to learn? Well, if it was possible to learn, she hoped she could learn fast. Abby took a slow deep breath and concentrated on believing she wouldn't crash into whatever was beneath, that she wouldn't die, that somehow something would break her fall. As if from a long distance, she heard the thrum-thrum, thrum-thrum, thrum-thrum of her heart. She locked onto it, chanting words of her own. "Safe landing. Safe landing. Safe landing."

Time telescoped; then another sound worked its way into her consciousness. It began as a far-away sighing noise, the sound of someone who realizes that pain has stopped. It grew quickly, becoming a steady roar that overrode the beat of her heart and the thump of the mountain. The pitch of the roar changed. It grew deeper, somehow slower.

Abby opened her eyes to see that the walls of the rock tube had begun to come into focus. After a moment, she saw the faces of Delacroix and Chillout, where before there had been only smudges of high-speed color. The sharp suction that had drawn them like water down a long drain became a gentle exhale. They drifted slowly, then touched solid ground.

"Oh." Abby stumbled and put out a hand. Chillout took it and steadied her. "Your very first trip on the Vorv," he told her. "Mega-cool, huh?"

The Vorv? She looked up, but saw only a rock ceiling, no open shaft, no sign of where they'd fallen from.

"Where are we?"

"A special place, ma cherie," Delacroix answered. "A place very near where you will help your brother repel the demon troll, Spid.

"Noah? Is he around here somewhere? Can I see him now?"

Delacroix's voice took on a note of deep sadness.

"Not yet, Abby. Soon. Many obstacles he must still overcome. There is much danger, but he will have help. An ally. And you, cherie, you must use the time well. Prepare yourself to play your part. As it is written."

"Written? Written where? How can I have a part, I've never been down here before? What is my part?"

"Shhh." He raised a stump and Abby imagined the missing forearm. She almost saw a finger raised to his lips. "You will look and you will learn, no? And then you will move. Just like in chess."

"But what will I—" Abby began to fire a question at him, but Delacroix ignored her and started down a narrow footpath. Chillout, scuttling quickly to keep pace with his master's long strides, stayed right behind. Abby, still quivering from the long fall, trailed behind, her mind racing. What was that thing they'd fallen down? An elevator shaft? No. An air flume? Ever since she and Noah came to Humbug Mountain, she'd been seeing things she would have never believed existed. From the old woman on the beach who seemed to have communicated with Noah using only her eyes, to the little hairless things that had carried her up the cliff. Not to mention the lights that appeared to be living things, and an armless drummer who had become the, what was it— Grand Exalted Pettifog of a world that existed inside a mountain. All of it defied logic. Or, she corrected herself, logic based on her previous perceptions; logic based on the world she'd known before.

She noticed Delacroix and Chillout had disappeared around one of the twists and turns in the passageway.

Picking up her pace, she caught sight of them outside what appeared to be the entrance to another chamber.

"Welcome to Cave-Mart, little chickie," rasped Chillout, pointing up at a crudely lettered sign over the opening in the rock wall.

"Cave-Mart?" She glanced at the sign. The letters spelled a phrase that looked totally foreign to her. It said:
Thela stpla ceyo ulook

A second look changed her perception a little. The language looked vaguely familiar, like the Greek and Latin phrases she'd seen in books on mythology. "What does the sign say?"

"It says what it says, little one." Delacroix answered with a shrug. "It will all become clear soon. Or it will not."

As usual, his patient philosophy infuriated her. "All you do is talk in riddles. It drives me crazy. Just say something that makes sense, for once."

Delacroix smiled, then shook his head slowly. "Could I, would I, Abby. But, I find myself as boxed in by fate as you, *cher*. I can only do what I can do. I can only tell you what I can tell you. What the sign says is your riddle, your first quest. For us to push Spid back to his dark hole, you must discover the path. I cannot the brush clear from your way, you see?"

Abby seethed. "Spid. Spid. Spid. You keep throwing his name at me and I don't even know who he is. How can I help defeat him if I don't know who he is?"

"Oh," Delacroix's smile faded to a grim-lipped frown. "Spid will appear to you soon enough, ma petite. Too soon, I fear. Now inside, shall we go?" He ducked through the doorway and Chillout followed. Abby, still angry and frustrated, trailed them, taking a last look at the sign, memorizing the order of the letters and the spacing so she could try to decipher them later.

She found herself inside a huge chamber, large enough to accommodate ten or more of the one where Delacroix lived and held court. As she glanced around, her eyes widened in amazement. Everywhere she looked were stacks and stacks of what she could only describe as stuff. Everything imaginable. She walked around gaping at hundred-foot-high stacks of men's wallets, a virtual mountain of car keys, a matching peak constructed of eyeglasses. She fingered one of thousands of woolen mittens. "What is this place? Where did all of this come from?"

"Pretty trippy, huh, little chickie?" Chillout chortled. "It's everything-o-rama."

Delacroix's frown loosened. He waved a stump at a creeping avalanche of paperback books. "You see Abby, this is where what is lost ends up. Have you never misplaced something? You could swear it disappeared into thin air, no?"

Organized as she was, Abby remembered a homework assignment she'd mislaid and never found. She'd looked for days, taken an incomplete rather than do it over—that would have been admitting she was fallible. "Um, once. But you can't mean that everything that gets lost—"

"—ends up here?" Delacroix shrugged. Believe what you want, but it's true, ma petite. Everything. Look around you, is it not fantastic?

Abby had to admit it was. It reminded her of a truckload outlet store she'd visited once in search of a kitchen table with her father. She strolled around the cavern, peeking at stack after stack. Sure enough, against one wall was a huge hillock of papers. She pulled a few loose and found bills, report cards, stock reports and what looked like finished homework assignments. She wondered how long it would take her to find hers. A part of her wanted to try, but as she studied the pile, she realized that was totally illogical. She could be there the rest of her life. Besides, she'd mislaid the paper three years ago. What did it matter now? Still, just to set the record straight . . .

Delacroix chuckled. She looked up at him furtively and he winked, as if he'd read her mind. Embarrassed, she moved on quickly, watching Chillout as he scrambled from pile to pile, checking out things and chortling. He came up with a Seattle Mariners' baseball cap and stuck it on his head with the bill pointing to the rear, then bolted on toward a stack of cellular phones.

She moved farther into the chamber and found an enormous pile of socks of all colors. Aha, she thought. That's where they end up when you can't find them in the dryer. Just past the socks, she found a similar-sized pile of unmatched shoes. She turned to Delacroix; again, he seemed to read her mind. "Did you not ever puzzle, Abby, why the single shoes you always see along the highway?" Delacroix waggled his eyebrows and shrugged. "Where did the other shoe go, you ask yourself. Before you, you see the answer. They are all right here."

An amazing array of things was crammed into every available space inside the huge rocky chamber. There was even a pile of musical instruments; saxophones, French horns, clarinets, flutes, drums and the like. Abby saw a pile of discarded drumsticks near the mound of instruments. She thought about picking up a couple for Noah, for when she saw him. The thought made her want to cry. Noah. Would she ever see him again? Would either of them ever escape from this crazy-mirror world deep inside the mountain? Would they ever see Dad again, walk on the beach, or go to school? She fought the panic that began to rise in her chest. Faith, she reminded herself. She had to believe that she would find Noah, and they would go home again.

"It is sad, no?" Delacroix mused. "A whole world of music never created because the means to make it was lost and now forgotten." He touched a drumstick with his toe. "Come, we must ride the Vorv back."

They circled the back of the chamber – past baby clothes and beach towels, scissors, pins and needles—and turned back toward the entrance. "Why did you bring me here?"

"Because the prophecy said I must."

"The prophecy?"

"Oui. The story as it is being told."

"You're doing riddles again." Abby stamped her feet in anger. "Talk so I can understand you."

He sighed. "I know you are frustrated, ma cherie. But I am only a guide, you see. What you seek must be revealed by time, Abby. And by your own ingenuity, yes?" She scowled at him and he shook his head mournfully. "Soon, you will know more, Abby. This promise, I can make."

Give it up, the logical side of her brain told her. If he doesn't know, he doesn't know. And if he won't tell, you can't make him. She sighed and followed him past stacks of alarm clocks and radios and a huge pile of dolls and other toys. Farther along, they came to another opening in the rock. They turned down the tunnel and came to a doorway with an actual wooden door.

"What's in there?"

"Open it and find out." Delacroix suggested.

Nervously, Abby reached for the shiny brass doorknob and turned it slowly. The door opened without a sound, revealing a chamber shrouded in darkness. She peered into the gloom, waiting for the tiny ceiling lights to come on, as they always did. Somewhere in the distance, one person began to laugh. The lonely sound echoed off the walls. "Who's there?" Abby called. "Come out where I can see you."

The laughter continued, and, in a moment, another voice joined in. Then another. Soon she was surrounded by the eerie, disembodied laughter of hundreds of men, women and children. They chuckled and chortled, giggled and guffawed. It sounded like the laugh-track from one of those unfunny sitcoms, but multiplied by a thousand. Spooked, Abby slammed the door shut.

"That's creepy," she commented. "Are there people trapped in there?" She thought of what she'd just seen in what Chillout called Cave-Mart. "Lost people?"

"No," Delacroix said. "But something they have lost.

Something you must be careful to hang onto, Abby, even to the very end."

Chillout mimed the posture of a stand-up comedian holding an imaginary microphone in front of his mouth.

"And then the parrot said that'll be two bucks, lady. And next time, skip the birdseed. Thudaboom-chick. But seriously folks, take my wife . . ."

Abby giggled at the impersonation "I see now. That room was filled by people who had lost their senses of humor. Laughter sure sounds weird all by itself."

"Yes," Delacroix agreed. "You need the smile to make the mirth real, yes?"

As they left the chamber, Abby again studied the sign over the door of the storehouse of lost things.

Thela stpla ceyo ulook

Hard as she tried, she couldn't figure out why the letters looked familiar. She felt like it was some kind of code. She stared at the first word again. Greek, she decided, definitely. That would make it difficult, maybe impossible to decipher. She didn't have a Greek/English dictionary. And Delacroix had made it clear he couldn't help her.

The trip back to the top was, in its own way, a reverse duplicate of the trip down. But Abby was so preoccupied with her riddle, she barely flinched as they leaped toward the hole that appeared in the ceiling of the chamber and hurtled upward, riding the Vorv.

After a dinner of nuts, rootburgers and orange soda, she became very, very sleepy. She laid down on the gelbed, but tired as her body was, her mind wouldn't turn off. The letters kept sliding behind her eyes. *Thela stpla ceyo ulook, Thela stpla ceyo ulook.* She tried reading the phrase back to front. She tried counting the number of each distinct letters. If you knew which letters were most common in a language, it helped crack a code. But nineteen letters was hardly a decent sample for that process. She tried substituting other letters for the ones in the phrase, hoping it might be a cipher. But it wasn't. Or at least not one she could decode.

She got up, went to her backpack and dug out a pen and small steno pad she'd thrown in. As she did, her fingers touched the translucent stone she'd found on the beach. She pulled it out, rubbed her hands over its smooth cool surface, then set it down on a ledge.

Flopping on the bed, she opened the pad and began playing with the letters. She filled three pages before, exhausted and frustrated, she flung the pen and pad to the floor and drifted into a fitful sleep.

Chapter Twelve

The burning that had begun in the wound on his lower leg now seemed to encompass Noah's entire body. Wild images jumped and jangled through his delusional mind like remote-controlled snatches of television shows clicked in by someone with an itchy trigger finger. Nebulous mental pictures flickered and danced across the back of his eyes, lingering only long enough to register before being replaced by the next equally frightening and perplexing flash.

He saw Abby being chased across a barren landscape by a leering, ugly thing with immense arms. He saw the hermit, shaking a finger at him for ignoring his advice, saw someone's hand placing a cool cloth on his forehead; saw Old Hannah, dancing a wild and frenzied dance, sending her thoughts across to him: "Don't forget the steps, Noah, don't forget the steps." Another picture flicker brought him Dad holding hands with Mrs. Ramsden, kissing her and smiling happily. He felt his body tense, heard himself sob. The image faded.

Sounds and sensations mixed with the visuals. The stench of the mold monster. Uh-oh's voice, "This is bad, Noah, really bad." The earthy taste of scrubbage stew, spooned into his mouth by an unseen hand. And penetrating through all of it, the fire, licking at his leg, the burning sensation radiating up to cocoon his entire body.

Sweating, then freezing, then sweating again, cold and heat interchangeable. Through it all, he felt his own hands moving, in sympathetic rhythm with a beat coming from somewhere inside the mountain or inside himself. Ta-ta-ta-ta ching ta ta . . . ta ta ta . . . da-ding ta.

He also felt other hands, pushing his arms to his sides, heard a woman say, "Go back to sleep, Noah, it'll be all right." He thought he recognized the voice. Mom? Could it have been Mom? He tried to open his eyes, but the lids felt enormous, thick and heavy, and he couldn't move them.

At one point his stuttering mind generated an image of himself clutching Uh-oh's leg and falling, falling, falling.

He flung an arm out to try to stop the fall, but couldn't. A different female voice, higher pitched and anxious, broke through the wall of fever. "Will he make it?" Then the first voice again. No, not Mom, he realized, but calm and reassuring like her. "Yes, of course he will. He must. He's needed."

Finally, the waves of fever began to recede. The sensation of falling stopped and Noah felt as if he were floating on a calm and cooling sea. Carefully, he rubbed his eyes. The dry and gritty eyelids scratched and grated and then opened to a blur of light. He blinked and blinked again. He was in a small room. Not rock, but some other kind of material. Brown. Kind of reedy. A massive, carved wooden chair stood beside the arched doorway, lights twinkled on the ceiling, growing brighter as his vision cleared. He plucked at the light quilt that lay across his legs and realized someone was sitting on the bed beside him. No one he knew. A young woman, a girl really, about his age.

She regarded him with raised eyebrows and a faint smile. "You're back." She peeled a warm damp rag from his chest and replaced it with a cold fresh one.

He tried to speak, but managed only a croak. "I . . . uh . . . guess so."

"Shhh." She put a finger to her lips. "You're still very weak. Don't try to talk. Here, try to swallow a little of this." She turned to a small table beside the bed, dipped a wooden spoon into a bowl and brought it to his lips. The pungent aroma of the stuff reached him before he felt the warm liquid against his cracked lips and swollen tongue.

He first tasted a familiar, organic flavor. But, as he sucked at the second spoonful, several other flavors crowded out the first. They were unlike anything he'd ever sampled, or even imagined. Sweet and bitter at the same time, with a zest that made him tingle. "Scrub . . . scrubbage?" He croaked.

"Yes." She put her finger to her lips again. "With some monga root and violet toadstool mixed in. One of mother's most potent recipes. It will have you up on your feet in no time. Which is good, because you're behind schedule. You took the wrong tunnel. But you're here now, and as soon as you're better, we'll make up for lost time."

Schedule? The only thing he had to do was find Abby. But that old man, and now this girl, talked as if he had to follow some kind of a plan, as if this were some kind of a treasure hunt game. Why was it everyone down here seemed to know where he was supposed to be and what he was supposed to be doing except for him? Why did it feel like things had spun so desperately out of control?

Why was he so helpless?

He wanted to lash out at the young woman, but instead he accepted another spoonful of the thick broth and studied her carefully. Actually, he thought, she's really just a girl. Probably about my age. She had smooth skin the color of an oatmeal cookie, and short hair a strange shade of brown that reminded him of the beach at first light. Large, expressive hazel eyes, a strong nose and a generous-sized mouth that always seemed turned upward in mild amusement made for a face that was not beautiful, but definitely interesting. She wore some kind of khaki coveralls, with a long-sleeved flannel shirt underneath.

"Who are you?" This time the words didn't hurt as much coming out, but they still sounded strange to him, as if another person had spoken.

"Deidre," she murmured, as if it didn't really matter.

110

"Here, eat another spoonful. Then you need to sleep some more."

"Where am I? How did I get here?"

She ignored the first question, but answered the second as she spooned another dollop of stew into his mouth. "Your little gray friend." She got up, putting the spoon down beside the bowl on the small table. "He must care about you a lot. He carried you a long, long way after you escaped from the Skeezbo's lair."

Skeezbo? She must mean the mold-monster. Noah shuddered, remembering the writhing things in the stomach revealed by that gaping mouth. He'd thrown a rock, hadn't he? And then Uh-oh pelted the beast and he found the taffy in his pack and then— "Is that thing, the mold-monster, is it dead?"

"Oh yes. We call those things Skeezbos around here. Nasty things. Your friend told us about your name for it. Anyway, you're a hero. You and the little gray guy."

"He really carried me?" Noah tried to imagine Uh-oh with a hundred and fifty pounds draped across his shoulders struggling down the rocky pathway.

"Well, I think he kind of dragged you some of the way. You're a lot bigger than he is. But he's a determined little creature, your friend. Good to have on your side."

Amazing, Noah thought. Why hadn't Uh-oh just left him there? After all, he didn't seem to know where they'd been headed. He'd have had no idea how far he'd have to drag Noah before he found help, or even whether he'd find help at all. Friend. Deidre had used the word three times. He decided she was right. He and Uh-oh were friends. Friends by fate much more than by choice, but friends nevertheless. And friends did things like that for friends.

Deidre stood. "I've got to go now. You get some sleep, okay."

The lights on the ceiling began to dim. Noah nodded, but didn't close his eyes. Watching Deidre stride across the room, Noah realized she was probably only an inch or two short of his own six feet, trim and athletic looking.

As she turned to go, she picked up something lying across a chair by the door and began to strap it on. It took him a moment to realize that it was a scabbard. As he watched, she slid a kind of two-pronged sword into it and settled the belt on her hips.

A girl with a sword? Or was it really a sword? The prongs hadn't looked that sharp. "Why do you have that?"

"Spid," she mumbled.

Noah tried to struggle to a sitting position. "Who's Spid?"

"Shhh," she ordered, her finger on her lips again, her mouth curling upward into a sly smile. "You'll know soon enough. And you'll wish you'd never asked."

Chapter Thirteen

"The last place you look!" Abby's own voice woke her. She sat up in bed, suddenly wide awake. The answer had come to her as answers often did—when she shut down her mind and let her subconscious take over. Of course! Thela stpla ceyo ulook. The last place you look.

Smiling, she sank back against her pillow, remembering other times when she'd blurted stuff out loud and woke up in the middle of the night. Mom and Dad used to rush into her bedroom, certain she was having some horrendous nightmare. They would return to their room, bleary-eyed and shaking their head after she explained to them she'd just figured out the value of x in some complex algebraic equation, or finally understood how to use the conditional tense in Spanish.

The lights above her danced and twinkled into a pleasant glow as if they shared her excitement. She smiled up at them. They must be what Delacroix referred to as Darksuckers. But what were they? She thought again about standing on her bed and trying to get a closer look, but decided to wait until morning. She smiled again. That implied this was really night. Night as she knew it. The opposite of day. Neither term had meaning inside the mountain. Or perhaps, she thought, stretching her mind and abandoning her former logic, they had new meanings. Having faith, she realized, could still mean believing in an order and structure—just a different kind than the ones you were used to.

Still, part of her felt very dumb that she hadn't figured out the phrase before. It was simple, really. Obvious.

Thela stpla ceyo ulook. You just took the whole thing, squished it together, Thelastplaceyoulook, then put the spaces in the right places. The last place you look.

People always said that when you were searching for something. "You'll find it in the last place you look."

Kind of a "Well, duh," really, if you thought about it, since nobody kept looking *after* they'd found something.

You were always going to find it in the last place you looked. Or, she realized, you wouldn't find it at all. And it would end up on a stack of other things like it in the storeroom down below. She thought instantly of Noah and Dad and her room at home. Faith trickled away. She felt small and afraid.

All at once, the lights began to flicker. The gel bed rocked beneath her. Abby felt a finger of fear jab her stomach. Was this an earthquake? Were the tectonic plates off the coast shifting as one slid beneath the other?

Would the rock walls and ceilings collapse on her? Frantically, she looked around for somewhere safe. Couldn't get under the bed, it was gel. And the rickety table where her pack sat wouldn't protect her from rain, let alone falling rock. Weren't you supposed to stand in a doorway? She started to move, but her eye caught something that froze her in place.

Over on the stone ledge opposite her bed, the orb Delacroix had called the Chameleon Stone began to throb with color, strobing streams of red, blue, green and bright white onto the wall beside it. Soon the colors ran together, darkened, then turned midnight black. A funnel of dark blue beamed from the stone. Above her, the twinkling lights she'd come to know as Darksuckers seemed to flee toward her, leaving the ceiling above the orb dark.

The bed quivered again. The orb strobed faster, the dark blue beam rotating, swirling into a vortex. Paralyzed with fear, Abby couldn't tear her eyes from it. A figure slowly materialized in the beam. The Darksuckers fled down the wall behind her, casting her shadow out to meet the intruder. Abby shrank back against the wall, terrified yet fascinated.

This person, this thing, was huge; an enormous head, with eyes like black holes and ears that dangled to its chin, emerged from the neck of a nicely-cut pinstriped business suit. The arms hung past the creature's knees, and where the trousers ended, instead of polished shoes, were bare . . . Well, Abby guessed they were feet, although they were nothing like any human feet she'd ever seen. These were reptilian, with webs between the toes and folds of loose skin.

She swept her eyes upward and gaped at the creature's grotesque face, at skin like wet, hairy leather that had been left to dry in the sun, skin that was kind of purple colored.

A major wart protruded from one cheekbone, wiggling around almost like it had a mind of its own. In contrast, the thing had neatly-combed, straight dark hair that looked like it had been professionally cut. Dangling from the long-lobed ears were dozens of earrings and studs – ornate, jeweled and jangly.

Abby squealed and shrank further back into the corner.

"A most predictable and understandable reaction, Miss Keene, but lamentable. You have nothing to fear from me. I am Spid The Devious, the Grand Exalted Garboon of the Land Below Skin, the Land of Beneath."

The precise, effete, slightly bombastic tone of the voice surprised her. It seemed out of place, practiced, as much a façade as the expensive suit. The Darksuckers glittered, making her shadow twitch like a broken puppet.

Her voice quavered as she responded. "They, uh, they warned me about you."

"Warned?" Spid's voice grew in volume, but remained falsely smooth. "Warned? Why would they need to warn you, my dear? And why would you want to listen to their lies? All I intend to do is apply my superior intellect, logic and highly evolved moral certainty to set things right with the world. He puffed out his chest, straining the buttons on the vest and thrust one lizard-like hand high into the air. "Only I have the answers to mankind's profound dilemma. Only I can provide the ethical center from which all good things must spring."

"Dittos, boss. You're exactly right, as usual," a growl-gargled voice agreed. An even uglier figure materialized beside Spid. This one was shorter, with a dark red, scaly body and beady, leering eyes. He was squat and wore a military-type uniform with epaulets and braid. As he stared up at Spid adoringly, Abby saw some kind of green gunk bubbling from his lips.

"Yurk," Spid informed her by way of introduction.

"My assistant and leader of my armed forces." He lowered his voice and leaned toward Abby as if confiding in her. "Not too bright really, but very loyal. Like most of my followers who have found themselves converted by my unmatchable oratorical style and the inarguable rightness of everything that comes out of my mouth. Am I correct, Yurk?"

"You duh troll, dude. You duh troll." Yurk wiped a potentially monumental green booger away from his nose with the edge of his sleeve.

Spid grimaced. "I've got to stop Yurk from watching professional golf on the Shadow Stone. "Still," he sighed, "it's good to be Garboon."

"You're a troll?" Abby forgot her fear for an instant and leaned forward. "A real, like troll, like in . . . like in that billy goat story?" From this new angle, she realized she could see the wall behind Spid, and concluded that she wasn't looking at flesh and blood creatures, but very lifelike holograms created by the dark light funneling through the Chameleon Stone on the shelf. Could the Shadow Stone Spid referred to be somehow connected to the orb she'd found in the surf?

"Vicious rumors and gossip spread by—" Spid stopped and swiveled his head back and forth as if looking for enemies. Finally he sputtered, "—Delacroix. That's who, and him an outsider who wasn't even born in the mountain. And the hermit and the 'Shroomers and all kinds of other wackos. Scaring everybody with stories about how evil I am and how much destruction I'd wreak and . . ."

"You go, boss, you go." Yurk, the ogre chimed in.

"Tell it."

"They'll stop at nothing to prevent me from taking my rightful place on the great throne." The troll paced, hands clasped behind his back. Then, almost as an aside, he muttered something Abby could barely hear. "Besides, my people haven't lived under bridges and eaten children for hundreds of years."

"Really?" Abby fought her revulsion and probed, watching Spid wrinkle his face in concentration. Now that she knew he was only a hologram, wasn't actually here with her, her fear had subsided, giving way to scientific interest.

"Not since the Dark Ages. We were . . . misunderstood, you see? And so we were all banished to Beneath. All of us. Trolls. And ogres too." He gestured at Yurk, who tried to make a deep sweeping bow and promptly fell on his keester.

Spid shook his head in dismay and continued, "Banshees, demons, gronnks, skrees, gammits and—"

Here, a sly smile crept onto his face. "Well, you'll meet them all soon enough. How long, Yurk?"

The ogre consulted what looked like a kind of crude wristwatch on his arm. "Uh, let's see now, carry the seven, divide by two, subtract eight . . ."

"Any day now, Yurk." The troll tapped his foot impatiently.

"Move the decimal over four places . . . uh . . . little more than four days, boss."

Abby cringed as Spid drew back a scaly arm and prepared to backhand the stubby ogre. At the last minute, he caught his downward motion with the other hand, took a deep breath and intoned calmly. "Use the correct tool next time, Yurk. The watch appears to be . . . defective."

"Oh . . . o . . . kay, boss. Next time, for sure." The ogre shrank back out of range.

"In . . . something less than five days, my dedicated army of creatures from the land of Beneath will pour through the Skin and I will lead us in the glorious conquest of the land of Above Skin. Soon after, the United States of America will become known as the Unified Spid Association. No point in changing all the letters if we don't have to. Inefficient. Washington already wastes enough money."

Abby calculated quickly. The attack he bragged about would happen on the solstice.

"First we'll capture everyone inside Humbug Mountain and then we'll fan out. We have the men, uh creatures, and the tools, and of course," he tapped his own chest, "the leadership."

"Except Noah will stop you," Abby blurted. "And I'm going to help him."

"Noah? Noah? Don't make me laugh! There is no chance that whelp will be able to challenge the awesome power of Spid The Devious," the troll thundered.

"Hallelujah, praise Spid." Yurk bellowed, striking a threatening pose, his mottled face turning a bright crimson.

"That's enough, Yurk." Spid elbowed his cohort to the rear and turned back to Abby, lowering his voice to a soft, courtly, almost apologetic rumble. "Noah's only a boy, after all. And you, Abby, should know as well as anyone, that he's not a very, shall we say . . . focused, kind of boy. Is he?"

"He's a real airhead, boss," Yurk burbled. "You could outwit him with one lobe of your brain tied behind your back."

Like you're a rocket scientist, Abby almost screamed. But she bit back the words. As much as it irked her, she decided to play along with Spid and captain ugly, to figuratively send out a pawn to gauge their strategy.

She'd see if she could learn anything that would help her, and ultimately, Noah. "Noah, tends to be a little scattered," she admitted.

"Scattered would be an excellent way to describe him." The troll smiled. Abby supposed he was trying to infuse some warmth into the conversation, but he succeeded only in making his face lopsided. "And in a little more than four days, he will face the challenge of his life. If indeed, he lives to make it to the Skin in time.

"He'll make it." Abby heard her voice ring off the rock. Behind her, the Darksuckers glowed like tiny suns.

"Ah, loyalty. And love for your brother. Both admirable qualities, Abby. Truly. You are a paragon. I have, in my own way, revered you from afar, you know."

"You have?" This didn't sound good. Creepy, even. Could he, through his Shadow Stone, have been watching her at home? While she slept and ate or even . . . a shiver of revulsion ran down her spine . . . while she took a bath.

Did this ugly, evil brute have plans to kidnap her, maybe even torture her?

"Oh yes." Spid rubbed his webbed hands together. "I've been able to observe you, through the Chameleon Stone, since you began the fulfillment of the prophecy by plucking it from the surf."

"That's disgusting. You have no right." She shuddered and pulled the blanket around her. Darksuckers gathered closer to her, laying a more intense light across her shoulders.

Spid put a hand on his chest and took a step back. "Miss Keene, I am appalled that you would think I would take advantage of the magical link between my Shadow Stone and the orb which you possess for any other than the most noble motives." Spid offered a sly smile and raised one bushy eyebrow. It reminded her of John Belushi from that old movie, *Animal House.* "You can be assured that I always closed my eyes at any, um, indelicate moment."

"Peeping Tom," Abby mumbled. "Pervert."

"What was that?" Spid's voice held a tone of menace.

"Speak up." He took two steps toward her.

Forgetting the image was only a projection, Abby felt a cold chill of fear. "I, uh said . . . 'Chameleon Stone, you've subverted it."

Spid stared hard at her and scratched his head with one claw.

"Uppitty little thing, ain't she, boss?" The ogre licked his lips and wiped another green gob away from his nose with his sleeve.

"She is indeed, Yurk," Spid agreed. "But she'll learn to respect my superior powers soon enough. Learn that male domination is a part of the true word my minions will spread."

"Dittos, boss. Mega dittos."

Anger overrode the last of the fear Abby felt. "So what are you doing here? Did you just come to gloat or what?"

Spid raised one eyebrow again and put an even softer, more wheedling tone into his voice. "Gloat? No, indeed, there is no need to dwell on my upcoming victory. I came to propose a battle of wits with you. I have observed your sharp powers of logic and deduction, your extensive vocabulary, your outstanding visualization skills."

Abby forced herself not to react to the flattery. "So?"

"Yurk! Bring out the board." The ogre snapped to attention as Spid snapped his fingers.

"Coming right up, boss." The squat figure of Spid's henchbeast faded into the blue light, finally disappearing entirely.

"Do you like word games, Abby?"

She thought about it for a moment. Was this some kind of a trick question? "You mean like unscrambling words? Like in the sign over the door of the storehouse?"

"You mean *Thela stpla ceyo ulook?*" Spid's voice took on a puzzled tone as he rubbed his chin.

"Yes, The Last Place You Look."

Spid's jaw dropped open for a moment. "What?"

"The last place you look. If you squash it together and put in spaces at the right places, it spells The Last Place You Look." The Darksuckers twinkled around her, making her shadow dance.

An astonished expression splayed across Spid's face. A finger wrote imaginary words in the air. She heard him mumble, "The Last Place You Look."

"Pretty simple, isn't it?"

Spid sniffed. "Of course. I knew it. Of course. I just wanted to make sure you really knew."

"Sure you did." Abby felt a sudden jolt of confidence.

Maybe Spid wasn't all that sharp either. Maybe his belief in his brainpower was his fatal flaw. Plus, the fact that he hadn't overheard her when she discovered what the words meant, told her that Spid wasn't watching her every minute.

With a loud popping sound, Yurk's image reappeared from the blue funnel, clutching a large game board to his chest.

"Ah, yes, here we are." Spid rubbed his hands together. The ogre set the board up on a sort of tripod arrangement and produced a large leather bag, cinched closed with drawstrings, which made a clacking sound when he shook it up and down.

Curiosity got the best of Abby; she slid out of bed and edged closer to the two grotesque figures. "Why, that looks like Scrab—"

"No, don't say it!" Spid interrupted.

"Why not?" Puzzled, Abby glanced at the board again.

"It does. It looks just like Scrab—"

"No! Do not say that word!" Spid made a chopping motion with his hand. "Spid the Devious, the Grand Exalted Garboon of Beneath, the all-seeing and all-knowing ruler of the armies of darkness and soon to be the conqueror of all of Above Skin, quakes at only one thing."

What thing? Abby stepped closer. This could be the way to help Noah.

"Lawsuits. Right boss?" Yurk croaked.

"Absolutely, my churlish one. I don't want to get into copyright infringement litigation."

Abby sighed. This was silly. "But it sure looks a lot like—"

"Superficially," Spid interrupted hurriedly, "perhaps, but there are major differences; innovations I have personally added to provide more depth to the game, to make it more challenging to my undescribable mental skills."

Abby sighed, tugged the quilt from the bed and wrapped it around her. If he played like he talked, they could be here all night. "Indescribable," she corrected him. "What?"

"Indescribable would be the correct usage."

"Oh. Of course. I knew that."

"I know. You just wanted to see if I knew. Sure."

She rolled her eyes as Spid nodded. "So if you don't call this game Scrab—"

"Put a sock in it, kid." Yurk growled.

"Anyway, if you don't call it that, what do you call it?"

Spid took a step forward and made an imaginary frame with his fingers. "The game's name is every bit as original and descriptive as the play is fast-moving and intriguing. Which is understandable, since it was I, Spid, who invented it."

Modesty is not this guy's strong suit, Abby thought.

"Soon," Spid continued, "every day, every man woman and child in the world, when they're not paying homage to me, will be playing—" he paused dramatically "—Spiddle."

"Spiddle?" Abby asked, trying to keep a straight face.

"Spiddle," Spid confirmed.

"And you think every man, woman and child in the world is going to *want* to play a game called Spiddle?"

"If they don't want to die screaming, they will," Yurk croaked.

"Well, of course the game *will* be mentioned in the decree of martial law," Spid confirmed. "So, would you like to play?

Abby perused the board once again. "Uh, I guess. What are the rules?"

"The rules? Oh, don't worry about those. I'll just tell you as we go along, shall I?" Spid's voice reeked with false heartiness. "Okay?"

The Darksuckers behind her flickered. "Um, okay," Abby decided. After all, it was only a game. And Spid was only a hologram.

"Good, then," he attempted another smile, making the wart on his cheek jiggle. "We'll play. Only one thing remains to be decided."

"What's that?"

Spid narrowed his eyes and rubbed his hands together once more. "What shall we play for?"

Chapter Fourteen

This sleep was deep, dreamless and restful. He emerged slowly, aware that he was waking, aware that waking meant leaving the safety of sleep. A gentle but persistent hand shook his shoulder and a soothing woman's voice drew him toward consciousness, toward responsibility.

"Time to wake up, Noah." The voice reminded him again of his mother. She used to tease him about how hard he was to wake up, how much he loved his sleep.

"Just let me sleep five minutes more. Then I'll get up." He mumbled.

"No, Noah. Now. You must be back on your pathway soon. Your friend is waiting. And time is very short."

He dragged his eyelids up, noting that this time they didn't scrape and his vision was clear and sharp. He looked up into the twinkling eyes of a woman with honey-blonde hair streaked with silver and a reassuring smile.

She seemed to be about the age his mother had been when she'd—

"Up and at 'em now," the woman coaxed. How do you feel?"

Noah took stock. Actually, he felt much better; a little stiff, but no longer feverish. He slid a hand down his leg and ran his fingers along the spot where the mold-monster's spit had burned him. Other than a sort of rough place on the skin, the wound had disappeared. The swelling had gone down too and he couldn't feel any soreness. How long had he been here? "I'm, uh, okay."

"Good," the woman continued in a no-nonsense tone.

"I've made you some breakfast. After you eat, you can go down to the water and bathe. You've gotten a little whiffy." She said this with a tone of amusement. "When you get out of bed, chuck your drawers over there in the corner so I can wash them along with everything else. She gestured to a robe that hung from a hook by the door. "Throw that on and come on out for breakfast. After your bath, Deidre will be along to chart your course."

"Deidre?" The girl with the two-pronged sword? "My course?"

"My daughter," the woman said in a voice both proud and wistful. "My headstrong and fearless daughter, I might add. She's decided to accompany you on the next leg of your journey. To the Temple of Cheltnor. It will be very dangerous."

Noah sat up and ran his hand through egg-beatered hair. "Listen, everyone keeps talking about some kind of a journey. I don't want to go, okay? I just want to find my sister and get out of here."

"And you will." The woman seemed to look into a distance inside her head. "If all goes as I hope." She stood, shaking out her long, quilted skirt. But you will need an ally. Someone strong and who knows the way. The prophecy allows for you to take another companion, and Deidre insists she be the one." The woman frowned. "And when Deidre insists, you might as well be arguing with a shitake tree."

"A what? That's a kind of mushroom. Mushrooms don't grow on trees."

She laughed. "Not where you come from, no. You'll find out what I mean when Deidre takes you through the forest."

Noah shook his head. It was all too much. Everything he'd already faced seemed like a distant dream, unreal and shrouded by mist. Surely, with all the twists and turns he'd made, he couldn't be that far from home. This woman got in here somehow. So did Deidre.

Why couldn't he just get out the same simple way? Without going on a journey. Without meeting strange creatures like— "Uh-Oh! Is he all right?"

"Quite exhausted, I'm afraid." The woman raised her eyebrows. "But I think, with another dose of distilled wormroot and freemish blossom, we can get him up and ready for your departure this afternoon. Now, hurry."

Noah waited until he was certain she'd left before he flexed his legs and arms, stumbled from the bed, put on the robe, belted it tightly and then stepped out of his undershorts. She was right. He'd begun to smell like Uh-oh.

She fed him a huge breakfast, featuring blue pancakes with lumps of some strange kind of nut or grain, scrambled eggs with cheese and a delicious juice that reminded him of a cross between apple and strawberry.

His appetite had returned and he polished off five pancakes and three glasses of the juice.

"Not to rush you, but . . ." she handed him his clean clothes, his pack, a rough-weave towel and a bar of what looked like homemade soap. It was green and gray and smelled like freshly cut grass. Smiling, she pushed him toward the door of what he realized was a sod house.

Sod? Down here? Another mystery.

"Just take the left-hand fork of the path, walk about a quarter mile and turn right at the oatmeal tree," she told him. "Careful, the slope to the wish pool is pretty steep."

Noah's head swam. "Oatmeal tree? Wish pool?"

"After you take your bath, make a wish. It just might come true. As for the oatmeal tree, you'll see when you get there. But don't eat any. It's poisonous until it's cooked."

"Okay. Thanks for the warning." He turned to go, then stopped and said, "Thank you. For everything."

"You're quite welcome. I ask only one favor in return."

"What is it?"

"Later. When you meet with trouble, keep an eye on Deidre. She's very, very brave and very, very able and," her frown betrayed her concern, "sometimes a little impetuous."

Noah pushed his doubts aside and said what she wanted to hear. "I'll do my best."

Her eyes locked on his and he felt a sizzle, like electricity, in the back of his head. "I know you will."

He nodded, started for the door again, then turned back. "You saved my life and I haven't even asked your name."

"Names can shift like the breeze," she laughed. "But I'm called Eve."

"Just Eve?"

"Just Eve."

"How did you get here? Why do you stay underground? Why don't you go," he pointed toward a wall, "out into the other world."

Her eyes surveyed a distance he couldn't see. "I'm in many worlds, Noah. This is just the one I'm occupying at the moment."

"Huh?"

"You see, Noah," she locked her eyes on his again and he felt the sizzle, now at the top of his head. "There are those who will tell you I am a witch."

* * * *

Self-consciously, Noah looked around, then peeled the robe away and stepped into the water. "Brrr uhrrr uhrrr," he cried out. Teeth chattering, he forced himself to take three more steps into the deep blue pool, going in up to his bellybutton. Quickly, he started to lather up with the soap, wishing all the while that the water were warmer.

As he scrubbed his arms, the surface of the water glimmered and swirled, then began to steam. Suddenly, it was almost too hot.

"The wishing pool, huh?" The water rippled around him. "I wonder if I wished for Abby and me to be out of Humbug Mountain and back home, if it would grant the wish?" He stopped scrubbing and concentrated, fixing a picture of Abby and himself walking down the driveway to their house, Dad hurtling off the porch to greet them.

"It only grants small wishes." Deidre's voice echoed around him.

Aware of his nakedness, Noah dropped the soap and splayed his fingers across his groin.

"Warmer water, a candy bar, your favorite song," Deidre continued. "If you want something major, you've got to be prepared to make it happen yourself."

Noah glanced behind him to see her standing on an overhanging rock a few yards away. He squatted, duck-walking toward deeper water. His feet slipped and he went under.

"Oh, get over yourself, Noah," Deidre told him as he emerged flailing at the surface. "I'm not trying to scope you out or anything like that."

Angry, Noah didn't answer. He treaded water, both hands anchored again over his groin. "How's the water?"

Ignore her, he thought. She'll get tired of tormenting you and go away. He kicked harder, gasping for breath and turned his back on her.

"Hey, you know, I could use a bath too. Maybe I'll peel off my clothes and jump in with you. Here goes my shirt!"

Heat flooded up Noah's neck and onto his face. He spun toward her.

"Made you look." Deidre threw her head back and laughed.

"Very funny." Noah panted. His legs were tiring fast.

She stopped laughing and fixed a steady gaze on him. "You need to lighten up, Noah. Laugh while you can. Laugh now. Because there's lots of serious stuff on the way. Life and death stuff." With that, she spun on her heel, jumped from the rock and started up the slope toward the cottage.

"I'll laugh when something's funny." He yelled after her.

"Fy-ine." Noah heard her trill. "By the way, nice buns, Noah."

Fuming, Noah waited until her throaty giggle faded completely, then retrieved the soap and finished his bath. He'd get even, he decided. He'd get even when she least expected it. Meanwhile, he'd pretend this never happened.

The thought of revenge made him feel stronger. After drying off, he got into his clean clothes and even hauled his toothbrush out of his pack, found the toothpaste and brushed his teeth. As Abby would say, he thought, he "scrubbed the moss off his chompers." He felt confident he'd find her soon. The witch had said he would.

Witches knew stuff like that, didn't they? They could read the future with crystal balls. Or was it gypsies that did that? Whatever. He combed his hair, tied his shoes and set off for Eve's cottage, whistling a little syncopated tune. He stopped to catch his breath at the oatmeal tree, a tall, broad, wide-limbed growth that did indeed have the texture of a huge stack of raw breakfast cereal. He was careful not to touch it.

When he arrived at the small sod house, he found Eve waiting in front. His gray, stumpy friend leaned against the wall beside her. Uh-oh's eyes were sunken back in his head and his dreadlocks hung limply from his head like tired black worms.

Noah felt like hugging Uh-oh, but decided that might be a little geeky. He took his hand instead, shaking it rapidly. "Thank you, Uh-oh. Thank you for throwing the rock at the mold-monster. Thank you for carrying me here."

"You're welcome, Noah." Uh-oh rasped. Something resembling a smile crossed his face.

"So you *can* talk." Noah felt his heart leap with excitement. "You understand what I'm saying and you can answer me?"

"You're welcome, Noah." Uh-oh repeated.

"Welcome, Noah."

Noah sighed, defeated again. Uh-oh must just pick up bits and pieces, he decided. Or else he's holding back. But why would he do that? Unless he doesn't trust me yet.

As he mulled that over, Deidre strode around the corner of the house. She now wore an outfit that resembled lightweight armor: loose-fitting pants covered in what looked like tortoise shell platelets and a top made of the same material. Her sword hung from a belt at her waist, prongs up, and she carried a pair of leather and metal harnesses and a second two-tined sword in its own scabbard.

Eve raised her eyebrows, walked over to kiss her daughter on the forehead and went to the door. "Play nice, Deidre. I'll be inside," she said. "Putting your provisions together."

"Thanks, Mom." Deidre called as her mother disappeared into the cottage. She handed the long-handled twin-headed weapon and a harness to Noah.

"This is a sonic sword, also called a battle fork."

"What do you do? Hit people with them, or stab them or what?"

Deidre made a "you're too dumb to live," face at him as he drew the sword from its scabbard and examined it, feeling its heft and balance. The shaft seemed made out of some kind of light metal with a leather strip wrapped around its center. The prongs were metal too, not sharp-edged, each a different color, one kind of brass-like and the other more bluish.

"This is how you wear the decibelt." Deidre strapped on her harness so the circular metal plate protected her chest. "Come on, hustle up," she told him, "we don't have time to waste."

With Uh-oh's assistance, Noah strapped on the harness, pulling the leather straps tight across his chest and shoulders.

"What the sonic sword is, Noah," Deidre instructed, "is a gigantic, highly sensitive tuning fork." She thrust the blunt end of the shaft against the metal breastplate with a clang. Noah heard a low, escalating hum emanate from her weapon. Copying her, he activated his own battle fork by whacking it against the metal. It began to vibrate.

He struggled to hold it upright. Uh-oh's eyes widened and he scuttled away a few yards.

"Alright, pay attention, drum boy." Deidre stabbed at the air with the sonic sword. "And I'll show you how you can knock down a charging wormonocerous with this thing. If you can learn the right moves."

Noah gripped the sonic sword, his arms thrumming. I'll learn them, soldier girl, he thought. And then I'll use them to kick your butt. He smiled. Revenge might come sooner than he'd thought.

Chapter Fifteen

"What do I get if I *win*?" Abby's voice quavered as she asked Spid the question. "Can Noah and I go home? Will you let us leave the mountain?"

"Ah, but if I had the power, I would do that anyway, Abby. Win or lose." Spid tried what she thought he fancied as an empathetic smile. It made his face look like an evil prune with ears. "As little chance as there is of your brother thwarting my designs to make the world a better and, may I say, more Spidlike place, ahem . . ." He paused, his mouth twisting into a frown. "Nevertheless, I would send you home in a trice, if I could. Half a trice, even. But fate has decreed the challenge must be met before the assembled multitudes at the Skin. So there you have it."

There I have what? Abby stared at the holograms, trying to make sense of what she'd heard. He'd let us go if he could, but he can't until the challenge is met. And what part would Noah play in this challenge at the Skin? What could he possibly do? His only real talent was drumming. "So why should I play Scrab—"

"Spiddle!" Spid sputtered. "It's Spiddle. And why should you play with me? Well, because by using the powers of both the Shadow Stone and your Chameleon Orb, I can allow you to see your brother, to reassure yourself that he is indeed alive and well and, as ill-conceived as it might be, following the path to our final confrontation."

Abby felt tears sting her eyes. She'd have to play the game. If she could see Noah, figure out where he was, talk to him, maybe she could devise a plan to get them both out of this madhouse.

As if he had read her mind, Spid broke in.

"Unfortunately, you will not be able to speak with him, you understand. Just observe him." The troll sighed heavily. "He's in is an area where we have reception problems."

"Reception problems? Magical stones have reception problems?"

Spid sniffed in disgust. "How little you mere humans know. Magical stones are not unlike cell phones, Abby."

Abby nodded. She still had to take her shot, even if she could only see him. "And if I lose?" Fear of the answer tightened her stomach. What kind of twisted thing could Spid have in mind?

"You could fill a small employment need. I've had, er, recruiting problems. I need someone to act as," he paused and stroked his chin as he thought, "researcher. Yes, that's it. A researcher."

Abby didn't like his manner. He sounded sneaky, like somebody trying to sell her something she didn't want or need. "Researcher?"

"Exactly." He rubbed his hands together. "Let me explain. By now, you have surely noticed that the light around us," he gestured to the roof of the cavern, "is provided by living creatures."

She nodded. "I suspected."

"Indeed. They are called the Zezzue. Or, in your language, Darksuckers."

Zezzue. The troll pronounced their name like saysyou. Abby practiced it in her mind. "Why are they called Darksuckers?"

"Because that is literally what they do. You have probably learned in your school that darkness is the absence of light, am I correct?"

"Yes, although the nature of light is one of science's continuing mysteries." She almost giggled. She sounded serious and scholarly like her teacher, Mr. Brinman.

"Your experts are in error," Spid declared. "Darkness is, in and of itself, an entity, a living presence. It exists in nature in varying quantities."

The concept boggled Abby's mind. "You mean . . ."

"Precisely. Certain things can literally destroy areas of the darkness. Fire, electric lights, the sun, the moon. But as soon as light is extinguished, darkness instantaneously reproduces and reclaims its territory."

Could Spid be correct? "And the Zezzue?"

"Can inhale many, many times their own body weight in darkness."

Abby looked up at the light on the wall and ceiling around her. It glowed a sort of amber color, then shifted to a more reddish tint. She wished she could get closer to them. "Where do they exhale it? The darkness?"

An eyebrow went up. Spid cleared his throat. "An excellent question. One I am hoping you can find out for me through, er, um, research. There is reputed to be an immense catacomb of chambers, a maze within a sealed cavern, somewhere in the mountain. According to legend, the Zezzue, at regular intervals, fly in through an entrance only they can access and expel their accumulated darkness."

Abby felt a sudden chill. All that darkness. She remembered her Snoopy nightlight. Mom bought it for her second birthday. She still used it every night at home.

Again, it felt like Spid had intercepted her inner thoughts, probed her mind. "You are not alone in your fear of darkness, Miss Keene. It is shared by many." He gnawed at the tip of one green fingernail. "And, in the Realm of Exponential Darkness, if indeed it exists, what the Zezzue exhale is compressed a million, billion times. It is darkness so intense it swallows all the other senses. In its presence, it is told, you cannot hear yourself breathe, feel your heartbeat, or smell your own fear."

"Yegggh." Abby jumped at the gargly growl of Yurk. "Stop it boss, you're scaring me."

Spid ignored his toady. "And there you have it, Miss Keene – the reason I need your, er, assistance. I don't want my troops accidentally wandering into the Realm of Exponential Darkness. It would be detrimental to them, and it would upset the Zezzue. They are very important to my future plans."

"So what you want me to do is watch where they go, spy on them."

"Never!" Spid took a step back. "Merely observe and report, that is all. The Zezzue communicate with Delacroix. And with the hermit."

"The who?"

"Oh, that's right, you've yet to meet that charming individual. That will come soon enough. At any rate, the Zezzue may decide to convey information to you. And should you lose the Spiddle game—"

"You want to know everything they tell me." Abby finished his sentence. "Well, I won't have anything to do with your evil plans for the world. I won't help you defeat Noah, and open the Skin and conquer the earth and make everyone play Spiddle. I won't!" She stomped her foot.

Spid sighed again. "Naturally. Of course you won't. Your ideals and loyalty prevent you from taking part in my grand plan. Besides," his fleshy lips pushed in and out, "I really don't require your assistance in that matter. That situation is totally under control. All I ask is your help gathering research data about the Zezzue. When you lose the game."

"Spying." She insisted. "*If* I lose the game."

"If you must." Spid shared an oily smile. "But only for the best motives. For the good of the world. Trust me."

Her mind raced. Did this grotesque, ugly egomaniac really have the resources to conquer the world? Could he read her mind? Could he tell if she lied? It was worth a gamble. If she lost the game. "Just the Zezzue? What they do and say? That's all?"

"Correct."

Okay, he hadn't read her mind that time. "All right then, fine. Let's play Scrab—"

Spid held one thick finger to his lips. "Shhh. Remember. The lawyers."

"Oh, right. Spiddle then. How do we get started?"

"Yurk!" Spid howled for his hench-monster.

The ogre stepped forward with the canvas sack, cleared his throat and began to growl the rules. "Each player draws nineteen letters. The value of each letter is written on the tile. After you have put a word down on the board, the mystery spaces beneath the letters will light up with bonus values and your score will be posted on the automatic scoreboard." Yurk gestured at an oblong black area that had appeared with the names Spid and Abby written in glowing script at the top of two columns.

"After you play, you draw letters to bring you back up to the original nineteen. When the bag is empty and one player uses all of his or her tiles, the game ends. The player with tiles remaining must subtract the total from his or her score."

"Very good, Yurk. Shall we begin, Miss Keene?"

Spid took the bag from the ogre and offered it to Abby."

She reached for it, then realized she couldn't touch it because it was merely a projection. "How can I—"

"Just say the word draw," Spid smiled. Your letters will appear in front of you."

"Draw."

As Spid had said, the bag opened and nineteen tiles flashed rapidly onto a three-dimensional tray that appeared in front of her. The letters were a motley assortment, fairly evenly divided between vowels and consonants. The most striking difference she noticed between this and a conventional Scrab—she caught herself—that other game, was the value of the tiles. For example, the U counted as seven points instead of one. And the Z was only two. P's apparently were highly thought of, with a value of seventeen points. She had several E's, ranging in value from four to eight points.

Confused, she studied her letters while Spid commanded "draw" and got his own set.

"I'm sure you've noted that you are unable to rearrange the letters by hand because they aren't physically in the same space you occupy," Spid offered.

"All you need do is point at one and then at the new spot you want it to go. When you're ready to lay them down, just visualize the word and the place on the board and Voila!"

Spid pronounced the French word Vo-ill-uh instead of Vwoy-lah.' Abby considered correcting him, but checked herself. No need to irritate him, not if she wanted to find out what had happened to Noah. Following his instructions, she tried rearranging the letters to form possible words. Finally, she decided on one. "Who goes first?"

"Ladies, Miss Keene." The troll gestured toward the board. "Fire at will."

"Does it matter where I set the first one down?"

"Not in the slightest."

Visualizing the word P-E-R-A-D-V-E-N-T-U-R-E, she examined the board. This was a tough game. Not only were there more letters from which to make words, but you didn't know what bonus you'd get until after you'd laid down your letters. The squares on this board were all the same gray color, unlike the other game where colored squares announced the availability of extra points.

Finally, she made her choice. To her amazement, the letters instantly flew from her tray in single file formation and plopped down on the exact spot she'd pictured.

Both Spid and Yurk twisted their heads down to examine the word. Yurk used a sausage-sized finger to scratch his forehead.

Lights lit up under three of the letters and numbers rolled up on the scoreboard—three hundred and forty seven points for her eleven-letter word. She got two triple word scores and one sextuple letter score on the D, which already had a nine-point value.

The Troll hissed in annoyance. Yurk produced a thick book and began to thumb frantically through the pages.

"Is that a dictionary? Does that mean you're going to challenge?" Abby hadn't heard Yurk mention challenges. Were they allowed?

"Ahem, well, I was considering . . ." Spid paused and appeared to be deep in thought. Finally, he decided. "I think not. Not this time. But I should have Yurk explain the rule about challenges."

"Oh boy. Oh boy, oh boy," the ogre growled. "Good move, Boss. Peradventure *is* a word. It means," he pointed down at the page, "perhaps, maybe, a possibility."

"Of course." With a self-satisfied smirk, Spid prodded Yurk to continue. "I knew that. The challenge rule, Yurk."

"Right, Boss." Yurk took a step forward and droned.

"Each player shall have one challenge of the other player's played word without penalty. After that, an unsuccessful challenge shall lead to the challenger having their choice of being immediately thrown into the river of molten mildew, or being eaten alive by giant loamsters."

The ogre drew in a deep breath and then rapidly and in a very small voice, tacked on a disclaimer. "Unless aforementioned challenger is Spid, the Grand Exalted Garboon of Beneath."

Abby gasped. "But that's not fair!"

"Fair?" Spid did the Belushi eyebrow thing at her again and shrugged. "All right. To show you how flexible

I am," he paused and squinted down at her word again. "I will waive the death penalty and instead stipulate that the second unsuccessful challenge, whether by you—an ordinary, if somewhat advanced mortal girl—or by me, the Grand Exalted Garboon of the—" Spid drew a deep breath. "Well, you get the idea. At any rate, that wrongly made second challenge will result in immediate victory by the party whose honesty and intellect was assaulted. Is that fair enough?"

Sure, thought Abby. If you considered any game where one of the participants could change the rules as the game went along as fair. "I suppose," she answered.

"Your turn." She looked at the bag. "Draw." Seven new letters flew from the bag. This time she got a Z, which scored only four points and three V's which ranged from two to eighteen points. Very strange.

Spid studied the board for a moment, pointing his finger at different letters and shuffling them around on his tray. Finally, he nodded and a river of letters flowed onto the board. Using the V from her word Peradventure, the troll had laid out a perpendicular word that looked like utter garble to Abby. G-V-L-E-E-X-B-M-A-O-G-R-N-TH.

Fifteen letters in all. She looked at the board and saw six spaces light up under various letters. The scoreboard blinked and brought up Spid's score. Seven hundred and eighty-nine points. He'd hit two sextuple letters, three double words and the eleven point value of the X had been squared.

"Horsehockey!" She yelled her father's favorite word for something he thought was a lie or nonsense. "That's not a word."

"So, then Abby, is this a . . ." he paused and gave her an evil leer, "challenge?"

"Of course it is. Everybody knows that can't possibly be a word." Even as she said it, a weevil of a premonition gnawed at her brain. She heard her mother's voice.

"Impulsiveness always leads to trouble. Don't ever forget, Abby."

"Yurk!" Spid thundered. "The dictionary."

The Ogre quickly flipped through the pages and found the G's. "Here it is, boss. You spelled it exactly right, G-L-E-E-X-B-M-A-O-G-R-N-T-H. A sound made by a charging Vorkal as it steps on a slippery mound of Rimosaurus droppings."

"Just as I suspected," Spid smirked again and examined his fingernails.

"If you'd added L-Y you could have made it an adverb, boss," Yurk noted solemnly. He turned to Abby and scrunched his face into a smile. "That's one, brat."

"What kind of dictionary is that?" Abby snapped. "That word is not listed anywhere I've ever seen."

Yurk turned the cover of the book toward her so she could see it. It read *Spid and Wagnall's Unabridged Dictionary of Modern English and Beneathese.*

"Beneathese? We're allowing words in this other language?"

"It's the language the whole world will be speaking some day very soon, Miss Keene. Our language. Right, Yurk?"

"Vrgamisptk, boss." This appeared to be some kind of private joke. Both Spid and his ogre sidekick slapped their thighs and laughed uproariously.

To Abby, Yurk's comment sounded like someone talking with a mouth full of oatmeal. She fought back her anger, reminding herself she hadn't expected Spid to play fair, not for a minute. "All right, I've used my challenge.

By the way, how do you pronounce that word?" She pointed at the board.

Yurk consulted the dictionary again. "It's pronounced Geks-Moh-rith."

"In other words, just like it's spelled, eh, Yurk?" Spid smirked and the two of them fell into a third small fit of laughter. "Our language can be a bit tricky, Miss Keene. Some letters are not always pronounced. And others are pronounced differently than you might think. Draw."

Letters flew from the bag.

Abby felt her hopes of winning at Spiddle diminish greatly. But she had to continue. What other choice did she have? And so they played on, for a very long while. Abby had no way of telling how long, but it felt like several hours. As she'd feared, despite her valiant efforts, Spid built a huge lead. Several times, he used all of his letters, a move Yurk notified her, paid off with a thousand point bonus. She searched the far corners of her mind for long words, but found out they didn't always score big. It all depended on which bonus lights came on.

Biting her tongue several times, Abby fought off the urge to shout "horsehockey" again. Often, it seemed that Spid was just throwing letters down at random, knowing she would be afraid to let Yurk go to the dictionary.

Second challenge and it's over, she thought. I become a spy for a power-mad troll.

Surprisingly, despite having mostly ignored her plays, Spid did challenge her once, when she laid down the word H-E-G-E-M-O-N-I-U-S and earned herself a nice six thousand points. The M had been a seventeen point tile and it fell on a value cubed square. The six thousand had drawn her to within five hundred of Spid and he'd squirmed and picked at his nose with one long green fingernail. Finally, in a loud and confident voice, he challenged. Yurk looked up the word and shrank back as he gave Spid the bad news.

"Are you positive, Yurk?" Spid roared at the hapless ogre. "Are you saying that The Grand Exalted Garboon of the Imperial Kingdom of Beneath, a personage who controls your fate, can decide whether you will be allowed to live or die—that I, Spid, the son of Glaub the Wrathful and Dismalia the queen of the gammits, has made an incorrect challenge?"

"It, uh, appears so, boss." Yurk looked as though he might bolt into the dark cone and disappear as Spid loomed over him, his normally purple-cast skin a bright violet, his breath sounding like a steam engine that had been over-stoked. "It says here that it means leadership or dominance, especially in a nation or—"

"Zip it, Yurk!" Spid bellowed.

"Prounounced hedge-uh-moe-nee-us," Yurk babbled.

"Maybe the dictionary is wrong, boss."

"The-dictionary-is-not-wrong," Spid muttered from between clenched teeth. "I wrote it. I should know." He stomped to the back of the image and Abby wondered if he was about to end their game, go back Beneath and rob her of a chance to see Noah.

"Listen," she offered, "I could put down a different word if . . ."

"No. No, of course not." Spid huffed. "I wouldn't think of it. I knew hegemony was a word. I just thought perhaps there was a D in it." He seemed to regain a little control, his skin returning to its original purple. "I, um, thought it only gentlemanly and sportsmanlike to even the challenge count to make a game out of it. I thought you looked a little downcast."

"Humor him," a little voice counseled her. "Okay, thanks. It's your play."

What seemed like several hours later, Abby saw the bag fold itself up after Spid drew his letters. Yes, she thought. If I can find a word that uses all nineteen of my tiles, I can end the game and he'll have to deduct his letters. She peeked at the board and her heart fell. She was more than nine-thousand points behind. 97,384 to

106,415. There was no way to catch him. Unless she got incredibly lucky.

Once again, Spid seemed to read her mind. "You've played well, Miss Keene. There is no shame in losing to the finest mind on the planet."

Finest mind! She'd almost been ready to consider throwing herself on his mercy, asking for a chance to check on Noah, even though she'd lost. But Spid's smirking face made her clench her fists. She would finish the game, play it all the way out. Nobody could say Abby Keene was a quitter. She studied the letters for what seemed to be hours, working them back and forth in her mind. It seemed hopeless. Fourteen letters was the maximum she could arrange into a valid combination and there was no way the word would score her enough.

She glanced up at Spid and Yurk who had bent toward each other and carried on a hushed conversation in the Beneathese language that sounded like words chopped up in a blender. The light in the room seemed to dim and flicker. She rubbed her eyes. The light flickered again.

She tipped her head and stared at the ceiling directly above her. Then she rubbed her eyes again. The Zezzue had swirled and eddied into different colors and formed into letters—the exact same letters that Abby had left.

The lights switched and shuffled until they stopped suddenly, forming a word unlike anything Abby recognized. More like the strange combinations Spid had been laying down.

Actually, she realized, she was one letter short. She smiled at the lights, slid her eyes to the board, and spotted a place where she could lay her letters out, tying them to an X in one of Spid's words to form her own.

She hesitated and tilted her head to gaze up at the Zezzue again. They were trying to help her. What did they know? This strange clump of letters couldn't possibly be a word, could it? On the other hand, Spid had built an insurmountable lead with a steady stream of words that made her want to holler "horsehockey."

Abby glanced at the lights. They twinkled. She made her decision. Pointing at the tiles on her rack, she moved them around until they took on the exact order written by the lights. As soon as she had arranged them correctly, the lights twinkled again, then scattered. Looking up, she saw Spid and Yurk were still in a huddle. "Here goes," she whispered. She visualized the location on the board and the tiles played follow-the-leader and dropped into their proper places.

The scoreboard flashed and the numbers rolled. Spid and Yurk looked up from their conversation and down at the word Abby had placed on the board.

T-I-R-K-D-E-S-C-X-O-S-L-K-N-U-R-P-L-V. Abby felt a little less confident as the mystery squares lit up and her score blinked under her name. She'd done pretty well, with three triple words, a cubed eleven point K and a quadruple seventeen for the third Z. Her final score flashed on the screen. 106,381. If Spid had more than thirty-four points on the letters on his rack, she would win.

"Challenge." Spid hissed, pointing down at Abby's word. "Most obviously, the last gasp of a desperate player. I challenge."

Abby felt her stomach clench as Yurk flipped dictionary pages at high speed, looking for the word.

Spid glared at her, rubbing his hands together.

The ogre stabbed at a listing in the huge book, pulled his hand back and rubbed his eyes vigorously, then found the place again. His tiny beady eyes darted back and forth from the page to Spid and back to the page. Brackish perspiration began to dribble down his forehead and across the bridge of his mashed-potato nose.

"Well, Yurk!" Spid ordered. "Tell this girl her bluff has failed and let's get on with it. I have things to do, demons to see, torture to supervise."

"Errr." Yurk's usual growl was reduced to a distant rumble. "Uhhh."

Spid had returned his attention to Abby. "Be sure to try to get up very close to Delacroix when he's talking to the Zezzue. That way you can—"

"Err. It's a word, boss." The ogre whispered. Above Abby, the lights twinkled at high speed.

"—find out how they manage to—" Spid turned and stared at his hench-beast. His jaw dropped open, his eyes widened in amazement and Abby heard him draw a ragged breath. "Ridiculous! It can't be."

"I know, boss. But it's in the book, boss. Look. Right here." He pushed the book toward Spid, who snatched it from him and scanned the page. His complexion began to change, first going to an ash white, then rapidly mottling with a reddish tinge.

Abby scurried to her bed and shrank back into the far corner, watching Spid grow angrier and angrier, looking as though he might explode at any minute.

"Look here, boss." Yurk pointed to Spid's letters, trying to make sure he wouldn't be the target. "If you wouldnta challenged, you would have beat her."

"Don't you ever tell me I'm wrong!" Spid thumped Yurk alongside his head, then became a raging volcano, spewing what must have been dirty words in his language, hitting Yurk again and again. Abby pulled her quilt around her, grateful that the two beasts were not really in the room with her. Tears welled in her eyes. She'd never get to see Noah now.

Finally, after what seemed like an eternity, Spid appeared to calm down. "So, Miss Keene," he intoned.

"It seems you have won a battle. Just a skirmish, really, but still . . ." He put both arms out to the side palms up in a gesture of acceptance.

I should apologize, Abby thought. Maybe then he'll let me see my brother. "I—"

"No!" Spid pointed down at her. "You will not speak. The time for words has passed. You won at Spiddle and you will be able to observe your brother as I promised. There." He gestured to the Chameleon Stone. "But mark my words, Miss Keene. We will meet again in—" He snapped his fingers at Yurk, who was gingerly rubbing his head where Spid thumped it. Scowling at his boss, Yurk pulled out his calculator.

"Four days, nine hours, twenty-two minutes and fourteen seconds, boss," he groused.

"And, Miss Keene, the next time we meet, it will be face-to-face." Spid's voice dripped menace. "And I will hold the three stones: your Chameleon, my Shadow, and of course, the Methuselah which your brother has been sent to procure. With their combined power, I will rule absolutely. And there will be no mercy. Then, and only then, we will speak of winners and losers."

Abby watched the troll and the ogre fade and the black shadow draw into itself and finally disappear. She crouched on the bed, cold fear bumps erupting on her skin. Finally, with teeth chattering, she wobbled over to the Chameleon Stone. As she peered into it, colors swirled and melded until finally, an image appeared.

"Noah!" She reached a hand out toward the stone as if she could touch him. Her brother stood in a green area, grasping some kind of strange spear-like thing. Like one of those tridents except with only two prongs. What would you call it? A Duodent?

As Abby watched, Noah leaped toward a dark-skinned girl decked out in some kind of crude armor and with a two-pronged weapon of her own.

The girl raised her weapon.
Noah fell to the ground.
Abby screamed.
The picture within the Chameleon Stone winked out.

Chapter Sixteen

"Attack me." Deidre commanded.

"With this?" Noah swung the humming sonic sword in a wide arc, fascinated by the Doppler effect the motion created.

"No, with your shoe," the feisty girl taunted, thrusting her own battle fork toward him. Noah heard a sharp sizzle as a soundwave passed inches from his head. "Of course, with that." She crouched, holding the sonic sword slantwise to her body. "Come and get me, bun-boy!"

Noah felt a blast of heat blaze up his neck and scorch his face. "What did you call me?"

"Bun-boy," she smirked. "Too formal for you? Would you prefer just Buns? Ummm. Maybe Bunny Buns. How about that?"

Something snapped in Noah. "Yaaahhhh!" He charged headlong toward Deidre, sonic sword extended in front of him like a lance.

He was nearly on top of her when something slammed into his chest. His feet left the ground. He catapulted backwards, spinning around and landing hard on his stomach in a bed of moss.

"Pfoooooooo." He felt all the air rush from his lungs.

A bolt of pain shot along his spine and into his head. He tried to heave in another breath, but his diaphragm seemed paralyzed. Panicked, he rolled onto his back, wheezing. Tears of fear and rage streamed from his eyes.

A hand grasped his harness, tugging him upward.

"Just knocked the air out of you," Deidre said. "You'll be fine in a minute." She pulled him to a sitting position and held him there. "Try little breaths. It'll come."

He gasped and shuddered, gasped again and heard himself moan.

Deidre bit her lower lip and frowned. "Sorry. I didn't mean to hit you that hard."

Noah drew in another painful breath, avoiding her eyes. Geez, how humiliating, he lamented. I'm sure glad Abby didn't see this. He sucked air again. This time it went down easier.

Frowning, Deidre slowly eased him back to the ground and walked a few yards away. As he concentrated on the breathing that until a minute ago had been purely automatic, he watched her pace in a tight circle. As she walked, she muttered to herself and looked at him out of the corners of her eyes. Noah strained his ears and above his labored breathing he caught one word: "Hopeless."

Heat rose from the tight center of his chest. Rolling over and pushing with quavering arms, he got his feet under him. He'd show her. He spotted the battle fork a few yards away, stumbled to it and hoisted it into the air. Banging the butt end against the metal plate on his decibelt, he set it humming and turned to face Deidre.

"Again," he demanded. "Let's go again."

She stopped pacing and looked over at him, a bemused smile pulling the corners of her mouth up. "You sure? You were flopping around like a gutted cave fish."

"Fooled you, didn't I? You just winged me. C'mon, let's rumble." He amazed himself with his own reckless show of bravado.

"All right!" Deidre banged her sonic sword against the decibelt plate and Noah heard it begin to vibrate with a high-pitched whine. She grinned. "If you've got the heart to fight, the moves will follow. Now, hold your hands like I've got mine and bend your knees. Stay loose, but stay ready." She began to circle around him. "I'm going to shoot a bolt of sound at you. You've got to block it."

For the next several hours, they skirmished with the sonic swords. Noah felt jolts of energy replacing his exhaustion as he learned the moves that could save his life, or slay an enemy. He discovered that each of the tines on the fork hummed at a different frequency. The bluish one was used to attack, and the other, brass-colored, to block soundwaves from another battle fork or even deflect more conventional weapons.

Within an hour, he grew adept enough with it that he could make Deidre give a little ground when he attacked. He began to anticipate her next move and turn aside her attack wave. After one particularly heated exchange of blows, blocks and counter blows, they collapsed beside each other on the mossy ground.

"Much . . . foof . . . better." Deidre wheezed. "You're starting to . . . huff . . . get it."

Gulping air, Noah just nodded. Finally he found enough breath to respond. "I . . . gasp . . . feel like maybe I am. But you're not . . . puff . . . going full speed."

"'Bout seventy-five percent," she conceded. "Fyooo. But you're still not doing that . . . *whew* . . . bad."

A gray hand reached out to hand him a cold mug of pale yellow liquid and he looked up to see Uh-oh standing over him. Eve handed a similar drink to Deidre and stood watching them take long swallows of it. The flavor, a mix of sweet carrot and a kind of citrus, refreshed him instantly. He drained the mug and stood.

"Time for lunch." Eve said quietly. "And then you'll need to be back on the path.

She took the mugs from Noah and her daughter without further comment, but a look passed between them; Noah saw misgivings in her eyes. Deidre squared her shoulders and fumbled with her decibelt harness, reaffirming her determination. Noah suddenly felt strong pangs of jealousy and loss. He didn't have a mother. In fact, since he and Abby got separated, he really didn't have a family. No one to care about him. Unless you counted a strange gray creature that smelled bad and mimicked everything he saw, a warrior-girl who teased him about his tush, and her mother, the witch. An All-American normal-as-apple-pie group.

He followed Eve and Uh-oh into the hut where they ate thick slabs of earthy brown bread, cheese, fruit and some kind of vegetable Noah couldn't identify. He ate silently and voraciously, a result of the violent exercise and his body's demands for more fuel. As he finished his fourth slice of bread and cheese, he remembered how his mother would tease him, saying they would need to take out a second mortgage on the house just to pay their grocery bills. He wondered what people used for money in the Mushroom Forest, and if they had mortgages.

"Time to stop stuffing your face and hit the road, B.B."

Ignoring Deidre's taunt, he swallowed and turned to thank Eve. The chair at the head of the table was empty.

"Where did your Mom go? I didn't see her leave."

The girl pushed back her chair and picked up a provision-stuffed pack from beside the door. "She does that. She always has. Just goes off. Kind of blinks out like a light. I think she didn't want to watch us go. She's worried."

"Where does she go?"

Deidre shrugged. "I don't know. Whenever I ask, she just smiles and says, 'Out.'"

Noah felt a spark of hope bloom in his chest. "Out of the mountain?"

Deidre stared. "You're raving again, Bun-boy. What are you talking about?"

Noah stared back. "The world," he said. "The world outside Humbug Mountain."

"Why would she want to go out there? Everything we need is here."

Noah opened his mouth. There were so many things he could tell her about his world and its beauty, but he decided not to. Right now they needed to focus on the path before them. He nodded, swinging his pack to his back and shaking it to settle and balance the contents.

Eve had even provided Uh-oh with a small knapsack and the gray creature had it slung over his shoulders and was silently looking down the path that rapidly twisted out of sight.

Noah hefted his sonic sword and remembered Eve's request that he watch out for Deidre. How on earth could he help her if they got into major trouble? Sure, he'd improved with the battle fork, but it would be a long time before he reached her level. And what else could he do? He didn't have any other weapons. Only his drumsticks. And a lot of good they'd be in a fight. What could he do with them? Poke an enemy's eye out? Ha. The old feeling of hopelessness flooded back through him.

Deidre seemed to read his thoughts. She reached over and tousled his hair. "Cheer up, drummer-boy. Everything will be fine. I guarantee it."

"Yeah? Are you offering a money-back guarantee?"

She flashed a smile. "Don't be silly. If we screw up, we'll all be dead. I won't be able to pay and you won't be able to collect. But on the bright side, if we're dead, we won't need money." With that, she set off down the trail.

Noah hitched his backpack up another couple of inches and started after her with Uh-oh on his heels. As they scrambled down the trail through the towering brown and white fungi of the mushroom forest, he heard an approximation of his own voice from over his shoulder.

"Too late to turn back now, Noah. Big trouble ahead. Big trouble."

"Shut up," Noah growled at his companion. "Save your breath. You may end up dragging me again before this trip is over."

Far above the narrow trail leading into the dense woods, two figures stood on a rocky ledge. Cool, dank air streamed from an opening in the rock behind them as they watched the quick-striding girl, the thin blond boy, and the gray creature called Uh-oh. "Well rested, he looks. Ready for the next challenge, no?" The muscular, armless brown man nodded at the figures passing below.

The disheveled, ragtag man beside him just grunted noncommittally and tapped a sturdy walking stick against the rock. "They will sleep for the night among friends and then it is on to the unholy river. Pfhaaa. Can he cross with them, do you think?"

Another grunt as the hermit snuffled in his sleeve and looked up at the ceiling. The lights above them glowed and faded and glowed again in a slow, syncopated rhythm. Around them, the soft thud of the mountain's rhythm beat in counterpoint to the Zezzue's twinkling.

"Thuh-duh-rum-puh, thuh-duh-rum-puh, thuh-duh-rum-puh."

"And once they cross the fire, there is the Temple of Cheltnor. And its guardians. Has the warrior girl trained him well enough, do you think? Will he find the correct stone? What do the Zezzue say?" Delacroix lifted his face toward the roof of the huge cavern.

"The Zezzue do not reveal their thoughts about the matter, Pettifog," the Hermit growled. "You should know that. They are enigma."

"True." Delacroix watched the figures below grow smaller and smaller and finally disappear around a bend in the trail. "Their role they will play in the end game. As we will. But only they know what that may be, yes? The Zezzue allow us to use them, for light, for guidance, to communicate with one another. But they are truly, how you would say, the wild card?"

"We can't count on them to help us." The hermit agreed.

"C'est vrai. We must hope the boy can get the stone quickly. Time is short."

The hermit ran his hands through unkempt, greasy hair. "What of the girl? The little one?"

Delacroix chuckled. "She has sent Old Spid and his grotesque sidekick back to Below Skin with their tails between their legs. Beaten him at his own game, s'il vous plait."

"Will she be ready?"

"I think so, yes. She has a most formidable mind. Questions upon questions, you know. Her curiosity, I think, will help her discover the answers to the most important riddles."

"All right then," gruffed the hermit. "I'm going. Anything you need from the outside? Records, maybe? Some more of those snack cakes?"

"Not now, my friend. I can think of nothing but the solstice and our fated meeting with Spid and his horde of demons. But for the asking, I thank you."

"Welcome. At the Skin, then?"

"Oui," Delacroix nodded as he watched the decrepit codger shuffle down the hill along a trail that seemed to appear before him and disappear behind him. "We meet again at the Skin." With that, he turned, walked through the opening in the rock, and disappeared into the mountain.

Chapter Seventeen

Abby lay on the gel bed for a good long time, gnawing on her fingernails and trying not to freak out because of what she'd just seen. Shortly after watching Noah being flung to the ground by a blow from the ferocious-looking girl in armor, the Chameleon Stone had faded to black, leaving her to imagine what had happened next. Noah might have been badly hurt and there was nothing she could do. Nothing. All of the possibilities swirled through her mind, and her helpless feeling grew and grew.

Her first glimpse of Noah in days shocked her. He, too, had been dressed like a warrior, looking somehow taller, more sure of himself, older even. For a brief second, she'd ceased to worry about him. Until the fierce-looking girl zapped him. Abby shuddered. Had the girl captured him? Or was he—she shuddered again and allowed herself to say the word that filled her mind.

"Dead." Dead, like her mother.

Feeling very small and alone, she dabbed at her eyes with the back of her wrist and tried to analyze the other things she'd seen in the cruelly short episode Spid had allowed her to watch. Before Noah advanced on the girl, she'd seen him bang the end of his forky thing against a large metallic disk that hung from a harness across his chest. She'd seen his arms vibrate a little as he tried to wield the two-tined spear. Sound. That had to be it. Soundwaves. After all, the thing looked like a tuning fork.

Satisfied with that explanation, she tried to recreate the picture of the girl. She'd looked intent, focused, but not angry or vindictive. In fact, it seemed that her lips might have been about to flex into a smile.

Abby pounded her fists against the bed and felt the gel shimmy under her assault. God, it was so frustrating. What had happened? Noah! If only she knew.

She paused, panting, and flopped onto her back. If Noah hadn't survived the fight, maybe she should try to escape, save herself. The thing with Spid really wasn't her battle after all. Or was it? She recalled the troll's gloating remarks about taking over the world outside, his parting threat. "There will be no mercy," he'd roared.

No mercy. That meant when he broke through the Skin and took over, he'd kill them all. Delacroix, Chillout and all the other grungoids. He'd kill Noah, if her brother still lived. "And me." She trembled and pulled the quilt tight around her shoulders.

And then Spid and his demons would surge out of the mountain. They'd overrun Port Anvil. Kill her father. Kill everyone she knew.

She rolled into a tight ball and surrendered to her fear and grief, sobbing miserably. What on earth could she possibly do? After all, she was just a girl, barely a teenager. And everybody expected so much of her, piled so much responsibility on her head. Looking out for Noah. Keeping the house clean and now stopping an evil troll from conquering the world and inflicting pain on everyone. Life just wasn't fair.

Around her, the Darksuckers glowed brighter. On its shelf, the Chameleon Stone throbbed with a pale green light. She sensed the Zezzue suddenly swirl, flicker and swirl again. A little voice nagged at her. "Stop it, Abby. Stop feeling sorry for yourself. Do something."

Abby sat up and rubbed her eyes, knuckling away the tears. She stared at the color-shifting orb on the shelf.

Spid would have to capture the Chameleon to consolidate his power. That's what he'd said. The troll wanted to link it to his Shadow Stone and to the stone Noah would bring back. If Noah had survived being nailed by the sound fork. If he . . . she forced the negative thoughts to dissolve. Emotion is your enemy, her logical self told her. Observe, think, analyze. Don't let your heart get in the way.

The Methuselah Stone. The oldest stone in the world, Delacroix had called it. Maybe even older than the world. Where would Noah find it? What would it look like? Was it big or small, heavy or light? And most importantly, how could they harness its power—connect it up with the Chameleon Stone to block Spid?

Abby's mind shifted to overdrive. Thoughts overlapped, conclusions were drawn, considered and rejected for lack of evidence. Above her, the Darksuckers stopped swirling and began to twinkle in microscopic flashes of red and green. Like Christmas, Abby thought. Like the lights on the tree. She smiled. "Thank you for helping me win the game," she told the Zezzuc. "Thank you for helping me beat Spid."

The lights blinked out, then seemed to fall around her in a burst of gold and blue and silver, like the cascading sparks that follow the explosion of fireworks on the Fourth of July. She couldn't see these tiny creatures, couldn't touch them, but now, surrounded by them, she felt she wasn't alone anymore.

Despite her overall pessimism, Abby felt herself grinning. Maybe Spid's towering ego, and his overconfidence could be turned against him. The idea of Noah stopping him from breaching the Skin seemed to amuse Spid. Clearly, the demon troll didn't take Noah seriously. But he hadn't been worried that she would beat him at Spiddle, either. Not that she could have done it without the Darksuckers, but still, Spid had clearly underestimated his competition. And clearly over-estimated his own knowledge and skill. Chances were, he'd do it again. Abby knew she needed to be ready to take the advantage.

This game wasn't that much different than chess. Not really.

She sat up in bed, reached for her backpack and dug around for the small notebook with the ballpoint pen clipped onto it. In neat block letters she inscribed the word the Zezzue had given her on the last move of the Spiddle game. *T-I-R-K-D-E-S-C-X-O-S-L-K-N-U-R-P-LV.*

She stared at it for a few moments, making sure she had the right letters in the right order. What could it possibly mean? How did you pronounce it? Maybe, along with being an actual word in Beneathese, it could be broken into smaller words. Kinda like The Last Place You Look. She took a stab at dividing it. "Turk-deskexosall-knurp-love," she mumbled and then tried repeating it faster and faster. It sounded like somebody trying to talk with an entire cheeseburger stuffed in his mouth. Made no sense. But then, as Spid had pointed out during the Spiddle game, in Beneathese, some of the letters didn't get pronounced. And some of them were pronounced totally differently than in English. The whole thing made her head hurt.

Abby played with the word, dividing it different ways and working it from the back to the front. It could be a cipher, she thought, like those puzzles next to the crossword in the newspaper. Letters standing in for other letters. She messed with it for an hour or so, substituting first in a logical manner and then at random, but couldn't come up with anything that looked even vaguely familiar.

Frustrated, she returned to nibbling at her fingernails.

"Hola little chickie. Like, what's the haps?"

She looked up to find Chillout standing in the doorway of her room, appraising her over the tops of his Ray-bans. "Oh. Hello. I was just," Abby gestured at the pad, "trying to figure out what—"

"I can dig it, baby. What a flipped out cat, that Spid, huh? Like double bummer to the ninth power."

"Huh?" Her mind scrambled to sift this new information. The grungoid knew about her visit from the troll. Did he know about the Spiddle game? And Spid trying to turn her into a spy? Had the grungoids bugged her bedroom? Or had the Darksuckers told Delacroix about her encounter with the troll?

Chillout acted as if she hadn't spoken. "Lix requests your presence, chickie. You're playin' the big room. "

Abby nodded and followed the gray creature through the corridor into the immense chamber where she'd met Felix Delacroix the first time. Chillout led her around a couple of boulders and back to a different corner of the room. Abby found the massive, bald, armless man lying on his back in front of a very strange apparatus.

Some kind of leather-like material had been stretched tight between two stalagmites about twenty feet tall and twenty feet apart. Elevating his legs, stomach muscles rippling, the Grand Exalted Pettifog swiveled his hips back and forth and up and down, drumming out a series of complex rhythms with his feet.

Ta-boom-ta-tee-tee-bum-bum? Delacroix's left foot beat out the musical question. The right foot answered. *Tee-dee-bum-tee-dee-bum-tee-dee-bummity-bum.*

As Delacroix played, the patterns grew more rapid and more complex. At times, he drummed so quickly, Abby saw his legs only as a blur. Fascinated, she leaned against a nearby rock and watched him.

Finally, after increasing the speed to a level she wouldn't have dreamed possible, he finished with a flourish.

Ta-dibbity-dum-dum-dibbity-boom-bummity-bum.

Panting, sweat rolling from his chest, he lowered his trembling legs.

"Some crazy groove, daddy-o," Chillout rasped. "I brought the chickie. I got to be fadin' now. Hasta." The grungoid swiveled on his heel and returned in the direction they'd come.

159

Delacroix wiped sweat from his eyes with the stump of his right arm, turned his head to look over at her and smiled broadly. "Just an old drummer trying to learn new tricks, ma cherie. Practicing for my part of the ritual."

He sat up and used his big toe to snag a nearby towel and blot some of the perspiration from his body.

"Your part? You mean there's more to it than that? It sounded pretty complicated all by itself."

"Counter rhythm, little one. Backbeat, if you will. Noah will have to play the hard part, the rhythm that matches and challenges Spid's best drummer. That's the rhythm that will keep the Skin from going liquid and the troll's nightmare army from riding roughshod over everyone up here.

Abby barely heard the last part. She'd fixed on her brother's name. "Noah? Is Noah all right? Have you heard anything?"

Delacroix shrugged. "Not specific, you know. He continues his quest for the Methuselah Stone. He has, how you say, acquired another ally."

Abby felt some relief at the giant man's words. "So he's alive, then? He's okay?"

"At last report, oui. Let us hope he regains the time he has lost, because if not, we are, as they say, in deep doo doo. For only he can drum against Spid's best."

"You mean the challenge is about drumming?" She felt her heart leap. Yes. She pumped a fist into the air. Spid was in big trouble. "Noah is just the best. He practices nonstop for hours and hours. He can really play fast and loud."

"Ah, yes, fast and loud," Delacroix smiled. "I remember once, my ownself, thinking fast and loud and music were the same thing. But soon, I learn that sometimes you must play slow and soft. Or perhaps fast and soft. Or slow and loud. The drum, we must remember, began its existence as a way for people to communicate, to convey news, and plans, and emotions, to imitate the natural world they found themselves in."

"So what song does Noah have to play to win? To beat Spid and keep him out?"

"Ah," Delacroix lay back on the stone floor and gazed at the ceiling. "It is not just the playing, little one. Noah must learn to listen. To turn loose of everything and hear the earth, the mountain, the ocean beyond." He gestured toward one of the walls of the mountain. "And he must tune in to his own heart, let its beat join with the others. Only then can his hands define the rhythms to keep darkness from us all."

Abby felt a sudden chill pass through her. Could Noah learn to listen? To listen hard. Or would he argue? "No way." She could almost hear his defiant half-alto-half-baritone voice, the obstinate teenager dragging his feet at every suggestion from anyone. It made her feel helpless and small again. "And me? What can I do?"

"What you do best, ma petite. Seek knowledge, try to untangle the many puzzles. Look for strengths and weaknesses. Observe, organize and strategize. But . . ." Delacroix raised the stump of an arm in her direction and Abby could almost see a phantom hand with a finger raised in warning.

"What?" Abby felt Delacroix's brown eyes lock onto her own.

"You must be careful, no? It can be possible to mistakenly let your sense of logic and proportion, and your skepticism, dismiss the mysteries of the unexplainable. You too, Abby, must learn when to listen to your senses, your instinct, your heart. Not merely your estimable brain."

Abby felt tears well in her eyes. Could she do that? She was just a girl. A girl in a world she could barely believe existed. "Why can't someone go for help?" She remembered she'd asked the question before and hadn't gotten an answer. "Why can't you tell the police about Spid. The police have guns and stuff. They can kill him."

Delacroix laughed. "It is not easy to kill a troll, Abby. And who on the outside would believe in that troll, anyway? Or in his ogres and demons? No, the prophecy says those of us who inhabit the mountain must fight this battle. With your brother. And you. And the prophecy will be as it will be."

But I'm just a kid, Abby thought again. How can I make a plan to stop Spid, to stop entire armies of horrible creatures?

Delacroix seemed to anticipate her thoughts. "You can only try, Abby. That is all anyone can ask of you. Or of me, or Noah. We may not succeed, but we must try. Not to try is to abandon hope. We cannot, we must not, do that."

Abby nodded. She could try. She *would* try. "What should I do next?"

"That is the question, no? The prophecy only provides the outline and leaves for us the details." The drummer slid back onto his shoulders and the stumps of his arms and prepared to kick at the tightly-stretched surface again. Looking over his shoulder, he winked at her. "I believe you should explore your environment, Abby. Find whatever is out there for you to find. You are free to go wherever you want, follow any of the routes through the many openings in the cavern. In fact," his head and eyes moved right toward a narrow natural indentation in the rock, "you will find that one, cherie, leads to the outside. A short walk and voila, you are breathing the sweet clean air of Oregon. A short climb down and you walk the beach again. You are free to use that door, Abby. You would not be blamed if you chose to go home, little princess."

Home! Her own room. Her father's arms. Jennifer Ramsden's cookies. A part of her, a frightened, confused voice screaming to be heard, pleaded with her to take Delacroix at his word. Leave this madness, this upsidedown world and the terrifying prospect of the days ahead, the battle to come.

"No." She heard herself say the word. She couldn't leave. To her surprise, it wasn't just her concern for Noah that made the decision. Within her was a steely determination she hadn't known she possessed. Spid could not win. Not if she could do anything to stop him.

"No," she repeated firmly. "I'm in. And I'll stay in until the end. Until we send Spid back where he belongs."

Delacroix thumped the drum-skin with his right foot, starting a steady "thoom, thoom, thoom," rhythm. "Most excellent," he grinned. "Explore, and think your deep thoughts, ma cherie. Do not dismiss anything you discover, because it could prove useful, yes?" Abby nodded. Delacroix used the tips of his toes on the left foot to tap light counter beats, adding another dimension to the sound. "As for me, I must work very hard. The moment, it is less than four days away." With that, he began a series of complicated patterns, making each hit on the drum crisp and distinct. Abby noticed he used contrasts between louder and softer beats to create different effects.

"Is there a map of the tunnels?" Abby pushed herself to a squat, then stood, feeling her muscles protest the movement.

Delacroix, without missing a beat, turned to smile gently at her and chide. "A map will only take you where others have been, not where you may need to go.

Sometimes the journey itself is the discovery you seek. A map can only extinguish the curiosity, no?" Brown leg flashing, Delacroix shifted to a wild, exotically syncopated rhythm. The sound reminded her of a beach on a Caribbean island.

Abby wanted to scream. Talk sense. How can I be expected to come up with a plan, to find out anything, if you won't give me a map? How could a map keep anyone from finding the way? Ridiculous. Unless, she thought, it was a very old map. Or a badly drawn one. Or the wrong map. She sighed. The point was, even if a map existed, Delacroix didn't intend to give it to her. She picked an opening in the rock wall at random. Here goes, she thought. All alone, wandering through the inside of a gigantic mountain with no idea where I'm going or how things will come out. Perfect.

After taking in a deep breath, Abby ducked into the natural doorway and started down the dim tunnel. Cold, damp air raised goosebumps on her arms as she advanced carefully, testing the rock before she put her feet down.

After a few hundred feet, the subterranean passage split into two branches. She stood for a moment and seemed to feel a pull to her left. Shortly after that, she had three choices of directions to go, and then four. Each time, she stopped and tried to turn off her brain and turn on a connection to the mountain. She had no idea if the almost magnetic pull she felt was real, or a figment of her imagination, but she kept on, one slow step at a time.

The relatively tight spaces and the twists, turns, descents and rises didn't bother her at all. Neither did the almost imperceptible light. She knew she could find her way back. She memorized the direction she'd turned each time, which choice she'd made, recognizing that all she needed to do to return to the main chamber was reverse her movements on the way back. Piece of cake. She grinned.

She wondered what she might discover if she kept going long enough. Was there yet another magical stone to be found and would she find it as she had found the Chameleon Stone? She thought about that glowing orb and then about all the wonderful jewels that came from under the ground—diamonds and emeralds, sapphires and rubies. Was that what Delacroix had meant when he said she should find what was there to be found—jewels? But no, she knew enough about geology to know she'd be unlikely to find any of those here. Agates, yes. But no precious gems. Not the ones she knew about, she reminded herself. Maybe there were dozens of types of precious gems yet undiscovered.

She set that thought aside, pulled her jacket closer and focused on her trek and keeping track of the different twists and turns. But her mind drifted again. She visualized the letters from the Spiddle game, Noah raising the strange forky spear to fend off a blow from the onrushing warrior-girl. Where was he right now? What dark tunnel was he marching along? She felt a heart-wrenching pang of homesickness. And where was her father? Was he looking for her? Or had he given up? Did he think she and Noah were dead?

"Mom." The name escaped from her lips involuntarily. Surprised, she choked back tears and bit her lower lip, then leaned her head against the tunnel wall. "What should I do, Mom? How can I help Noah? It's so hard."

She listened, as Delacroix had instructed her, knowing she wouldn't hear her mother's voice, but hoping she would feel something, some fleeting sense of reassurance, of another presence. "Will I know it if I feel it?" Her whisper seemed to dissolve into the darkness, dissolve into a silence that made her feel even more alone.

Got to go back, she thought. The only things the tunnels seemed to lead to were other tunnels, more choices. She felt like she was in a maze, and suddenly she wanted to scream, to run, to get out of the mountain or back to Delacroix. She heard her heart pounding, her breath quickening. Get a grip, Abby, she told herself. Running won't do any good. And fear will just make you forget how you got here. Calm down, turn around and start back, very slowly. Just reverse the directions.

165

Where you turned right, turn left. If there were three tunnels and you took the one to the left, take the one to the right this time. No problem, it'll take you back to Delacroix.

She took a deep breath and began to walk. She took a right-hand tunnel, then one to the left. She felt confident. She walked faster and faster. Her legs grew tired and twice she stumbled on the uneven floor. The light seemed to grow dimmer and take on a dirty, yellowish cast.

Colder air lapped her ankles and she shivered in spite of her jacket. "Just around the next bend," she whispered several times. "Just along the next tunnel a little way. Just a few more steps."

But strangely, even though she knew she had the order down perfectly, when she'd completed the final leg of the journey, she didn't emerge into the immense chamber where she'd started. Instead, she found herself in a smaller chamber with a rocky bench in the center. Four other tunnels opened from it.

Panicked, she looked around. She'd forgotten a step somewhere. While she'd been daydreaming about jewels and home, and Noah and Spid and all of her troubles, she'd mentally misplaced one of the turns.

"Think," Abby encouraged herself. "Go over it all again." She sat on the cold stone bench and retraced it all in her mind. No, she was sure she hadn't forgotten a turn. The chamber should be here. Right here. But it wasn't.

But it had to be.

She stood. Maybe if she went just a little way down one of these new tunnels she'd find it. Okay then, she'd take the one to the right.

Fighting tears, she trudged into the tunnel and came almost immediately to another junction, a three-choice crossroad. That wasn't right. She went back the way she came and took the next tunnel in line. No good. She emerged into another small room she'd never seen with five tunnel openings. The room was about the size of her bedchamber back at Delacroix's and had a high ceiling looming so far above her in the gloomy light that she couldn't see it.

Returning to the original chamber, Abby chose the third branch tunnel. Surely, this one had to be right. Surely, this one would bring her to something she recognized. Her heart thudded in her throat and she wondered if Delacroix would send someone out to look for her if she didn't return soon. What if he didn't? What if he was so intent on his drumming that he forgot all about her? Hunger gnawed at the pit of her stomach. She hadn't eaten for quite a while. How long did it take someone to starve to death?

The tunnel she'd chosen emptied into the same high-ceilinged chamber with five entrances. A loop.

Adrenaline pouring through her, Abby ran back and found the chamber with the bench again. Still on the dead run, she scrambled down the fourth tunnel, the only one she hadn't tried, racing toward the growing light at the other end. Hope began to build. This is right, she thought. I can't be lost.

Lost! The word filled her mind. If she was lost, that meant that she hadn't been smart enough, hadn't paid attention, hadn't marked the map in her mind correctly.

Above all, being lost meant she'd failed. She began to cry and gasp at the same time, sucking air in and choking on it. Tears partially blinded her and she bumped into the wall and hurt her arm. No. She couldn't be lost.

Finally, after what seemed like forever, she stumbled out of the tunnel and into a large room. Drying her eyes with her sleeve, she looked through reddened eyes at her surroundings. Her heart seemed to squeeze to a stop and she plopped to the floor and began to sob again. It wasn't possible. She'd taken another loop. She was back in that high-ceilinged chamber again. She was lost. Absolutely lost.

For the first time since the grungoids kidnapped her, she felt truly frightened.

Chapter Eighteen

Noah craned his neck so many times to check out the gigantic mushrooms towering around him that it grew stiff and began to ache. But he couldn't stop to take off his pack and knead his muscles. The long-striding Deidre set a killer pace and if he lagged, she ragged on him pretty good. So he hustled on, even jogging at times to keep up.

Behind him, he heard Uh-oh panting and worried that the little creature would drop of exhaustion. He wondered if he could carry his pack and his weapon and somehow drag his friend, too. If he had to, he would. He wouldn't leave Uh-oh behind.

The trio had followed the wide path through the shade-darkened mushroom forest for nearly half an hour, and Noah saw no signs they were anywhere near the end. All around them, fungi a hundred or more feet tall and up to twenty feet in diameter thrust upward from the sodden, moss-covered ground. Above, bell-shaped caps spread out to two or three times the diameter of the trunks, totally blocking any view of the enormous cavern's ceiling.

Smaller mushrooms, ranging in size from thirty feet or so tall, down to the grocery store variety of Noah's experience, grew thickly among the giants. Not all of them took the stem and bell shape. Some resembled real trees with thick reedy trunks and fuzzy green growth hanging from the limbs. The dank, cloying perfume of decay filled the air, a reminder that the vital life of the enormous fungi depended on the death of other organisms.

"Are they edible?" Noah's voice sounded muffled, cushioned by the soft vegetation surrounding them.

Deidre, about twenty yards ahead, must have heard, though. She paused and looked back over her shoulder.

He stopped, flexing his neck and shoulders, seizing a chance to rest for a few seconds. Uh-oh collapsed on the trail, wheezing and holding his sides.

"Sure. Some of them," Deidre yelled. "Others will kill you within seconds. Trick is knowing which ones are which. Come on, let's go."

She stood, hands on hips, tapping her foot impatiently as Noah helped Uh-oh to his feet and they struggled to catch up to her. He angled for more rest time. "So, do you know? The poisonous ones from the others?"

"Some." She shrugged her shoulders. "Some of them, though, even if they wouldn't kill you, you wouldn't want to eat. Taste like cardboard. The big ones are too tough. Like eating wood. People build houses out of them. Some of the others will turn you into a raving lunatic. But a lot of them are yummy. My Mom knows them all."

Noah detected a note of pride in the warrior girl's voice.

"It's pretty amazing." He commented, peering up at the corrugated undersides of the mushrooms caps. Uh-oh sprawled on the ground again, closed his eyes and began to sigh deeply. Deidre looked down at him with annoyance, but then her face softened and she plunked to the ground beside him. Relieved, but trying not to show it, Noah eased his pack off his shoulders and dropped beside a mushroom that smelled like a compost heap.

The ground squished beneath him and he quickly scuttled back to the graveled trail that cut its way, like a dry river, though the forest.

"Amazing? I guess they are," Deidre mused. "I've been around them all my life, so I kinda take this forest for granted, you know." She pulled her canteen out, took a swallow and offered it to Noah. Gratefully, he took it, rinsed his mouth, and passed it back to her. She handed it over to Uh-oh, who, opening one eyelid, then the other, accepted it and took a short pull.

"We can rest here, I guess. We've made pretty good progress. We should arrive at 'Shroomtown way before dark."

"Shroomtown?" Noah laughed at the name. "Are there like, people living there?"

"Like people?" Deidre wrinkled her nose and then responded. "Like fer shurr, dude," she laughed. "They're like really gnarly, you know."

Noah felt himself blush with annoyance. "I only meant—"

He felt her hand on his shoulder. She grinned. "I know. I'm just yankin' your chain. Keeping in practice, like."

"Thanks a lot."

"You're welcome a lot." She took her hand away and stared straight ahead. A few minutes passed with only the sound of Uh-oh's slowing breaths. Deidre finally broke the silence. "Actually, I spent a lot of time in 'Shroomtown when I was growing up. Mom would go off and leave me with Uncle Benny. He's very cool. You'll meet him and the others pretty soon."

"Oh," was all Noah could think of to say. And then something else she'd said struck him and he realized it had been puzzling him all along.

"You said we'd get there before dark. We're inside the mountain, right? Sunlight doesn't reach in here, right? But there's light. Not much, but there is light. But it's not sunlight. So how can it get dark?"

"When the Zezzue decide it's time," Deidre gestured upward, "it will get dark."

"The Zezzue?" Noah looked around. "Do they control the light switches?"

She chuckled. "You haven't been paying attention, have you? The Zezzue. The Darksuckers. Tiny creatures that inhale darkness and take it somewhere else."

"Huh?"

"They hang out on the ceilings." She waved toward the tops of the giant fungi.

Noah's mind clicked into gear and he flashed back to the hermit carrying on a conversation with the lights on the rock ceiling of his chamber. He remembered how he'd ignored the arrow formed by the winking lights when he and Uh-oh had begun their journey. That seemed so long ago. Years. He wondered what would have happened if he'd followed the Zezzue's directions, where they would be now. "The darkness. Where do the Zezzue take it?"

"Nobody knows for sure. Legend has it there is a place in the mountain where they, they, uh . . ." She struggled for the word. "Regurgitate it, I guess. Spit it out, like something that tastes really bad. Anyway, they say there's a place, darker than anything you could imagine. They say the darkness swallows all your senses. There are stories of people stumbling into it and never being heard from again."

"Wow, creepy." Noah tried to picture a place like that and found he couldn't even begin. It was like thinking about how empty space was and how far it was to a star. Your brain couldn't handle it.

"Chhht . . . chhht . . . chhhht." Noah and Deidre turned to see Uh-oh standing upright. He pointed up the path and made another small "chht" sound back in his throat.

"Shhh. Someone's coming." Deidre levered herself up quickly and pulled her sonic sword from its scabbard.

Less gracefully, Noah clambered to his feet, drew his own weapon and took a position in front of Uh-oh. He heard the hoof-beats and felt a strong vibration on the trail. It sounded like a herd of horses, or cattle, approaching rapidly. That's stupid, Noah, he scolded himself. How would horses end up down here in the middle of Humbug Mountain? "Deidre . . ."

"Galloopapede." She banged the battle fork against her decibelt, setting it humming. "Only one, I think."

"Galloopa-what?" Noah asked, incredulously. Getting no answer, he activated his own fork and brandished it in the ready position as she'd taught him.

The sound of many legs hammering into the gravelly surface of the path filled heavy air. Soon a form emerged around a bend in the trail. Noah took a step back, colliding with Uh-oh, and rubbed his eyes in disbelief.

Closing in on them rapidly was a creature about thirty feet long with a long neck ending in an almost lizard-like face with floppy ears and a prominent, beaky nose. Dozens of pairs of legs, in a blur of motion, catapulted the beast along, raising a cloud of mud.

"Be ready," Deidre commanded, raising her fork. "It could be bandits."

Bandits! Noah's heart thumped rapidly in his chest and he felt a charge of adrenaline run along his arms and legs. Raising his weapon higher, he waited, nerves jangling. He felt Uh-oh's warm breath against his back and heard his trademark "Uh-oh," drowned out by a loud bellow from the rider of the Galloopapede.

"Pull up, Sznorspap. Pull up!"

Noah stared in amazement at a young man, probably not much older than himself, perched at the base of the beast's long neck, red hair streaming behind him. The rider yanked back on what Noah at first assumed were ropy reins, then realized were the swept-back whiskers of the multi-haunched animal.

"Stop, damn your hide," roared the rider. The Galloopapede, now less than twenty yards from them, showed no signs of slowing down. Noah pressed himself between a pair of huge mushrooms and pulled Uh-oh in beside him.

Deidre didn't move. She lowered her fork and covered her mouth with one hand.

"Sznorspap, please, stop!" The rider's plea was almost drowned out by the thunder of what had to be a hundred legs and an echoing goat-like "waaankkk" from the charging animal.

The runaway Galloopapede pulled abreast of them and Noah smelled it—a cross between dead crab and sewer gas.

As beast and rider swept past, Deidre called out a giggled greeting. "Halloo, Peitr. Good-bye, Peitr."

"Hello, beautiful . . ." came the return call, fading even as it left the rider's mouth. By the time Noah heard the faint follow-up, "I'll be right baaaaack!" the Galloopapede had stormed out of sight down the path.

"You know him?" Noah returned his battle fork to its scabbard.

"I grew up with him. He's very nice, really. You'll like him. If he, uh—" she broke into a whole-hearted laugh. "If he can ever get Sznorspap to turn around."

"Isn't riding that thing dangerous?"

"I broke my collarbone twice training him. But he's fine if you know how to talk to him. Peitr just doesn't have the tone of voice right." She smiled and gestured down the trail where the beast had disappeared. Noah heard pounding feet again.

"You'll see." Deidre beamed. Sznorspap will behave. I'll drive him on the way back to 'Shroomtown and he'll mind his manners and get us there in no time."

Us? You'll get me up on that thing when clams tap dance, thought Noah. "No. No way I'm riding that Galloop-a . . . Gal . . ."

"Galoopapede." Deidre shrugged and examined her fingernails. "Fine, Bun-boy. Have it your way. You can ride on Sznorspap for half an hour or walk another three.

Makes no never mind to me. I'll have a bath, eat dinner and be on my third truffle beer by the time you show up. Hope there are some leftovers for you."

Noah had a nasty retort on his tongue when the Galloopapede and the freckled, lanky red-haired youth reined in beside them with a heavy clatter of iron-shod hooves stopping at different speeds. The boy leapt from the creature's neck, took two steps and gathered up Deidre in a bear hug.

"Welcome home, little sister."

"Urrrfen mfrrrk bdnrk." replied Deidre, so scrunched in his grasp she couldn't form a word.

"Oh, sorry." Peitr relaxed his hold a little and set her back down.

She brushed at her tunic and straightened her belt. "It's good to see you, Peitr. How is Benny?"

"Good. Better, once he's seen your face." He turned to examine Noah and Uh-oh. "Who are your friends?"

Deidre pointed to Noah. "His name is Noah. He drums at the Skin when the sun marks the solstice and the mountain's heartbeat fails."

The red-haired boy's mouth formed an O shape. "He is the chosen one, then? The message the Zezzue delivered from your mother said he would come." There was no mistaking the slight tone of disappointment in Peitr's voice. "But somehow I expected him to be—"

"He is the one," Deidre interrupted. "And old Spid will be sorry he tried to breach the skin when we're done with him."

Deidre sounded confident, but Noah wondered how much of that was an act. He pictured her later, in the presence of her friends, confiding her doubts and qualms about his abilities. Not that he blamed her.

Peitr shrugged. "As you say. And the other one?"

Noah spoke up. "His name is Uh-oh. He saved my life back a ways."

"Then he will be a good soldier. As we all must be. The others of his kind will be glad to welcome him. Come. They are expecting us.

'Shroomtown proved to be a small settlement with a couple of hundred residents. It sat against one wall of the

175

immense cavern, hemmed in by the edge of the Mushroom Forest and a tumbling waterfall that veiled a tall cliff. People lived either in shallow caves, or in houses carved out of giant mushrooms or built of other fungi stacked up like logs. Where the small settlement ended, a pathway led alongside the waterfall, away from the forest and toward another series of openings carved into the rock wall.

Riding in on the back of the Galloopapede, which obeyed Deidre's every command, Noah observed clusters of people, men and women both, skirmishing with a variety of weapons. Some brandished sonic swords, much like the ones he and Deidre carried. Others held mock battles with more conventional swords, spears that looked like small metal porcupines mounted at the ends of short poles. They're getting ready, Noah thought. In case I fail. Or maybe getting ready for when I fail.

Peitr led them to his father, who watched over a group of about twenty people practicing hand-to-hand combat.

Benny Vlavnosk, a burly man who shared hair color, eyes and smile with his son, waved a greeting. "Go wash up and get a little rest. I'll catch up with you at dinner, Dee-Dee. Welcome, Noah. And your friend, too."

"All right, Uncle Benny. See you then." Deidre blushed as she hopped off the Galloopaped and helped Noah and Uh-oh down. Dee-Dee, Noah mused. Must be an old name from when she was a baby. Something told Noah that Benny was the only one who called her that to her face without risking a quick zap from her sonic sword. He filed the name away for future reference. Might come in handy next time she starts in with that Bun-boy routine, he thought.

Later, after cleaning up and taking a brief nap on a spongy bed inside the spacious mushroom apartment of Deidre's Uncle Benny, they met for a communal dinner.

As the lights dimmed overhead and the air cooled, Peitr and others built a large fire. Men, women and children sat around it, sharing food and talking into the night. The fire emitted a loamy-smelling smoke and Noah decided they were burning chunks of fungal stuff he'd seen lying in the forest. Deadfalls, he guessed. Just like in a regular forest. A few days ago he would have dismissed the idea as impossible, but now he accepted the fact that somehow dead mushroom trees dried out enough to burn.

The food was good; a savory mushroom stew with other vegetables and some kind of meat in it. When he asked Deidre what the meat was, she rolled her eyes and told him he'd be better off not knowing. He put down his spoon but then hunger overcame squeamishness and he emptied his bowl and asked for more.

Much to Uh-oh's delight, several dozen gray-skinned dread-locked creatures like him lived around 'Shroomtown. Uh-oh gravitated toward them and become the center of their attention. He seemed to be telling them the story of his journey with Noah, in between eating what looked very much like large insects. Something else, Noah decided, he was better off staying ignorant about.

"So, Mr. Keene. You have an appointment with destiny at the Temple of Cheltnor, do you not?"

Benny Vlavnosk leaned toward Noah, one eyebrow raised. He was burly, with wide shoulders and the beginnings of a paunch. His bushy red hair, approximately the same shade as his son's, was streaked with gray. He wore a neatly trimmed gray-red beard, and had huge bushy eyebrows that seemed to have lives of their own.

"I . . .uh . . . guess so." In mid mumble, another memory overtook Noah. The Temple of Cheltnor. The hermit had been talking about it to the lights on the ceiling. The Zezzue. He'd been talking to the Zezzue.

So maybe, Noah decided, if he'd listened to the hermit, or if he'd taken the tunnel the Zezzue pointed at, he could have taken a short cut.

Benny Vlavnosk smiled at him, eyebrows wriggling. "Yes, it seems that all roads lead here. Some just twist and turn more before depositing you."

Deidre chimed in. "How long will it take to reach the temple?"

Benny stroked his beard. "Depends." He looked up at the tunnel openings above them. "No one here has ever been to the temple. In fact, we are not even sure it exists.

All we have to go on is the prophecy. It tells us you take the middle pathway up there. He elevated his chin an inch. "But along the way, you must cross Pfhaaa, the river of fire." The way he pronounced the name of the river, it sounded like a long, hot exhalation of air.

"River of fire?" Noah's voice squeaked and he heard a small ripple of laughter radiate around the circle. "What's that?" He looked over at Deidre. She just shrugged.

"Despite what you might have learned in school, Humbug Mountain is volcanic still. Melted rock flows at various points through its interior." Benny threw another chunk of fungus onto the fire. Flames crackled and sparked, burning blue and silver, shadows danced in tempo with them. "Pfhaaa, the molten river, is wide and deep and white hot. Any attempts to cross it have ended in tragedy, I'm afraid. But the prophecy says that's the way you must go."

"You knew about this, didn't you?" Noah flung the accusation toward Deidre. "A river of fire! How did you possible think we could do it?"

"I thought we'd cross that Pfhaaa when we got to it."

Her feeble attempt at a joke fell silently into the circle. Noah glared at her and she bit her lower lip and looked hurt. He turned his head away, freezing her out for the rest of the meal. Later, tossing and turning in his bedroll, he decided that being angry took energy better used for other things. After all, she had meant well. She was just going by the prophecy.

"Deidre?" He called softly into the darkness.

No response came from the girl in the bag next to his. He looked over to see her eyes closed and heard her deep and regular breathing against the stillness of the night.

"Deed, Are you awake?"

"What a stupid question," she mumbled. "If I wasn't, I couldn't answer you now, could I?"

"Oh. Right."

"What do you want, Noah?"

"I'm sorry for hollering at you earlier."

A brief silence. "It's okay. I understand. I'm scared too."

This amazed Noah. "You are? I didn't think you were ever afraid of anything."

"Anybody who says they're not afraid of danger is either stupid or lying."

Noah thought about that. "You're probably right."

Deidre turned to face him, leaning on her elbow.

"How did . . ." Noah paused, hoping she wouldn't be offended by what he was about to ask. "How did you come to be in here? In the mountain, I mean?"

"I was born here. Mom and I have lived here all my life."

"Oh. And your Mom, was she born here too?"

"I . . . uh . . . don't really know."

Noah thought of the stories his own mother used to tell, stories about the Nebraska town where she grew up.

"Didn't you ever ask her?"

Deidre grew silent for a moment, then locked her eyes on Noah's. "One time."

"And?"

"She said she didn't know. She just woke up one day, she was like a grownup already. The 'Shroomers said they'd found her wandering around the forest, all cut up, and brought her here. Mom says she has no memories of anything before that."

"Wow, that's really mysterious."

"It used to bother me, not knowing where we came from, but it doesn't any more. But I do wonder sometimes . . ."

Noah waited for her to continue, but then had to prompt her. "What do you wonder sometimes?"

"Why she'll never tell me where she goes."

"Did you ever try to guess?"

Deidre scrunched her face up. "What kind of silly question is that? Of course, I try to guess. But she won't say." She hunched the sleeping bag around her shoulders. "Go to sleep, Noah," she commanded him.

Noah didn't acknowledge her order. Propped up on his elbow, he studied her shape in the darkness.

"Noah?"

"Yeah?"

"About tomorrow."

"Uh-huh?"

"Pfhaaa. The River of Fire?"

The scorched sound of the word made fear surge into the pit of his stomach. "Yeah?"

"I don't have a clue how we get across," she admitted. "Do you have any ideas?"

For a long moment, Noah lay silent, sorting out his thoughts, feeling some of his earlier anger seeping into his brain. He could just say the obvious. No, not even a glimmer, thank you very much for asking, now leave me alone. What did they expect of him, anyway? Who did they think he was? But as he thought of all the snide things he might say, a shred of an idea—half memory, half premonition—began to wiggle at the base of his brain. He groped for it, but it wafted away, leaving a feeling of confidence—confidence like he'd never felt before except when he was drumming.

"Deidre? You know this River of Fire thing?"

"Right."

"Forget about it; I've got it handled." The bravado in his own voice amazed him.

She didn't respond for a moment, and then he heard her impish giggle. "You are such a liar, Noah Keene."

"Hey, you asked."

"Such a liar," she repeated. "But at least you're learning to lighten up."

Chapter Nineteen

In her mind, Abby retraced her route again and again a dozen times. She couldn't understand where she'd gone wrong, couldn't figure out how, even distracted as she'd been, she could have forgotten a tunnel connection. But here she sat, cold and hungry—no, starving—and feeling totally lost. Her brain had let her down. She'd left the lens cap on her photographic memory.

What should she do? She studied the mouths of the tunnels that converged in the high-ceilinged room. Two of them would lead her back to the room she'd been in before. But which two? She couldn't remember.

"Ohhhhh!" She clamped her hands to the sides of her head. "Think, Abby, think!" If only she'd taken something to mark her route, chalk or string or even pebbles like the kids dropped in that fairy tale with the wicked witch and the gingerbread house. Gingerbread?

Her stomach growled and she dropped her hands to clutch her middle. She could almost smell it. Her dry mouth filled with saliva and she swallowed quickly. Her stomach growled again.

Don't think about food, she coached herself, think about how to get out of here. There had to be a way to make a smart decision. No way could she just go wandering along, hoping she'd learn something important. That couldn't possibly be what Delacroix meant. She searched her memory for the exact words.

Closing her eyes, she drew back his low, rumbling, musical voice. "You too, Abby, must learn when to listen to your senses, your instinct, your heart. Not merely your estimable brain."

But how do you do that? How do you let go of what you've always trusted and grasp something you're not sure of?

Abby moaned and rocked back and forth, the chill beginning to spread through her body. She couldn't just stop thinking, could she, just turn off her brain?

She rocked some more. "I'm only a kid," she whispered.

So was the Dalai Lama, once. The thought leaped into her brain. She'd seen him on television, an aging man without a country, but a man who radiated such a sense of peace and completeness, self-fulfillment. She felt herself smile and remembered reading how masters of meditation talked about focusing on one object or one sound, a mantra. They talked about breathing very slowly and repeating the mantra, over and over again.

A part of her, her intellect, instantly rebelled at the idea. How could that accomplish anything? Maybe it would really relax you or maybe unlock some hidden memory or something, but what real good could come from it? Meditation couldn't possibly help her now.

Could it?

Abby eyed the five openings in the rock wall and realized she couldn't even remember which one she'd come out of. Not only was she lost, but her mind felt all tangly and fuzzy edged. All No-way's fault. Why couldn't her bonzo-brained brother have just stayed home and talked it out with Dad? But noooo. He had to run away from home and dance with some old crone on the beach and . . .

She stood and screamed at the top of her lungs. "Darn you, Noah!"

The words echoed eerily back at her, toneless but somehow taunting. "Darn you, Noah, darn you Noah, you Noah, u Noah, Noah, oah, ah." The words ran together, then dissipated, like smoke in the wind.

"Darn you, Noah!" She yelled again. The words echoed around again, chasing each other, colliding and somehow cleansing her mind. Her mantra? Feeling foolish but desperate, Abby clenched her eyes shut and began to chant the words over and over, melding them together. "DarnyouNoah, DarnyouNoah, DarnyouNoah, DarnyouNoah."

As she chanted, she tried to breathe in and out as slowly as she could. Folding her legs into an approximation of a lotus position, she repeated the words until they became a continuous string without beginning or end. Gradually, the cold seemed to leak from her body and she felt a warm glow tingle up her arms and legs and center itself somewhere between her eyes.

As she chanted the phrase faster and faster, something very strange occurred. Even though she knew she was saying "darn," all she heard back in her ears, or maybe just in her mind, was "you-Noah, you-Noah, you-Noah, you-know-uh, you-know-uh."

"You know-uh how to find your way back."

The voice was a quivering whisper, a faint hum of sound.

Abby opened her eyes to find herself floating near the ceiling of the chamber. Below her she saw a girl, sitting in the lotus position on a large rock, mumbling the same words over and over. Youknowuh, youknowuh, youknowuh, youknowuh . . ."

She studied the girl with detached interest and realized with no surprise that it was herself. This can't be, the rational side of her brain told her. You can't be there and here too.

"Why not?" The hum of sound filled her head, wiping her brain. "Why not?" She whispered back to the voice and rolled onto her back in mid-air. Above her, the ceiling glowed with a strange tint of violet. The Zezzue.

She was talking to them. Or perhaps just listening. The rock seemed to throb as more words appeared in her head.

"You know-uh the way, Abby."

"I thought I did," she whispered. "But I got lost."

"Not lost. Nothing is ever lost. You can find yourself. You have the map in your soul. Trace the route with your finger. Then use your finger to lead your body to the place you began from."

Above her, the lights began to dance, and swirl. She watched a map appear, a series of tunnels begin to take shape, tunnels linked by larger chambers. Turning her head, she saw herself, still sitting cross-legged on the stone, still chanting at high speed, breathing slow and deeply.

"Youknowuh, youknowuh, youknowuh, youknowuh."

Turning to face the Zezzue, she extended her arm and let her forefinger circle the map. Finally, she touched a spot on the light map, a chamber with multiple entrances.

The lights flashed a bright blue and she smiled. "You know-uh the way." Dreamily, she dragged the finger along the simulated tunnels until she had moved it to a huge cavern. The lights flashed again.

"I know," she whispered proudly. "I know how to get back."

With a heart-wrenching jolt, she found herself back inside her body, arms tingling, legs cramping, feet growing numb. She continued to chant, almost afraid of what would happen when she stopped. "Youknowuh, youknowuh, youNoah, youNoah, arnyouNoah, darnyouNoah." Without her brain commanding it, she stood, opened her eyes, flung out her arms and screamed again. "Darn you, Noah!"

The words echoed back at her once, then all sound died. She nodded. No longer afraid, she stretched, yawned, and stomped circulation into her feet. Time to go. Confidently, she jumped from the rock and took six steps toward a tunnel entrance, then froze. Was that the right one? She looked at the tunnel beside it. Maybe that one? Yes, it looked right. Or did it? She felt a wave of panic and returned to her rock, breath coming in long, shuddering gulps. How could she have forgotten already?

"You must keep your eyes closed, Abby." The vibrato murmur from overhead seemed to swell inside her head. "Close them and begin walking."

"Close my eyes? But how will I see where I am going?"

"Your eyes have deceived you. Now trust your other senses. Follow your finger."

"Follow my finger?" She held up her right index finger and studied it. "You'll get even more lost," an angry voice inside her brain shouted. "You're just dreaming those lights and voices. They don't really exist. Trust yourself. Forget about them. You can think your way out of here."

"No! I can't think! I have to know!" She closed her eyes and began to breathe slowly, regularly and deeply.

In a moment, she opened her mouth, freeing the words she knew would realign her consciousness. "I know the way. I know the way. Iknowtheway—Iknowtheway—Iknowtheway—Iknowtheway—Knowtheway—"

Extending her right arm in front of her, Abby let her finger drift through the air in a slow circle. When it stopped, she took a deep breath, swallowed her fear and began walking slowly in the direction it led. She stopped whispering and concentrated on keeping her mind empty except for the words, concentrated on opening her other senses, on seeing in other ways. She heard her shoes brush and pat against the rock, heard the fabric of her jacket whiffle as she moved her arm, tasted metallic air on her tongue as she filled her lungs.

After a while, she noticed that her feet were moving faster, that she'd stopped testing each step before she put her weight down. She smiled. She'd let go of all her fears. She'd learned to trust the Zezzue.

Once she felt her arm swing to the left, moving without her control like a water witcher's wand. Her body followed automatically and she felt the air tighten around her. As she went on, it felt warmer, too, and smelled different, like growth and decay. Was something growing here? She wanted to reach out and touch the walls, but forced herself to keep her left arm at her side. A little further along, she felt her knees bend automatically.

Something brushed against her head and she realized she'd ducked to enter a low-ceilinged chamber or passage. More than once, she fought a strong desire to open her eyes. The left-brain voice kept nagging at her. "You'll bump into something and hurt yourself. What if there's some ferocious animal just ahead of you? What if the ground just opens up, and you fall?" Abby blanketed the fears with her mantra, chanting faster and squeezing eyes more tightly shut.

"Knowthewayknowthewayknowtheway."

She felt something like a cobweb brush her forehead. An image flashed across her brain—cascades of diamonds, rubies and emeralds. Was it her imagination, or had she walked through the energy of her own previous thoughts? Was that possible? Was this the place where she'd daydreamed about finding precious gems? If it was, her journey was nearly over.

Suddenly, her knees began to pump, her feet lifted higher with each step. She began to run, faster than she'd ever run before, with her eyes still closed. The chant matched the rhythm of her pounding feet, became an endless string of sound with no beginning or end. Like a mobius strip. Like the symbol for infinity. Her right arm bent sharply and she took a corner on the dead sprint, never even brushing any of the walls of the stony maze.

Abby felt a warm wind current pass over her body, smelled vanilla, cinnamon and hot grease and heard the raspy voice of Chillout.

"Whoa, little chickie."

187

She stumbled and stopped, bent double, gasping for breath.

"Cool your jets, baby. You almost made this homeboy assume the prone position."

Opening her eyes, she shrank back from what felt like an automobile headlight pointed squarely into the face. She blinked furiously and the bright glare became the normal light of the cavern.

"What's the haps, Abster? Where's the fire? I was, just like, you know, bopping along minding my own biz when you pell-melled into my personal space. Dig?"

"Oh. Sorry." Abby swiveled her head to look around. "I'm really here then?"

Chillout cocked his head. "Far as I can tell.

Everybody got to be somewhere. You hungry? Almost time to tie on the feedbag."

Abby's stomach answered before she could, delivering a rumbling growl. "Excuse me. Yes. I'm very hungry. Where is Dela . . . the Pettifog?"

"He'll be boppin' in momentarily, if not sooner. Could you scarf down a heapin' helpin' of chicken fingers and cinnamon buns?"

"Sure. Great." Fleetingly, she wondered again about the food supply, about the items that clearly came from outside the mountain. She remembered the tunnel Delacroix said would lead her home. They must have a regular supply train. What did they use for money? What could they barter for chicken fingers and cinnamon buns?

"Me, I don't mind what happened to the wheat and sugar cane," Chillout interrupted her thoughts, "but I feel kinda bad some chicken's not gonna get a shot at bein' Van Cliburn, you know, but hey."

Abby groaned at his silly joke.

The grungoid shrugged his shoulders, gestured for her to follow and began to walk to the other end of the chamber.

Before she followed, Abby craned her neck at the haze of lights on the ceiling and mouthed the words, "thank you."

The lights flickered. A rainbowed wave of colors passed across them and broke with a shower of gold sparks. She heard the tremolo whisper a final time. "You knew the way."

Chapter Twenty

Deidre stopped five yards ahead of Noah on the rocky trail. "Pfhaaa. Hear it?" She turned and held two fingers to her lips in the universal shush gesture.

He shuffled to a standstill, listening for the sound of the River of Fire. Had they arrived already? A part of him had hoped this journey would take longer, would give him time to crystallize a plan for crossing the boiling stream.

Uh-oh, his baboon-like face creased with worry and exhaustion, shook back his hair. The once tightly bunched dreadlocks had loosened into a mound of unwinding and unruly clumps.

Straining his ears, Noah first heard the hollow quiet of the immense cavern. But then he picked up the faint undercurrent of sound—a constant hissing, like steam escaping from a kettle, interspersed with whip-crack snaps and pops and a nasty rolling gurgle. The river's audible signature created an instant understanding of why someone gave it the name Pfhaaa.

He wished he was back in his bedroll in 'Shroomtown. Then he wished he was back in his bed at home, where the very worst that could happen would be that he might be grounded for staying out too late or not getting his chores done. Instead, after wearing himself out hiking through twisting tunnels and across a rocky plain strewn with boulders, he now had to figure out a way to get himself and his friends across a river so hot it could boil the skin off their bodies in seconds. Suddenly all the problems he'd had before he came to Humbug Mountain seemed as insignificant as mosquito bites.

He rubbed his eyes and tried to remember if he'd slept at all last night. Maybe a little. But just at the very end.

His brain wouldn't seem to turn off. For most of the night, he'd stared up at the distant ceiling of the chamber, sorting fragments of memory, trying to find the one that could help them meet the challenge ahead. But the harder he labored to extract the deeply embedded information, the more elusive the mental tidbit became. Frustrated and exhausted, he'd given up. And then, what seemed like seconds later, Deidre shook him awake.

His traveling companions hadn't rested well either. Deidre's usually glimmering hazel eyes seemed to have become red-rimmed dark marbles and Uh-oh's usually nimble pigeon-toed scuttle had slowed to a syncopated scraping of hairy feet across the rocky ground.

Noah nodded to Deidre. "I hear it."

She pursed her lips and held his eye for a moment. She said nothing, but her body language and slightly raised eyebrows asked the question. "Have you thought of a way across?"

Noah bent down and fiddled with his shoelaces. He knew she wouldn't like the answer. Not the honest one. He couldn't tell her about the parade of crazy ideas and wild schemes that had bracketed his sleep. Deidre didn't want to hear that an elusive memory, dangling just out of reach, might or might not provide a way across the molten flow ahead. But most of all, she wouldn't want to hear the scream, building inside him, waiting to reverberate across the rock ceilings and wall around them:

"Heeeeeelp! Mommmmmm! I'mmmmmmm scared!"

Noah took a deep breath, swallowed the panic rising in his throat and forced his mouth into a tight smile. "Let's get down there," he gruffed. "I'll get us across." Right, he thought. All I've got to do is figure out how to make us sprout wings.

Deidre nodded, hitched at her pack and started off. "You're such a liar, Noah, such a liar." Noah heard Deidre's voice from directly behind him.

The rangy warrior girl spun, eyes darting. "Who said that?"

191

Noah turned, shook his head and then stepped aside so she could see Uh-oh, frozen in a perfect Deidre pose, hands on hips, head held defiantly high, eyes steely. The gray creature's lip curled in a sneer. "You're clueless, Noah, clueless." He stalked back and forth, aping the girl's muscular, arm-swinging gait perfectly.

Noah felt a laugh erupt from his throat.

Deidre frowned for a moment, then began to giggle. "I . . . oh . . ." unable to contain it, she fell into a laughing fit, pointing at Uh-oh, still tromping back and forth.

Finally, Uh-oh's face reformed into its normal, lost-in-space expression. The moment passed.

"How did he learn how to do that?" Deidre narrowed her eyes in anger, but her grin betrayed her. "Did you teach him?"

"No. He does me too. Imitates how I sound and look." Tears of laughter streamed down Noah's face. He coughed, fighting for control. "He must have heard us talking last night."

"Very funny, Uh-oh." Deidre thumbed her nose at the final member of the trio. Uh-oh responded by shrugging and waggling his thin eyebrows up and down. "It's good we laughed now," she told Noah in a serious tone. "It could be our last chance. Ever."

He nodded grimly and she turned and started along the trail. Within a few hundred yards, the hissing, snapping and crackling melded into a steady roar, echoing through the immense chamber. Noah smelled the rotten-egg reek of sulfur. It grew stronger as they walked, mingling with the odor of hot metal. Waves of heat undulated over him.

The air seemed to grow thicker every moment, making it harder to breathe. His throat felt raw, his eyes watered. As they crested a small rise, Noah saw the angry orange glow of the river for the first time.

"Maybe a half mile more," Deidre shouted back at him. "Are you all right?"

Wiping sweat from his forehead with the back of his wrist, Noah nodded and forced himself to keep walking, keep moving forward. Glancing back, he saw Uh-oh plodding along, perhaps twenty yards behind, huffing and stumbling, sweat dripping from the ends of his snarled curls. Noah waited for his friend to catch up and offered his arm for Uh-oh to lean on. "Don't look at it," he advised. "Just take it one step at a time." The creature gave no signal that he'd heard or understood, but kept moving.

Finally, they stopped on an overhang fifty yards shy of the molten flow. Noah cupped his hands over his nose, trying to shield out the intense heat and the venomous stench of liquid rock, trying to draw a normal breath into his scorching lungs. A mixture of sweat and tears flooded his eyes and he fought the impulse to turn and run. Not only did he not know how they would cross the red, orange, yellow and white ribbon of pure heat gurgling through the deep cut in the earth below; he wondered how long he could stand there before his blood came to a boil and his brain exploded and blew his head apart. His skin was already scarlet and the hair on his forearms smoked.

"Be logical. Use that thing on top of your neck, Noway."

Above the unending roar and the pounding vibration of the rock on which he stood, he seemed to hear Abby's voice. It carried the chiding tone she used when they played chess, when he'd impulsively knock off one of her knights with his queen, only to watch her capture the royal lady with a bishop or rook. "Think, big brother. Look at the board. See what I'll do after you've made your move. Better yet, try to think a couple of moves ahead."

Okay, I'll think, Noah told himself. But this isn't chess. He squinted his burning eyes and tried to focus on the path of the molten river. There didn't appear to be any way around it. To his left, it flowed for what looked like miles, twisting and bending to conform to the sheer rock face of the chamber. To the right, perhaps a quarter mile from where they stood, the gurgling, spitting, hissing flow ran over a ledge and plummeted, creating a waterfall of fire. The crash and crackle of millions of gallons of super-heated, falling rock escalated the noise level to a painful threshold. If there truly was a hell, like some of the preachers on television insisted there was, this must be what it looks like, he thought.

He felt a gentle tap on his shoulder. Turning, he saw Deidre, her face glowing with sweat, her ears as red as flames, her hair wild with static electricity. He felt a sharp tug on his pants leg and looked down to see Uh-oh clinging to him, struggling for oxygen like a landed fish.

Think, Noah, he commanded himself. He looked to the left again. Not that way. They'd be worn out before they reached the edge of the horizon, and there might be no crossing when they arrived. Maybe the right? Perhaps they could climb the rocky face beside the waterfall and edge their way over the molten lava upstream. No. The rock wall looked slick and without many footholds. It would be an ascent for trained climbers. Not for two exhausted kids and whatever kind of creature Uh-oh was.

Blinking his eyes to clear the sweat, he peered directly across the flow. Was it his imagination, or did the river narrow there? And was that a kind of rocky beach on the other side? He rubbed his eyes and squinted hard, trying to block out the waves of shimmering heat that rose from the river. Yes, it was a flat spot. And beyond it he saw a tunnel cut into the rock wall. That had to be the way then, directly across the river.

A crackling boom erupted from the river and a finger of fire shot fifty feet into the air. Globs of molten rock spun free, swirled and arched, then crashed back into the flow with a prolonged "Tsssssssss."

The memory he'd dug for flashed across Noah's mind. A fire. The beach. Music. There was music. And the sound of the mountain. He could hear it now, even over the steady roar of Pfhaaa, the rushing river of fire.

Thoomp Thoomp. Thoomp Thoomp. Thudda-Thoomp.

Noah reached back into his pack, groping through the clothes and bundles of food until he found the drumsticks. Grasping them, he looked around for a likely rock. There. He balanced the sticks in his hands.

Deidre's hand dropped to his shoulder again, this time an insistent grip, pulling him to face her. She put her mouth next to his ear and snarled. "What are you doing, Noah? We're about to become crispy critters and you're messing around with—"

He whirled away from her, found a flat place on a nearby rock and began to beat time to the music churning through his mind. Hannah. The old woman on the beach. Moving with her to the rhythm of the music playing on the boom box. He remembered it all now; the scene was the only thing his mind could hold.

The sticks seemed to move by themselves as his memory took control of his arms and hands. On the movie screen that filled his brain, he watched himself spin and backpedal and lunge and retreat in the strange dance on the sand. As he saw himself and Old Hannah change directions, his hands moved the tips of the sticks to alter the rhythm.

He closed his eyes tighter, then opened them wide and saw Deidre, a panicked scowl on her face. She pointed to the river and shouted something at the top of her lungs, but he couldn't hear. What he heard was Old Hannah and the words she'd left him with. "Don't ever be afraid to dance, Noah. Remember the steps."

Crazy, Noah thought. Why am I remembering this now? How is dancing going to get us across a river of lava? He thought of the mold-monster, brought down by a bag of candy. Before that happened, it would have seemed impossible.

Springing to his feet, he jammed the drumsticks back into his pack. He shoved past Deidre and started down the path toward the river. "C'mon. Follow me," he bellowed over his shoulder.

Deidre didn't move. Uh-oh, on hands and knees, continued his battle to draw breath.

"Trust me," Noah yelled back, knowing he could never explain the insane idea that drove him closer and closer to the scorching heat of Pfhaaa. He wondered if his companions would have enough faith in him to follow his lead, to let go of their doubts. He wouldn't blame Deirdre if she decided to scramble back to 'Shroomtown for help. That would make more sense than what he wanted her to do.

His sonic sword began to glow an eerie orange, the hair on his arms scorched, his fingers swelled like broiling hot dogs and the sulfurous smell bent him nearly double with each breath. Across the river, on the sheer cliff face, he saw shadows flicker and dance as flames spit from the molten flow of rock. Noah stopped at the edge of the current and turned to see Deidre half carrying Uh-oh toward the brink. They came, he thought triumphantly. They believe in me. They trust me.

He felt himself crest a wave of elation and slide into a trough of depression. What if this doesn't work? He turned to Deidre. She tightened her cracking lips and shook her head. Uh-oh turned his back and began to crawl away from the river.

Noah spread his arms over the roiling lava and began to hum the music of Old Hannah's dance. Within seconds, flat, round, metallic blue stones, about the size of large dinner plates began to appear on the volcanic river. Each one surfaced for a few seconds, floated until another popped up alongside, then slid beneath the surface with a sharp "tsssst." Shielding his eyes against the relentless heat, Noah watched them rise and sink, in what seemed to be a random sequence, across the width of the lava flow.

Humming louder, he peeled off his backpack and ran to Uh-oh, his lungs screaming with the effort, his legs trembling. "Get on my back," he yelled, working the words into the music.

Uh-oh shook his head and tried to scuttle away, but Noah seized him and tossed him over his shoulder as easily as if the creature had been one of Abby's dolls. Uh-oh instinctively flung his arms around Noah's neck and squeezed his legs around Noah's waist. Noah retrieved his pack and slung the straps over his right arm. He no longer seemed to feel the heat, his thirst or his exhaustion.

He advanced on Deidre, humming louder, and put his right hand around her waist and grasped her right hand with his left. Was that the way he'd danced with Hannah? Was that where he'd put his hands? He hoped it didn't matter if he didn't get this part exactly right.

Deidre recoiled and struggled to pull away, but with a strength he didn't realize he had, he clamped his hand around hers, pulled her close against his chest. He stepped to the edge of the river and eyed the rhythm of the appearing and disappearing rocks. Uh-oh's breath steamed in his ear. Deidre's large and frightened eyes stared up at him. He began to hum the song from the beginning again, the sound a mere whisper over the roar of the molten torrent at his feet.

"This is crazy," Deidre shouted. "What are you doing? We can't—"

Her next words were interrupted by a scream as Noah spun her around once and backed them onto a flat blue rock as it surfaced inches from the bank.

Chapter Twenty-one

"Once Bravo Company has completed the pincers movement, cutting off the supply line to Delacroix's force, we'll march toward 'Shroomtown and perform a flanking operation on their defenses." Spid used a long, thin pointer to indicate broad red X's marked on the huge map. This was propped up by two small gammits squatting on one end of the oval stone table.

"Brilliant, boss. Patton couldna' come up with a better plan." Yurk growled the anticipated and demanded compliment at his boss.

Spid beamed and blinked through the acrid haze of the oil-lamp-lit chamber to see if the gathered generals of the combined Beneath forces agreed with the appraisal.

Freghzpad, the gammit commander, sat staring into his mug of mud-colored coffee, multiple wrinkles of confusion writhing across his broad, leathery face. His assistant, Stozalg, had fingers stuck in three of the ears on the right side of his face and seemed to be trying to dig something of substantial size out of them.

Farther down the table, Krellep, the huge skree who led the air forces, hunkered with his head tucked beneath one wing. Spid felt his stomach tilt and roll and wondered how the flying demon flesh-shredder could stand being that close to his own underarm. But, he decided, the unbelievable stench of the skrees as they flapped their wings could be a deciding factor in the battle to come. If he, Spid, could barely stomach it, imagine how the odor would affect the Above Skin defenses He smiled grimly and turned his gaze to a trio of ogres, Yurk's field commanders, who drooled on the table and themselves. Their slack-jawed, glassy-eyed expressions betrayed their nearly non-existent attention spans. But once the killing started, Spid knew they'd acquit themselves well. He'd seen Yurk's forces in action before, hundreds of years before, at the great conflict in the coal beds where the ogres had triumphed over the gronnks and cemented the forced alliance that stood to this very day.

"Could I offer you a scone?" A four-armed gronnk appeared beside Spid's right shoulder, bearing a tray stacked with flaky, dark brown pastries.

"Scones?" The demon troll commander looked up suspiciously even as his stomach rumbled and saliva pooled beneath his tongue. He cocked his head at Yurk.

"Scones?"

"Sure, boss, you told me to come up with some goodies for this here final planning meeting, so I had Glemmis whip up a little something special."

"I hope they're better than the cappuccino, Yurk. That tasted like mud."

The ogre's small beady eyes darted back and forth, meeting the gronnk's for a moment. The multi-limbed creature shrugged and used one of the arms not balancing the tray to hand two scones to the suddenly uncertain ogre. Yurk set them in front of him and cleared his throat twice. "It, uh, was mud, boss. We don't have any real coffee down here."

"Delightful." Spid stared at the liquid in the cup at his right hand. He couldn't wait to get Above Skin, couldn't wait to march up to an espresso stand and demand a latte with a dusting of nutmeg, and a chocolate chip cookie with real chocolate chips, not chunks of coal.

"Uh, try a scone, boss." Yurk nodded toward the tray. "And could you, uh, try not to hurt Glemmis' feelings? She spent all day in the kitchen."

Spid sighed loudly, and took a pastry from the tray, forcing himself to smile into the pointed face of the gronnk. The scone felt grainy and heavy. He sniffed it tentatively. It didn't smell half bad. At least, not compared to the underarm of a skree.

Beside him, Yurk munched energetically on a substantial chunk. Lifting the scone to his mouth, Spid bit off a small section. For a moment, the sensation was pure texture, a not-unpleasant biscuit-like flakiness that ground between his teeth. And then the full impact of the flavor assaulted Spid's taste buds, rocketed to his brain and exploded.

"Pffffutuuuui!" Spid spat out the wad of masticated dough. The globby projectile caught one of the ogre generals flush in the face. The squat, ugly creature reached up with a two thick fingers and scraped the goo off his hamburger-like face. He jerked a knife from his belt, bared his teeth at Spid and growled a warning.

The troll was too busy blowing the remaining fragments of the partially chewed scone out of his mouth and onto the rock floor beside him to notice the threat or acknowledge the displeasure of one of his underlings.

"Pfuii, Pflagh, Pfuii," Spid sputtered. He slammed the uneaten portion of the scone to the table and gargled with the remains of his mud coffee in a vain effort to clear his palate and salve his taste buds. "Yurk," he gasped, pointing at the scone. He tried to say more, but the horrible taste seemed to renew itself. He choked and spat some more.

His second-in-command chewed contentedly on the final portion of his own pastry with a look of innocence and delight. He wiped his mouth on his sleeve and pointed to the remains of Spid's scone. "So, you're not going to finish that?" Without waiting for an answer, he reached over, snatched it and stuffed it into his mouth.

Spid coughed and spat, wishing he could ram his hands into his mouth and rip out the taste buds that continued to send their message of distress to his brain. "What in the devil is in that, Yurk?" Spid thought his voice sounded like it had been burned, like only an ash of sound remained. He wondered if the damage was permanent.

"It tasted like dried Stegalope droppings."

A wail of despair erupted from Glemmis, the scone-serving gronnk. She dropped the tray with the remaining scones. It clattered to the stone floor. Yurk's generals dove for the scones in a blaze of knives, battle clubs and spiked brass knuckles. Glaring at Spid and muttering incoherently, Glemmis stalked from the chamber. Just before she disappeared through the entryway, she used all four hands to flip him a rude gesture.

"Aw boss, you gave away her secret ingredient. And you insulted her food. Now she'll never cook for us again." Yurk looked with obvious distress at the few crumbs remaining on the table, then began to lick them up.

Spid heard a grumble of annoyance swell from the assembled demons, ogres, skrees, gammits, gronnks and trolls. He'd broken one of the few rules of protocol in the land Below Skin. He'd have to act quickly or his leadership would be undermined, his orders wouldn't be obeyed, the alliance would fall apart. "Yurk!"

"Yeff, boff?" The ogre, his tongue scraping the table, turned one eye toward Spid, then snapped to attention.

Spid swallowed and forced what was left of his voice to be calm and reasonable. It wouldn't do to show any signs of weakness. He had to appear totally in control. "When we have finished our strategizing, Yurk, I want you to find Glemmis for me."

"I'll make a note, boss." The ogre pulled out a piece of slate and a sharpened bit of charcoal and began scribbling. His strokes made a grating sound and several gammits moaned and covered their multiple ears with their arms. "Find Glemmis. Got it." He licked the charcoal and awaited further instructions.

"If you would, please apologize to her for me and tell her I meant no offense."

201

"No offense," Yurk wrote on the slate. "I like that, boss. Nice touch. It takes a big man, uh troll, to admit when he's wrong. That's what makes you such a great leader. Your humility."

The rumble from the other end of the table swelled. Spid thought he heard a small giggle from one of the gammits. He ignored it and concentrated on controlling his breathing and resuscitating his damaged voice.

"Would you also please remind her that my show of disrespect was inappropriate, but that hers was more so. Seeing that I am the Grand Exalted . . . well, you know. Tell her I would appreciate it if she would not repeat it at any point in the future."

"at any point in the . . ." Yurk turned the slate over.

". . . future. Right, boss. Anything else?"

"Just one thing further. After you've gotten her solemn promise . . ."

"Solemn promise," Yurk scratched the word onto the slate

"Then have her—" Spid leaned back in his chair and took a deep breath. His roaring, venomous voice, almost as strong as it ever had been, filled the chamber with his uncontrolled rage. "—THROWN FROM MY PERSONAL STALAGMITE!!!

A gasp rose from the assembled generals. The ogres sat up straight and cut looks at each other from the corners of their eyes. Even the skree withdrew his head and eyed Spid with a look that might have signaled respect.

Yurk gulped and dropped his slate. "Do what, boss?"

Spid swallowed painfully and lowered his voice. "You heard me, Yurk. Now obey!"

Yurk gulped, saluted, and tucked his slate and charcoal back in a pocket of his blousy field jacket. "Y . . . Y . . . yes, boss. I'll get right on it."

202

"Good." Spid smiled at his minions. He continued in a controlled, almost salesman-like oily tone of voice.

"And Yurk."

"Yes, boss."

"I'll want to know exactly how many times she bounces."

A second gasp from the assembled generals assured Spid his point had been made. The skree blinked its reptilian eyes. "Yes, boss," Yurk mumbled.

"And have her strung up over the main archway as a reminder to any who might consider any form of rebellion."

Yurk pulled out the slate and charcoal again and made a note. "Any form of rebel . . . rebel? Two L's in rebellion, boss?"

"Yes, Yurk, two L's." Spid smiled at his commanders. They were with him again, he could feel it. "Now then, gentlemen, if I could have your attention here at the map, we'll proceed."

Practically stampeding over one another to get to the front of the room, Spid's commanders formed a half-circle around the young gammits who held the map. They straightened their stilt-like legs and gripped the edges with clawed hands the color of phlegm.

"Here," Spid tapped the pointer against a large green area on the hand-drawn representation of the world Above Skin. "I'll need your forces, Freghzpad, to create a diversion while Krellep and his skrees provide air cover for a blitzkrieg by Monghelk and the first platoon of ogres. When the enemy begins to fall back, I'll want . . ."

After nearly an hour of discourse, Spid stopped and fingered his prodigious wart, rolling it between his fingers. No doubt about it, he was a military genius. In millenniums to come, young trolls would read about the way he'd deployed his troops, the way he'd anticipated each feint and rally by his enemies. He would become even more of a legend. "I think we're all on the same page, now, are we not?" He tipped his head toward Yurk and the ogre took his cue.

"Brilliant, boss. You are Napoleon, Genghis Khan and Alexander the Great all rolled into one."

"True as it may be, Yurk, thank you for saying it. Are there any questions?"

Freghzpad raised a timid paw and Spid pointed at him. "Yes, my friend?"

In a series of grunts, squeaks, groans and sputters, the gammit framed some kind of question. Spid, of course, could not make heads or tails of it, even though his mother had spoken gammit. The language, filled as it was with triple negatives, idioms and constantly-changing slang, was difficult to master. Not that he, Spid, had had time to try. His talents had been turned to more vital objectives. "What did he say, Yurk?"

"Well, er, uh . . ." The ogre chewed at a lower lip that reminded Spid of a picture he'd seen of bratwurst.

"What?" Spid prompted. "Out with it."

"Well, he says he likes your plan. It's a great plan. The best battle plan he's ever seen. But, um, well, he was just wondering if, instead of going through all the maneuvering and coordinating and stuff, could they just rush in and kill everything in front of them?"

Spid felt angry blood rush to his brain. "Weren't they listening? Don't they understand why I've spent years on this plan? Everything depends on split-second timing, on teamwork, on knowing the signs and signals! They can't just rush in and—" He paused, eying the group gathered around him, the gronnks and gammits alternately scratching themselves and picking lice from their bodies with their teeth, the ogres staring open-mouthed at the ceilings, walls and each other. He, Spid the Devious, the Grand Exalted Garboon, deserved better than this.

204

He sighed heavily, plucked the battle map from the young gammits' hands and began slowly to roll it up. Tucking it under his arm, he decided he'd be better off concentrating on training the mutant five-armed gronnk who would drum their way through the Skin and into the land of Above. He shook his head and turned to Yurk.

"Tell them that will be satisfactory. But ask them not to harm that brat, Abby. She's mine."

Chapter Twenty-two

As their feet settled on the first stone, it sank slightly beneath them. Deidre let out a little gasp and dug her fingers into his shoulder.

Noah ignored her. Half closing his eyes, he focused only on the music, the memory of the steps, how quick and how slow each one had been, how long and short each stride or shuffle. Uh-oh snuffled into the collar of his shirt and clung to his shoulders like a tick. Heat radiated from the boiling magma scant inches from their toes and the pungent skanky-egg smell mixed with the rank odor of their fear. White-hot rock popped and exploded, sending red and orange contrails into the air around them.

Planting his right foot, he pressed Deidre tighter against his chest, pivoted and placed his left foot where he prayed the second stone should be. For a fraction of a second, he felt only the rising heat, then with a slap, his shoe struck a solid surface and he spun the three of them safely onto the second flat rock. It felt almost cool beneath his feet. "Yes," he breathed into Deidre's hair.

He hesitated for a half second, then stepped backward onto another surfacing rock. Glancing over Deidre's shoulder, he saw the stone they'd just left sinking rapidly into the bubbling orange liquid. Deidre turned her head, her mouth opened and he felt her chest compress against his as she screamed. The bubbling roar of the river smothered the sound. Uh-oh's grip tightened to a band of pain.

For one desperate, short moment, Noah's attention wavered. He stopped humming. He forgot the steps. The stone beneath them begin to sink.

His toes felt like they were on fire. He started to scream himself and then he seemed to be overtaken by a cool silence, within which he heard only the old woman's voice commanding him: "Dance, Noah, Dance. The steps. Remember the steps."

The stone beneath them wobbled and tilted.

"Don't look," he shouted to his friends. "Hold on tight. It's gonna get hairy." Humming again, he swiveled them all to the left, pushed off and guided them through three long steps, a stutter, a spin and another three backward steps. During the sequence, their feet touched seven different stones, each of which sank just after they'd danced to the next.

Faster and faster, the stones rose and fell. Louder and louder grew the roar of the river and the explosions of rocks split apart by the heat. Noah could barely hear himself hum. He knew that if they stopped now, for even a second, they be boiled in the scalding river. He wondered if he'd have time to scream. Time to feel more pain than he already felt.

He swung his friends to another stone, and another. His legs seemed to move on their own, with no direct connection to his brain. He danced faster, dipping and swaying, feeling the jolt in his spine each time his feet struck a surfacing stone.

Noah looked back at the shore they'd left, then toward their destination. The advance and retreat of the dance had taken them only a quarter of the way across Pfhaaa. His back ached. Sweat stung his eyes. He blinked frantically to clear them and gasped for oxygen in the roasting air. No way would they make it. He couldn't do it. He wasn't strong enough.

"Promise me you'll never give up, Noah." His mother's voice. As clear as if she were standing beside him. "I'm with you, Noah. Dance. Dance."

He looked around. He saw nothing by the steaming, swirling river, but he felt a change in the air. A sort of mental mist clouded his surroundings and he could no longer feel the heat of the river or taste the acrid sulfur

207

smoke. His worries about where they were on Pfhaaa or whether the next stone would appear ceased to have any meaning. His entire being, every molecule, focused only on the music now filling his mind, sharper than ever before, its rhythms more clearly defined.

He straightened, took a deep breath, dipped and stepped. Deidre, as if she sensed his transformation, seemed to meld into him, to become one with him and even anticipate his next series of movements. Even the burden of Uh-oh seemed to lighten, to become as insignificant as the weight of his shirt.

They glided across the molten river, dancing for their lives. Inside Noah's head the music built, the beats becoming more and more rapid. As the melody swirled toward a crescendo, he and Deidre spun first one direction and then another, back and forth. The river of fire became an orange blur and he felt himself getting dizzy, felt a sudden cold emptiness in the pit of his stomach and saw the darkness beginning to creep in around the edges.

"Hang on," he told himself. "Just a little more." He fought to stay conscious as the song inside his head climaxed with crashing cymbals and blaring horns. His field of vision narrowed and crimped.

He felt himself begin to sway, felt his center of balance shift. The putrefying smell of sulfur assaulted him. I'm going into the river," he thought, and I'm taking Deidre and Uh-oh with me. If Uh-oh hasn't already slipped off somewhere halfway across, he thought. He could no longer feel the gray creature's hands.

"Don't give up," he heard himself croak through cracked and parched lips. His field of vision narrowed to a pinpoint, then blacked out. He felt himself falling, burning.

"Hey, get off of me." Deidre's yell sent Noah swimming toward the edge of consciousness. His eyes fluttered open.

208

"Come on, Noah, move it!"

Hands pushed at his chest. Others pulled at his shoulders. He looked down to see Deidre pinned beneath him on a flat boulder a few yards from the edge of the tumbling, hissing edge of the river of fire. The rock beneath him felt cool. Or at least less hot. He felt Uh-oh's long fingers clamp around his shoulders again, trying to lift him. We made it, he thought. But how? I was sure we hadn't.

"Noah, c'mon, you're heavy for a scrawny little goof. Move it," Deidre yelled as she pushed again at his chest.

He tried to obey, but it seemed to take hours for his body to respond to the command from his brain. Finally, he managed to roll away from her. As he did, he sent Uh-oh sprawling. The gray creature, now streaked with soot and with half his hair singed off, tried to stand again, but his legs wobbled and wouldn't hold his weight. After three tries, he plopped back down on his rear end with a groan.

"We got to have water," Deidre gasped as she sat up.

"We're dehydrated." She clawed at the canteen on her belt and twisted the cap. It opened with a hiss and a puff of steam shot out. She put the canteen to her lips, then jerked it away. "Too hot to drink. Come on, let's get out of here as fast as we can."

Noah tried to get to his feet, but he couldn't feel them. His socks and shoes were little more than blackened scraps of fabric and melted rubber. Inside them, his feet throbbed. The hair on his arms was black and crispy and broke away at a touch. He felt another huge wave of dizziness and fell to the ground again. "Can't."

"Can!" Deidre shouted. She lurched to her feet, steadied herself, and stumbled toward Uh-oh. The gray creature clung to her arm, trembling; together they tottered back to Noah. "Come on, Bun-boy. On your feet."

"I can't," Noah moaned. How much more did he have to go through before he could just go home? Why had he ever left in the first place? He couldn't remember what had been going on in his mind when he snuck away. It all seemed so trivial, so silly.

"Get up! Get up or you'll die here." Deidre seized his hand. "Get up or I'll drag you." She began to tug at him. "Do you want to be dragged around by a girl? What will all your friends say?"

"No problem, don't have any," Noah muttered, but he realized that wasn't true. He had at least three. Abby, Uh-oh and Deidre. He shook off her hand, heaved himself up and reeled after her, panting. With each painfully slow step away from the Pfhaaa River, the air and ground grew cooler. Before them, the tunnel they'd seen from the other side opened. The air rushing from it seemed almost frigid, and they inhaled deeply and gratefully and drank the now-tepid water from their canteens. Noah peeled off this shoes and socks and threw them away. The rock beneath his burning feet felt marvelously cold and soothing.

"You might need your shoes later." Deidre started to retrieve them. "I can carry them."

"No." Noah shook his head. "They're worthless. He glanced over at Deidre's feet. Her sturdy boots, although scorched in several places, seemed to have survived intact. "Leave them, we don't need the extra weight.

Besides," he pointed at Uh-oh, "he's been barefoot all along."

Deidre opened her mouth as if to argue, then seemed to change her mind. As they started into the dim tunnel, Noah felt Deidre's lips brush his ear and heard the smiling whisper of her voice. "That was fun. Let's do it again sometime."

Noah grinned, found her hand and squeezed it. "Great. Next time we'll make it a slow dance." He noticed that she didn't pull her hand away and he grinned again.

An hour or so later, they emerged into a small chamber. A stream of water slid from a crevice in the

210

ceiling and pooled in a natural basin in the wall before overflowing into a crack in the floor. They flopped down, opened their charred packs and dug out the sandwiches Eve had packed for them. Noah bit into his and marveled that the heat from the river hadn't spoiled it. Instead, the ingredients between the slabs of a rough-crusted wheat bread seemed to have melted together into a tasty filling, almost as if that's what Deidre's mother had intended. He swallowed the first few bites quickly, but then chewed more slowly, detecting some kind of mushroom, onions, tomatoes and a green that resembled lettuce but probably wasn't. The mushroom had an almost meat-like, salty flavor, reminding Noah of bacon. After they finished the sandwiches, they ate cookies redolent with molasses, or something akin to it, and carrot.

Uh-oh fell asleep clutching his second cookie. Deidre fought a yawn and looked over at Noah. "So, Fred Astaire. Nice moves out there."

Noah blinked. How did she know about Fred Astaire? Where would she have seen the graceful, thin, tuxedoed man with the slicked back hair who still floated across the television screen with a leggy blond woman in his arms.

"You weren't half bad yourself, Ginger."

She giggled. "Thanks. I never danced much before. They have some kinda half-baked dances in 'Shroomtown. Mostly klunky boys stepping on your toes and like that. Everybody kind of doing their own thing. Not real dancing."

Noah nodded. "Sounds like junior high back home."

The thought of home sobered him a little. Home was where he'd seen Fred Astaire. Old black and white movies on late night TV. His mother had loved watching the dancer's effortless movements. "Hey, how do you know about—"

"Fred Astaire? Mom has an old magazine. About movies and people who were in them. It's kinda ragged

211

and tattered. It's been around our place for as long as I can remember. I asked her about it once, where it came from, but she said she didn't know, that she'd always had it."

They both sensed movement and turned to see Uh-oh, up from his nap and on his feet, clutching an imaginary dance partner. He advanced and retreated, twirled and high-stepped. Flinging his remaining curls back, he spun his invisible counterpart out and away from him, then brought her back with a flick of his wrist. Bending her over backward (at least Noah assumed it was a her), Uh-oh posed, face tilted toward the imaginary applause from an audience. Noah and Deidre rewarded him by clapping enthusiastically. Uh-oh bowed deeply from the waist, spun in place and plopped back on the ground, grabbing a cookie as he landed. Munching contentedly, he waggled his eyebrows and growled one word. "Tadah!"

"What a clown," Deidre rolled her eyes and laughed.

"He really is pretty amazing," Noah agreed.

"So are you. I gotta tell you, I was pretty freaked out when you grabbed me and stepped out on that rock. Where did you get the idea to dance across? Did it just come to you at the last second, or what?"

"Not exactly." Noah stretched out on his back and closed his eyes, enjoying the feel of cool and solid rock against his spine. "Something happened. Earlier. Before I came into Humbug Mountain." He turned his head to look at her.

Deidre asked "and" with her eyes and he told her the story of Old Hannah and the music on the beach, how Abby had been kidnapped, and how he and Uh-oh fell into the ocean and woke up in the hermit's cavern. "I've seen him. The hermit." Deidre told him. "Just at a distance. Up on some of the high shelves above the main caverns. I asked Mom about him and she said he was just

212

another lost soul down here. Like the ones in 'Shroomtown."

"The ones in 'Shroomtown?"

"Sure. That's how they got here. They're all descendants of people who disappeared from somewhere. You know, lost hikers, children who vanished on their way home from school, people who never returned from vacation."

Noah realized he hadn't wondered about where the 'Shroomtown residents had come from, just accepted them as another part of the underground landscape.

"That's what we all are down here. Lost souls." This time, Deidre laid back and closed her eyes. Neither of them spoke for awhile and Noah had nearly drifted into sleep when she broke the silence. "Noah?"

"Yeah?"

"What's it like? Out there?"

Out there. Home. Abby. Dad. His room. His drums. The smell of the ocean and the forest. The town, with the little stores selling junk to the tourists. Highway 101 with all of the cars zooming by on their way to Gold Beach and Brookings and California. The mall in Coos Bay. None of the words he could think of seemed to be right to describe it. And where would he begin? "Well, in here you go only so far and you run into a wall. Out there, it's very . . . unbelievably large . . . open . . . with no boundaries."

"Really?"

"I can sit at night, on the bluff by the lighthouse, and look up at the sky and see a billion stars."

"Stars. What are those?"

"They're huge balls of burning gas that are trillions and trillions of miles away, so they only look like little pinpoints of light in the sky."

"What's the sky?"

"It's . . . well, it's miles and miles of air, going up and up and up." Noah put a hand up as if pointing at the sky.

213

"And one of those burning balls of gas isn't that far away from us and the whole planet circles around it, spinning while it does, so that sometimes it's dark outside and sometimes it's light. Dark and light. In a regular pattern. And when it's dark, we turn on electric lights so we can see what we need to."

"Get out of here. Really?" Deidre's eyes opened wide and she thought for a moment. "So you don't have any Darksuckers out there?"

"Not that I know of. Just the sun and the moon."

"The moon? What's the moon?"

"It's a big dead chunk of rock that circles around Earth. The earth is what we're all on. Sometimes you can see all of the moon and sometimes only part of it. It glows at night and you can see the face of a man on it."

Noah could hear Deidre breathing quietly beside him. She remained silent for a moment. "It must be beautiful."

"It is."

"Will you show me some day? When all this is over?"

He felt himself blush. "Sure. Definitely. Yeah. I'll show you the moon and we'll watch a Fred Astaire movie and eat popcorn and I'll even let you tease my little sister." Yeah, he thought. And all I've got to do first is figure out a way to keep some evil thing called Spid from killing all of us.

As tired and played out as Noah felt, he forced himself to his feet. "Maybe we'd better get going again."

"In a second," Deidre mumbled. "Noah?"

"What, Deidre?"

"Is there evil out there? Like Spid? Like the nasty things that live Beneath?"

Noah took a moment before he answered her. "Yeah. Of course there is. There are bad people, or even regular people who sometimes do really bad things. And sometimes . . ." He felt his eyes mist up. ". . . really bad things happen to really good people. Like my Mom."

214

"Oh."

That was all she said, but Noah didn't need any prompting. He wanted to tell her. "My mom died. A little more than a year ago. She had cancer. Evil stuff that grows inside your body and hurts you and kills you."

"Noah, I'm so sorry. It must have been tough to lose your mom. Especially like that. But . . ."

"But, what . . ." He snapped, and was immediately sorry.

She took a breath and looked away. "At least you had her for a while. You had both of your parents. I've never known my father."

The words hung in the air between them. Slowly, Noah let go of his anger and thought about what she'd said. He decided not knowing your dad was probably as bad as what he went through with Mom. "He's never been around?"

"No," she answered, sadness tingeing her voice. "I don't know where he is."

"Have you asked Eve, your mom?"

"Yes, but she doesn't remember. Something happened to her. I don't know what. Her life before she had me is a total blank."

Noah couldn't think of a thing else to say. He looked down to see Deidre lift her hand. He took it and helped her to her feet.

"Time to hit the road," she said gruffly. "The Temple of Cheltnor can't be much farther."

"Hope not," he said, not really meaning it. He felt like he could sleep for a week.

"You got another vision, like the dance, for what we do once we get there?"

"I'll think of something," he answered, knowing with cold certainty that he'd run completely out of ideas. His mind felt empty, as if all ability to think had been fried out of it by the heat from the river. Maybe, he hoped,

215

something else that had passed between him and Old Hannah would surface. He'd have to think about it while they walked. Or maybe he shouldn't think.

"Great." Deidre sounded a touch sarcastic as she helped Uh-oh to his feet and turned to stride ahead into the tunnel. "You do that. Because I've got bad vibes about marching into Cheltnor and carrying the Methuselah out of the temple. Somebody's not gonna like that. And whoever or whatever it is probably won't be dazzled by your footwork."

Chapter Twenty-three

Lix Delacroix picked up a chicken finger from the platter in the middle of the table, trapping it expertly between his big toe and the next one. He paused to dunk it into a container of sweet and sour sauce, lifted it to his mouth and devoured it in one bite. Abby forced herself not to gawk and nibbled at a sweet, yeasty cinnamon bun running with butter. Eating with your feet? What would Mom say about that? Actually, Abby smiled to herself, she probably would have gotten a kick out of it. At least Delacroix's feet were clean. She'd watched him meticulously wash them in a basin before they'd begun dinner. The grungoid Chillout appeared at her elbow, refilled her mug of lemonade, then moved to his own spot at the table.

Abby felt a sudden heavy weight of homesickness press down on her. Gathered around the table, eating dinner with Delacroix and Chillout, reminded her of family times back home, before Mom got sick. Dad would often stop for take-out food on his way from work. The four of them would sit around the dining room table, munching their burgers, or tacos, or sharing Chinese food from those little white boxes and talking about how their days had gone.

Mom always seemed to have a funny story about one of her customers at the supermarket. Dad and Noah would talk about music. Sometimes, after they finished the food and helped Mom clean up, Noah and Dad would go out to the garage and jam together. Gosh, she'd completely forgotten about that. She and Mom would play chess or two-handed pinochle and listen to the wail of Dad's saxophone over the rhythmic thunder of Noah's drums. After that, they might crowd onto the couch together and

217

watch a movie on videotape, passing a bowl of buttery popcorn back and forth.

It felt so real, so close, that Abby wanted to cry out. But she couldn't, she told herself. She had to be strong. She had to be ready to help Noah when he returned with the Methuselah Stone. Noah where are you? What are you doing right now? I hope you're all right.

Abby had asked Delacroix what he knew before they sat down to eat but he'd only directed a sympathetic smile in her direction and shrugged his shoulders. "No word, ma petite. Maybe good news is no news, you know?"

Maybe so. Maybe she'd just have to be content with that. She wiped a drop of butter off her chin and guessed that patience was another lesson she needed to learn.

Only a few days remained until Spid would try to break his way through the Skin. Delacroix insisted it was critical that he and Noah have time to practice together before that happened. He said if her brother didn't show up sometime in the next day or so, they were sunk. All of them. She wouldn't be spared, she knew. Not according to what she heard during Spid's post-game temper tantrum.

Not that the residents of Above were giving up. During the meal, several visitors approached Delacroix, carrying on hushed conversations with him in languages that sounded like words whirled in a blender. Some of those who'd huddled with Delacroix were human or humanoid and some were grungoids. But there were also some creatures she'd never seen before. One of them resembled a large, brown anteater with two eyes on either side of its triangular face. Another towered over the table, a hair-covered bear-man at least seven feet tall with glowing orange eyes and furry feet so large they would make ten of hers. Even though Abby could understand none of the words exchanged during these whispered confabs, she could easily interpret the tone. War.

Everyone was preparing for the invasion of Spid and his demons. And they would fight in the tunnels to the last man. Or beast.

She nibbled half-heartedly at one of the fried chicken chunks, watching as Delacroix extended his leg and wiggled his toes over the platter, preparing to help himself to another portion. "Don't you ever miss them? Your arms, I mean?" Abby heard herself blurt out the words.

Instantly, she brought both hands up to cover her mouth, as if she could stuff the rude question back in. As if he hadn't heard, Delacroix plucked another morsel from the platter, dipped it, popped it into his mouth and dabbed at his lips with a napkin he'd captured with the other foot. How does he do that, she wondered?

He's got both feet up near his face. I'd fall on my rear.

Delacroix smiled broadly at her, set the napkin down and arranged his legs into a lotus position. "Of course, I miss them, cherie. They are, or were, a part of me, after all. And for a drummer, a very important part."

"But it's as if you've never had them," she marveled. "You've learned to do everything with your feet. You're amazing."

"Merci," he acknowledged. "But of course, for some things, nothing can replace your hands and arms."

Abby nodded. "The drumming, of course."

"But many other things too, Abby. I miss having my elbow to lean on and my hand to hold my chin when I daydream. I miss doing the spider on a mirror thing with my fingertips when I am trying to solve a particularly perplexing problem, you know? And . . ." His face took on a wistful expression. "I especially miss the hugging."

Abby felt a lump constrict her throat. Funny, she thought, the things you take for granted. Mom had been a great hugger. Dad too, until— She couldn't stop her next question, any more than she could the first. "Did you lose them in the plane crash?"

219

Delacroix sighed and raised his foot to scratch his ear. "You don't really want to hear this story, cherie. It is a very old and sad one and it can change nothing."

Chillout stood and gaped at both of them, swiveling his head slowly. Then he made a faint chhht, chhht, chhht sound, gathered up the remainder of the dinner and disappeared with it. Abby was surprised. She couldn't remember the grungoid using anything but jivespeak since she'd met him. Perhaps he'd had something to say that he didn't want her to understand.

A profoundly long silence stretched between her and Delacroix. Then she heard him clear his throat. "There once was a musician, a young man who learned to play drums on his native island in the Caribbean, by listening to the rhythms of the world around him. There, on that green, green island in that blue, blue sea, he listened to the surf, to the breezes in the trees, to the beating of birds' wings and the rush and rumble of streams after a rain."

Abby could almost see it. She gathered her legs beneath her in imitation of his lotus position and watched him as he spoke.

"He came to America and found success, this boy, this man, no? Other musicians, they liked his sound, and they invited him to play with dem. He recorded his music and people bought it and he made a great deal of money. Before he knew it, he had become famous. A person celebre, you see."

"How old were you then, when you were famous?"

"By the time I bought and learned to fly the aeroplane, I had passed my twenty-seventh birthday, ma petite.

Always, I had desired to fly, you know." His voice dropped and she heard bitterness in the next words. "To soar with the birds."

"How old are you now?" Another question blurted out.

A bemused smile drew his lips back. "I am not sure, not knowing how much time has passed. You have

220

probably noticed there are no clocks here, and the sun does not rise and set. Probably the downhill side of forty, I am guessing."

Abby hesitated, thinking before asking the next question. "Where were you going, when the plane, uh, crashed?"

She saw his lower lip push out and heard him draw in a ragged breath. "I was returning from my honeymoon," he said softly. "With Melanie."

"Noah told me she was an actress."

"Oui. A very fine young character actress, she appeared in plays in New York. She was to begin work on her first movie when we—" He choked and dabbed at his eyes with the napkin.

Crashed. Abby mentally filled in the missing word.

Silence once again filled the chamber and she shifted her legs uneasily. Forget it, she told herself. Obviously, it's way too painful for him to tell. A part of her—a very large part—wanted to get up and go to him, to give him a hug and tell him everything was all right. But before she could, she heard his low, rumbling musical voice pick up the thread again. He told the story as if it were happening at that very moment, not years ago.

"We were to fly from Portland to San Francisco. About four hours. An easy flight. But suddenly we find ourselves in the middle of a storm. The wind, it howls. My little airplane, she is punched and pummeled. I pull her up, to try to go over the storm, but the storm is stronger than my engine. The wind swats us down like you might swat a fly. The rain, it falls so hard we cannot see."

Abby shivered as she visualized the scene. Two people, Delacroix as a young man and his pretty young bride, huddled together in terror, strapped into a small airplane, not knowing whether they would crash or not, whether they would survive if they did. She felt like she

221

should say something, anything to ease his pain. But all she could do was nod.

"I see the mountain in front of me only a few seconds before we hit. I get the nose up somehow, so we would not strike head-on. I aim for what looks like a clear spot.

And then . . . I remember how it felt to smash into this mountain. It was like nothing I could have imagined, nothing I could ever have prepared for. There were trees all around and a grinding crash and a bright flash. And pain. So much pain, ma cherie. And after that, I have no memory until I awaken in the middle of the wreckage."

"Oh, God, how awful." Abby shivered.

He went on quickly, as if now that he had begun, he was compelled to complete the tale. "I could not move at first. Rain fell and wind blew and my body hurt in ways I did not know it could hurt. In the darkness, I feel beside me for Melanie and find her seat empty. But when the morning comes, I see the blood. Everywhere there is blood."

Abby gnawed at her knuckles, watching Delacroix's eyes grow distant, lost, in another place. But if he'd reached for Melanie, she thought, he still had his arms.

When had he lost them?

"I had to find her, you know? Maybe she was in the woods somewhere, among those enormous trees, trying to get down the mountain, trying to find help. I knew she must be hurt very badly. How could she not be? I crawl out of the crumpled aeroplane and begin to drag myself through the brush. Inch by inch, I move down the mountain as the sun grows hotter. I call her name until my voice gives out. And then, just when I think I can go no farther, I hear a rustling in the brush behind me.

Melanie, I think. My heart leaps."

"Was she all right?" Abby leaned forward, feeling her eyes widen.

Delacroix shook his head. "Alas. I do not know. The rustling in the brush, it is made by a large creature, a creature that stalked me, coming to hasten my demise. A cat. I hear it snarl. A big cat who thinks he has found his dinner." He smiled a little. "I am large enough, he could have invited friends, non?"

The dark humor made Abby smile despite herself.

"What happened? How did you get away?"

"I climb to my feet and shout with all of the power I can gather." He threw his head back and boomed the words across the cavern. "You go away, Monsieur le Chat. I am not ready yet for to be your dinner."

Abby giggled. "And did it work?"

"I am alive today, non?"

"But . . . your arms?"

"Yes." He held out the stumps that ended above his elbows. "My arms. I do not know how long I searched for her, Melanie. I only know I would not give up. But then, I fall. It had begun to rain again and I crawled into a cave, thinking perhaps she sought shelter there. The cave it is dark, very dark. The ground gives way beneath my feet. I begin sliding, down, down, down. My head hits rock and everything becomes darkness. And when I wake up, I have no arms."

Abby couldn't imagine how someone could fall down and wake up without arms. "Were they broken off when you fell?"

"No. Melacherub removed them. To save my life."

Delacroix's tone changed as if the events he spoke were now from the distant past.

"Melacherub?" Abby swiveled her head to see if Chillout had re-entered the chamber. He hadn't. "You mean one of the grungoids operated on you?"

"No, cherie, Melacherub was not a . . ." He used the ancient name for grungoids that sounded like gargling.

"Melacherub was a very old, very wise wizard. He was before me, the Grand Imperial Pettifog."

"A wizard?" Abby scoffed. "You mean, with a great long flowing beard and a magic wand and like that? C'mon now."

"You don't believe in the magic?"

"No. What people think is magic is really all sleight of hand, misdirection."

He laughed. "Ah, my little scientist. How do you explain how we fell down that airshaft and remained uninjured? How then do you explain how you found your way here from the maze?"

He had her there. Maybe the magic he was talking about wasn't rabbits-out-of-a-hat stuff. Maybe it was a whole lot more.

"Melacherub was short and bald. He reminded me of the man who I had hired to watch after my money in New York. A what you call it . . ."

"Accountant?"

"Yes, accountant. And he did not use a wand. But he had the magic, of that there is no doubt."

"So he cut off your arms."

"While I was unconscious. Without anesthetic. But I did not feel a thing. Melacherub saw I had developed the gangrene. He could not cure it with any of the potions or spells he attempted. So, yes, he took my arms from me.

But not with a knife. He used only his mind."

"Really."

"Really." He held out the stumps. "Look and you will see there are no scars, no marks from stitches. It is as if the skin, it grew that way when I was inside my mother."

Abby reeled at the concept. A wizard. Psychic amputation. Unreal. Another question popped into her brain and immediately to her mouth. "So after you healed. Why didn't you come back out? Into the world, I mean?"

Delacroix flexed his legs and rose smoothly to his feet.

Abby attempted the same move and tipped over, falling onto her rear end.

Delacroix grinned. "Getting up with no hands is like anything else, little one. It takes the practice. I long ago perfected the move, you see?"

Scrambling to her feet, she asked the question again.

"Why have you stayed here? All of these years."

"Because, I . . ." He sighed. "I decided my sweetness, my Melanie, must have perished up there," Delacroix lifted his eyes toward the ceiling, "on the mountain. She could not have survived. By the blood, I knew she had been hurt very badly. And the animals . . . that enormous cat . . ." He shrugged. "I could not leave her. And without my arms, I did not have the music, I could not play. So I decided I would live my life here, alone, inside the mountain. Except, I found I was not alone. There were others here. And they accepted me and became my family. Eventually, after I learned the ways of Humbug, Melacherub moved on. I became the Pettifog."

"Where did Melacherub go?"

"Some think he went somewhere to die by himself. Others think he lives on. No one for certain knows."

Delacroix turned to go, then stopped and looked back. "Have I satisfied your appetite, ma petite? Have you asked me every question generated by your hungry mind?"

Abby felt remorse and bowed her head. "I'm very sorry. I didn't mean to pry."

Delacroix smiled warmly and chuckled. "Your curiosity is a blessing and a curse, is it not? But on balance, I think it serves you well. Do not stop questing, Abby."

"One more question, please. Do you ever miss it? The outside."

Smoothly lifting his leg to scratch his chin with his foot, while balancing effortlessly on the other, Delacroix thought about that for a moment. "Not so much, any more. Perhaps a little, at odd times. You have noticed, have you not, the food. A friend brings me food from the outside, sometimes. Eating the grubs and worms and tiny bugs like Chillout and the others has a limited appeal, non?"

"Definitely," Abby agreed with a shudder.

"Truth be told, I think Chillout has become addicted to cuisine le refuse also. I have ruined him. But other things I do sometimes miss. Birds. Train whistles in the middle of the night. The smell of the food cooking at the stalls in the marketplace in my hometown. The exquisite green-blue water of that warm sea.

"Do you ever think about going back?"

"Oui. Sometimes. But then I realize that life there, without my Melanie, would not be complete. And I remind myself that my life here is complete, in its own way. I belong to Humbug Mountain." With that, he turned, ducked his head to enter the passageway and walked away.

After a moment, Abby walked to the other side of the chamber and entered her own room. Notebook in hand, she propped herself up on the bed and began again to try to untangle the word the Zezzue had given her at the end of the Spiddle game. *T-I-R-K-D-E-S-C-X-O-S-L-K-N-UR-P-L-V.*

She played games with the letters, trying to rearrange them into another word or words she could recognize. For a while, she toyed with the theory that perhaps each letter stood for the next letter above it in the alphabet or the next one below.

All the while she worked on the problem, her mind kept wandering back to Delacroix's story, to Noah and the upcoming battle between the forces of Spid and the innocents who lived Above Skin. Everyone seemed to be missing something, she realized. Delacroix missed

226

Melanie and, of course, his arms. Noah missed Mom and the tight connectedness they'd all enjoyed before she died.

Abby missed her mother, too, but she'd forced herself to shove her feelings into the background because Noah mourned so deeply and openly. Somebody had to be the strong one. And Spid. Was Spid missing something?

Perhaps that was the key. Perhaps if she could figure that out, she could use it to defeat him, to keep him Beneath where he belonged.

She sat up and stared at the word. Maybe that was it. Maybe there were letters missing. She stared at the jumble for a moment, then tossed her pencil down in frustration. How could she possibly know what to put in, that wasn't there? She flopped back down and chewed on the eraser, thinking about Delacroix's story and what it meant. Maybe, she thought, it's not about what I'm missing. Maybe I need to think about what I do have, and figure out how to use it." Reality made her glum. What I have, she admitted, is letters that spell no word I can recognize and that defy any attempt at pronunciation. She brightened. But I also have my brain.

I have my heart. I have the friendship of Felix Delacroix, the Grand Imperial Pettifog of Above Skin and his be-bop man Friday, Chillout. I have a wonderful, talented brother.

T-I-R-K-D-E-S-C-X-O-S-L-K-N-U-R-P-L-V

She examined the word again, letting it bounce around inside her mind without running into the walls and corners thrown up by her logical self. Remembering the floating, out-of-body state she'd reached while finding her way back from the dead end room in the twisted maze, Abby wondered if she could do it again. She began chanting, closing her eyes and mouthing the words.

"Youknowuh, youknowuh, youknowuh,youknowuh."

She kept it up for at least half an hour, but felt no transformation, no shift in her consciousness, no emergence of an alternate self to guide her. Finally, frustrated and sleepy, she wrapped herself in her quilt and began drifting off to sleep. The Zezzue dimmed themselves and she almost thought she heard them hum as she yawned and rolled over. She hovered for a moment between wakefulness and the edge of sleep

"You know the way," the Zezzue whispered. "Follow your heart."

She tried to pull herself out of the spiraling darkness, tried to ask them what they meant, but she couldn't.

When she woke up, the tiny lights seemed cold and distant and she wondered if she might only have dreamed it.

Chapter Twenty-four

Noah's feet were tender and blistered when they first caught sight of the Temple of Cheltnor. They'd been walking for an hour, with Deidre setting a merciless pace through twisting, turning passageways of the inner mountain that eventually opened onto a rock shelf overlooking a broad plain strewn with immense boulders.

In the distance, they saw a wide crack in the earth with a vivid violet glow rising from it.

"Cheltnor," Deidre declared. "And the Methuselah Stone. According to the prophecy."

Uh-oh pointed to the radiance flowing up through the far-away fissure, made a nervous chhht . . . chhht . . . chhht sound and scuttled behind Noah. Deidre smiled, but her eyes revealed the unspoken question that hung between them like a cobweb. What now? What do you think we'll face? What's the plan?

You'd be better off asking Uh-oh, Noah thought ruefully. Or asking one of those boulders down there. I am major clueless to the forty-second power. Abby was the brains of the operation. Planning to me is like the way I play drums; listen and try to pick up the beat and then improvise. Make it up as you go along.

"Bout half an hour more," Deidre looked away from his eyes.

"Uh huh," he grunted. He started to walk again, each step sending needles of fire up his legs to his brain. Maybe he should have kept his shoes. Any protection would be better than none at all. He gritted his teeth as they worked their way into the boulder field, weaving between the massive rocks. The ground was rough, and although he tried to avoid them, Noah stepped on several small, jagged stones that nicked his feet. He noticed he was leaving a trail of blood. Uh-oh followed that trail,

229

looking back over his shoulder from time to time, as if afraid somebody or something was pursuing them. Noah wondered if the creature had seen or heard something, or if he just had a bad case of nerves.

In twice the time Deidre had predicted, they stood on the rim of the crevasse, peering down at the temple.

Cheltnor hulked on the far side of the rocky floor of the crevasse. The temple itself was broad, several stories high, and appeared to be carved right into the rock wall that defined the other side of the narrow canyon. Its surface was jewel-like, sparkling and glimmering, catching light and spinning it in different directions. The aura was largely violet, but Noah saw twinkles of orange and green and blue and practically every color he could imagine.

"It's beautiful," Deidre gasped.

"Sure is," Noah agreed. And scary, he thought. Like those pretty flowers that snap their jaws around unsuspecting insects. He studied the crevasse. Several hundred feet deep, at least. "How are we going to get down there?"

"Very carefully." Deidre peeled her pack from her back. "We'll leave these here. The climb back up will be tough enough without them."

"Makes sense."

"I've got some rope." She produced it from a deep pocket on her pack. "We'll tie ourselves together in case—" She didn't finish the sentence, but the implication hung in the air. Noah dropped his own pack and Uh-oh followed suit. He trembled, casting eyes glazed with exhaustion back and forth between the temple and Noah. Deidre roped them together, looping the sturdy cord through their belts and knotting it around Uh-oh's waist, leaving about twenty feet of slack between them. "One of us must always be anchored," she said. "In case the others lose their footing."

230

Uh-oh looked again at the long drop and shuddered.

"You'll be good at this," Noah told him. "Remember the day we met? You only fell because I grabbed you. I'm depending on you to help me. Just don't look down."

Uh-oh nodded and took a deep breath.

"Let's do it," Deidre said, and led the way over the edge, easily finding hand and footholds.

The girl must be part mountain goat, Noah decided. So agile and sure-footed. He started after her and was surprised to find that, if he studied the rock carefully and took his own advice about not looking down, it was relatively easy. But thirty yards from the bottom, they ran into trouble—a wide slide of small, loose rocks that funneled down to the floor of the basin. "Can we get around it?" Noah shaded his eyes against the violet glow and peered at the boulder off to his left.

Deidre studied the hulking blunt-nosed stone to the right. "No. We're in a layer of shale. It fractures easily, that's why this sheared away. We'll have to descend through the rock-fall and hope it's finished shifting. She took a few tentative steps as Noah anchored her. "Feels firm," she called.

He followed her onto the slide and Uh-oh trailed him, lagging at the full length of the rope.

"It's getting looser," Deidre called back to them after they'd gone a few yards. "Careful. I'm going to move down and toward the edge."

Noah nodded and took a few more baby steps down hill, setting each foot carefully. Suddenly, his ear picked up a soft cracking sound from above him. It was followed by the grating of shifting rock. He looked up to see Uh-oh, arms flailing, feet digging wildly at a stream of stones flowing downhill.

"Deidre. Look out."

Uh-oh tumbled backwards and began to shoot toward Noah, hands and feet still searching for a purchase. Noah

231

tried to plant his feet, but felt the shale swirling beneath them. No-way, he thought. No-way can I stop him. Uh-oh bounced and skidded past, his eyes wide with fear.

Noah leaned back into the slope, gripping the rope. It played out between them quickly. Noah leaned back farther, turning his upper body, scrabbling for a handhold on the shifting surface. The rope snapped taut. Noah's feet slipped on the rasping rock. Uh-oh's momentum yanked him out of place and propelled him down the slope like a water skier on a gravel lake.

"Aaaaaagh," he screamed as he slid down toward Deidre. "I can't stop." He tried to dig his heels in, but only managed to lose his balance and fall onto his side.

"Get ready to grab me," Deidre screamed as Uh-oh careened past just out of her reach. She laid down on the slide and flung out one arm toward Noah. "Now."

Reaching desperately, he felt their forearms slap together. He grasped at empty air, then felt her fingers clamp around his wrist. Through rising dust, he saw her face contort as she strained to hold him. He rolled onto his stomach and dug in his toes, searching for a hold beneath the soft surface, trying to swim against the stonefall. He wished again that he'd kept his shoes.

He heard Uh-oh squeal and turned his head. The rope had snapped tight across the lip of an overhang. Uh-oh was nowhere to be seen. Noah heard another squeal. His own. He saw the rope twitch. Realized Uh-oh was still secured, still alive. But for how long? They were still sliding.

For a moment, Deidre supported all of them. Noah saw sweat bead across her forehead as she strained to stop the momentum. Finally, his bare foot found a solid spot beneath the shifting rock shards. The sickening slide stopped.

"Bad news, Noah," Uh-oh's voice rose from the end of the rope. "Very bad."

232

"Hold on, Uh-oh," he hollered down. We'll pull you back up." He torqued his neck and looked up at Deidre.

"Won't we?"

She nodded, chest heaving as she drew in a series of breaths. "Uh-oh, stay as still as you can. Don't wiggle. Don't try to climb back up the rope! We'll rescue you, but it will take a little while." Without waiting for a response, she addressed Noah. "Have you got a good hold? Can you support Uh-oh for a bit?"

"I think so." He dug his free hand and both feet into the rockslide, ignoring sharp fragments of stone that sliced his fingers and toes.

"Let's find out." Noah felt her grasp on his arm loosen. He slid half an inch, an inch, then felt the motion cease. "There's a ledge just below you and to your right."

Deidre said. "Turn your head slowly. Don't make any sudden movements."

"I see it." He began to loosen one foot from the grasp of the slide. "Should I—"

Her voice cracked like a whip. "Shut up and listen to me."

Uh-oh whimpered.

Noah forced himself to stay still. "Shutting up now."

"Good. You hold Uh-oh. That's your job, your only job. Got it?"

"Got it," he agreed.

"Okay. I'm going to work my way over to that ledge.

Looks like I've got to go up a few feet, and then I think I can pick my way without falling."

Noah thought she sounded less confident than when she'd told him to shut up. "Is that plan A?"

"Right."

"What's plan B?"

"We all fall down and hurt ourselves," she said, matter-of-factly.

He forced himself to grin, remembering a scene toward the end of *Ghostbusters* where they decide to do what they'd concluded earlier shouldn't be done. "I'm wild about plan A."

"I thought you would be. Soon as I get to the ledge, I'll help you scramble over and we'll double-team Uh-oh. Okay?"

He forced bravado he didn't feel. "Sure. Piece of cake. Take it slow."

She released his arm and he dug the freed hand into the slide as he heard her begin to move. A spray of loose gravel rained down on him. If Deidre fell, he couldn't stop her, couldn't stop Uh-oh who dangled on the end of the rope like a puppet. Don't think about it, he coached himself.

He heard Deidre exhale sharply and grunt and then she reassured him. "I'm okay. I found a handhold."

Out of the corner of his eye, he saw her clamber to a position about ten feet above the ledge. He heard her mutter something unintelligible, then suddenly saw her hurtle past him.

Oh God. She's falling. The thought hit him like a punch in the stomach. He turned his face into the rockslide and prepared for the sudden yank on the rope that would signal the start of a body-chewing slide and fall to the floor of the canyon.

"Oof." Deidre grunted as her boots slapped a solid surface. Noah risked a look and saw her crumple to the ground. For a moment, he wondered if she'd broken a leg. What would they do then? Would he have to go on without her? Could he?

"Are you hurt?"

It seemed an eternity before she answered. "No, not really. Just shook up a little. Let's get you over here."

Deidre helped Noah scramble down to the ledge. From there they could see that Uh-oh dangled thirty feet above

234

the ground. "It will be easier to lower him," Deidre decided.

When he was safely on the ground below, they roped themselves together again and eased down the rest of the slide without incident. At the bottom, they rested for a moment, sipped from their canteens and took stock.

Noah's pants and shirt were shredded and his feet and hands were raw. Uh-oh had a number of deep oozing scrapes and Deidre had twisted her ankle. Lucky, Noah thought. We were very lucky.

Five minutes later, they stood at the entrance to the Temple of Cheltnor. This close, the colored light reflecting from the surface created a glare that made Noah hood his eyes with his hands. Squinting, he saw the walls were comprised of thousands and thousands of crystals like the ones in the chunks of amethyst Port Anvil gift shops hawked to tourists.

Inside, they found themselves in a high-ceilinged room with smooth and polished walls. The air grew colder and the echoes of Deidre's footsteps seemed to hang in it as she strode across the gleaming translucent floor. At the far end of the room, four stone statues depicted figures seemingly flash-frozen while in action. Made of red-tinged stone, they ranged in height from twenty to thirty feet. They're kinda crude, Noah thought. Don't really look like people. More like what little kids make out of clay.

One stone character, a boy or man, with some kind of sticks in his hand, beat on an imaginary surface. The second statue showed the same character running or perhaps climbing. One foot was planted on the ground, the other poised at knee level. He held the sticks in one fist and used the other hand to aid his climb.

Noah and Deidre turned their heads at the same time to examine the third statue. He saw her shiver a little and he felt a chill run down his own spine. This creature was short and squat and had five arms, each grasping a stick.

He, too, seemed to be striking a flat surface. The final stone figure, the tallest, loomed over the other three, watching them. Even though he couldn't see much detail, Noah felt ugliness and violence radiate from the smirking, cruel countenance of his face.

"Troll," said Uh-oh in a voice they'd never heard before. It sounded like that of a very young child. "Maybe Spid, maybe not Spid."

"Is this what a troll looks like? What Spid looks like?" Noah asked. The gray creature just shrugged his shoulders and hugged himself.

"If it's not Spid, it's one of his ancestors," Deidre confirmed.

"You've seen Spid?"

"Kind of. For quite a while now, he's been appearing at different places in the mountain. But it's not really him. It's kind of a ghost of him or something. It moves and talks, but you can put your hand right through it."

"Like a hologram?"

"Maybe. I don't know what that is."

"It's like a projection." Because he can't really transport himself up here, Noah thought. That's why he needs to get past the Skin. Whatever that is. It must be a portal between where he lives and up here.

"When he appears, he says we must obey him or die," Deidre scoffed. "He also says that those who join him and are loyal will become wealthy beyond their wildest dreams and possess all that they want."

"That's some incentive. How many have joined him?"

She looked at him in amazement. "No one. No one here would join Spid. Especially not for money. It means nothing inside the mountain. We have all we need, and we share all we have. We enjoy life and take care of one another."

Noah wondered how Deidre's view of what she needed might change if she spent a few hours watching one of the television shopping channels while thumbing through a fashion magazine. Her life seemed so simple. Almost too simple. He looked up at the statues again and saw something he hadn't noticed before. Perched on the shoulders of the troll, other creatures huddled, wings folded, beady eyes surveying the room. Their faces were wrinkled and deformed, and they had pointed ears, webbed feet and talons for hands. Human, birdlike and reptilian. They emanated pure evil.

He had a sense that he'd seen them somewhere else—in a book, a movie or a nightmare. What were they called? As he cast about for the word, another image popped into his mind, a fuzzy memory that focused instantly and he knew he had to take on this portion of the quest alone. The girl warrior wasn't going to like it, but he couldn't risk her life, or Uh-oh's, again.

Deidre noticed the menacing creatures and pointed toward them. "Ugly suckers, aren't they? Good thing they're just stone, right?"

Noah nodded numbly. In a minute, he'd tell her his decision.

She peered into a dark opening between the statues. "Looks like there's a set of steps going down. Pretty narrow, we'll have to go down one at a time." She pulled her sonic sword from its scabbard. "I'll lead and you—"

"No, you won't."

"—we'll spread out when we get to the—" She paused, then her voice grew sharp, the anger apparent. "When did you start giving orders? Ten minutes ago you were whimpering on the landslide."

"I know, but I've got to go down alone."

She shook her head. "Bad idea, Bun-boy. Vetoed. You'll need help."

"No. I have to go alone. Remember when I told you about dancing with the old woman at the beach, and she

237

sent a bunch of stuff into my head, pictures and words and . . . and . . . I don't know, like feelings?"

"Yeah. So?"

"So I saw this place. Exactly. Every detail. I saw you, and Uh-oh and the statues and all of it."

"So now you can see the future?"

"I saw this future," Noah said firmly. "And you weren't with me. I walked down those steps, " Noah pointed at the opening in the floor, "alone. You and Uh-oh have to wait here."

"Wrong! I don't care about any crazy dream, or vision. I'm going with you."

Noah felt frustration buzz in his head. Eve had warned him how obstinate Deidre could be. No way she'd give in. Unless . . . "Sonic swords."

"What?" An amused smile formed on her lips.

"You're loopy, Bunster. You can't carry my lunch." She leveled her weapon at him.

"Probably not, but I've got to try." Noah pulled his own fork from the scabbard, banged the butt against the metal plate on his decibelt and started it humming. In a flash, Deidre followed suit. They stood, ten feet apart, weapons and nerves vibrating. Uh-oh, muttering his own name, took refuge behind a statue.

"Before we start, we need to talk about the rules." Noah lowered his fork and took a step toward her.

"Rules?" Deidre scowled and dropped her fork to waist level. "There aren't any rules in a fork—"

Kuh-zap. Noah caught her a glancing blow with the attack wave of his weapon and sent her sprawling. Her weapon clattered off in the other direction. Stunned, Deidre stared up at him through glassy eyes. Noah disengaged his fork with another tap on the decibelt and slung it back into its scabbard.

"Sorry. You're right, Deidre. There aren't any rules in a fork fight." He instantly felt guilty. Gosh, I hope I didn't

238

hurt her, he thought. That was really awful to pull that old trick Paul Newman did in *Butch Cassidy and the Sundance Kid,* but I couldn't let her come.

"Keep an eye on her, Uh-oh," he told her. "I'll be right back with the Methuselah Stone." He turned toward the passageway.

"And then I'll kick your fanny, Noah." He jumped at the sound of Deidre's voice, reaching for his sword. Then he realized the voice had come from Uh-oh who stood, hands on hips, beside Deidre.

Noah laughed. "I'm sure she will, Uh-oh. I'll just have to risk it."

His laughter died quickly as he descended the stone stairway into a musty passageway. The air grew warm and muggy, and he felt sweat start to dribble off his forehead and down his face. Every so often, a short landing sent the stairs in another direction, but they twisted ever downward. Crude drawings were inked onto the walls and he strained to see them in the dim dust-flecked light. In one, the boy represented by the statue stood with a group of other beings, gathered around some kind of immense upright circular thing, which he hit with sticks. On the other side of the thing, the character Uh-oh had called Spid stood behind the five-armed creature, who also hit the skin with his sticks. An assortment of ugly animals stood on their side of what Noah concluded must be a drum. On another stretch of wall, a girl holding an object from which rays emanated seemed to be calling out to a figure racing up a narrow path to a smaller, circular object. Very strange. He wanted to stay and examine the pictures more closely, but he had a feeling he should hurry.

Finally, the stairs ended and he found himself in a stuffy, cobwebbed chamber about the size of the inside of his house, except with much higher ceilings. As he paused to catch his breath, he became aware of the mountain's

239

rhythm again, the muffled, bassy, *thoomp-thoomp, thooomp-thoomp, thoomp-thoomp.* Noah's own heart fluttered, then seemed to find the cadence and match it.

He looked around and saw three carved stone arms protruding upward from the floor at the center of the chamber. Each arm had a hand, and each hand held a stone of some kind, offering it to Noah. Edging closer, he heard the mountain, or his own heart in his ears.

Thoomp-thoomp, thoomp-thoomp, thoomp-thoomp.

Suddenly, he became aware of the things that squatted on thick pedestals on either side of the array of arms and hands.

"Gargoyles." The sound of his own whispered voice made him start. He remembered a book on mythology he'd checked out of the library and the pictures inside. Flying demons from hell. The carved stone creatures in this underground place were much larger and more detailed than the ones that perched on the shoulder of the Troll statue in the upper temple. Hewn from some kind of smooth, green-gray rock, they scowled down at him, wings half-folded and foot-talons fully displayed. A gruesome picture appeared in his mind. Himself. Razorsharp claws ripping at his skin. Agony.

"Stupid, Noah. They're just stone. Lighten up." That's what Deidre would say, he thought. Thinking of her made him feel better, not quite alone. He thought about how mad she'd be when he returned and, ignoring the gargoyles, advanced to examine the hands and their stones.

The first hand held a dazzling, pure, clear, multi-faceted rock about the size of a tangerine. Diamond? It would have been worth millions. Maybe billions. Out there.

Put it in your pocket, a small, greedy voice urged. Take it with you. If it's not the Methuselah Stone, you can sell it. You'll be rich.

240

He stretched out his hand and heard Deidre's voice in his head: "We enjoy life and take care of each other. That's all we need." He'd smiled at her before, but now, staring at the diamond, he admitted that wealth wasn't about getting what you wanted; it was about having what you needed. All the money in the world couldn't bring back his mother, or make his father say he loved him.

Besides, wealth wouldn't mean squat if he couldn't deliver the Methuselah Stone to the Skin. If Spid triumphed.

Moving to the next hand, he examined what lay in its palm. This stone resembled an inverted flask, wide at the top, narrow at the bottom. At the bottom, the pure green neck of the flask vanished, melded into another stone, a brilliant red, with dancing light playing across its surface.

Noah couldn't relate it to anything he'd ever seen or experienced.

The next stone, propped on the palm of the third hand, looked like nothing more than a sickly cantaloupe-colored rock replica of a human brain. Its only distinctive feature was thousands of tiny pores. It didn't glow, it didn't sparkle, it just sat there.

Which one is the Methuselah Stone? He looked at all three again. Maybe the diamond-looking thing, he thought. He'd read diamonds were very old. They'd once been coal. And before that, what? The plants that dinosaurs ate? What about the green and red one? Maybe the way it's shaped meant something. And then there was the brain-stone. He tried to think, but couldn't decide. His head began to throb. Abby, he thought, where are your little gray cells when I need them? Maybe he should take all three stones.

But no, the prophecy said the Methuselah Stone. One stone.

He tried to remember where he'd heard the word Methuselah before. The Bible. That was it. Methuselah.

241

He was very old, like nine-hundred something. He had lots of children. Goo-gobs of begats. Hundreds.

Suddenly his choice became obvious. Methuselah!

Wisdom born of age. Wisdom. Brains.

Snatching the brain-stone from the upturned hand, he tucked it under his arm like a football and raced up the stairs, taking them two at a time.

"Noah." Deidre's angry voice echoed down the twisting passageway.

He grinned. When she saw he had the stone, she'd cool off. His aching bare feet slapped on the warm stone steps, but now he didn't mind the pain. He had the stone, the mountain and his own heartbeat in his ears.

And then he heard other sounds—scuffling and snuffling and growling.

Just as he hit the first landing, he felt hot breath on the back of his neck, smelled a putrid odor worse than rotting garbage, more pungent than dead fish, as foul as burning oil. Behind him, something scrabbled and scratched at the stone steps. Run, he told himself. Don't look back. He forced his tortured feet to move faster, felt his heart pump harder.

Near the top of the next long flight of steps, something sharp raked at the back of his leg, ripping his tattered jeans from his knee to his ankle, snagging on the hem. He tore the cloth loose without slowing his pace, but he couldn't stop himself from risking a glance back over his shoulder. What he saw petrified him. He was certain it would be the last thing he'd ever see.

Two living, breathing gargoyles crouched below him, ready to spring.

Chapter Twenty-five

"Have they ripped the flesh off of his body yet, boss?"

Yurk entered the smoky chamber, rubbing his hammy hands together in glee.

"Momentarily, my impatient friend. When he turns to run again, they'll have him."

Spid turned away from the image of the boy being chased up the steps by gargoyles. Dark light from the Shadow Stone projected a three-dimensional miniature version of Noah's desperate situation onto the tabletop beside the demon troll. Chortling low in his throat, he pulled out the chair beside his own. "Come in, Yurk.

Make yourself comfortable. In a moment, they will pick young master Keene's bones clean and proceed to his misguided friends to further quench their thirst for blood."

"It's a good day, huh, boss?" Yurk sidled toward the table.

"Indeed, Yurk, indeed."

"I brought him, boss." The ogre extended a hand to someone behind him in the entranceway. "The gronnk. Your drummer. Up from the depths of Colongurg."

"Thrndur? He's here?" Spid leaped to his feet. He could barely contain his excitement. He peered beyond Yurk to the figure whose face was obscured by a shadow thrown from the sputtering oil lanterns. "Come. Come. Step forward, so we can see you. Your Garboon has spoken."

Obediently, the creature trundled into the room. "My Lord," he intoned, his voice a sly whine. The gronnk bowed deeply from the waist and flourished four of his five arms. The fifth arm, the one growing from his forehead, slapped onto the stone floor as his upper body became parallel with the floor. When he straightened again, Spid saw that he stood almost a head and a half

243

above average for a gronnk, nearly six feet tall. He remembered that some said Thrndur's mother had been pure gronnk, but his father had run with the abysswolves.

No one ever said that to Thrndur's face, but Spid could see the canine features in the long nose and prominent front teeth. The fifth arm, Spid decided, must be purely a mutation.

"At your service," the gronnk rasped.

"Ah, yes, Thrndur." Spid tipped his upper body a few centimeters in an imperial bow. "So gratifying that you could join this noble effort of ours. For you have been chosen to stand at the Skin when the sun touches the northern sky. You will drum the rhythms that will open the way for my hordes. You are the key to upholding the honor of Beneath and extending our lofty goals to the slacker creatures of Above, to harnessing the power of the Darksuckers for the greater good of . . ." Spid hesitated, wondering if he should blush. He decided not to. "Well, to be quite honest, for the greater good of me, Spid. But I will be most generous in sharing the wealth. When and if that becomes convenient, of course, and after the auditors have been through my books, naturally. But I welcome you and thank you for volunteering your services."

Thrndur grunted, scratched his head with two of his hands and looked down at Yurk, as if asking him to explain. The ogre just shrugged and said in a stage whisper that Spid couldn't avoid hearing, "You've been well paid, already. Just play along."

Thrndur nodded, satisfied. "For my lord Spid, the Grand Exalted Garboon of Beneath, I take up my weapons willingly, to give my all for the cause." He reached into a long, narrow skin bag hanging from his waist and extracted ten drumsticks. They were white, highly polished and unmistakably the bones of some unfortunate creature. Taking two in each of his five hands, he began to twirl and juggle them, slowly at first, then at lightning speed, moving them from hand to hand to hand, spinning them behind his back and through his legs, tossing them high into the air.

After a few moments, he set five of the sticks aside and began beating out rhythms on the walls, tabletop, and other available flat surfaces, creating different tones and different levels of rhythm with each hand. The stone around him began to vibrate with sound and Spid felt a renewed sense of confidence, of purpose, of destiny.

As he watched Thrndur, he caught flashes of movement from the projected images thrown by the Shadow Stone. But he no longer cared whether Noah Keene would be devoured by the guardians of the Temple of Cheltnor. It no longer mattered whether the boy lived to join with that armless, ineffectual dark-skinned buffoon from Above to try to defend the Skin. He, Spid, would deploy the ultimate drumming machine. The Skin would open before you could say Vlorspak Morkphoy. His minions would make short work of any opposition. All those who dared oppose him would pay the ultimate price.

The world would soon fully realize the talents, the towering intellect and, of course, the modesty of Spid the magnificent.

As if sensing his mood, Thrndur stopped the manic many-handed drumming and set down all but two of the drumsticks. Bowing his head in a posture of solemnity, he began a slow, funereal roll on the hollow-sounding surface of a nearby chest.

"Thuhdutdutdutdutdutdutdutdutdut." Individual drum hits soon became a continuous mournful drone, extending into forever. Spid smiled as he recognized what they symbolized. The walk of the condemned to face the blade of the executioner.

245

Chapter Twenty-six

"Noooooah!" Deidre's voice floated down the passageway toward him. She sounded angry. He wanted to call back to her, but his mouth was dry with fear and his heart pounded in his throat. He couldn't speak or move.

On the step just below, a gargoyle crouched, poised to strike, its evil lizard-like eyes glaring, its mouth twisted into a cruel leer. Beyond it, a second gargoyle waited to join in the carnage. Poisonous orange drool dripped from the corner of its mouth.

Noah's heart beat faster and faster. The rest of his body seemed frozen solid from fear. He couldn't feel his feet, couldn't feel the stone beneath them.

The gargoyles held as still as he did. Their eyes seemed to burn into his.

He drew in a fluttering breath, felt himself shudder. The gargoyles didn't move. Their eyes didn't flicker. He drew in another breath, all the way to the bottom of his lungs. The air, or maybe simply the motion of breathing it, seemed to trigger his survival instinct. He kicked out with his right foot, catching the first gargoyle squarely in the forehead.

It teetered, then tipped back into its companion, knocking it off balance.

Noah didn't wait to see how far they rolled.

"Deeeeeeidre!" He screamed as he began to run, clutching the Methuselah stone more tightly under his arm. Behind him he heard a heavy thump, thump, thump.

He fought the temptation to look back. He had to get to the next landing, get his sonic sword out and get ready to fight. But even as he made his plan, a voice within told him they were too big and too powerful and he wasn't really that good with the battle fork. He needed Deidre.

246

Ragged sobs of breath exploded from his lips as he forced himself up the steps. From below, a bloodcurdling, shrieking hiss of pure rage and hatred surged around him. Feet clawed at the steps behind him. The powerful stench filled his nose and made his eyes water as he turned at the last landing. Why did all the monsters down here have to smell so bad? He pounded on tortured feet toward the last twenty steps.

"Oh my God," Deidre screamed. "Noah, hurry, they're right behind you."

He heard her clang her sonic sword against her decibelt. "C'mon, c'mon," she screamed.

He looked up. He stumbled. He went down, one knee slamming into the edge of the fourth stone step from the top.

He heard a gurgling growl and felt a sharp talon prodding his backbone as if the gargoyle was trying to decide where to beginning ripping him in half. An instant later, he heard the whistle and hum of a bolt from Deidre's battle fork pass his left ear.

"Hugnnn." The beast behind him growled.

The sharp pressure against his skin eased. He stretched out his arm and felt the heat and strength of Deidre's hand closing around his. With a single yank, she pulled him up into the temple.

"Draw your sword, Noah. We'll have to make a stand here." Deidre waved the two-pronged weapon back and forth, creating a warped ringing sound in the close air of the temple.

Noah secured the Methuselah stone under his shirt, anchoring it between his belt and breastplate, then drew his weapon and banged the butt against his decibelt. The battle fork vibrated. He braced his feet and locked his knees, waiting for the two hellish creatures to emerge from the hole. He felt himself trembling. He willed himself to stop, but he couldn't. The mountain's heartbeat

247

matched perfectly, the hammer thumping against his chest. Thoodah- thump, thoodah thump, thoodah-thump.

He glanced at Deidre. "Where's Uh-oh?"

She shrugged. "Dunno. He was here a second ago."

Noah turned his head away from the opening in the floor, scanning the temple for their companion. A sudden disgusting whiff of something profoundly rancid made him gag. Claws scrabbled against the stone steps. He could barely hear Deidre's scream over the snarling, screeching, hissing sound of the approaching demons.

"Noaaaaah! Here they come!"

"FOOOOF! FOOOOF!" The expulsions of rancid gargoyle breath seemed to suck the oxygen from the temple.

Jerking himself around, Noah saw the fearsome creatures, claws extended from scaly green arms, catapulting through the air. "Rrrrggghhh!" Their blood-curdling shriek of victory and blood-lust filled his ears.

"Take the one on the left!" Deidre's voice cracked with the command as she turned her fork to the right.

Noah raised his weapon. But before he could fire, the two gargoyles fell with a loud and solid thud. Staring in disbelief, he saw a strange sight. One beast sprawled, fully extended, on its belly, a fearsome snarl frozen on its face. The other teetered for a second on its hind legs, then crashed to the floor.

Noah heard Deidre let out a long breath. "What the . . ." She stepped forward and prodded one with her sonic sword. It didn't move.

"Got me," Noah whispered. "They're statues again. Stone. Like when I first saw them in the bottom chamber." Like when we were on the stairs, he thought.

"Why? How?" Deidre tapped her knuckles against one and then the other.

Noah shook his head. "No clue." From the corner of his eye, he spotted Uh-oh edging out of the shadows. I

248

don't blame you for hiding, little pal, he thought. I'd like to hide too; like to put my head into my pillow and wake up and find this was all a horrendous nightmare, that I've never been pursued by stone statues that could come back to life at any moment and tear me into bloody hunks.

Statues. Statues. The word reverberated in his memory. The game. The one they'd played in elementary school. Statues. All of the kids but one would line up at one end of the schoolyard. The person who was "it" would stand at the other end, her back to them. The other kids would start creeping toward her. Some would even run, trying to get there before she yelled "statues" and opened her eyes. That's when everyone had to freeze in place, pretending to be a statue. Anyone caught moving, even slightly, was out. Was it possible that this was a deadly version of that same game?

"Deidre. Uh-oh." The authority in his voice amazed him.

"What?"

Uh-oh gave a nervous "chhht-chhht-chhht," then mimicked Deidre. "What?"

"I want to try something. Both of you turn away for a moment. Turn toward the entrance to the temple. Don't look at the gargoyles."

"Are you nuts?!" The voices of the girl-warrior and the gray creature came as one.

"Maybe, but do it anyway."

"But what if . . ."

"Do it!"

From the corner of his eye, he saw Deidre wrinkle her nose and roll her eyes. "Who put you in charge?"

When he didn't answer, she backed away from the gargoyle a few feet and nodded to Uh-oh. They swiveled and looked the other way.

249

Noah clanked his battle fork against his decibelt again, giving it a fresh charge. He'd need it to ward off the gargoyles if he was wrong.

But he wasn't.

The horrifying beasts remained statues.

"Okay, turn back around." Noah grinned and gave Deidre a thumbs-up sign. "I think we're going to be okay. They didn't move. I can control them."

"What are you talking about?"

"I think they can only come to life if I turn my back or if I don't look at them."

Deidre shook her head. Uh-oh followed suit. "That's absurd. It can't be that simple."

"I think it is," Noah argued. "Let's try another experiment. Get your battle fork ready."

She shrugged and banged the butt end against the decibelt to recharge it.

"Let's move back a little for this." Carefully keeping his eyes trained on the gargoyles, Noah backed toward the outer door. Deidre and Uh-oh did the same. They stopped about twenty yards from the stone demons.

"Okay, be ready, here goes." He squeezed his eyes tightly shut. Instantly, he heard a screeching, hissing growl rise up from the statues. Clawed feet scrabbled at stone. He heard Deidre gasp. He forced himself to keep his eyes closed.

"Uh-oh." He heard the gray creature mimic his voice.

"Okay. Enough. I believe you." Deidre whimpered softly. "Open your eyes."

Not yet, he told himself. He heard the beasts talking to one another in a guttural gargle-growl-chant. Claws scrabbled harder, faster. Rancid breath made his head ache.

"Noah! Open your eyes! Now!"

He stretched his lids open wide and watched the gargoyles turn back to stone in the time it took for his

250

brain to acknowledge them. One froze with its hind legs flexed, front legs clawing the air. The other, caught in mid stride, apparently had been attending to an itch in an embarrassing place. Uh-oh laughed and pointed at the beast.

"So, that's really how it works, " Deidre breathed a sigh of relief. "As long as you look at them, they won't move. Well, let's just back on out of here." Battle fork at the ready, she began to step backwards.

Noah followed. "Backing now. I wonder if it works because I have the Methuselah?" He patted his midsection and felt the reassuring hardness of the brain-shaped stone. Once they got away, he'd wrap it carefully in the center of his pack. It would definitely be the pits to go through all this, he thought, then lose the stone or drop it and crack it. "Guide me when we get to the steps so I can keep my eyes on them."

"What about when we go out the door and you can't see them anymore? Or what if they split up and you can't watch them both at once?"

"Hmmm." He hadn't thought about that. But then, fifteen minutes ago, he hadn't thought statues could come to life. "I guess if we get out of sight, we'll turn and run like hell until they're right behind us and then I'll freeze them again. And if they split up, I'll turn my head back and forth real fast."

"Good," Deidre said sarcastically. "For a minute there, I thought you didn't have a plan." Facing behind him, she linked their left arms. "Uh-oh, take his other side. We'll go faster."

With his friends leading him, Noah backed across the huge room, keeping his eyes trained on the stone gargoyles that seemed to shrink with each step. Finally, they passed through the archway and the gargoyles became mere dots. "Run," he ordered. "They'll be on us in a few seconds."

251

He turned, leaped down the stairs and sprinted behind his companions toward the canyon wall they'd descended. Within seconds, he heard pounding, growling and hissing close behind him. He ran a few more yards, snapped his head around and halted the creatures in mid leap. Again, they clattered to the ground.

Noah stared at them for a few moments, feeling a new emotion—pride at his sense of power. He, Noah Keene, had the ability to turn these creatures to stone or back into living creatures. It was exhilarating. He felt bigger, stronger, smarter.

"Good one." Deidre put a hand on Noah's shoulder and gave it a squeeze.

Uh-oh echoed her. "Good one, Noah. Whew." The gray creature made an exaggerated gesture, wiping his brow with the back of his arm.

"Thanks." As he backed away from the statues again, a wicked idea popped into Noah's head. He would test his new power, use it to get something he wanted.

"Deidre?"

"Um-huh?"

"Did I mention how tired I'm getting of being called Bun-boy?"

"It's just a nickname, Noah." She laughed. "Get over it."

"I'm not going to have to get over it, Deidre. Because you're going to promise to stop using it. I'm closing my eyes." He squeezed his eyes shut and instantly heard the stirrings of the gargoyles, the sound of them shaking the cobwebs out of their heads and preparing for another charge.

"Noah! This is crazy. Open your eyes." Her voice was shrill.

"Not yet." Heavy feet thudded toward them.

"All right. All right. No more Bun-boy," she snapped.

"Really?" He opened his eyes and froze the gargoyles fifty feet from them.

"Yes. Grow up." Deidre just made a *foof* noise with her lips. "This isn't a game."

"Hmmm, I don't think I heard the 'I promise' part of that promise, Deidre." He squeezed his eyes shut again. A hissing screech rose from the gargoyles. Noah could almost hear Deidre grinding her teeth in frustration. He smiled. This was great.

"Oh, all right, I promise," the words spilled from her mouth. "No more Bun-boy."

For the first time ever, Noah heard a tone of meek acceptance in her voice. "Thank you, Deidre." He opened his eyes and halted the gargoyles at twenty feet.

"You're welcome," she said. Then, under her breath, "Creep."

"Creep I can live with," he grinned. "C'mon, let's get out of here."

As he backed the rest of the way to the edge of the rockslide, Noah felt a twinge of regret for what he'd just done. What if he'd taken it too far? What if the gargoyles had moved faster than he thought and had hurt Deidre or Uh-oh? He could never have forgiven himself. Or, worse yet, what if there were only a certain number of times he could freeze them and he'd exceeded the limit? He felt a chill at the back of his neck and realized he'd learned something about power. It shouldn't be used for his amusement. I shouldn't be abused.

When they arrived at the beginning of the long climb, Noah cut his eyes quickly toward the canyon walls. How were they going to get out of here? It had been dangerous enough coming down, and now he'd have to climb backwards.

As if she'd read his mind, Deidre sheathed her battle fork. "Here's what we'll have to do." The snap of authority had returned to her voice, the docile tone of a few moments a distant memory. "We'll move over there."

She pointed at a spot ten yards to their left. "Looks like the footing's better."

"How are we going to do this? I've got to go up backward so—"

"Right." She ignored him, directing her comments to Uh-oh. "Since his lordship has to keep staring at those ugly muthahs, we're going to have to drag his cute little buns up the hill." She directed a smirk at Noah. "Notice I didn't violate our agreement."

Noah made a face at her, being careful not to take his eyes completely off the frozen gargoyles.

Deidre unlooped the rope from her belt and ran it under the straps of Noah's decibelt where they crossed in the middle of his back. She secured one end around her waist and the other around Uh-oh's. "Okay, Uh-oh, you'll have to climb a little ahead because you're shorter. We'll stay about fifteen feet apart. Noah, you'll be the point of the triangle. Keep your eyes trained on those things and help us climb with your heels and hands when you can. It'll be slow going, but we'll make it."

She was right. It took nearly two hours for them to inch their way up the slope. The route she picked proved easier than the one they'd taken down, but much of the time she and Uh-oh had to literally pull Noah up as he struggled to keep his eyes locked on the gargoyles.

At the top, they hurried to where they'd left their backpacks and then all three of them collapsed on the ground. Noah's thigh, shin and calf muscles felt like they were on fire and the breastplate had bruised his chest when he'd hung suspended between his friends. He guzzled water greedily from his canteen and poured some on his bleeding feet.

"Noah?" Deidre set her canteen down and stared at the rim of the canyon, her eyes wide with fright. "Noah. You stopped looking at them! Those suckers had wings!"

Fatigue forgotten, both of them leapt to their feet and snatched their sonic swords from their scabbards. In unison, they banged the weapons against their respective decibelts and scrambled to the edge of the canyon.

Far below, Noah saw two distant dots scuttling back across the dusty plain toward the open maw of the Temple of Cheltnor. He felt relief flood his veins. Either the creatures couldn't follow, or else they wouldn't. Beside him, he heard Deidre sigh and deactivate her battle fork by bringing it in contact with the ground. He did the same, draining its charge.

Deidre returned her sword to its scabbard and dug some nuts and fruit from her pack and passed them to Uh-oh and Noah. "Can we see the Methuselah Stone?"

Noah nodded, untucked his frayed shirt, pulled the stone from beneath it and passed it to Deidre. She turned it over and over in her hands, examining it from all angles. Uh-oh moved near to get a look, scratching his head with puzzlement. "Doesn't look like much," Deidre commented.

"I'll say." Deidre's voice again, this time from Uh-oh. "Are you sure it's the right one Bun—" she caught herself and handed the stone back. "I mean, Noah."

Well, I was in kind of a hurry and it was pretty dark and there weren't any nameplates or anything under the three I had to pick from, but . . ." he put the stone back into his pack, "yeah, I'm pretty sure, this is it. Seemed to get those 'goyles pretty fired up when I snatched it."

"True. But they'd might have come to life whichever one you took."

Self-doubt eroded Noah's temporary feeling of confidence. "Yeah, could be. But this is the Methuselah.

255

Has to be. Now we've just got to figure out where to take it."

"The Skin." Deidre sounded confident.

"You know the way?"

"Maybe." She looked flustered. "Kinda." Her face scrunched into a grimace. "No, not really."

"Great!" Noah threw a nut at a rock. "Just great. I'm getting tired of wandering around down here. Don't you have a map or something?"

"There aren't any maps down here. And no directions, either. At least none that I know of. There's only up and down and across. You have to remember where you've been and what people say about where you're going. But, I think I can get us to the chamber of the Grand Imperial Pettifog."

"The who?"

"Pettifog. He's like a . . . a . . . kind of wizard or something. I've never met him. But people talk about him. He's a part of the prophecy."

"What part?"

"He's supposed to help you drum. Help you keep out Spid and the demons."

"Well then," Noah got to his feet. Uh-oh made a big sigh and did the same. "We'd better find him. Which way?"

Deidre pointed with her finger. "Up."

"Up? Can you be a little more specific? How far up? Which way up?"

The dark copper of her skin glowed with a reddish tint and she answered him defiantly. "No. I just told you. All I know is up. But I'll bet you don't have a better idea."

He didn't. That was a fact.

"So, we'll go up." Deidre got to her feet and brushed herself off, avoiding his eyes. "That way." She pointed up and to the right. "Try to keep on the pace."

Noah grunted and stretched a little. He felt aches and pains in places he didn't even know existed.

"And another thing." Deidre's defiance took on an angry edge as she shouldered her pack. Uh-oh cringed away from her. "I owe you. For that little trick down on the plain. As soon as this Spid thing is out of the way, I've got serious plans to knock you on your keester. Repeatedly."

"Yeah?" Noah replied belligerently. "You and whose army?"

"I won't need an army. Write it on your calendar, drummer dude."

"I will!" Noah found himself suddenly grinning. Why worry about whether she could beat him up? There was probably no way they'd survive the battle with Spid anyway.

"What's the silly grin about?"

"Tell you sometime," Noah chuckled. "Let's go. Up."

He laughed, throwing his head back. As he did, he saw movement on a shelf of rock above them and to his left. He blinked hard, trying to focus his eyes. Either he was imagining things, or he'd just spotted the tattered, raggedy, gray-bearded hermit. As he watched, the figure turned and, leaning on a walking stick, started along a path that angled upward from the ledge.

Noah tapped Deidre on the shoulder and pointed.

She craned her neck. "What?"

"Didn't you see him?"

"See who?"

"The hermit. He was up on the trail. There."

Deidre scanned the upper reaches of the cavern. "You're seeing things."

"I think he wants us to follow him."

"I think you're nuts."

But Noah was sure he wasn't. Running from the hermit had been a big mistake. He wouldn't make it again. "I'm

257

going. You're free to follow me." Without waiting to see what she'd do, he started striding toward the steep pathway that would take him up the inner face of the mountain.

Chapter Twenty-seven

In Abby's dream, she saw herself at five years old, drowsy and cocooned in a fluffy blanket. Mom sat beside her on the bed, reading her a story from a tall book filled with colorful pictures and words that began with immense first letters. She felt warm and secure, lulled by the familiarity of her mother's voice, her clean, apple-soap smell, her light touch as she stroked Abby's hair. "Which story would you like to hear next?"

"Tell me one about Noah, Mom. A happy story." Her voice had a first-lost-tooth lisp.

Mom beamed down at her and pulled another book from a shelf beside the bed.

"This is the story of Noah and the troll," Abby's Mom read aloud, shifting to a trilling, high-pitched, "story lady" voice very unlike her own.

"No, Mom, I don't want that story," the five-year-old Abby protested. "I want a different story. I don't like the way that one ends."

"Now, Abby, you know very well this story has a very happy ending. A happy ending for me, that is."

The soft, loving smile of Abby's mother dissolved. It became an evil leer on the broad-nosed, blotchy-skinned, wart-encrusted face of Spid. The little-girl Abby clapped her hands over her eyes, but the vision of Spid didn't go away. He opened a thick, blood-red, leather-bound book to a random page, and put a long, pointed fingernail on a figure drawn on the stiff parchment. "Look here." The voice transformed itself into Spid's oily smarminess.

"Look what's happening to Noah now."

Curiosity got the best of her. Peeping between her fingers, she saw colorful inked drawings come to life on the page. There were gigantic, ferocious flying dinosaur things, and ugly, squat four-armed monsters, ax-wielding

259

ogres, and Spid himself, chasing an inch-high cartoon of Noah across the parchment.

"Run, Noah, run," She heard herself scream.

The full-size story-telling Spid laughed diabolically and turned page after page, each one featuring different nightmare creatures chasing Noah toward the margins of the paper. From time to time, the drawing of Noah would stop and drum on a flat surface and the inked creatures would pause and watch. Then, as if hearing a prearranged signal, they'd chase him again.

"Help him, Mom. Help Noah," the dream girl cried. "They're going to catch him."

"Your mother cannot help you, Miss Keene. She's gone. Noah is living out his destiny." Spid's voice dripped with malice. "And mine."

"Can I change things?" The little girl asked the troll. Spid reached a claw-fingered hand toward the dream-Abby's face. She cringed and shrank back. She closed her eyes.

Soft fingertips stroked her cheek. "Of course, dear."

Abby felt Mom's hand cup her chin and heard the reassuring smile in her voice. "You know the way, don't you?"

"I . . . I . . . think so. But I'm so sleepy." The girl in the dream pulled the covers around her and yawned.

"Don't worry, baby," Mom began to sing an old Beach Boys song she'd used as a lullaby when Abby and Noah were small. "Everything will work out all right. Don't worry baby."

Fighting sleep, the five-year-old felt her eyes close. She couldn't see Mom now, but she heard the song. She yawned again and Mom's song began to fade, becoming less and less distinct. Finally, it melded into a musical hum that began to grow louder and louder. It filled Abby's ears, her head; it filled the entire room.

Abby sat up in bed. The humming seemed to fill her whole body now, making her ribs vibrate. What was it and where was it coming from? A rainbow splash of color panned across her face and then continued around the room in a circular pattern. Her eyes followed the color burst to its source—the Chameleon Stone. It spun in place on its natural shelf, throwing off shafts of multi-colored light and emitting the hum that seemed to increase every moment.

The sound seemed to scramble her thoughts. She put her hands over her ears, but it made no difference. Surely, Chillout or the other grungoids would hear it soon and come to see what was happening. Maybe they'd know why the stone was humming, and how to make it stop. Or maybe the walls muffled the sound. Perhaps she could turn it off herself. Or take it to Delacroix and have him look at it.

Abby eased back the covers and stood up. As she did, the orb changed color, from rosy pink to a honey-spun gold in the blink of an eye. Looking up, she noticed the Zezzue had adjusted themselves to the same exact tint as the globe. The humming grew louder, deeper. Her whole body seemed to vibrate now. The rock beneath her feet seemed to shake. What was happening?

As if answering her question, the Chameleon Stone levitated and spun across the room. Wide-eyed, Abby watched it orbit around her, then hover above the chair where she'd laid her neatly folded clothes before going to bed.

"You want me to get dressed?" She felt foolish talking to a rock, but to her surprise, it bobbed up and down and zipped into another orbit around her head.

"I'm thinking that means yes." Abby put aside her self-consciousness and walked to the chair, yanked off her nightgown, slipped on her jeans and shirt and sat to pull on her socks and tennis shoes. The moment she'd

261

finished, the rapidly rotating Chameleon Stone orbited her a final time, then spun quickly through the doorway.

Abby put hasty double knots in her shoelaces and ran into the main chamber. The stone, now sapphire-colored, hovered near Delacroix's practice drum skin. The Zezzue emitted only minimal light, and she heard nothing except the humming of the floating stone, now much fainter than it had been in her chamber. Everyone else must be sleeping, she thought. As she moved toward the stone, another sound penetrated through the humming.

Thuddah-thoom, thuddah-thoom ,thuddah-thoom. The heartbeat of the mountain began to fill the cavern, overriding the buzz of the stone. As she neared the Chameleon Stone, it bobbed once, then darted toward the entrances to a series of tunnels that opened onto the ledges above her.

Thuddah-thoom, thuddah-thoom, thuddah-thoom. The pulse continued to throb, just loud enough to be a constant presence as she stumbled up the dark pathway behind the now translucent turquoise orb. Once again, as she was about to touch it, the stone darted away, disappearing into a darkened tunnel.

Abby took a deep breath and followed. In front of her, the Zezzue seemed to wake up, and lit the tunnel with a soft orange glow. "Thank you," she told the tiny lights. They flickered in response and increased the intensity of their glow.

She followed the tunnel for about a hundred feet before it ended in a small, bathroom-sized chamber like the one that had transported her along with Delacroix and Chillout to The Last Place You Look. Another Vorv, she thought.

Faith elevator, she'd taken to calling it in her mind, because it was the place where she learned to trust that Delacroix wouldn't allow her to be hurt.

The Chameleon Stone drifted into the elevator, spinning in place as if waiting for her to enter. "Where are

262

you taking me?" The sound of her own voice echoed eerily back to her. Once again, she felt utterly ridiculous, talking to a chunk of rock. The Chameleon didn't answer.

Not that she had expected it to. It just hummed quietly. Abby felt her nerves jangle and her stomach quiver at the memory of her last experience riding the sucking air down at a speed she didn't even want to guess at. Maybe she shouldn't go. Maybe she shouldn't follow the Chameleon Stone. Maybe Spid was controlling it.

She took a step back, trembling. Above her, the Zezzue glowed brighter, pale blue now, like the sky she hadn't seen since the day she and Noah ran away. She felt tears burn the rims of her eyes and rubbed them away.

What should she do?

Thrum-thrum, thrum thrum, thrum thrum, the mountain seemed to answer. The beat grew stronger by the moment. A low hum of a voice, maybe real and maybe her imagination, synchronizeded itself with the rhythm. You know the way, Abby. *Thrum-thrum, thrum-thrum, thrum-thrum, thrum-thrum..* Youknow, youknow, youknowtheway, theway, theway.

She took three tentative steps, positioned herself beneath the Chameleon Stone and looked up into the bottom of the spinning orb. Colors seemed to swim in a milky ocean, darting across its diameter, swirling along its edges. She felt her mind emptying, her muscles relaxing, felt herself borne along by some cosmic tide into a trance-like state. With one tiny functioning corner of her mind, she searched for the words Delacroix had used to make the rock melt beneath their feet. Alameezos gravititos? Or maybe Gravameezos Alvitos? Or even Alvagravos Meezotos?

Abby forced herself to blank her entire mind and just open her mouth and let the words tumble across her tongue. "Alameezos gravitos," she intoned. Alameezos gravitos. Alameezos gravitos. Alameezos gravitos. Over

263

and over she repeated it, until the words began to stick together, to melt into each other.

This time she squeezed her eyes tightly shut as she chanted; this time she didn't watch as the rocks dissolved from the edges in. She felt the chamber vibrate, heard the steady thrum-thrum, thrum-thrum, thrum-thrum of the mountain beating in synch with her chant. She felt she was twisting in a gentle breeze. Don't think about what comes next, she told herself, chanting harder and faster.

"Voorrrrrvvvvv!"

A sudden rush of air and she felt herself plummeting. Her eyelids started to fly open, but she clamped them closed. She fell and fell and fell, hoping every second to hear the growing roar that would drown both her heartbeat and the percussion of Humbug Mountain and signal that she had almost touched bottom.

Finally, she heard it. Then she felt it, the sensation of gliding to a stop. Her stomach twitched. She opened her eyes. The walls swirled around her for a few seconds and then the nausea passed. She blinked away the blurriness.

A tunnel stretched ahead of her, an oval of light promising only a short walk to a larger chamber. Abby took a few wobbling steps and then halted. The Chameleon Stone. Where was it? She craned her neck, but knew before she looked that it wasn't hovering overhead. No hum tickled her ears, no splashings of color lit the walls. Her heart sank. She'd lost the orb.

She felt sick with dread. Delacroix had told her the orb could be critical when they met Spid at the skin. Now it was gone. Maybe Spid had tricked her, had gotten her into the elevator so he could steal the stone.

No. The rational side of Abby's brain took over. Not possible. Spid couldn't come up into the world of Above. Not yet, anyway. And there had been no one else around. Except the Zezzue. And they'd never cooperate with him.

At least she didn't think they would. Not if they had a choice.

But where had the Chameleon Stone gone? Maybe it fell out on the way down. Maybe she should go back up.

She started to step back into the Vorv, then paused. Maybe the stone had arrived before her. Maybe it had spun along on its own through the tunnel ahead of her.

She decided to look. If she didn't see it, she'd go back. It only took her a few moments to emerge from the passageway into a high-ceilinged cavern. The chamber was enormous, the sloping ground littered with rock and boulders, crisscrossed by crevices. It stretched for half a mile or more, sloping gently downward to the opposite wall. She looked in all directions. There was no sign of the Chameleon Stone.

Abby plopped down on a rock, scanning the broken landscape and wondering why she had been led there. Was she meant to cross this cavern? And if so, for what purpose? She looked to the Zezzue for advice, but the lights were far away, spread out along the distant ceiling. She couldn't tell if they flickered an answer.

A warm breeze lifted her bangs. She licked her forefinger and held it up. Wind. Definitely. The first time she'd felt this strong and steady an air current since coming to the mountain. Was this chamber so huge that the air currents rose along the slope of the plain? Or was there a tunnel that led outside? Was that what she was meant to find? Was she supposed to leave the mountain? To leave without finding Noah?

Standing, squinting across the plain, she searched for a shaft of light, then shook her head. No. She wouldn't go without him. She started to turn to go back into the tunnel, but something caught her eye. At the very bottom, not far forward of the opposite wall, a small dark dot of movement danced into her vision. The Chameleon Stone?

No, she could never have spotted it at this distance. And it wouldn't appear dark, would it?

Clambering to the top of the rock, she rubbed her eyes and concentrated on the dot. It zigged and zagged, but moved steadily toward her. For a moment, it disappeared behind a ridge of rock and when it emerged it had become three distinct dots. Definitely not the stone. Before much longer, the dots seemed to grow heads and arms and legs and she saw that two of them were people. Humans. Like her and Delacroix. The third looked shorter, grayish. Like Chillout. Who were they? Friends? Or enemies? Should she go out to greet them? Or should she hide?

She settled for climbing down off the rock and crouching beside it. Had they seen her? How fast could she get back to the air elevator if they weren't friendly? And how long would it take to activate the Vorv?

Aware that the wisest course might be to run now and find out more later, Abby continued to hunker beside the rock, eyes glued to the steadily-growing figures picking their way across the plain. A tall, muscular, cappuccino-colored girl clad in some kind of armor led the way. Abby thought she resembled the young woman she'd seen in the Chameleon Stone after the Spiddle game. A boy limped along beside her, his clothes in tatters, his tangled hair lying across his forehead, his head bent forward with the weight of his pack. A grungoid scrambled to keep up with the others, dreadlocks bobbing.

Abby studied the boy again and felt a stab of disappointment. She realized she'd been hoping it might be Noah. But it wasn't. This boy, despite his limp and obvious exhaustion, seemed taller, surer, stronger than the brother she'd last seen on the ledge overlooking the Pacific. This boy, who matched the Amazon-like girl stride for stride even though he had no shoes, couldn't be the sulking young-for-his-age brother who lived so deeply within himself. This boy had confidence, power.

266

The boy looked up.

Abby's heart jumped in her chest. On her feet and running before she could think, she screamed his name.

"Noooooooooah."

As she pounded down the plain, Abby saw recognition flash across her brother's face. He halted, raised his arm to wave, said something to the girl and broke into a hobbling trot. "Abbbbby."

Screaming and laughing at the same time, Abby collided with her brother, wrapped her arms around him and squeezed as tightly as she could.

"Oof." He recoiled. "Take it easy, Abby. I'm kinda sore."

"Too bad," she squeezed harder, sobbing against the metal plate harnessed to his chest. "I'm kinda glad you're alive."

"I'm kinda glad too, Abby. Real, kinda glad," Noah chuckled, wrapped his arms around her and returned the hug.

That's different, too, she thought. Noah didn't hug. Not since Mom died.

"Hey," she heard his voice, a deeper steadier tone than she remembered. "You're almost impossible to lose, you know. How'd you find me, pest?"

She released him and knuckled away her tears. "Like I told you, bro. Somebody has to be the brains of this operation. Where have you been? Who's the girl? And the grungoid? Are you hungry? Delacroix is waiting for you." She took a step back to take a good look at him and saw his blistered and bleeding feet, the rips in his pants and shirt and the bruises beneath them, his blow-torched eyebrows. "Noah. You're hurt."

"It's nothing, Abby. I'm okay." Noah put a hand to his sooty face and ran his fingers over a couple of healing scrapes.

"Yeah, he just cut himself shaving. With his sword."

The brown-skinned girl and the gray grungoid trudged toward them. She looked like a gladiator, but she was pretty, Abby decided. Not beautiful, but naturally attractive, with strong features and an aura of energy.

She, too, looked bruised and beat up. She halted and the grungoid stopped a few paces away, panting.

Noah chuckled and turned to smile at the girl and she grinned back.

"Well, Bunny-buns, are you going to introduce me to your sister or what?"

The girl's lips hadn't moved. She and Noah exchanged glances and she began to laugh, pointing to the grungoid who stood, hands on hips, tight curls brushed back from his forehead. The girl shrugged and tipped her head at Noah. "Hey." This time the voice came from the actual girl. "I promised I wouldn't call you that." She crinkled her nose. "Can't help what Uh-oh does."

"You put him up to it," Noah accused her.

"Me? Would I do that?" She turned from Noah and stuck her hand out toward Abby. "Doesn't look like he's going to get to it, so I'll do it myself. Hi, Abby, I'm Deidre."

"Deidre." Abby repeated as she took her hand. The grip was firm but warm. "Pleased to meet you. What happened to you guys? Where has Noah been?"

Deidre opened her mouth, but Noah interrupted. "No time to explain, Sis. I've got to get to the Skin."

"I know." Abby told him.

"You do? How?"

"Hello-oh. Brains of the operation." She tapped on her forehead with an index finger. "Leetle gray cells hard at work." Abby chortled. "You're not the only person who has a story to tell, you know."

"Yeah?" Noah raised what was left of his eyebrows.

"Well, we'll catch up later. Do you know the way to the Skin?"

268

"No. But I can take you to somebody who does. Come on."

A few minutes later, they stood in the semi-circular chamber at the end of the short tunnel. "Ready to rock and roll?" Abby grinned at her brother.

Noah touched the walls and the solid ceiling. "Rock and roll to where? This looks like a dead end."

"It's not." Abby couldn't wait to see Noah's reaction when they were swept aloft. "It's the Vorv. Everybody hold hands," she instructed.

Deidre clamped her hands together. "Not until I know what the Vorv is," she said suspiciously. The grungoid, Uh-oh, made a small chattering sound and snapped his head around as if looking for an escape route.

"Trust me." Abby patted her brother on the shoulder and felt him flinch. She must have hit another tender spot. "Sorry."

"'S' all right," he answered, but she saw him clench his teeth, reacting to the pain. He touched the walls again and he and Deidre exchanged a glance and a shrug. "Are you sure this is going to work?"

"It's how I got down here," Abby said. "Join hands. Everybody ready? Close your eyes and take a deep breath. As deep as you can. Then do it again." She heard them inhale slowly.

"Alameezos gravitos," she began the chant, closing her eyes tightly. The words ran end-over-end-over-end, becoming a pulsing hum. She felt the lightheadedness of the trance-state. In a matter of seconds, the ground begin to vibrate and she sensed the rock above their heads dissolving. The only things that pricked her concentration were Uh-oh's panicked sounding *chhht, chhht, chhht,* Deidre's small squeal of anticipation, Noah's whooshing exhalation and the distinctive "Vorv" sound that signaled the beginning of the pneumatic ride. Then they were

269

sucked upward, riding air to the chamber near Delacroix's cavern.

"Here we are," Abby told them. Deidre took a step and fell to her knees. Uh-oh careened into a wall, and Noah gripped Abby's shoulder. "The twirly tummy and light-headedness pass in just a moment. Just take a few more deep breaths and then I'll take you to Mr. Delacroix. He's the Pettifog."

"Delacroix?" Noah cocked his head.

"Right," Abby grinned. "Step right this way and meet your hero." She trotted along the short tunnel that led to the drumming practice area where Delacroix lay on his back, thumping rhythms on the stretched surface. At the end, she stepped aside and motioned Noah to go ahead of her. As he passed, she saw his jaw drop and his eyes bug out.

"Y...y...y...you're Delix, Feelacroix . . . I mean, Fecroix Dela-lix, but-but-but I thought you were d...d...d... dead, I mean how could you possibly...wh...wh...what happened to . . . uh, I mean . . ." He leaned against the rock, shaking his head in wonderment.

Delacroix never paused. He continued thumping out the steady beat on the skin in front of him. But he turned his head, smiled broadly and winked. "I'll 'splain it all, my man. Just get out your sticks and join in. We got lots of work to do, if we gonna ruin old Spid's party."

Chillout, who'd been watching Delacroix practice, piped in. "Crazy, man. It'll be like stereo, daddy." He snapped his fingers to Delacroix's rhythm, then spotted Uh-oh, who'd emerged from behind Noah. A rapid exchange transpired in grungoid-speak with a series of rapid *chhht, chhht's*, a number of clicks, gargles and chatters. Finally, Chillout took Uh-oh by the arm and began to lead him away. "This cat needs nourishment, dig? Wants to lay some wacked out tale on me about dancing on fire. Now, that's entertainment." The

270

grungoids walked through an opening in the wall and disappeared.

Noah began to advance toward the practice skin, fumbling with his pack.

"Hungry?" Abby asked Deidre.

The tall girl grinned. "I could definitely eat something. Like a large animal or a small building. And I wouldn't mind a bath."

"Chillout will turn up with some food. Let's go to my room." Abby put a hand on Deidre's arm and guided her toward the outer chambers. "And I'll show you where you can bathe."

Abby noticed Deidre had to duck her head a little to get into the sleeping chamber where the bed had been made and a table set for two was laden with dishes filled with potato chips, smoked salmon and oatmeal cookies. Abby had expected that. She hadn't expected to see the Chameleon Stone, back on its shelf, glowing with a muted shade of ocean blue.

Abby stared at it, feeling awash in guilt. In the excitement of finding Noah and bringing him back to Delacroix, she'd forgotten all about the orb and her fear it had been lost forever. But here it was, and Noah was safe and she had two new friends and she felt that everything was going to be all right. How could it not be? As Delacroix often said, it was all a matter of faith.

Chapter Twenty-eight

"I know the way out of Humbug Mountain. At least I think I do." Abby answered her brother's question. "Maybe we should just go home."

Noah frowned and took another tentative bite from the strange fruit Chillout had brought them for breakfast. It tasted a little like pineapple but had the texture of an apple. The grungoid had also brought thick slabs of brown bread identical to the kind he'd eaten at Deidre's mother's house. Everybody down here must make it, he thought. Probably the flour comes from some root or something that grows underground, maybe even from mushrooms.

He contemplated the night he'd spent in 'Shroomtown with the residents preparing for the battle. Abby could be right. The smart thing might be to run from this craziness. He shouldn't let her stay here and get hurt. And she would, if Spid broke through the Skin. They should find a tunnel to the outside and go home.

Biting another hunk of the fruit and munching on it, he marveled at how strange it was that his memories of his house, his room and even the garage had muzzed up in his mind. So much had happened since the hermit rescued him that it was like his head no longer had room for other memories. One thing he did remember clearly, though, was the situation with his father. But he couldn't think about it now. He had to focus on the drumming challenge. When he got home—if he got home—he'd be a different person. Maybe his father would be different, too.

As important as it was to straighten things out with Dad, he knew he wouldn't leave Humbug Mountain until it was all over. If he left, any chance the people of Above had of holding off Spid would vanish. From what Delacroix told him, the collection of trolls, ogres, demons and other unspeakable beasts that made up Spid's army vastly outnumbered the volunteers preparing to defend the tunnels and caverns of Above. If Spid's forces overran them, they were all doomed—Deidre, Uh-oh, Eve, Delacroix, Chillout and all the others. They were family now, too. No way he could abandon them. Not after what they'd been through.

Noah knew his sister must be frightened of what might happen if he failed. She'd witnessed Spid's wrath, or at least the wrath of his image when she'd beaten him at that word game. Spiddle? Noah remembered playing Scrabble with his sister and getting so frustrated he'd given up and thrown some of the tiles at her. She was too good, too smart. But would her brains, the "leetle gray cells," be of any help if the Skin opened and the fighting began? For that matter, Noah thought, would he? One of Spid's demons would probably make short work of him, battle fork or no battle fork. Between drum practices today, he had to have Deidre show him more techniques.

"Well?" Abby gripped his wrist as he conveyed another hunk of fruit to his mouth. "Do you want to try to get out?"

Staring at her darting eyes, Noah wondered how long he'd zoned out. "You go." He ordered. "Find Dad. Tell him what's going on. Tell him to send help."

"Hah!" Abby snorted. "As if. Trolls, ogres, demons, an armless drummer and a pack of grungoids—who will believe that fairy tale? They'll lock me in a loony bin."

"Well, then at least get out. Tell Dad I went to California."

"No way." She curled her lip in the same determined pout she'd adopted when he'd tried to send her home the night they ran away. "You may have walked across a river of fire and fought off gargoyles and all that, but if it wasn't for me showing you the Vorv, you'd still be out there wandering around in the middle of the mountain."

273

Noah decided to try another appeal. "You really should go, Abby. I don't know if Dad can take losing both of us."

"Then you come with me. It's all or nothing, Noah."

"I can't. I feel so connected with . . ." he gestured around him, "this place. I feel like it's my destiny. I've got to drum."

"I know." Abby suddenly grew quiet. "Same here. There's something I've got to do, too. It's in the prophecy. I just don't know what it is yet." She took a solemn bite of her fruit and said between chews. "We fight Spid then?"

Noah knew then he couldn't change her mind, not if she was in the prophecy too. "Guess so," he responded, dispiritedly.

"Well then, big brother, you'd better go practice some more. Delacroix's waiting. The summer solstice is tomorrow."

Their eyes met and Noah felt his chest constrict. He wanted to tell her how much he loved her. What a great little sister she was, and how much he really admired her. But he didn't. Neither of them spoke. Finally he got up. "See you after a while."

"Right," she said. "After a while."

He found Lix Delacroix just where he'd left him before the armless drummer had insisted he get some rest and food. The giant brown man lay on his back, feet spanking a syncopated series of rhythms on the tightly stretched surface of the practice skin. Noah stood for a moment listening, watching, marveling at the perfection of the sequences, the seemingly effortless shifts from one time signature to another. Even without hands, Delacroix was still the greatest drummer ever.

At first, Noah had been in total awe of his skill, almost unable to lift his sticks to play alongside him. But Delacroix had put him at ease, speaking to him in the language they both understood so well. The beat. They

274

talked without words, using taps, thumps, clicks, bops and booms.

"Noah, mon ami. Where are your ticklers, my man? We must practice, non? We have less than a day."

Noah fished the tapered wooden drumsticks from under his belt. They'd been scorched when he crossed the river of fire and the tips were chewed up from all the times he'd drummed on rocks along the way. He hoped they would be worthy of the rhythms Delacroix created.

As he took his place beside the practice skin, Delacroix began patting out a beat with his left foot, adding accents with his right. "The ritual is a simple one, my young friend. Call and answer. I am thinking Spid's drummer will probably lead with something like this. What should we respond?"

Starting with one stick, Noah picked up the beat, then automatically slid into a counter-rhythm with the other stick. Call and answer. What you played had to exactly duplicate what was laid down by the other drummer or team. Then, using their original rhythm, you spun it into an improvisation of your own. Then they had to answer you while you listened to the rhythms and hoped your arms remembered. It seemed to Noah that after awhile the beat bypassed his brain. It came from somewhere else. His heart, maybe? His dreams? Somewhere outside of him? He didn't know.

Now he took his place at the practice skin, and thought about the challenge to come. Depending on the fluctuations in the rhythm and who had the upper hand, the Skin would either soften or grow more rigid. Delacroix knew from the prophecy that if it got too flexible, if Noah and Delacroix fell behind, some of Spid's forces could push their way through the soft spot. If Noah and Delacroix failed entirely, the Skin would disintegrate and evil would be set loose in the world. At one point, he'd asked Lix what the Skin was made of.

275

"We do not know. No one has seen it for hundreds of years. Since the last time."

"Oh."

"But I think it is more an energy than a solid thing, you know? A portal between worlds. Made of the stuff of the universe."

Noah sat quietly for a few moments, letting his head bob to Delacroix's rhythms, letting his fingers start to twitch, to itch to hold the sticks. When he could stand it no more, he picked them up. "We could try this."

Doubling the rhythm his left hand played, he worked a three-hit attack in between beats.

"Good." Delacroix shifted effortlessly to put a bottom beat under Noah's lead. "And then to the 12/8 beat, I think. Ooh, that would be a fat groove." Shifting gears, he slid into a wildly syncopated bass pattern, his legs and feet moving so fast they seemed like a total blur.

"I got it." Noah moved faster to parallel Delacroix's acceleration. "And then maybe a slide-hop here."

"Ah. Yes!" Delacroix grinned, his teeth a flash of white against his glistening skin.

They practiced non-stop for what felt like hours, until Noah's right hand cramped and he dropped his stick. As if he'd been waiting for that cue, Chillout appeared with a tray of lemonade and some chocolate chip cookies. He also brought a couple of towels to dry the sweat from their bodies. Both of them were drenched.

It was a moment, Noah decided, he would remember for the rest of his life. The lemonade was sharp and tangy, the air cool and clean, the cookies sweet and crunchy. Despite his exhaustion, Noah felt contented, satisfied with himself, at peace. At least, he thought, if I die tomorrow, I will have played with my hero. And he hasn't treated me like a kid, like an amateur. Me and Lix Delacroix. Amazing.

Delacroix flexed the stumps of his arms, easing his back. "You must promise me you will remember something, mon ami, remember it when at the Skin we attempt to send Spid back into the depths."

Noah took another sip of the cold drink and nodded.

"What is it, Mr. Delacroix?"

"Please, no. Lix is what you should call me. We are partners, here, before the drum of truth."

Partners? And he wants me to call him Lix. Feeling awed and uneasy, Noah took him at his word. "All right. Lix? What do I need to remember?"

"Although we practice many of the variations that the other drummer may play, he can choose from millions of others. Is not true?"

"Yes." The thought sobered Noah. "True."

"There is no way, in the time we have, we can practice even a tiny percent, non?"

"Yes. I mean no. We can't." His elation of a moment ago seemed to crumble beneath him like coarse sand. The weight of the other drummer's words pressed down on him. All this practice might be a complete waste. So many things could go wrong tomorrow. He could drop a stick, lose the beat, play too fast or too slow, work into an improvisation that became a dead end.

"So." Delacroix stood and stretched to his full height, tilting his head upward and raising the stubs of his arms toward the sky. "We must, both of us, listen. We must hear completely. We must take the sound of the other drummer into us, and let it saturate every pore in our body. And then we must let the energy flow back through us, into our hands," he raised his leg and wiggled his big toe at Noah, "and into our feet."

"Concentration." Noah nodded. He wondered if Abby had told Delacroix that his mind tended to wander. He felt a flash of anger. What did Abby know? His mind never wandered while he was drumming. Never.

277

"No!" Delacroix adamant denial rang from the walls of the chamber. "Not concentration. Surrender. Total submission. What we must not do, my friend, is let our brains speak louder than our hearts. The drumming, she is not thinking. The drumming, she is pure feeling. Pure emotion."

Noah hoped he knew what Delcroix meant, hoped that the feelings he'd had while drumming were the same as what the armless man experienced. "Yes," was all he could manage to say.

It was enough for Delacroix. He nodded. "You have already proven your bravery several times over. All anyone can ask of you is that you do your best."

"I'll try. I'll do the best I can."

"I know. As I, too, will try my best. And if we should fail . . ." He shrugged his shoulders and got back into position in front of the practice skin.

"Are you afraid?" Noah picked up his drumsticks, rolling them between his hands. He realized this might be his last full day on earth. Or under the earth.

"Afraid to die?"

"Yeah." Noah bent his head and beat a slow rhythm on the practice skin. He heard Delacroix sigh and then flutter kick the drum with his left foot.

"Oui. Of course. Not of what comes or does not come after we have ended this gig, you know." He rolled his head, as if to get a good, long last look at the cavern where he lived. "But only the pain and that I may not be as strong as I want to be, that I may not bear it as well as I hope. But . . ."

The word hung for a moment. "But what? Noah asked in a quiet voice.

"Something I am more afraid of than death."

"More than death?"

"Oui."

"What?"

278

"To die knowing I have not truly lived."

Chapter Twenty-nine

Abby sprawled on her bed and squinted at the Spiddle word for the thousandth time. Admitting defeat didn't come easily to her. She hated that moment at chess when you had to tip over your king and concede that your opponent had maneuvered you into a hopeless position. Not that she'd had to do that often. In fact, she'd hardly ever lost. But she was losing now. She might as well admit she couldn't win. There was no way to figure out what the Spiddle word meant or even the right way to pronounce it. She didn't know Beneathese and didn't have an English-to-Benethese dictionary to refer to. She couldn't ask Spid. Not that he'd tell her.

She closed her eyes, remembering the troll's reaction when she'd laid the word on the board. His instantaneous challenge. The stunned, then enraged expression on his face when Yurk told him he'd found the word in the very reference book, which he, Spid, had compiled.

But neither of them had pronounced it, nor had they told her what it meant. In fact, she remembered Spid clamping his hand over Yurk's mouth to keep him from saying it out loud. So it must be important. Even dangerous to Spid. But why? What was its function?

One thing she'd decided. The word wasn't code. It wasn't an anagram or a substitute cipher or anything else. It might be a phrase instead of a single word, but it was just what it was, a jumble of consonants with a few vowels sprinkled in. Like vegetable soup spilled on a tabletop. With no frame of reference, no knowledge of Spid's language, she had no way of discover how to pronounce it.

And she had to know. She had to know soon. Before the event that would determine the rest of her life. She felt like crying. But she wouldn't let herself. Not now. Too late for tears. Or perhaps too soon.

Frustrated and angry with herself, she climbed off her bed and went to the massive outer cavern to see how the last minute preparations were going. At the far edge of the arena-sized room, she saw Noah and Delacroix at their practice. Even at that great distance, she could hear the throbbing beat. Once again, she noticed how confident Noah appeared. She felt a burst of pride that he'd been chosen.

Toward the center of the cavern, on a broad level area, Deidre and several of her friends from 'Shroomtown scrimmaged with battle forks. Fascinated, Abby listened to the sizzle and warp of the weapons as the combatants circled each other, thrusting and blocking, ducking and attacking. She considered asking if Deidre could train her, give her a fork to use against Spid, but decided she couldn't learn enough in a few hours to be any more than a momentary nuisance to the demon troll and his soldiers if they broke through the Skin.

In another corner of the immense room, Abby found Uh-oh with a cluster of grungoids gathered around him. Although they only communicated in grunts, whistles and the almost snake-like *chhht, chhht, chhht*, sound, she got the impression he was lecturing them on battle tactics.

Abby wandered the chamber, gathering a wave from the boy Deidre said was named Peitr, who practiced fighting imaginary attackers from the back of his many-legged Galloopapede, Sznorzpap. A little further along, a man who'd been introduced to her as Benny Vlavnosk talked earnestly to a small group of men and women about the tactics of tunnel fighting. She felt like a fifth wheel. There didn't seem to be anywhere she could help out.

Finally, she migrated over to where Noah and Lix Delacroix toiled, as they had almost non-stop since her

281

brother arrived. They drummed with an intensity that totally overshadowed any Noah had reached in his garage-haven back at home. Amazing, she thought, they've almost melded into one person, one drummer. Noah, his long hair flying like sweaty spaghetti around his head, darted from place to place, striking his sticks on different areas of the tightly-stretched practice Skin, creating a universe of sounds. His eyes were closed in concentration and his lips pushed in and out with the rhythm. He seemed to be speaking a musical language with his drumsticks, and speaking from another place, a place where no one else could go.

Delacroix nodded his head rapidly, keeping time with the bass beat that anchored the bottom of the controlled fury Noah delivered to the quivering drum. "Here, Noah," he said." This is where you must take this moment and fly."

Abby couldn't believe it. Her brother, already drumming at a speed that seemed superhuman, moved it up yet another notch. He hammered the practice skin with a ferocity that sent a crackle of electrical excitement up her backbone. He hammered harder, faster, nailing the beat.

Kuhrack. Kuhrack.

Not one, but both of Noah's drumsticks snapped in half. The rounded tip ends flew in different directions. One whizzed by Abby's head at near-supersonic speed, thunked into the wall behind her and shattered into splinters. The other went straight up, like a bullet shot into the air. Noah, eyes and mouth open wide, watched it.

Delacroix stopped drumming. The projectile hesitated, began to fall. It seemed to take an hour to spin past them and land, making a *tink, tink, tink* sound as it bounced against the floor.

The jagged edges of Noah's drumsticks protruded from his clenched hands. Delacroix furrowed his brow, tapped

282

the drum twice more with half-hearted kicks, then arched his back and snapped himself to his feet in one motion.

"The sticks. They could not take the stress. You have another pair, yes?"

Noah just shook his head slowly back and forth. "No. Just these." He opened his hands. The fragmented wood clattered to the floor.

Abby saw his face crumple. He looks just like he did that night on the road when I caught up with him, she thought. "We'll get another pair. Don't you have . . ."

Abby realized how silly the question was, even before Delacroix raised his eyebrows and the stubs of his arms.

"No, I guess not. But can't somebody make a pair? How hard could it . . ."

"It is a long way to find wood, ma pctitc. And no proper tools to carve the sticks with." Delacroix's chided her somberly. "Non. We must think of something else."

"I . . . I . . . could play with my hands." The quivering in Noah's voice betrayed his fear and uncertainty.

Something tickled at Abby's brain. A memory. A picture. Drumsticks. But where? Ah! There! "Wait!"

Abby shouted, hearing her voice bounce back to her from the cavern walls. "I know. I know where there are drumsticks."

Delacroix arched himself to his feet. "Where, Abby? Where will we find these sticks? I will send someone to retrieve them, quick like the wink."

Abby smiled at the image. "They're in The Last Place You Look," she said smugly. "A whole bunch of them."

"Huh?" Noah stared at his sister. "The last what?"

"Place you look." Delacroix raised an arm stub and pantomimed striking his forehead with his palm, then laughed at himself. "Alors! I am so into the drumming, I forgot all about it. It's the place where all lost things go," he told Noah. "It's at the bottom of the Vorv."

"The Vorv we rode up in?"

283

"No, another one. There are many Vorvs. Or perhaps the same Vorv many times. They are a mystery onto themselves." Delacroix turned his attention back to Abby. "Tell me where you saw the sticks, ma petite, and I will send Chillout for them."

Abby tried to visualize where, in the massive piles of luggage, car keys, school books, wallets, wristwatches, socks and everything else, she'd spotted the drumsticks. Were they near the mittens, or on the other side, next to the bracelets? She made a rapid decision. "I can't really describe where they are, and Chillout's busy training and scavenging provisions for his troops. I'll go by myself. I like riding the Vorv and I can walk right to the drumsticks once I'm down there. I'll be back in just a few minutes."

"You're not going alone," Noah insisted. "It's dangerous. I'll come with you."

"Go pound salt, big brother." Abby said defiantly.

"I've been there before. I know the way. You get something to eat. Take a nap. You're going to need your rest."

"She is a stubborn one, your sister, non?" Delacroix laughed. "But she is right. It will only take a few minutes. And it is perfectly safe. There are no monsters there. They are all behind the Skin as yet."

Abby stuck her tongue out at her brother. "If I'm not back in an hour, send out a search party." Before she could lose her confidence, she spun on her heel and headed for the tunnel that led to the first Vorv she'd ridden with Delacroix and Chillout.

She began to chant even before she stepped into the semi-circular room, and in a matter of seconds, felt herself spinning down the airshaft. Shaking off her dizziness within seconds after landing, she scuttled quickly under the sign that read *Thela stpla ceyo ulook*.

Inside, she looked around in the muted light, trying to get her bearings. She remembered Chillout cadging a pair of sunglasses. Yes, she thought, toward the back of the room, with all the instruments. She began to walk quickly, telling herself not to be distracted by the stacks of books and games, and a pile of cell phones. Still, she stopped and picked one up, wondering if she could use it to call her father. In a moment, she tossed it back in the pile. "Don't be stupid, Abby," she whispered. "You can't make a call through solid rock."

Trudging on, she found saxophones, trumpets, guitars, drums, harmonicas, flutes and other music-making paraphernalia piled in a stack three times as high as her head and as wide as her living room back home. She ran her finger across the cool brass of a tuba. How could somebody lose something as big as a tuba? And then she smiled. She remembered something she'd read once about a cellist who had accidentally left his three-hundred-year-old instrument in the back of a taxi. An honest cab driver had returned it. People just lost things. All kinds of things. Some of them much harder to replace than others.

She spotted a smaller mound of drumsticks, tangled like a game of Pick Up Sticks. Good, she thought, I'll just grab a couple and run back. She stretched out her fingers. Which ones should she take? Did it matter? The logical part of her brain told her it didn't. Drumsticks were drumsticks. And drummers didn't always need the real things. She'd seen Noah drum with everything from butter knives to chopsticks. The important thing was to grab two sticks, or maybe four or five in case another broke, and get them back in a hurry. She reached down, grasped several sticks, yanked them from the pile and began to stow them into her rear pocket.

"Fate is not random. Fate is the way." The eerie humming whispered voice of the Zezzue startled her. The sticks clattered to the floor.

"You know the way, Abby," the Darksuckers whispered.

285

She looked up to see the tiny creatures had formed a soft swirl of violet and golden light, a nebula that spun slowly in place.

Maybe the drumsticks she took *did* matter. Maybe this whole adventure, everything she and Noah had been through, was like putting together a giant jigsaw puzzle. The Chameleon Stone was one piece. The drumming was another. Noah had brought a piece back with the Methuselah Stone, and she'd found another in the word game against Spid. She didn't know where that fit yet.

But if you put in the wrong piece, the picture wouldn't make any sense. The right drumsticks, she decided, must be another important piece. She stared at the heap of sticks. Some were lighter and some were darker, but basically they all looked alike. How could she find the right ones?

A laugh almost snuck out. How had she found anything she'd looked for inside the mountain? By not looking with her eyes, that's how.

She tossed aside the sticks she'd picked up, sat beside the pile, closed her eyes and began to breathe in and out. In the darkness inside her mind, she searched for that perfect calm that had led her out of the tunnel maze. A picture began to form, Noah, his hair flying about his head as he hunted for the rhythm, the perfect rhythm.

Thrum-thrum, thuddahthrum, thrum-thrum. Abby heard the beat. It seemed to come from all around her, but she couldn't tell whether the sound existed only in her mind or she was really hearing it.

Thrum-fadit-ditthrum, ticketytick -thrumthrum. Thrum, diddah-boom, tickety-tick thrum-thrum. Inside her mind, Noah played a duet with the mountain, playing ever faster, and more insistently. She felt her arms start to move, her hands roll at the wrists, matching his movements.

Clackety, clack, clack, clack, clackety, clack.

286

She opened her eyes to see an amazing sight. The drumsticks, hundreds, if not thousands of them, were beginning to move, to spread out on the floor, rolling against each other, spinning, tumbling. The golden light from the Zezzue beamed down on them, like a spotlight on a crowded stage. Suddenly the sticks levitated from the floor of the cavern.

Abby gasped, jumped to her feet and shrank away from them.

Slowly at first, the sticks began to spin. They formed a spiral, then a tight circle. The center of the circle began to drop and the circle became a cone. As they moved, the swirling drumsticks made a soft, irregular clacking noise. It swelled to a steadier rumble as they picked up speed. The cone lengthened, rotating on its point like a tornado. Faster and faster it spun, revolving around her. She turned with the swirl, never taking her eyes off of it. The tornado lengthened and rose until the point was even with her shoulders. She realized the point wasn't a single stick, but two. While the others swirled around them, they were still. Was the drumstick cyclone protecting them, or revealing them?

She peered at the sticks through the swirling mass. She saw something gleam. She forgot her fear. These were the sticks she needed. But there was no way to grasp them without getting her fingers sliced off, or at least badly bruised, by the spinning galaxy of drumsticks.

Or was there a way? The same way she'd found her path out of the maze.

Taking a step closer to the ever-accelerating cosmos of swirling drumsticks, Abby closed her eyes, took another long, deep breath and extended her arm. She began to chant, "Iknowtheway, Iknowtheway, Iknowtheway," faster and faster and faster until it became a low-pitched hum in her mind, the words becoming sounds that melded with the high-pitched whine of the wooden maelstrom.

287

She opened her hand, turning the palm up. The chant tumbled from her lips, faster and faster and faster.

Smack. The drumsticks slapped against her palm. She closed her fingers over them and opened her eyes. The whirling mass caved in upon itself. The sticks clattered to the stone floor.

"I know the way," Abby crowed, staring at the sticks in her hand. They were made of pure white wood. Inlaid in mother-of-pearl on the butt end of each of them were the letters LD.

"Lix Delacroix?" She marveled. "It couldn't be, could it?" Could they really belong to the Pettifog? Maybe he'd lost them in the plane crash? After all, he had something more important to look for—Melanie. And when he lost his hands, he'd probably decided there was no point in searching for them. Well, there was no time to wonder about it now. Noah needed them. And he wouldn't need any spares. She was sure of that. She turned to start back.

"Most impressive, Miss Keene. You really have honed your mental acuity to a new level. I applaud you."

Spid's three-dimensional image blocked her way. He clapped with the tips of his horny-skinned fingers, producing a light, echoing *thuff, thuff, thuff* sound. "You are, of course, still not quite up to the pinnacle of thinking that I have attained but . . ."

"You can say that again, boss. Dittos. Mega-multiple-dittos." Yurk appeared beside his troll commander with a soft pop, saluting, bowing and scraping and all but kissing Spid's ring. The ogre and his superior were both in full battle regalia, with polished dark armor. Yurk carried a long, sharp spear and Spid had a spiky hammer and a hatchet-like club hanging from his wide leather belt. They looked fearsome.

Abby reminded herself they were only holograms. What a toady Yurk is, she thought. What an awful way to go through life, kissing up to a troll. The thought distracted her from her fear. "I don't have time to talk to you right now. I've got to get back."

"To take the drumsticks to your brother. Yes, yes," Spid smirked. "I know all about it. I must say, Abby, that your scrawny older sibling has also astounded me. He has shown a great deal of determination and courage. And now he has the Methuselah Stone. And he will drum at the Skin. But he cannot win."

"The little geek's in a heap of trouble, isn't he, boss?" Yurk chortled.

"I would not have phrased it in exactly that manner, Yurk, but yes, sadly . . ." Spid adopted a mock sympathetic tone, oily and unctuous. "Sadly, he and the accursed Pettifog will face a humiliating lesson in drumming delivered by Thrndur. It will be followed immediately by a painful and agonizing death. Unless . . ."

"Unless what?" Abby couldn't keep the anger out of her voice. "Unless I throw in with you, right?"

"The terms have not changed since our last meeting."

"Very generous of you, boss. Giving the little twirp one last chance to survive."

"Thank you, Yurk. And, Miss Keene, the offer extends to your brother. He could prove useful in the future. But it does not extend to Delacroix. The brown wizard is an annoyance that I wish to remove."

Abby almost blurted out something she'd heard her father tell a late-night telephone salesman once: "Not only no, but hell no." But as she opened her mouth, a thought occurred to her. It quickly grew, filled out, and became a plan. Possibly a futile plan, she realized. But a plan, nonetheless. To enact it, however, she needed to stay on Spid's good side—or at least not openly antagonize him.

"I really don't want to die." The truth of the statement lent credibility to her acting. "But I can't speak for Noah. And I won't betray him."

"Ah, yes, devotion—another fine quality, Miss Keene. One I encourage my many loyal subjects to develop. As least as it pertains to me. Well then, let me frame my offer in practical terms."

Abby felt her skin crawl. "Practical terms?"

"Yes," Spid smirked. "In fact, you might call them terminally practical. You will have one final chance to come to me. At the Skin. There, I will accept your abject apology for opposing me when the Skin is breached and my actual physical magnificence breaks through . . ."

Buh-ruthh-er, what a swelled head he's got, Abby thought, biting her tongue to keep from blurting out, "So, who's going through the Skin first? You or your ego? You both won't fit at the same time."

"Am I clear?" The threat in Spid's voice and his poisonous dagger-like glare vanished all thoughts of making a flip remark. She had to get back. Noah needed the drumsticks. And he'd be worried about her.

"Yes," Abby said petulantly. "Can I go now?"

"Of course. Give my best to the boys. Ta ta."

Ta ta? Bu-ruthh-er. She turned to start across the *Thela stpla ceyo ulook* chamber. But Spid's purring, smirking voice stopped her.

"One little thing further, Miss Keene."

She turned. "What?"

"Even though you're considering joining me, you still represent a threat to my success."

Abby tried for her best little girl voice. "Me? A threat?"

"Granted, the chance you'll ruin my plans is miniscule, but I can't risk it. Remember when we played Spiddle and I told you I had devised the most masterful and fair rules."

Abby swallowed hard and willed her feet to move. They wouldn't.

"Well, I dictate the rules for this game too. The larger game." He sidestepped to expose the image of the

Shadow Stone on a pedestal beside him. "Maculostis Astigmaneesus," Spid commanded. He pointed a long green fingernail at Abby's face, while rubbing a spot on the gem.

A beam of dark light sprang from the stone and lanced into her eyes. Spid's image seemed to explode in a bright flash within her brain. She shrieked in pain. Her knees buckled. She fell to the floor.

The pain receded like a wave on the sand. She opened her eyes. She blinked. She couldn't see Spid. She couldn't see the mounds of stuff piled high in the room. She could make out only very faint shapes behind a wall of blackness. "No," she moaned.

"Yes," Spid laughed. "You are nearly blind, Abby. I hated to do it. When you present yourself to me, in your abject humility, admitting defeat, we will talk of bringing light back into your eyes."

"I'd rather die."

Spid guffawed cruelly. "That, too, can be arranged."

Abby heard a sharp pop and sensed Spid's image had disappeared. She was alone. Tears dribbled down her cheeks and her teeth began to chatter. Alone. In the absence of sight, other sensations became more vivid. She felt a faint current of air wisp across her face. The always-present rhythm of the mountain amplified.

Thrumm, thrumm, thrumm, thrumm, thrummm.

She smelled the lemony soap she'd washed her face with that morning and the unique tang of the oil that lubricated the pads and joints of the brass instruments on the stack near her.

Blind, she mourned. Maybe for life. Or for the few hours remaining until Spid charged through the Skin, whichever came first. Her dark joke strangely squelched her temptation to give up. Stop it, she scolded herself. Self-pity sucks. She blotted her face with the sleeve of her sweatshirt and tried to clear her mind. What to do?

291

She had to get the drumsticks back to Noah. Unless she did that, nothing else mattered. I can do this, she told herself with a burst of confidence. I know the way. Heck, I could find my way back to the Vorv with my eyes closed. Which, she thought, thanks to Spid, was exactly what she'd have to do.

She didn't even need to chant, she decided. She'd just use her memory and common sense. How hard could it be to pick her way around the various mounds of misplaced miscellaneous and make her way back to the Vorv? She began walking, extending her arm in front of her so she wouldn't bump into anything.

Ten steps, she thought. Piece of cake. I should be alongside the pile of hair dryers. Turn right and go another eight steps to the mound of hair barrettes, then another ten steps or so to the small mountain of paper. She remembered glancing at them on her early visit. Homework assignments mostly. Must be the ones the dog didn't eat, she thought to herself, smiling.

After a series of twists and turns, she found herself at what felt like a doorway. A strange sound emanated from it, a kind of low level buzz, something she hadn't noticed before. Some kind of energy radiated by the Zezzue, maybe.

She stepped through, already planning the rest of her route to the Vorv. About twenty yards, a right turn, and then into the tunnel. Piece of cake.

Frazzzz! Abby's hair crackled and stood on end. Her skin prickled as she passed through some kind of energy curtain. *Fzlooorp!* The sound of the force field was immediately replaced by something else.

Laughter.

"What the . . ." Her words were drowned out by more laughter. She spun around as a cascade of chuckles, chortles, giggles, guffaws, snorts, sniggers and haw-haws reverberated around her. The hilarity of hundreds of men, women, children and what she could have sworn was a small pack of hyenas created an eerie cacophony.

She slapped her hands over her ears. She must be in the room where lost senses of humor went. The one with the sign that read: *Tak emyw ifepl ease.* But that was impossible. She'd been so sure of her route. And besides, when she'd come here before, the entry had been that weird wooden door and doorknob. How could this be?

As she wrestled with the problem, the volume and intensity of the laughter grew, creeping her out, making it harder and harder to think. "I must have come in another door," she yelled. She could barely hear the words. "I'll go out the same way."

If you can, a negative little voice screamed inside her mind.

"I know the way," she yelled back. She took two steps. Her hand struck rock. Don't panic, she told herself. You spun around when you first heard the laughter. It must be this way. She made a quarter turn, walked another two steps and found another solid surface. As if hearing the punch line to a particularly funny joke, the laughter swelled and roared around her. The panic she'd fought overtook her in a dizzying flood. She darted left and right, sliding her hand along the wall, frantically searching for an opening.

Nothing. Around her, laughter rang, louder and louder.

Nooooo! Her head swam. Her thoughts seemed to break loose inside her brain, they flitted like light-drunk flies dive-bombing a glowing bulb, they collided and crashed. But there's got to be. A way out. Doesn't . . . but. . . . where? Am I going . . . it's crazy . . . How did I . . . ?

Stumbling along now, the tears freely running down her face, Abby groped at the cold rock of the chamber's wall. "Stop laughing!" She shrieked at her disembodied tormentors. The demonic hilarity only grew more manic, a waterfall of mirth crashing down around her. She forced

293

herself to stop running, tried to take slow, deep breaths. She was panting like a thirsty dog.

Chant, she thought. Chant, Abby, chant. She tried. "Iknowtheway,Iknowthe way,Iknowthe . . ." She couldn't hear herself. Laughter clogged her mind, her throat. Her lips stopped moving. She clutched the drumsticks to her chest.

I screwed up, Noah. I'm so sorry. She tried not to think what would happen at the Skin when she didn't arrive with the drumsticks, but that's all she could see—Spid and Yurk, flailing at her brother with their weapons, laughing, laughing, laughing.

Something brushed lightly against her upper arm. She flinched. A spiderweb? Ick. She hated spiders. It brushed her again. Not a spiderweb. Fingers. Hairy fingers. She opened her mouth to scream.

A hand clamped down on her shoulder.

Chapter Thirty

Noah knew he needed down time to gather strength for the coming challenge, but he couldn't shut his brain off long enough to fall into any real slumber. It wouldn't have mattered if the sandman had shoveled sleep-dust under his eyelids; he was too worried about Abby to relax.

After she'd gone to find the sticks, he and Delacroix had resumed their practice. Noah tried slapping the practice skin with his hands, using his fingertips and the heel of his palm to achieve different sounds. It felt futile, but he'd kept at it, losing all track of time. Only when a worried-looking Chillout appeared had he remembered his sister.

"Uh, Lix?" The dreadlocked grungoid, as Abby called the creature, had cleared his throat and croak-growled. "The uh, little chickie is like, major latesky. Bad trip, no? You want I should go check?"

"Abby?" Noah had immediately jumped to his feet.

"She's not back? I'll go too."

Lix had arched his back and leaped to his feet. "Not a good idea, mon homme. You do not know the many tunnels and blind alleys of Humbug Mountain. And you are needing the rest. We are only a few hours from meeting Monsieur Spid, non? If you are exhausted, we will have no chance."

"But . . ." Tired or not, Noah had to go. He'd done a crappy job of protecting Abby so far. If anything happened now that they'd found each other . . .

"Chillout will find her. I am confident she has just gotten turned around."

Before Noah could protest again, Chillout had dashed away, zipping through a nearby tunnel.

295

Noah flopped to the other side of the sleeping mat and closed his eyes again. He knew he'd dozed a little, but wild cookie-cutter dreams had prevented his sleep from being even remotely restful. He'd seen the magma dance, the gargoyles, the scraggly hermit talking to the Zezzue.

Now he caught a flash of himself, Deidre and Uh-oh straining their way up the cliff. He saw the Methuselah Stone, Mom, Dad, Abby, home, his bedroom. The fluffy pillows on his own bed beckoned, and he sank his head into them. So comfortable. So soft. Maybe he would sleep, really sleep, just for a minute. And then he'd get up.

"Wake up, brother monster. Time to spring into action." The voice seemed part of his dream. Ab-normal. Bratty, brainy, little sister. "In a minute. I'll get up in a minute. I can still make the school bus."

"No, doof." He felt a hand shaking his shoulder.

"Wake up now. It's time to go kick some serious troll tush."

"Huh?" He opened his eyes to see his grinning sister.

"Hey. You're back."

"Terrific grasp of the obvious, bro. Did you miss me?"

"Chillout found you?"

"Not before he scared the whoosymajoos out of me, but yep, our favorite beatnik grungoid turned up just in the nick of time."

Noah sat up, nerve endings jangling. "What do you mean, nick of time?"

Abby backed away, hands sweeping the air behind her. "Later. No time now."

Standing, he took a tentative step toward her. "What's wrong, Abby?"

"Nothing." She backed away a few feet. "C'mon, get going, Delacroix's waiting. We've got to ride another Vorv down to the Skin. Hustle up."

296

In two long leaps, Noah closed the space between them and locked his hands around her forearms. She tucked her chin. "Abby, look at me," he commanded.

She sighed, then raised her head. He saw what looked like inkblot contact lenses blanketing the irises and pupils of her eyes. "Oh my God. What happened, Abby? Are you blind?"

"Very politically incorrect, brother mine. I'm visually challenged. A little parting gift from our friend, Spid."

"You saw Spid? You said you'd be safe from him."

"I thought I would. I thought— Anyway, Spid cast some kind of spell on me with the Shadow Stone."

Noah wrapped his arms around her and pulled her against his chest. "Abby. I'm so sorry. If I'd just stayed home. Or if I'd taken you back there, then none of this would have happened."

"Know what, big bro?" Abby pulled away from him. Her voice sounded almost cheerful. "Even with this," she brought her hand up to touch her cheek, "and being scared half out of my mind three or four times, I wouldn't change a thing. It's been amazing, hasn't it? The stuff we've seen. The things we've done. It's incredible. No one will ever believe it."

Noah thought about that for the first time. If they ever got back to the world, they'd probably have to keep all this to themselves or their father would have them talking to psychologists for the rest of their lives. "Well yeah, but . . ."

"Shush." Abby put a finger to her lips. "Let's just go finish it. Here," she reached back to her back pocket and drew out a pair of slim, ghostly white drum sticks, "you'll probably need these." She held them out. "If you can't beat Spid with those, big bro, then the contest was rigged against you from the start. Check out the monogram."

297

Noah took the sticks and twirled them between his fingers. He spotted the letters LD inlaid in mother-of-pearl.

LD. It couldn't be. Lix Delacroix. "But how?"

"Found 'em, downstairs. Or maybe they found me," she amended. "Just when you thought things couldn't get stranger, huh?" Abby grinned.

Noah stared at the sticks for a moment, then flipped them between his fingers again. He grinned back at his sister, but then frowned, remembering she couldn't see his smile. "Tell Lix I'll be right out."

The earlier ride up in the Vorv was nothing compared to the ride down. It felt like he, Delacroix, Abby and Chillout were being sucked into the very core of the earth. The force of the descent splayed the flesh on Noah's face; he couldn't prevent drool from escaping from his loosened lips. And then, as suddenly as the ride began, it ended with an emphatic "vorv." An updraft lowered them to the ground as softly as a feather drifting to earth.

"Ungggh." Noah tried a tentative step. His stomach somersaulted and he lurched to the wall and bent at the waist, trying to regain his equilibrium.

"Offer you a barf bag, my man?" Chillout put a hand on his back.

Is he kidding? Noah felt blood rush back into his head and decided that, from what he'd seen of the hipster grungoid's foraging ability, he just might produce an air-sickness baggie. Holding up a hand to decline, Noah straightened and felt his stomach settle and his head clear.

"Quite a ride, huh?" Abby waggled her eyebrows at him and patted his shoulder.

"Definitely an E ticket," he agreed.

They walked down a short tunnel in silence, but as they drew nearer to the opening at the far end, Noah heard the steady pulsating of Humbug Mountain. *Thrum-thrum,*

thrum-thrum, thrum-thrum. It seemed like the very heartbeat of the planet, radiating up and through him.

Thrum-thrum, thrum-thrum, thrum-thrum. Noah could feel the rhythm permeating his very core, vibrating through his cells. *Thrum-thrum, thrum-thrum, thrum-thrum.*

They were, he knew, very close to the source.

Emerging from the tunnel and onto a natural balcony hewn into the rocky wall of the drumming chamber, he halted, open-mouthed.

"Describe it to me." Abby groped for his hand.

"Huh?"

Her fingers dug into his palm. "Earth to Noah. Little sister. Blind as a bat. Hello-oh."

A flush of embarrassment and guilt warmed his face.

"Abby. I'm sor—" He noted the "cut the pity" grimace on her face and began telling her what he saw. "We're standing on a wide ledge about two-thirds of the way down into a really tall, tubular chamber. It's maybe fifty yards across at the bottom."

She cocked her head. "I hear other people, I think."

Noah confirmed it. "There's kind of a spiral trail that runs up the walls and there are tunnels every so often. And there are people, some of the 'Shroomers, and grungoids and some kinds of animals I've never seen before. They're all on the ledges, looking down at the Skin."

Delacroix added. "My little friend Chillout goes to join them. As with the others, he protects his home."

Noah glanced around. The gray, dread-locked creature with the Ray Charles shades had disappeared silently.

Delacroix continued his explanation.

"They will defend Above from Spid and the darkness on the other side. They will fight in the tunnels and caverns until Spid is vanquished or until . . ."

They were all silent for a moment, then Abby turned her face up and swept a hand through the air. "What's above us?"

"The shaft narrows," Noah answered. "I can't," he craned his neck, "really see where it ends."

"Somewhere up there," Delacroix pointed, "they say there is a portal to a place known as the Realm of Exponential Darkness."

Noah peered upward. "What is that?"

"It's where the Zezzue go," Abby said, reverence in her voice. "To purge themselves of the darkness they inhale to give us light."

"According to the legend," Delacroix added, "the Zezzue have regurgitated darkness in that place since the very beginning of our universe. The gloom is so deep, so intense, that if it were to escape, it could extinguish the sun."

"Like a black hole," Abby agreed.

Noah tried to imagine anything that dark, but his mind couldn't begin to grip the concept. He dropped his eyes to the people on the natural balconies around the chamber.

Thudda-thoom, thuddah-thoom, thuddah-thoom. The sound echoed around him, and he looked down at a natural rock platform that rose from the floor. At the rear of it, against the far wall, Noah saw the Skin, a tightly-stretched and almost diaphanous oval membrane. Light strobed across its surface, green and blue and red, casting an unearthly glow on three figures standing before it.

From her upright, combative posture, there was no mistaking that one of them was Deidre. The small gray figure beside her had to be Uh-oh. It looked like he'd chosen to be by his friend's side. Noah felt a twinge of something strong. The grungoid had stuck with him through thick and thin.

Unless Noah was sorely mistaken, the third figure, disheveled and leaning on a staff, was the hermit. Here to fulfill he prophecy, Noah thought. A tingle of anticipation skittered along his spine. This time, he almost welcomed fear. It wouldn't stop him. He knew how to use it, how to work past it.

"We must go, Noah," Delacroix said. "We must begin to drum as the sun approaches the solstice. As it passes into the constellation of the crab this year, there will be a moment when the moon and all planets will align, the seas will stop their ceaseless movement and all will be in total synchronization. That is when the mountain's beat will falter. That is when the Skin will open. Unless we succeed."

Noah felt the chill hand of fear around his heart as they followed the trail along the perimeter of the spiral chamber, descending toward the Skin. To take his mind off of it, he described what he saw to Abby. "The drum is huge. Maybe fifty feet across. There are steps in the rock on both sides of it. Deidre's standing next to it on a huge platform with Uh-oh and the hermit I met. From this distance, they look like toys."

"What color is the Skin?"

"Hard to say, it's several— Wait a minute, there's something— Whuh-what's that?" Noah turned toward Delacroix and pointed to a dark funnel cloud forming near the front edge of the platform. "It looks like a tor—"

"Spid," Abby whispered as she clutched her brother's arm. "I can feel him."

The dark funnel of light glimmered; the enormous armor-clad Troll began to materialize. Beside him stood a squat, ugly figure with a globule of green drool escaping from one corner of his mouth. Yurk, thought Noah, just as Abby had described him. Only the faint vibrating aura around them, and their translucency, betrayed them as three-dimensional images.

Noah heard a collective gasp from the assembled defenders of Above. Deidre drew her battle-fork and set it humming. "Get me down there," Abby told him.

"No. Stay here."

"Noah!" Abby clutched at his shirt, ripping the frayed fabric. "You must take me down there."

"Yes," Delacroix said. "She must be there."

Noah opened his mouth to argue, then gritted his teeth and led Abby down the trail to the platform. The intimidating images of the demon troll and his grotesque second-in-command snapped into focus and looked out over the arena. Spid cleared his throat and began to speak, his voice a round-toned, self-important, drone—a combination of boring school teacher and oily politician, "We have gathered here—"

"Tell em, boss. Lay it on thick," the grotesque ogre bleated.

"To witness . . ." Spid let the word ring. "To witness the demise of the ill-conceived, illogical and quite possible illegal regime of Felix Delacroix, the pusillanimous Pettifog of the astoundingly underachieving land of Above."

"You go, boss. You duh troll."

"Horsehockey," Abby hissed.

"You might reflect," Spid continued, "all of you gathered here, as you live out the final moments of your lives, how you transgressed against the all-wise, all-seeing, all-knowing most merciful and kind, soon-to-be ruler of the reunited realms of Above and Below . . ." He paused, looking expectantly at Yurk.

"Uh, that would be you. Right, boss?"

Spid cast a narrow-eyed poisonous glance at his hench-ogre, then continued. "Yes. I, Spid the devious."

He raised his hands and paused again.

No one moved. No one spoke. Yurk jumped into the yawning silence. "C'mon, let's give it up for the big guy."

He slapped his ham-like hands together. *Thungh-thungh-thungh.*

"Suck-up," Abby whispered. Noah put a hand over her mouth, but Spid had heard and swiveled his head around toward them. Noah saw the glint of demon eyes boring into him, felt them searching for weakness. He forced himself to return the stare, steadily, without blinking.

Spid smiled. "Well, then, the victims, uh I mean, our worthy opponents have arrived."

"Ignore him," Delacroix ordered. He took the steps to the platform with Noah guiding Abby right behind him.

The troll sniffed. "There is no need to be rude. Especially since you will be begging for my most munificent mercy in a matter of mere moments."

Man, Noah thought, this guy really loves the sound of his own voice.

The Skin began to vibrate and the lights of the chamber began to dim. The surface of the gigantic drumhead turned a burnished orange and began to throb.

"Ah, the solstice approaches." Spid gestured back at the Skin. "Soon we will know without question who has the greater power. All of our destinies will be sealed."

His image went static, as if he'd removed himself from it.

For the first time, Noah noticed a large recessed stone face carved into the rock wall beside the Skin. It glowered out at him, mouth pulled into a tight grimace, empty cavities for eye-sockets. A scooped-out area above the forehead formed a narrow shelf. Delacroix nodded at the visage. "The stones," he said.

Noah withdrew the brain-stone from his nearly empty back-pack.

"And Abby, you have with you the Chameleon Orb, no?"

303

"Right here." She drew the translucent stone, now glowing the same orange as the Skin, from her own backpack.

Noah took her by the arm and led her to the primitive face. They knew what they had to do. Delacroix had told them.

Abby went first. Noah helped her up the steps and placed her hands on the right-hand eye socket of the carved face. She studied it with her fingers, then set the stone inside. Noah helped her down, then climbed and placed the Methuselah in the second eye socket.

Reaching into his backpack again, he drew out the picture of his mother. He touched her face, then set the picture on the shelf made for the Shadow Stone. He nodded at his mother and led Abby back to Delacroix.

Suddenly he became aware of the piercing gaze of Spid. The image had become reanimated. Abby seemed to sense it. "Spid's pretty creepy, huh, Noah?"

"Yeah." He felt his stomach muscles jitter with the tension. He pulled in a deep breath. "Reminds me of Mr. Trangle." The mention of the high school football coach and gym teacher made Abby giggle a little.

Deidre appeared at his elbow. "Noah," she said softly, "you ready?"

"Hi, Deed," he grinned. "No problem. I've got a plan."

"What's that?"

"Play as loud and fast as I can."

She smiled with trembling lips, leaned toward him and kissed the corner of his mouth. He felt his breath catch in his throat. "Good plan," Deidre said. "You'll do your best. I know you will. And I'll be right here." She backed away and rejoined Uh-oh and the hermit, who stood placidly, arms folded.

Boooom! A single bass drum beat exploded the stillness.

"Noah." Delacroix tilted his head toward the Skin. "It is time."

Noah took off his backpack and fished out the drumsticks. Delacroix stared at them in disbelief. "Noah, where did you—"

Bah-Booooom! The second drumbeat reverberated through the chamber. The figures of Spid and Yurk, nearly transparent now, hovered at the front of the platform, looking back at the Skin.

Noah rubbed the sticks between his palms. "Abby found them."

"Ah, Abby. As always, she astounds, does she not? But we must hurry." Delacroix folded himself to the ground at one side of the Skin, rolled unto his back and raised his feet. Noah grasped the sticks, head spinning, nerve endings jangling, heart pounding. Totally unreal, he thought. A few days ago, I was just another kid finishing my sophomore year in high school. And now I'm in a battle for my life. And Abby's. And the world.

I hope I—

Bah-Boooooom!

Through the gathering dimness of the room, a thick column of light shot down around him; Noah found himself bathed in a yellow glow. He stepped to the Skin; through its now nearly transparent surface he saw, for the first time, their opponent.

Bizarre. That was only word that described the flat, jowly, pig-like face, with clumps of black hair sprinkled across its cheeks and wolfish snout. The creature pulled broad lips into a profane leer, exposing four sharp fangs.

Noah willed himself not to flinch, but what he saw next drove his confidence to a new low. Protruding from a body covered with armor-like platelets were five arms.

Two sprouted from each side. The fifth unfurled from the center of a bushy growth of hair on the creature's

305

forehead. Each of the hands clutched a jet-black drumstick.

"You're in way over your head, kid." Noah heard the growled taunt from the other side of the Skin.

"Play, Noah. Nothing can be done about what you see on the other side. Let your heart guide your hands. Play." Delacroix began to pat his feet against the skin, laying down a steady pattern.

Noah tore his eyes from the creature on the other side and focused on the sticks that had once belonged to Delacroix. He stepped up to the Skin and beat out an easy pattern, a place to begin—three hits with the left hand, two with the right, three more with the left. Repeating the three-two-three, he accelerated into a kind of early Ringo Starr style.

Instantly, the five-armed creature across from him began to play. Using his forehead-arm and one lower arm to mimic Delacroix's bass beat, he picked up Noah's lead beat with the other lower arm and one of the top ones. With the remaining arm, the beast played a series of short, sharp rolls, sliding them perfectly into the main beat.

Noah answered instantly, keeping a steady 5/4 going with the left hand and doing roll-punch-roll with the right. Delacroix picked up the change effortlessly, spinning the bottom end to a new counter rhythm. The Skin seemed to thicken.

A small cheer rose from the watchers on the ledges. The creature on the other side of the Skin faltered for a moment, then plunged into a volley of higher-pitched strikes, segueing into a Ginger Baker attack with two of the other hands. This time, it was Noah who was slow to respond. The Skin grew more transparent. The creature smirked. After a half-second's hesitation, Noah picked up the challenge, playing the answer in a syncopated 6/8.

The surface of the Skin grew milkier.

306

It senses what's happening, Noah realized. The Skin knows who's ahead and who's lost the beat. He drummed faster. The Skin grew milkier. He grinned.

The sound of chimes tinkled through the chamber. The milkiness diminished. Chimes? The Skin grew nearly clear. It seemed to grow slack. The creature leered.

"Think it," Delacroix commanded. "Think what you would play."

Chimes. Chimes. Chimes. Noah struck the Skin and heard the silvery notes. He followed the creature's lead.

The Skin tightened.

Congas, Noah thought. Before the second syllable had formed in his mind, he heard the hollow wood and leather thudding. Wow!

Chimes and snare, he thought, when it was his turn to answer the creature's rhythms. He heard the sound of chimes, jingling and tingling from the stick in his left hand, the staccato rattle of the snare from his right. The Skin grew milky again.

Bells and tympani, tom-tom and rim. His hands fluttered and flew. His feet and legs flew too, up and down the stairs, deepening and raising the tone of the beat. Back and forth, up and down – faster, slower – rolls, chatters, slides and slaps.

Noah's focus narrowed to a pinpoint; his concentration became absolute. He no longer felt the heat of the white light that poured onto the stage from above. No longer could he hear the gasps and applause of those gathered above the stage, watching, their fate in his hands. As it had been many times in his garage music studio, everything else blurred, faded into nothingness. His entire being became the beat. There was no sense of time.

His fatigue disappeared. His cloud of self-doubt burned away by the heat of the beat, the beat, the beat. The five-armed drumming dynamo across the skin became only a smudge of color in his consciousness,

Delacroix only a brown blur as he pump-shifted his legs to lay the solid bottom behind Noah's machine-gun improvisation. The Skin hardened and softened. It changed color constantly, shifting with the tempo and emotion of the drumming. Red, blues, greens, oranges and yellows flashed by Noah's eyes, but he barely noticed. The wet sweat-mop of his hair flopped into his eyes and he flipped his head to fling it away. Nothing mattered; nothing could shift his attention from the beat.

He found himself in a combination he'd first learned by hearing Felix Delacroix play it on his "Live at Carnegie Hall" album. He took the core of it and moved it to another level, mixing in right-hand hits as he thought of a steel drum. Across the skin, he felt the other drummer hesitate. The Skin stiffened. Maybe. Maybe he could turn this into an advantage that would—

Clack. Clack.

Noah stared in horror as his sticks collided in mid air as he tried to accelerate the tempo. He stopped dead. A mistake. He'd let himself get distracted.

The Skin began to clear. The five-armed wolf-piggy thing sneered at him as if to say "thanks, sucker" and riffed back into the correct rhythm, then shifted into an amazing combination of his own, dopplering a tympani and conga in a cross current that made Noah's head swim.

The Skin softened, wobbled like jelly, glowed with grayish tint. A fusillade of beats cascaded from the other side.

"Noah!" Abby screamed. "Play. Play!"

"Now!" Delacroix commanded. Inserting a six-note downbeat over the top of the other drummer's clustered beats, he cued Noah in with an emphatic nod.

Noah's hands reacted automatically. He echoed the back-and-forth syncopation created by his opponent, then inserted a muted tambourine counterpoint. The Skin glowed a faint turquoise and firmed a little. He felt the breath rush from his lungs and realized he'd been holding it. He'd nearly lost it all. For everyone. He drew in another breath and picked up the tempo.

For what might have been hours, it went on and on. He and the demon drummer took musical ground and gave it back again. Whenever Noah wanted to go on the attack, Lix anticipated him perfectly, helping him create seamless segues. But, though he tried to ignore them, the limitations of his body began to erode the wall of concentration he'd built again: a quick pang of pain when he raised his arm to hit a high counterbeat, neck muscles beginning to tighten with the strain, lungs beginning to struggle to draw in another supply of warm air as he raced to the top of the steps.

As exhaustion overtook him, Noah knew he had to make a move, gamble and try to end it. Like the split-second he'd chosen to step back onto the burning river with Deidre in his arms and Uh-oh draped across his back, this decision was born of non-existent choices.

With uncanny timing, Delacroix swung out of their opponent's most recent barrage and into a low, rumbling tympanic roll. He nodded up at Noah, and winked. Here we go.

They'd talked about it; that moment when one or the other of the lead drummers decided to end it. To put it all on the line in one final flurry. It was the musical equivalent of playing chicken in speeding jalopies, racing for the edge of a cliff.

Snare drum. Noah issued the official challenge with three sharp strokes. The hits rang out like gunshots.

Bang! Bang! Bang!

For the first time in a great while, Noah sensed the spectators again. He heard their mumble, a distant clatter of weapons being readied, and felt a rush of air that might have been a group inhalation. From the corner of his eye, he saw Abby, her sightless eyes looking off into space,

309

lips moving in and out as they did when she was working on some kind of problem. Deidre, battlefork at the ready, nodded. Ready. Do it! The hermit hovered behind her, arms tucked into the sleeves of his burlap robe, smiling.

Across the nearly-transparent Skin, Spid and Yurk stood glowering, weapons drawn, muscles bunched in anticipation.

Three whip-crack beats came back from the other side of the Skin. Challenge accepted!

The membrane itself began to throb. The color changed from red to orange to yellow. It flashed yellow again and Delacroix nodded three times. After the third yellow, it would go to green.

Noah took a deep breath and placed the rounded tips of the sticks over the area he intended to strike first. So much at stake, he thought, and it's all on me. But a strange peace came over him. Win or lose, he told himself, at least you tried. You did your best. You did all anyone could ask of you. And you never gave up.

Chapter Thirty-one

Thuddddddaaaa . . . thooommmp . . .
Thudddddaaaaaa . . . thoomp.

Abby felt the mountain's pulse slowing. The spaces between the beats increased and she feared each one might be the last. She dug her fingers into Deidre's arm and blinked her nearly sightless eyes. "What's happening? Tell me what's happening? Why isn't Noah playing?"

"He's about to." Deidre slung an arm around her and squeezed her shoulders. "He's holding his sticks ready. He's really tired. And the Skin, it's gone totally clear. It's vibrating like you wouldn't believe."

"Where's Spid?" Abby stood on tiptoe, then dropped back to her heels, shaking her head. That wouldn't help. Nothing would help. She might never see again. She might have to spend the rest of her life asking people to tell her what they saw, trying to remember the faces, shapes and colors she could once see for herself. She felt a burst of anger. It was all Spid's fault. She should have known he wouldn't play fair. "Can you see Spid?"

"He's right behind the other drummer. Ready to burst through. Man, he's even uglier in person. And he's got that squatty-bodied ogre beside him."

Abby felt Deidre's arm muscles ripple as the warrior-girl flexed them. "That's Yurk," she told Deidre. "He's dumb, but he's dangerous."

The snarling rattle of a snare drum sliced the air.

"Noah's starting to play," Deidre released Abby and clapped her hands. "Wow. He doesn't sound tired at all."

But Abby, who'd listened to her brother drum all her life, knew better. She heard the almost imperceptible hesitations, the strikes that were a little less than crisp.

She tugged on Deidre's arm. "Listen," she shouted over the ever-building thumping and crashing of the drummers.

311

"I may have to do something in a minute. Something radical."

"Something to do with the stuff you had me write on that scroll?"

With her free hand, Abby felt the rolled parchment in the back pocket of her pants. "Yeah," she hollered. "And you gotta trust me."

The snap-bang of a particularly violent exchange of drumstick gunfire drowned out Deidre's response, but Abby felt the older girl's hand squeeze her shoulder. When the thunder ebbed for a moment, Abby shouted to her companion. "How far from here to the Skin?"

"About thirty feet." Deidre's hands gripped Abby's forearms, turning her slightly to her left. "Straight ahead the way you're facing now."

Abby nodded. Thirty feet, she thought. Fifteen long steps. More or less. Another drum volley began, this one notching up the intensity to a level Abby would have thought impossible. But this time, it didn't back off; didn't diminish to gain momentum for a new skirmish of drum hits, cymbal rolls, bass thumps. This time, it just built and built and built and built. She could no longer feel the mountain's pulse and wondered if it was ceasing as the prophecy said it would.

Thutututututututututututututut–tha–a–boom-thutututututut-tutututut. The pace increased, the pitch climbed and climbed, stretching Abby's nerves to the edge. She tried to visualize Noah, his hair stringy with sweat, eyes clamped shut, wrists and hands flying faster than hummingbird wings.

Now a series of cymbal punches punctuating every third beat, kicked the already high-geared din up to another louder, faster level of highly compressed fury.

"Thututut, kuhrash, thututut, kuhrash, thututut, kuhrash."

312

Noah, she thought. You've been going non-stop. You've got to be stretched so tight inside. If you go any faster, you'll explode. But, big brother, I'm so proud of you. So proud.

Again, she put a hand back to feel the parchment. Still there. But what if she was wrong? What if, instead of fitting the last piece in the puzzle, she was forcing in a piece that didn't belong? What then?

The answer was simple. She would die. And so would Noah. Her knees went wobbly and she leaned against Deidre and screamed at where she thought the warrior-girl's ear would be. "Has the Skin changed?"

"No," Deidre yelled back. "It's exactly the same. Clear. But solid."

The drumming, seven hands and two feet already at warp speed, shifted up another impossible notch, and Abby knew this had to be the last burst.

Thutcrashthutcrashthutcrashthutcrashthutcrash. The tempo built and built, the volume swelling to totally fill the cavern. It grew so loud Abby's ears ached; so intense, she ground her teeth together. Oh God, Noah, she thought, how much more can you take? For that matter, how long before Delacroix's leg muscles cramped up or he missed a beat?

Crashthutcrashthutcrashthutcrashthut. The air around Abby felt thick, dense with soundwaves and ripe with the smell of fear and adrenaline. She felt Deidre tense beside her, and her own instincts told her the end had come.

As if by prearranged signal, the drummers on both sides of the skin trip-hammered one more rapid run up the ladder—*thututututututututututut*—and then crashed to a close. Kuh-woooom. Kuhrash.

The sound reverberated in her ear for what seemed like an eternity. Just as it was beginning to die, she heard Deidre yelp beside her.

313

"It's Spid. He's trying to push through." Abby felt Deidre pull away, then heard the ringing whack as the warrior-girl activated her battle fork against the decibelt.

If he breaks through, Abby thought. I have to act. She checked the parchment once more, thought about the words on the page and what they might mean. If she was right. If. If. If.

"Whew," Deidre sighed. "He just stretched out the surface of the Skin. It's gotten really rubbery. But it's holding."

Thudddaa. The mountain's pulse throbbed once beneath Abby's feet. Trembling, she touched Deidre's arm again. "Where's Spid? Where's Noah?"

"Spid's on his knees. His drummer's collapsed. He's trying to pull him to his feet, but he keeps slumping back down. Noah's on the ground, too. He's lying next to Delacroix. He's panting. And now there's a— Oh! It's beautiful."

"What's beautiful?"

"There's a drum. Up on a very high ledge, near the top of the chamber. And there's light, like inside of it. It's glowing. It's like gold."

Thoomppp.

Humbug Mountain's heartbeat. The golden drum. The prophecy. Images swirled through Abby's head.

"Noah's on his feet," Deidre told her. He can barely stand." Abby felt her start to pull away. "I'll help him."

Thud...da.

"No. He has to get up there alone." Noah had told her about the drawing on the temple wall: one boy climbing alone toward a high ledge with a drum.

"They're coming this way."

Abby heard Delacroix's urgent instructions, Noah gasping his understanding.

"The rhythm, Noah. Three beats, then four, then five. Once again, you strike it three times and then four."

"Uh-heff, huff-huhn."

"Not too fast. Let each one ring out."

"Whoo, heff, Uh-huhn."

"Noah!" Deidre screamed. "The five-armed drummer. He's up. He's running."

Thoom . . .

"Run, Noah! Run!" Abby screamed. She felt his damp hand squeeze hers, then heard his feet pound across the platform. She turned toward the sound, wishing she could watch him as he took on the final challenge. "Tell me," she commanded Deidre.

"I can't see the five-armed creature," Deidre responded. "He must have climbed out of my view," her voice was tight. "Noah's up on the first tier of rock."

Abby nodded. "Climb, Noah, climb," she whispered into the hushed silence that had settled into the chamber after the thunderstorm of drumbeats. She heard a pebble clatter off a rock and gasped. "Careful, Noah."

Thud. The mountain's heartbeat sounded even more sickly than before.

Beside her, Deidre stiffened, then bolted away. Abby heard the *wooorp* of the sonic fork whistling through the air. "Get back. Get back." Deidre's shrill demand was accompanied by another blow from the fork and an enraged snarl of pain and rage.

Spid, Abby thought. He must have tried to push through again.

She heard Delacroix's voice and realized he was beside her. He, too, seemed exhausted, panting between words. "The Skin, it is . . . *huff* . . . very soft, ma . . . *whuff* . . . cherie. I do not . . . *phew* . . . know if hold it will." He gulped more air, then continued. "But Noah is nearing the top. No more trail. He climbs straight up now. Very steep."

315

"The other one." Abby touched the stump of Delacroix's arm. His skin seemed to steam from his exertions. "What about the other one?"

Thooo . . . wump went the mountain, weakly.

She felt Delacroix twist away and then back. "Impossible, Abby. I cannot see far enough."

Abby heard another *woooorp* from Deidre's weapon and another roar of pain. Spid's venomous threat followed, clear even through the Skin. "You will die first. Within minutes. Prepare to perish."

"I prepare only to live," Deidre shouted back.

Abby felt tears of pride burn her blinded eyes.

Thd. The mountain's beat was only a flicker.

"Good girl," Delacroix whispered. "Strong girl."

"Where's Noah?"

"He is nearly there. He is climbing up over the—"

Faintly, a drum beat on the other side of the Skin.

Thump, thump, thump.

"The other drummer," Abby gasped. "He got there first. He'll start the mountain's heart and it will beat for Spid, for evil."

The demon's drum sounded again. *Thump, thump, thump, thump.*

"Hurry, Noah," Abby cried. Huddled against Delacroix, she heard the snark of Deidre's sword, another roar of rage from the Skin and then five hits on the distant drum.

Before the echoes could dissolve, Abby heard the sound of Noah's first strikes. *Thump, thump, thump.*

"Get back!" Deidre shrieked.

Abby heard a long stretching sound followed by a loud pop, then the sickening crunch of something heavy and solid striking flesh.

"Deidre!" Delacroix cried. "She's hurt. Stay here, Abby," he commanded as he left her side.

316

Deidre whimpered. Metal rang against rock. Spid roared with triumph, a roar that seemed to rattle Abby's ribs; a roar that was no longer muffled. He'd broken through. How many others had come with him?

"Now you will see whose power is supreme," the troll thundered. "The wrath of Spid will send you all into oblivion."

The echoes of the five-armed drummer's next-to-last three-beat stanza and the louder sound of Noah's second strike, four beats, punctuated the troll's threat.

Noah will never make it. He'll never beat the demon drummer back to the Skin, Abby thought. We've lost. Unless . . .

Thirty feet, she reminded herself. She strode toward the sound of Spid's voice. Six steps. Eight. Ten. And kneel. Quickly. A blast of fetid breath burned her eyes and nose, the odor like skunk armpits mixed with rotted fish and fresh manure. As her knees touched the cold rock, she heard Spid's oily, purring, patronizing tone.

"Ahhh. Miss Keene. So you've seen the light? So to speak," Spid laughed. "You've come to kiss the ring of your new master?"

Abby recoiled as she felt a long, thick, scaly finger trail across her cheek. The final four beats reverberated from Spid's drummer. He'll start down the cliff now, she thought. With his five arms, he can move much faster than Noah. He'll get to the Skin first. How can he not?

She heard the thump of Noah's five-beat midpoint. Right on top of that came the sound of Deidre's moan, Delacroix's curse and a rending noise Abby suspected came from the Skin. Perhaps Yurk was fighting his way through to his master.

"No time for that," she blurted at Spid, purposely running all of her words together in gurgling, lisping, scared-little-girl string: "Please don't kill me, I'll follow you and do whatever you want!"

317

Spid chuckled. "Well, I don't know, Abby. This comes at rather the last moment, you know?" Noah's three beats sounded from above. Spid took on an even more gloating tone. "A more cynical sort than I might judge you insincere."

Abby heard the malicious pleasure in his taunting voice. Where was the demon drummer? Nearly down? "Here." Abby reached into her back pocket, pulled out the parchment, unrolled it and thrust it toward Spid.

"Delacroix's plan to defend the tunnels from your troops after the breakthrough. I stole it."

She felt the reptilian hand pluck the parchment from her. "I see. A token of your profound esteem, eh?"

This is it, she thought, crossing her fingers. What if he doesn't read it out loud? What if I didn't divide it right? But it had to be. It had to.

"Let's see now. Thuh-dur?"

Good, she thought. T-I-R. Thuh-dur. He's doing it.

She heard Noah's final four beats. She wondered if he'd heard the other drummer's final beats, realized how far behind he was and had lost heart.

"Kuh-neh?" Continued the Troll. What is . . . "Kuhneh?"

Abby would have never guessed K-D-E-S, was pronounced "Kuh-neh."

"Ess-shull?" A small note of suspicion crept into Spid's voice as he read the C-X-O-S-L. "What kind of battle plan is this?"

"I don't know." Abby answered.

Pleasepleasepleaseplease, she prayed. The next two words. Say them. K-N-U and R-P-L-V. Say them. Say them!

"Nut-Prr? Revale? Gibberish. All of it." She heard Spid crumple the parchment. "This is worthless."

Not to me, Abby thought. The wheels whirred in her head. "Thuh-dur. Kuh-neh. Esshul. Nutpur. Revale."

She threw the whole thing together into one long string in her mind, then redivided it. At first, it eluded her. But then she made the connection from the last two words.

"Nut-pur-re-vale. Not prevail." The rest came in a flash.

Leaping to her feet, she threw her head back and screamed at the top of her lungs. "The darkness shall not prevail."

Instantly, a loud buzz sliced the air from above her. It sounded like a million angry hornets. Abby turned and stumbled away from the Skin. Hairy fingers gripped hers and a small voice said "Uh-oh." She heard Deidre's sonic sword wooorp through the air and a great roar from Spid.

The buzzing grew louder and louder. Uh-oh towed her to the edge of the platform. The buzzing spiraled into a loud *zeeezpop* sound.

Suddenly, everything was still. Then she heard Uh-oh say his name again, and Yurk howl in dismay. "Hey, what's the big idea, boss, who turned out the lights?"

"Yes!" Abby pumped her fist into the air. It had worked. But now Noah had to believe. Noah had to trust her. And there was no time for lessons, no time to experiment, like she had. Noah had to have instant faith.

"Jump, Noah! Jump to the Skin. Now. Do it. Jump!"

Her shrieked commands echoed back to her. The final word repeated over and over again as if it came from one of Noah's vinyl records stuck on the last groove.

319

Chapter Thirty-two

"Jump, ump, ump, ump, ump." The trailing echo of Abby's voice reached Noah in the darkness as he clung to a narrow shelf of rock just below the ledge where he'd finished banging the glowing drum. Abby's gone crazy, he thought. Jump? I'll smash onto the platform and die.

But, he thought, the whole thing has been nutso from the beginning. What could be crazier than dancing across flowing magma, riding the Galloopapede, battling gargoyles, or sailing up and down in the Vorv? A hodgepodge of images, emotions and questions bounced through his mind as he turned one foot and then the other and spun his body to face out into the chamber.

Two inner voices engaged in a stereo argument. "Why jump if you've already lost?" and "You have lost," the other voice argued. "The other drummer is way ahead. He'll be back at the Skin any minute hitting the final three drumbeats."

"But wait. Maybe he's lost in the dark," the first voice interjected.

Noah felt his knees bend even before he knew he'd made a decision. That other thing Abby screamed—the darkness shall not prevail? Did it mean he could jump into it and not get hurt? It must. Abby wouldn't do anything to let him get hurt. No way.

Relaxing his grip on the stone, Noah jerked his drumsticks from his belt and launched himself. He sprang up and out, swan-diving into the dark abyss before the last word of the last thought had registered in his mind. All of his exhaustion, all the tension accumulated over the course of his journey seemed to funnel out of his mouth.

"Ah-yooooooo!"

He spread his arms wider to embrace the air. Or the rock below. After the hours of drumming and all the practice that had come before, the silence of the chamber seemed deafening. He fell into that thunderous silence, feeling the cool air rushing by his face, feeling his hair trailing behind him, his shirt fluttering.

A low murmur hummed in his ears. Delacroix's forces preparing for battle? No, something else. A glowing cloud of hazy green light overtook him with a deepening buzz, zipped beneath him and disappeared from his field of vision.

Down, down, down he sailed. How far up had he climbed? And how fast did falling objects fall? Abby would remember the equation to compute that. Not that there was any point. He must be close to the bottom now, close to breaking his head open on the rocky platform.

Tears formed in the corners of his eyes and were swept away by the rushing air.

The green cloud appeared directly below him.

I'm going to hit it, he thought.

And he did.

The buzzing glow was all around him. He felt heat and something else—a force? Life? Thought? Yes, he could have sworn he could hear, within the now profoundly loud buzz, the distinct sounds of individual voices. They were faint, indistinct. He couldn't begin to extract what they were saying.

The downward rush suddenly slowed. Buzzing built around him, enveloping him in the sound.

His fall stopped. He hung in the air. His feet swung toward the platform.

The buzzing began to subside and suddenly he knew it for what it was—the sound of millions, no billions, of tiny wings whirring frantically. The Zezzue. Somehow Abby had harnessed their power. Or perhaps Abby had merely requested their help and they had consented to give it.

321

No time to think about that now, he told himself as he drifted toward the platform. Once they let you off this green cloud, you've got another problem. Where's Spid?

As he'd pounded the golden drum, he'd seen the assembled group on the platform—Abby, Delacroix, Deidre, Uh-oh and the hermit. He'd seen Spid break through and seen Deidre try to force him back through the rip in the Skin. He'd heard the voice of the ogre Abby said was called Yurk, and suspected that when the lights went out, others under Spid's command also broke through.

The green cloud cast a dim light, so dim he could see only the spot his feet would touch in a few seconds. How many more of Spid's demons had burst through the Skin? And how long would it take them to fall upon him? Would the Zezzue go to full light power so he could find the Skin and strike it the final three times and start the mountain's heart? Or would the troll reach him first and cut him to shreds before he could make a move toward the Skin? And what about the other drummer? How close was he to his goal?

Noah felt himself rotate with the motion of the green mass. A slender beam of light shot out into the inky darkness. It fell on one edge of the Skin.

The moment his feet touched ground, he sprinted, drumsticks clutched in his outstretched hands. The green cloud swept along with him, a mirage of dim light in a desert of darkness.

As he pulled back his stick to strike the first blow, he saw the shadow of another figure on the other side of the Skin. One of its five arms cocked. Noah snapped his arm forward and banged the drum.

Kuhboom. The sound rang out in the darkness.

A twin *Kuhboom* came so close behind it caused an almost shimmer effect.

Whose stick hit first? Noah honestly didn't know. And he couldn't think about it. He had to concentrate on the ritual. The three beats that had begun the challenge had come exactly five seconds apart. The last beats must be the same.

Light began to bloom around him as he counted it out in his head. He glanced over his shoulder and saw Spid, lips pulled back from teeth like spikes, hands gripping a five-bladed ax. The troll spotted Noah and strode toward him. Right on his heels came Yurk, wielding a long spear.

"One thousand five." Noah kept his eyes on Spid as he brought his stick down on the flaccid surface of the Skin.

The other hand, the other stick, hit the Skin, too.

K . . K . . Uh . . Uh . . Buh . . B . . Boom.

This time Noah heard a definite lag between strikes, but with his attention riveted on the advancing troll, he still had no sense of who hit first.

"One thousand one," he counted, his muscles tightening automatically as Spid raised the ax.

"One thousand two." He wouldn't move. He couldn't. Everything depended on him. If Spid cut off his right arm, he'd drum with his left.

"One thousand three." Maybe he could duck, take a glancing blow and—

He bent his knees and cocked his arm to strike the Skin. Something flew through the air. A pair of large brown feet caught Spid full in the chest.

"Ooof." The troll crashed to the platform. The edge of the Skin convulsed and three more fierce-looking demons squeezed through the rubbery surface with a "pop" before it resealed itself.

"One thousand four," Noah counted. Delacroix rebounded to his feet.

Voorp. The sound wave from Deidre's sonic sword walloped Yurk. The ogre yelped and scuttled away. Spid roared. He stood. He charged.

Crunch. Spid's ax found flesh. Delacroix fell.

Time. Noah struck the Skin.

323

Kuh-kuh-boom-boom. This time it sounded like rolling thunder, thunder that followed a hundred-mile lightning bolt. And this time Noah heard a definite separation of the beats. Perhaps an eighth of a second.

But Noah, his head turned, still hadn't seen who had struck first.

But the Skin knew. It began to throb and glow.

Noah's own skin began to tingle and he felt the hair on his arms ripple and prickle and stand up. Rainbows of color swirled across the Skin, racing and chasing each other.

Swiveling his head, Noah saw everyone else stopped in place, frozen like the gargoyles had been, all looking at the stone face where the two orbs had been placed. The stones, too, glowed. Color radiated in synch with the flashing strobe of the Skin.

And then bands of color began to fly around the room, flashing across the faces of all of those gathered on the platform. Faster and faster and faster they twirled until they no longer could be distinguished as individual tints, until they fused into unearthly blinding whiteness. Only Abby didn't squint or shade her eyes.

The light compressed, forming a thin beam that connected the orbs and the center of the Skin. The beam arched high above the platform. An image formed, a translucent figure. It was very thin, with a flowing robe.

"The convergent solstice has passed." A high, wavery voice delivered the information. The tone was flat, expressionless. "The drums have spoken. The prophecy is fullfilled. Humbug Mountain lives. Destiny has been satisfied."

"Melacherub," Delacroix said in a pain-tinged whisper.

The voice paused. Noah held his breath. Every muscle in his body seemed to quiver with suspense. The image of the departed wizard surveyed them one by one, its eyes without judgment.

324

"The Skin is now healed." The apparition spoke again. "Let those from Above and those from Beneath remain apart until the next alignment of the divergent elements of our universe."

As suddenly as it had appeared, the figure shrank into itself and vanished. The beams of light seemed to be inhaled back into the two orbs and the Skin. The electric crackle that had filled the air of the cavern diminished and died.

Noah put his hand out and touched the Skin. It felt like smooth wet leather. He tapped it gently with a drumstick and got only a dull *thunk*.

"You haven't won yet!" Spid roared.

Noah whirled. It wasn't over. Spid and Yurk and three of the troll's grotesque soldiers raised their terrible weapons.

"Noah. Here." Deidre banged a sonic sword against her decibelt and flung the vibrating weapon toward him butt-end first.

He plucked it from the air. His own weapon. He hadn't noticed she'd brought it. Automatically, he raised it to the ready position and scanned the platform. From above he heard the thudding of feet—the tunnel defenders rushing toward the platform.

Spid advanced on Delacroix, who lay on his back, feet raised to fend off an attack. Blood welled from one of his arms.

Yurk circled behind Abby, Uh-oh and the hermit, spear raised. "I've got the drooler," Deidre called. She backed Yurk away with a *voorp* from the fork. "You take them."

Noah swung his battle fork at three ugly, four-armed reptilian soldiers who'd begun to circle behind him. They fell like dominoes. He grinned. This shouldn't be too hard. He turned toward Spid.

Too late.

The troll sprang toward Delacroix.

325

Noah raised his battle fork. Deidre sprinted forward. Lix rolled away from the first blow. Spid's ax rang against the platform. Sparks and chips of stone flew.

Noah blasted wildly with the sonic sword. The troll dodged the wave and raised the ax again. Delacroix flopped and rolled. The blade caught him in the thigh with a sickening crunch.

Noah released a second wave. The troll roared and turned toward him. Deidre blasted Spid again and again, driving him away from Delacroix, who writhed in pain, a red stream running from his leg, spreading quickly across the platform.

Deidre raised her face to the ledges above them where grungoids and humans swarmed toward the platform. "Hurry."

Smirking, Spid halted his retreat. She aimed the sonic sword at him.

Voooooorrrrrpppp.

"I'm running out of juice." Deidre thumped the butt of the sonic sword against the decibelt. "It's not charging. Watch behind you!"

Noah spun to see Yurk and the reptilian soldiers closing in on him. He swung the sonic sword. The squatty soldiers fell once more. Yurk barely staggered.

"I'm getting low, too!" Noah backed toward Deidre and looked toward the ledges where warriors hurtled toward them. Could they hold out for another few seconds?

"Despite my most considerable skills as a commanding general, and my infallible battle plan, it appears we are outnumbered." Spid's voice rang out.

Huh? Spid? Giving up? Noah turned to look at the troll and saw his evil leer dissolve into confused jaw-drop.

"Throw down your weapons immediately and surrender to the Above-ite nearest you."

326

Three weapons clattered to the platform. Noah stared. The troll's lips hadn't moved. Either Spid was a ventriloquist or . . .

"He did it again," Deidre crowed.

Noah turned to see Uh-oh, stalking back and forth across the platform, chest thrust out, chin imperiously jutted skyward. "I, the Grand Exalted Garboon, command you," Uh-oh mimicked.

A dozen men from 'Shroomtown, Benny and Peitr in the lead, clattered up the steps and surrounded the reptilian soldiers. Chillout vaulted to the platform and raced toward Delacroix.

"You idiots!" Spid darted toward Uh-oh.

The grungoid zipped out of range, while perfectly mimicking the cry. "You idiots."

More of Deidre's compatriots, grungoids and other members of the Above population swarmed onto the platform and formed a bristling circle around Spid. Noah felt relief wash over him. He lowered his failing sonic sword and rushed toward Delacroix.

Something clattered to the ground. Deidre screamed.

Noah swiveled in time to see Yurk yank her back by her braided hair and put the point of an obsidian knife against her throat. With his other hand, the ogre pried her arm up behind her back. Noah saw Deidre try not to flinch from the pain, saw pure hatred in her eyes.

"Got her, boss," Yurk drooled. "Want I should slice her up?"

"Perhaps that would be best, Yurk." Oblivious to the weapons that corralled him, Spid continued to command. "An object lesson to these peasants to show them the futility of their opposition to the all-knowing and all seeing wisdom of my—"

"Noooooo." A woman's voice rose in a scream. A dervish in brown robes flew toward Yurk. Before the ogre could make good on his threat, the hermit brought the

327

wooden staff down on his head. Deidre twitched away from the knife, spun and kneed the ogre in the stomach. Yurk doubled over, covering his head with his lengthy arms. Again and again, the hermit struck. His hat flew away, revealing a clump of matted, unruly gray hair.

"Nooo," the voice, definitely that of a woman, screamed again. Noah stared in amazement.

"Unnhh!" Yurk dropped his knife and groveled on the platform. "I give up. I give up."

The hermit stepped back, panting and leaning on the staff.

"Go to your master," Deidre commanded Yurk. As the ogre belly-crawled toward Spid, Deidre bent to retrieve her sonic sword, then walked to the hermit and tugged at the mass of gray hair. "Mother?"

"Eve?" Noah took a step toward them as the wig tumbled to the ground. Yes, there was Eve's hair, pinned against her head. The hermit was Deidre's mother.

Without question.

"Mother," Deidre wrapped her arms around Eve. "Thank you."

Eve smiled, kissed Deidre on the forehead, then disengaged her daughter's arms. "Mr. Delacroix needs me." She picked up Deidre's battle fork and handed it to her, then turned toward Delacroix and Chillout.

"Give it up, Spid. You're done." Noah turned to see Abby, inside the circle of Spid's captors, her finger leveled at the glowering troll and the cowering ogre.

"Ah, Miss Keene." Spid's tone swung back to the salesman-smooth dulcet tones of his pre-battle persona. "Come to bask in the glow of your victory, have you? But you may be just a wee premature. Spid began to pat at his robes. "As long as I have the Shadow Stone, and can channel its power, I cannot be vanquished. I . . .uh . . .

I . . ." Spid frowned and turned to his aide. "The Shadow Stone, Yurk. Hand it to me. Now!"

328

The ogre's face twisted into a sickly grimace. "I don't have it, boss."

"You don't have it?!? What do you mean, you don't have it?"

"I mean you, uh, you left it." Yurk pointed toward the skin "Over on the other side."

"You're quite mistaken, Yurk. I would never make a blunder such as that." He snapped his scaly fingers. "Now hand over the stone."

"I can't, boss. You said you'd go back for it after you'd killed everybody on the platform. You said once the Skin opened all the way up you'd get it and—"

Spid's five-headed ax whistled through the air. The ogre ducked. "Cheez, boss, you almost got me."

Abby's voice, cocky, almost impudent, taunted the infuriated troll. "Like I said, Spid. It's over. At least be a graceful loser. Show some class."

"Class! Class! You impudent little pipsqueak of a girl. You won because you were lucky. Lucky!" The echoes from his roar careened crazily through the cavern.

"And we haven't lost. We have the will, the courage, and the conviction of the rightness of our cause. We will fight on. Many of you will die." He unsheathed a knife and handed it to the ogre. It isn't easy to kill a troll. Or an ogre. "And we will fight to the death, right, Yurk?"

Yurk cleared his throat and confirmed in a sickly quaver of a voice. "Uh . . . dit . . . dittoes, boss. To the . . . to the . . ."

"No!!! The darkness *shall not* prevail!" Abby's voice rang out, not as a challenge, but as undeniable fact.

Spid laughed. "No, you are wrong again, Miss Keene. The darkness most definitely *shall* prevail."

"Horsehockey," Noah heard Abby mutter quietly out of the side of her mouth. The lights in the chamber flickered. He tilted his eyes toward the roof and saw the Zezzue begin to roil.

Yurk tugged at Spid's robe. "Uh, Boss," the ogre pointed up at the ceiling, "I don't think—"

"The drumming hurt my ears, Mr. Spid." Abby cupped her ears. "I didn't hear you."

As if he were an actor who'd just gotten a cue for his soliloquy, Spid took a step forward, thrust his chest out, jutted his chin and projected his voice to the furthest ledge. "The darkness *SHALL* prevail."

As the echoes died, Noah heard the distant whirr of Zezzue wings. He looked up to see the wild and vibrant colors of the agitated creatures strobing across the ceiling.

Spid raised his ax above Abby's head. "In a moment, you won't need your ears, you impudent little brat."

The men encircling him raised their weapons, but before anyone could strike, the lights in the chamber blinked to near darkness. As Noah watched, a huge patch of white light peeled off the blackness of the ceiling. The buzzing of the Zezzue grew as the glowing blanket plummeted to a position directly over the troll and his second-in-command.

"Wait," Spid commanded. "You cannot do this. As the Grand Exalted Garboon of the—"

Before he could finish, Spid and Yurk were enveloped in a mass of furiously buzzing Zezzue. In the next instant, the tiny creatures lifted the troll and the ogre and hovered for a moment. All Noah could see of each of the villains was a sleeve and hand, one encrusted with a spot of green drool, the other bearing a thick ring.

"See yuh, Spid," Abby called out toward the cloud. "But I wouldn't wanna be yuh. Next time we play, I'll spot you a pawn."

The finger twitched. The ring clanged to the floor, rolled to Abby's feet and spun slowly to a stop. With that, the undulating sea of Zezzue shot upwards with a sharp *kzooorp*, speeding toward the very upper reaches of the cavern. Noah watched them rotate into a narrow beam, then shoot through a tiny opening in the distant ceiling.

For a few moments, total blackness filled the chamber, then the Zezzue returned and blinked on. Noah looked around, taking stock. Delacroix, wounds bandaged with strips from Eve's robe, lay with his head in her lap while Chillout massaged his feet. Deidre stood over them, staring at the armless drummer, her head cocked to one side, a finger against her chin. Uh-oh, following the 'Shroomtowners and the captive demon soldiers, marched toward the edge of the platform, scratching his stomach and pooching his lips in and out.

Abby stood alone in the center of the platform, her eyes tightly clenched. Noah strode over to her and wrapped his arms around her. She raised her face to his and opened her eyes. The dark screen across them had vanished.

"I knew the way, Noah. I really did know the way."

"Yes, you did, Abby." He kissed her forehead. "I love you, little sister."

Chapter Thirty-three

"That stuff she pours down us, it tastes nasty, yes?" Delacroix sat propped up against several pillows in a bed carved into the rock of his chamber.

Even the mention of the root – fungus, and of course, scrubbage – concoction Eve had been feeding them made Noah's taste buds shrivel. Mokblag, she'd called it. It sounded as bad as it tasted. "Yes. Nasty to the max," he answered, scrunching down into the beanbag chair Chillout had hauled up from The Last Place You Look. "But it seems to have worked."

Exhausted, dehydrated, and in general, shredded from his ordeal, Noah had regained most of his strength. Delacroix, who many feared would not survive the fearsome wounds inflicted by Spid, had amazed everyone with the speed of his recovery. What was it Eve had said? "Some people say I'm a witch?" Well, Noah didn't know about that, but he was living proof she knew how to heal people.

He and Delacroix were awaiting the return of Abby and Deidre, who'd gone off for a last ride in the Vorv. Since the battle, the two of them had become fast friends. And he and Deidre had become . . . well, he didn't really know for sure. He tingled as he remembered the kiss the warrior girl had given him just before he began drumming. The smile that crept onto his face must have betrayed what he was thinking, because the amusement in Lix' voice was unmistakable.

"She is quite a girl, non? My daughter?"

"No. Uh, I mean yes, she is. I like her a lot."

"And I know she thinks much of you, my friend. She has told me."

"Really?"

Delacroix winked at him. "But do not say that I told you so. She would forgive me not, yes?"

"Sure. Of course. Lix?" Noah had only been able to force himself to call the legendary drummer by his nickname after being scolded repeatedly for calling him Mr. Delacroix.

"Yes?"

"When did you know? That Eve was really Melanie?"

"Before I knew she was Eve."

"Huh?"

"As I lay bleeding on the ground, I began to drift and visions appeared to me. I could not distinguish what was real and what was not. It was like . . ." He paused, searching for a way to describe it. "Did you ever have one of those little books, that when you flipped the pages very fast it made for a cartoon, you know? A little scene you could make go faster or slower?"

"I think so." Noah vaguely remembered his dad making something like that for him when he was little. "It was like that. Except the little pictures were all different. Memories, hallucinations, real events. I could not tell."

"You were delirious. Like when you get a fever."

"Exactemente. And one of those pictures was my Melanie. And I did not know if it was only a memory. But then she smiled. That wonderful smile. And she told me everything would be all right. And she ripped parts of her raggedy hermit robe to make bandages. And I knew. Knew I had found her. Or perhaps she had found me."

"But you must have suspected . . . I mean, Deidre is . . ." Noah felt embarrassed trying to express it.

"She is beautiful, yes? A brown like coffee and cream, cafe au lait. Yes. But I did never see her very closely, Noah. And there were several other dark-skinned people who arrived from 'Shroomtown to fight Spid."

"She told me she knew you were her father the minute she got up close. She said it was like looking into a mirror."

Delacroix shrugged. "Most unfortunate she has not gotten less of me and more of her mother." He grew a little misty-eyed. "She helped Melanie dress my wounds, and when I saw them together, I knew. She came to me, my girl, and called me father and told me I must get well. Because there were many things she needed yet to tell me. So, I do as I am told. I drink Melanie's evil brew and I sleep. And now, I am almost ready to rejoin the world."

"How did it happen? How did she become Eve? And the hermit?"

"She has many gaps still. In her memory? She can recall only preparing herself for the crash." A faraway look filled Delacroix's face. "A blinding flash of light and then pain. Awakening, she crawls. A great distance she crawls, and then there is nothing. And she awakens to find herself inside the mountain. With the people of 'Shroomtown. They nurse her back to health, but she cannot remember where she came from. Or who she is. She needs a name. They call her Eve. And then Deidre arrives."

"Why did she call her Deidre?"

"The human mind it is a strange thing, no? Melanie's best friend, her bridesmaid, was named Deidre. Without knowing, she linked to her past."

"Pretty amazing." Noah heard the slap of shoes on stone and turned to see Abby and Deidre approaching. He scrambled out of the chair. "Here they are now." As they drew nearer, talking and laughing, he marveled at how comfortable they were with each other. Almost like sisters.

"So, it's decided? You'll come stay with us?" Abby asked.

Deidre, smiling answered. "Maybe. First I need to get to know my dad. But I would like to see the world. The other world."

"I can't wait till you get there. You can help me keep No-way here in line."

"But what will you tell your father?" Deidre put a hand out and touched Noah's hair with her fingertips.

Abby shrugged. "Dunno. Noah will think of something, won't you, brother?"

Noah felt himself blush. "Uh, sure, Deed. I've got a plan."

"He's got a plan, Abby." Deidre and Abby looked at each other, then broke out in giggles.

"Uh, maybe you better let me handle this, big brother." Abby grinned.

"Whatever," Noah scowled at her.

Deidre bent over Delacroix, and adjusted the bandage on his thigh. "Did you eat your mokblag, Papa?" Noah noticed she had picked up a little of the lilt of Delacroix's speech patterns.

Delacroix made a loud mock groan. "Sometimes the cure is worse than the sickness."

Deidre rubbed his bald head then planted a kiss on his cheek. "Stop complaining or when mother gets back she'll double your dosage. Hey, I had to take it too." She touched the bandage on her shoulder that covered the ax wound she received when Spid broke through the Skin.

"I will never forget that. Does Melanie return soon?"

Delacroix's voice took on a tone of fond wistfulness. "Don't know. Said she had to get a few things. You know how she is." Deidre smiled. "Maybe she'll bring you some of those little snack cakes."

"All of that time," clucked Delacroix. "The hermit would bring me things from the outside. And I did not know it was Melanie. Could not see her beneath the grit and the grime and the all the time scowling. She plays the

335

part well, yes? She tricks the audience. And with her amnesia, she did not recognize me. Except maybe faintly, in her heart." He touched his chest with the stump of one arm.

Noah and Abby exchanged glances. It was almost time for them to go. "Mr., uh, Lix. Here. I wanted to make sure you got these back." Noah extracted the monogrammed white drumsticks he'd tucked into his belt.

Delacroix shook his head emphatically. "No. No. Of this, I will not hear. You must keep them, use them. After all, of what good are they to an armless drummer?"

"But—"

Delacroix cut him off. "It is destiny, Noah.

Remember. We play our parts as they are written. Mine is to be here. With my family." He smiled at Deidre, who put a hand against his cheek. "And yours is to share your gift with others. To feel, and hear and play. The sticks must go with you." The finality of his tone made Noah bite back any further objection.

"Play that funky music, white boy." Noah heard Chillout's voice behind him and turned expecting to see him. Instead, a sunglass-wearing Uh-oh slouched in the doorway with the ultra-casual hipster stance of the other grungoid. Just as the real Chillout appeared from a nearby tunnel, Uh-oh added. "It's been a stone gas working the big show with you, my main man. Slide back soon, so I can grok you the most."

"Man, that cat is the eeriest." Chillout shook his head as he stopped in front of them. "But she's cute, so I may let her hang with me a while."

She? Her?

If there had been a competition for synchronized double takes, Abby, Deidre, Noah and Delacroix would have won hands-down.

Noah marveled. All that time traveling with Uh-oh and he never knew. Of course, he'd never asked either.

336

His mind spun as he tried to remember if he'd undressed in front of her. Then he smiled at himself. What did it matter now?

"Uh, little chickie," Chillout turned to Abby. "I got a little, like, token of my esteem to drop on you here. Kind of a going away thing, you dig?" The grungoid pulled out a small velvet-covered ring box and presented it to her.

"For me? Why Chillout, you didn't need to . . ."

"Open it, ma cherie." Delacroix commanded.

Abby took the box from Chillout's outstretched hand and eased the hinged lid open carefully.

What Noah saw gave him the shivers. The thick ring had been forged from what looked like polished iron. The stone, a gleaming eye of dark green, scattered light in all directions. "Spid's ring," Abby exclaimed.

The lights in Delacroix's chamber dimmed and transformed to a brooding red. Noah felt the apprehension swirl though his body.

Abby snapped the box shut. Instantly, the Darksuckers returned to a soft warm glow. "It . . . it's beautiful but kind of . . . of . . . I don't know, intimidating. I'm not sure what . . ."

Delacroix interrupted. "The ring itself is not evil. Not unless it lives on the finger of the evil one. Since the Chameleon Stone now must live with us, we thought the ring might be for you, a what do you call it?"

"Souvenir?"

"Yes. A memento of what we have gone through together. You will keep it safe, non?"

Abby looked thoughtful. "Yes. I will keep it." She slid it into her pocket, walked to Delacroix's bed, sat down beside him and hugged him warmly. Noah saw tears slide down her cheeks. "Thank you, Lix. For showing me. For trusting me."

337

Suddenly, Uh-oh took two quick steps and hurled herself toward Noah. Before he knew it, she'd wrapped herself around him and snared him in a tight embrace.

"Bye-bye, Noah," the grungoid croaked. "I'll miss you."

Just as suddenly as she'd sprung, she released her grip, dropped softly to the ground and darted over to pick something from Chillout's skin. Examining it for a second, she popped it into her mouth.

"Goodbye Uh-oh, I'll miss you too. And you, Chillout." Noah put a hand on Delacroix's shoulder. "Good-bye, Lix. Maybe we can drum together, again sometime."

"I would like that, Noah. Perhaps in better circumstances, no?"

"Right," Noah agreed. "And maybe I'll bring you some CD's for your collection.

"We'd better get on it, brother," Abby reminded him.

"You guys go ahead." Deidre jogged off toward her sleeping chamber. I'll meet you up at the tunnel."

As they walked away, Noah felt a sadness. It was the same sensation he'd experienced when he'd decided to run away from home. He was leaving something behind— something very special, something he might never find again. He was leaving a family. Another family. But now it was time to go back and try to repair the on he'd left before. He felt his feet begin to move faster and realized he was smiling through the tears that welled from his eyes.

Just as they arrived at the entrance to the tunnel, Deidre ran up. In her hands she carried a pair of boots. "Here. You're going to need these. You can't walk out barefoot. What would your dad say?"

As Noah accepted her gift, his eyes met Deidre's.

They held for a long time. When she blinked, he dropped his gaze to admire the boots. They were much

338

like the ones on her feet, made of some kind of plant fiber that felt like soft leather.

"And here," Deidre tossed him a pair of cloth socks. "Try them on."

Obeying, he sat on a nearby boulder, slid the socks over his feet, then slipped on the boots. They fit perfectly. "How did you . . ."

"Abby told me your size. I had Mikkal do a rush order. He makes shoes for all the 'Shroomtowners."

Noah stood and walked back and forth, feeling the boots conform to his feet like another layer of skin.

"Deed, they're great. Thank you. Thank you. I . . . I . . ."

"C'mon, for cripe's sake," Abby needled him. "Kiss her and let's get going. I'll wait in the tunnel." She stomped off loudly, laughing.

Deidre blushed and smiled at him. "Yeah, Noah, you'd better or I'm going to have to take out my battle fork and give you a little jolt." Deidre pretended to draw the weapon she hadn't worn since they'd returned from the Skin. "Now that I think about it, I still owe you one for that little incident at the Temple of Cheltnor."

Noah grinned. He took Deidre in his arms and pulled her close. He felt awkward and clumsy. He felt warm and wonderful. "Deed, I . . ."

"Shhhh." She put a finger against his lips, then removed it and sealed his mouth with her own. Noah felt a pleasant tingle vibrating throughout his body. He closed his eyes, enjoying the moment, enjoying her closeness.

After a few moments, she pulled away, kissing the tip of his nose. "You'd better go," she said, in an even huskier voice than usual.

"Yeah." He choked. "I'll miss you, Deidre."

"Knock it off," he heard her voice break. "Soldiers don't cry. Besides, I'm coming out there. To your world.

You're going to take me to a movie. Remember?"

339

"I remember."

"Careful, Deidre, he hogs the popcorn." Abby emerged from the tunnel.

The little sneak, Noah thought, she was watching the whole time.

"I'll remember that, Abby. And once I learn what popcorn is, I'll make sure I get my fair share." The warrior girl hugged Abby, took Noah's hand, gave it a small squeeze, then turned on her heel and started down the trail.

Noah watched her until she turned and waved. He returned the gesture, wanting to run back to her, but knowing he had to go home. "Let's go, Ab-normal," he told his sister. Together they turned and walked quickly along the tunnel. "Abby."

"What?"

"Remember. We can't tell anybody anything. About in here, right?"

Abby seemed to hesitate for a moment, then agreed.

"Yeah. Who'd believe us, anyway? We'd be in shrinksville getting our heads examined until we were old enough for social security."

"Shrinksville?" Noah chuckled. "You sound like Chillout."

Abby didn't respond for a moment, and then asked in a small voice. "What are we gonna tell Dad, Noah? About where we've been for—" He saw her glance at the wristwatch she'd rescued from The Last Place You Look.

Noah had one much like his original inexpensive sports watch on his wrist. Uh-oh had found it for him. Neither watch had been set. "However long do you think it's been?"

"Week. Week and a half. I don't know."

"Maybe, we could just say we went to San Francisco and hung out. Stayed with some people we met."

340

"Tell him we hitchhiked all the way?" Noah asked skeptically. "Don't think so, Ab-normal. That would really freak him out."

"So you're just going to wing it?" She sounded angry and incredulous. "My brother. Good old No-way. Making it up as he goes along right up to the end."

"All right, brain factory. You come up with something. Something that won't get us grounded until the next time we have to save the world."

Abby snorted and broke into a laugh and it triggered the giggle reflex in Noah too. Their laughter bounced, hollow-sounding through the passageway. Save the world. It sounded so ludicrous when he said it out loud.

Even if it was the truth.

A sudden thought sobered him. What if Dad was just as inflexible when they got back. He and Abby disappearing for so long probably wouldn't prove Dad could trust them with more personal responsibility. His mouth pulled into a tight frown. Things might even be worse than before he ran away.

Before long, the tunnel dead ended. "Your sticks, s'il vous plait," Abby commanded.

Noah pulled his drumsticks out of the backpack and listened for the heartbeat of Humbug Mountain. *Thrum-thrum, thrum-thrum, thrum-thrum.* He let it seep into his brain and radiate through his nerve endings.

Picking a flat spot on the wall, he began to tap out a counter rhythm. *Thrum-thrum, (tickuh-tum) Thrum-thrum, (tickuh-tum).* When the beat shifted, so did Noah.

Thrum-thrum, (tickey, tickey, tum) thrum-thrum. He heard the rock begin to groan and grate and heard Abby's jubilant cry.

"Noah. Smell it. The ocean."

The rock face slid back, revealing a ledge that faced the Pacific Ocean. The moon, a shade less than full, shone on the water. To the north, the lights of Port Anvil

341

twinkled in the distance. The beach he and Abby had walked stretched far below them. Somewhere, about a third of the way towards town, Noah saw the glow of a campfire and flashed back to his encounter with Old Hannah, the dance and the vision.

They stepped onto the ledge. The rock slid shut behind them with an almost inaudible hsssss.

"Home, Noah. We're almost home."

"Yeah," was all he could think to say. Carefully, they began to work their way down a narrow trail. Glancing up at the distant stars, Noah asked Abby the question that had been on his mind since they'd returned from the Skin.

"How did you know? How did you know how to break down the word from the Spiddle game to make the phrase that would persuade the Zezzue to catch me? How did you know?"

"Well, I didn't *know*. Not exactly," Abby said defensively. "I, uh, made a logical assumption."

"You guessed?"

"Uh, a little more than a guess, big brother. Here's the way I figured it. As crazy and out of whack as everything was in there, it all made its own kind of sense. You just had to figure out the rules. It was just like any math or science problem. I took the letters and divided them up the same way I did the scrunched up Thela Stpla Ceyo Ulook from the sign over the door of The Last Place You Look. Three letters, then four, then five. Then three and then four again. The same pattern as your beats on the high drum. It had to be right. Just had to."

"And it was," he said quietly. "It was exactly right."

"But the other part was that I had to believe it was right. And you had to believe in me."

Noah nodded, thinking again how big that leap of faith had been, and how tiny the amount of time in which he'd considered not taking it. They didn't talk for awhile after that. The trail widened and then emptied into a grassy

342

meadow near the bottom of the mountain. Noah knelt and ran his fingers through it. Grass. Not moss, but real grass.

Beyond the meadow, the trail wound through a stand of trees and then up a bank toward the highway and a small park. As they climbed the bank, Abby grabbed his hand and stopped him. "Listen," she whispered.

Voices, those of a man and a woman, drifted on the fading night. Noah didn't recognize the woman's voice.

But he knew the man's. Dad.

"We could try the west trail again." The man's voice. Dad.

"Whatever you think, Sean. But just rest for a few moments. You're exhausted."

"But they've got to be out here somewhere. They've got to be."

"That's Jennifer," Abby breathed.

Mrs. Ramsden, Noah thought. She was out here with Dad. And they were looking for him and Abby. He remembered the cookies he'd tossed in the trash and felt a pang of regret unrelated to the wasted treats.

"Let's go." He tugged free of Abby's grip, leaped up the bank and strode through a patch of moonlight toward the couple sitting across from each other at a wooden picnic table. Abby followed at his heels.

As they drew near, Mrs. Ramsden looked up. Her eyes widened, sparkling in the dim light. Her mouth opened, but no sound came out.

"If anything happened to them, I'll never forgive myself, Jen," Sean Keene told her. "Noah's been trying to tell me something was wrong for the longest time and I just didn't listen. I couldn't hear, I . . ."

Jennifer Ramsden gulped air and pointed across his shoulder. "Oh my God. Sean. Look. It's them."

"Wha . . .Noah? Abby?" He turned, legs tangling in the bench.

Noah saw tears flowing down his cheeks. "Dad," he heard himself say. "We're back."

Sean Keene raced toward them, arms open. "Oh God. Noah. Abby. I . . . I'm so . . . Oh, thank God you're safe."

Noah felt himself encompassed by his father's right arm as Abby was enfolded in the left. He returned the hug, the first since before his mother died, and felt tears rolling from his eyes. Over his father's shoulder, he saw Mrs. Ramsden blotting at her face with a tissue. He smiled at her. It felt good. It felt right. Now for the next step. He took a deep breath. "Dad."

The word came out with a crack in the middle. Noah cleared his throat and tried again. "Dad, there's something I need to tell you."

His father didn't release the hug. "Noah, you don't have to—"

"Yes, Dad, I do."

Noah felt his father unwrap his arm and he stepped back a couple of feet. Sean Keane's face began to harden.

He saw Abby turn to make eye contact with him, her brow furrowed, bottom lip beginning to pout. She thinks I'm going to blow it, Noah thought. Well, I guess she needs one more lesson in trust. He took the verbal leap.

"Dad, I want to apologize to you. I was so hung up on trying to get you to hear what I was saying, that I didn't realize I wasn't listening to you either. You were right about not giving me more responsibility. I hadn't earned it yet. And running away was a horrible, inconsiderate thing to do."

His father's face didn't change. Noah pulled in a breath. "Please don't get mad at Abby. She just came along to try to keep me out of trouble. And . . ." He and Abby exchanged glances. "And she did. Mostly. But it was my fault, not hers. I'm so sorry for all the pain I've caused you and I'll accept any punishment you have for me."

Mrs. Ramsden sniffed and blotted her face again.

344

Sean Keene's face didn't change.

Abby looked up at her father, then shrugged off his arm and took Noah's hand. "If you punish Noah," she insisted, "you'll have to punish me, too. I was the brains of the operation. So there."

Sean Keene threw back his head and roared with laughter. "Oh Abby. Noah. What a pair you are. What a pair." He rubbed tears away with his shirtsleeve. "I think we've all been punished enough since your mother died. I didn't realize how . . . Well, I didn't realize how selfish I've been, how wrapped up in my own sorrow. I forgot I still had a family. I've got a lot to be thankful for. And I need to start showing it." He held out his hand to Noah.

"And I need to listen better too."

Slowly, Noah raised his hand and grasped his father's.

Abby wrapped her arms around both of them and squeezed. In a moment, Noah felt other arms, and realized Mrs. Ramsden - no, he'd call her Jennifer—had joined the embrace. If she made Dad happy, he thought, that was what counted. Everybody's entitled to some happiness.

"So, um, where were you guys?"

The question from his father was unaccusing, almost matter-of-fact, but Noah felt his body stiffen automatically.

"We were lost, Dad. Really lost," Abby jumped in with an answer as she kicked Noah in the ankle. "But with the help of some friends, we found our way. We found our way home."

Sean Keene stepped back and studied them for a moment. His face started to harden. Jennifer Ramsden laid a hand on his shoulder. He shrugged and smiled.

"You're safe. That's all I really care about."

"Are you hungry?" Jennifer asked.

"We could eat," Noah and Abby answered together.

"A lot," Noah added.

"We'll stop for something at the all-night diner, Sean Keene laughed. "How about a clam basket?"

"Yum," Abby agreed. She darted ahead toward the truck, Noah in pursuit. It was a tight fit, but with Jennifer sitting in the middle and Abby perched on Noah's lap, they managed to wedge themselves into the cab.

Half a mile from the diner, the headlights illuminated a figure walking toward them on the shoulder of the road.

As they came closer, Noah saw it was an old woman pushing a shopping cart filled with plastic bags.

"Old Hannah," Sean Keene said. "Wonder where she's going in the middle of the night."

Abby nudged Noah and giggled softly.

As they watched, Hannah paused, one hand on the metal cart handle, the other around a thick wooden stick. Her fingers were long and delicate, not gnarled with age.

Noah wondered why he hadn't noticed that before, down by the campfire. He assumed it was because he simply hadn't opened his eyes and looked.

As they rolled past, Noah saw Hannah smile. Eve's smile. Melanie's smile. She raised the stick in a salute.

She winked.

As Noah looked back, she began to walk again, rolling her cart toward Humbug Mountain.

Epilogue

The Realm of Exponential Darkness surrounded Spid like a skin-tight, sensory-deprivation suit. The all-encompassing inky blackness was so heavy, so thick, that the only tactile sensation was a feeling of clamminess on his skin. He couldn't tell, when he lifted his hand, if he was touching his own face, or even if he'd actually lifted his hand at all. From the second the Zezzue had dropped him into the ultimate blackness, he hadn't been able to touch, see, hear, or smell anything.

But considering Yurk must be only a few feet away, that last loss could be called a blessing, he conceded, struggling to fight an unfamiliar emotion—fear. Unless he found a way out, he would die here. And why?

Because of a bratty little girl.

Anger, quickly escalating into rage, smothered his fear. "She cheated."

He thought he'd felt his lips move, but he heard nothing. He tried again. "She cheated."

His words rang inside his head, but no sound reached his ears. The utter darkness sopped up the words the instant he opened his mouth.

How could she have done this to him? After he offered to spare her life? And how could he, Spid, the Grand Exalted Garboon, the towering intellect of The Age of Trolls in the land of Beneath, a ruler so wise, so benevolent, so . . . so . . . inarguably right all of the time, be so misunderstood? After all, he'd only wanted the best. He'd only wanted to illuminate and enlighten the misguided souls of the world with his ultra-omniscience.

He felt a prickle in his mind, a sort of psychic vibration inside his skull. "Yurk?"

The sound was instantly extinguished, unheard by either of them. But the thought must have made contact.

He felt the psychic prickle again. It grew stronger. It seemed to buzz and tickle. Then it became a voice, a tiny and hollow voice from deep inside his ears. "Dittoes, boss. Dittos to the forty-ninth power."

"Yurk!" Spid probed the darkness with the thought.

"Here, boss," the ogre thought back.

"Ah." Spid imagined a smile. Or perhaps he actually did smile. Things would be fine. After all, he had Yurk. The ogre was practically family. No, closer than family.

He was more loyal. More caring. Of course, Spid admitted, it was easy to be more caring than a gammit mother who refused to look at him and a troll father who'd chained him to a rock for a hundred years just for using his battle hatchet without permission.

He tamped the memories down. This was no time to get into all that. No, he needed to think only positive thoughts. He had to remain in perfect command of his mind. His mind was the most powerful weapon ever devised. He would escape and he would triumph. The world would soon recoil in fear from the terrible revenge of Spid the Devious.

Filling his lungs with dense air, he opened his mouth and roared, "I'm the king of the world!"

The sound was so loud, it actually penetrated the darkness, but so much of it was absorbed he heard only "foof."

But Yurk must have sensed it. Spid felt the psychic prickle again, and the ogre's voice filled his brain. "You duh troll, boss. You duh troll."

About the Authors

Mike Nettleton grew up on the Oregon coast, not far from Humbug Mountain. A "radio gypsy," he's been on the air in Albuquerque, Eugene, San Jose and other cities around the west, but since 1994 has been in Portland. When he's not writing, he's playing golf or Texas hold-em poker and trying to avoid housework.

Carolyn Rose grew up in New York's Catskill Mountains and went to college in Arizona. After a stint as a VISTA volunteer, she became a TV news producer and tracked stories in Little Rock, Albuquerque, Eugene and Vancouver. Presently, she works as a substitute teacher and continues her efforts to train Bubba the ten-pound wonder dog, and Dudley, a dachshund-Lab mix who turns heads on their daily walks.

SynergEbooks

TM

Taking Books to New Heights!